A Life Not Lived

By

Michael Peter

Published by Michael Peter

ISBN 979-8-3711-3228-4

For my brothers who never got a chance at life

For the lives that never got a chance

For the voices that never got to tell their story

For the ears that never listened

For the mandem

And the women that hold us down every step of the way

For the culture.

"A life not lived for others

is a life not lived" – Mother Teresa

Prologue

To tell you how it ended, I guess I need to tell you how it started. I know it's a cliché, but fuck it, does that make it less sincere? Not in my opinion. But yeah, the start—the day they finally let *me*, Rakim Morrison, out of those prison gates.

Boy, it seems like a long time ago now, another life, another me. But I'll my do my best to explain.

I mean, isn't that the measure of a man—to do his best no matter what odds are stacked against him?

1

"Morrison!" a raspy voice thunders through the open door.

"Yeah, guv."

"You're being transferred. Pack up your gear and let's move," Mr F says.

"... Ninety-eight... Ninety-nine... One hundred."

I raise myself from the tacky green flooring, my hands mimicking that sound you make when you unwrap *Sellotape*. One thing I won't miss is these floors. I've cleaned this cell twice a week for the past fifteen months, and still, it finds a way of leaving its muck on my hands.

The place I've called home for the past twelve years wants to taunt me just a bit longer.

'You'll never get me off you, not until you're out that door,' it hisses.

And even then, every time I do a press-up, I'll remember the grimy floors of HMP Huntingley.

"You hear me?" Mr F says, poking his head into my cell like an unrelenting dog tryin' to sniff out where the treats are kept.

"Nice try," I say as I reach for my jumper.

I watch his face drop from an eager beaver with a smile that would scare off any woman, to pancake flat under a moustache that doesn't know whether it's coming or going.

"I'm being serious," he says, scratching at his bristles. "You're getting transferred, pal. The bus is—"

Mr F notices my steady glare. 'The death stare,' as Shanice used to call it.

Don't watch that. We'll get to her later.

With a puff of his cheeks, Mr F shakes his head and turns away briefly. "Couldn't get him, Wixie," he shouts before telling me he's going to collect another inmate who's due for release today.

"Back in ten, Morrison," Mr F says, then disappears.

'Thought he was gonna get me with that one? Must've thought I was a sucker.' I scoff as I filter through a clear plastic bag full of CDs, clothes, letters, and loads of other junk.

I can't blame Mr F for trying, though. He's blatantly new on the job. He still asks for directions once in a while. I've seen a few men on these landings send him on a wild goose chase. Maybe he thought he'd get one up on me before I leave this place. You know, make him feel a bit better about himself. A little something to brag about to the other screws on his lunch break before he goes home at eight to swipe right on Tinder for the rest of the night.

If he had any brain cells circling in his head, though, he would have realised two things. One–those rookie lines don't work on men who've done a bid like mine. We see them old tricks coming from a mile off.

And two, who I am. If Mr F didn't know, a quick name search on the prison system would explain. Or a simple observation of me and the mandem on association. Because if you don't know me in here, you most definitely know them man.

Looking around my cell, I have a weird feeling, like I'm leaving home. There's a faint rumbling in my stomach, just like when a car's parked fifty yards down the road with the engine still running. You can hear the thing vibrating, even feel the subtle anticipation. My stomach is doing the same thing right now.

I take a few deep breaths while sieving through a mountain of stuff. Until they call you to reception to be released, it's mad how much rubbish you feel you need when you're here. It means nothing on the outside.

As I run my hand over an old carving some spicehead did for me about a year back, I hear a voice that instantly puts a smile on my face.

2

"Oi, what, man like Rakz... Home time? Come on, my guy," Scribbler shouts, invading my cell like he's Hitler and I'm Poland. I'm about to turn around, but already he's on my back.

In rush the rest of the cavalry—Devonte, Jonesy, and Jamal.

"Oi, allow me," I hear myself shouting in between breaths as they pile themselves onto me, one after the other.

"Free fuckin' man," Jonesy yells, shaking me like a bottle of Fanta, hoping I pop.

"Don't let him go. Hold him down."

That's Scribbler. That nigga's got jokes for days.

I fight back, but he possesses that Nigerian strength, and with sixteen stone of Jonesy on my back and Jamal's arm around my neck, it's over before it begins.

"Ite, cool. I'm staying, I'm staying," I say, my hands raised like a truce flag.

Satisfied they've collectively shown me who's boss, they ease up. I untangle myself from the limbs around me and stretch my neck from side to side.

"You're going home, my brother," Scribbler says.

You'd think he was the one getting released by the way he's moving around.

"I know, fam," I reply.

I don't, though. It still hasn't sunk in. A part of me still thinks I'll reach that gate, and then somehow or someway, they'll find a way of getting me back in a cell.

"What, you don't need these, alie?" I hear Devonte cry. He already came here like a bailiff last week when I broke the news, taking a mental inventory of what goods are coming with him. "FIFA 18, yeah. Come on," he says as he cradles the game underneath his armpit.

"Take it all, fam," I tell him.

He winks and pats me on the shoulder.

"You got something lined up... Workwise?" Jonesy says.

By workwise, he means illegal activity.

3

"I'm good, ya know, my bro," I mutter.

And when I tell you that I say that with a heavy heart, you'd better believe me.

You see, someone like Jonesy offering you a role in his firm is like Alan Sugar inviting you to work for him. You don't turn down such an offer.

Jonesy joined our little family here a while back. Came in on a sixteen-stretch courtesy of dealing class A. As you can probably guess, I'm not talking about two grams for one-fifty. You don't get double-figure sentences for poncey street deals like that.

In a former life, Jonesy was more accustomed to five-grand-a-week Bulgari Hotels in Dubai than a bottom bunk on C Wing. And it's not just waffle like most of the guys here, making ten grand a week or shagging seventy-five girls a month on the outside. I'd seen the paperwork. When The Met came for Jonesy, they must have closed the local station for the day because they came hard. A real Big Time Charlie, excuse the pun.

He'd gone from Lamborghinis and yacht parties to four tokes on a spliff and a quick round of The Still up on the fours. (That's weed and alcohol on the fourth floor for those who aren't quite privy to the lingo).

How things change.

He wishes me all the best, gives me a hug that nearly takes my breath away, and he's off to education.

Meanwhile, Scribbler and Devonte are now arguing about who's getting my extension cord. That little gem went under the radar for a good six months. I know it might not sound like much, but believe me, when you've got to alternate between Match of the Day and cooking up rice and vegetable curry because you need two kettles, but you only have one free socket, an extension cord is like the Holy Grail.

"Rakz, on the level, my bro, tell my man before I bust his head," I hear Devonte call as he and Scribbler let their disagreement spill out onto the wing.

"Oi, keep that shit outside, man," orders Jamal as he finds himself a comfortable spot on the bottom bunk. "So, free man at last, bro. How you feeling?" Jamal asks. Slouched against the off-white brick wall, his feet stretch out. He looks like he could be sitting in his living room.

"I'm good. I just want them to hurry up and get me out, you feel me?" I say as I notice a warm smile form on Jamal's face. "Wa gwarn, bro?" I ask.

Jamal shakes his head. "It's just you, fam."

"How you mean?"

"Just you."

He doesn't want to admit it, but he's being coy.

Prison is a place where men rarely show their vulnerable side. The walls. The screws. The food. It all just seems to have a way of numbing you. Chipping away at those emotions and feelings you carried in here with you, bit by bit, day by day, until one day you decide they don't serve any purpose and just bury them deep inside.

You see, the world outside doesn't exist here. Well, it does, but only in your head and only if you allow it. And then again, everyone's head is different. So, my perception of the outside world may differ far from what Jamal thinks.

You could argue that manipulation applies to everybody's perception of reality to some degree, and you'd have a point. The only thing I'd tell you is this. The advantage you get from being on the outside is that you see the world changing as time goes on. You get to feel, touch, smell, taste, and ultimately experience it in its total capacity as you somewhat change with it. A feeling you come to realise is so precious only when it's taken away from you.

From those sensations you can establish an authentic feel for the world around you. Where you belong, what you like and dislike, who does what, and how the whole thing keeps turning, which allows you to make an informed decision about what serves you well to keep turning with it.

We prisoners, we don't have that luxury. We see the world through a TV screen or apps like FaceTime and Snapchat. And if you're not one for all that social media stuff, then, boy, you're certainly in another world.

Believe me, if there's one thing I've learned over my twelve long years away, it's that society doesn't care about a murderer. We're like that psalm in the Bible my mum always used to quote.

Every Sunday, I'd be hovering around the kitchen, pining after the oxtail or curry goat, and she'd be deep in her prayer, '... but the wicked are like chaff, that the wind driveth away.' That's us, the chaff.

'Rah, rest in peace, Mum.'

It's mad how things change rapidly nowadays. When you're serving a long-term—anything over ten years—then any memories of the outside world that still linger, become irrelevant.

I mean, think back to fifteen years ago. The world before Netflix and Instagram. An era where you actually needed natural beauty and not just have a fake bum, fake boobs, and fillers to be called a model (or influencer, whatever the fuck that means). It was a world where you needed some sort of talent to make money.

Nowadays, you can just film yourself acting like a knob on your phone, and people will subscribe to your channel or whatever they call it. I swear I miss my era. You know when men and women spoke, not just messaged and hit the like button below pictures on a screen. Nah, man, you had to have game.

But I'd be a fool for thinking it wasn't a different world now. I've seen posts online about a man getting charged with harassment because he tapped a woman on the arm. As I said, that's that world, and this is ours.

I straighten my jumper and take a seat opposite Jamal.

"You want one?" I ask, offering him a digestive.

"Nah, it's calm, family."

There's an awkward pause.

I sense Jamal's got something on his mind, so I probe. "What you tellin' me, though?"

Jamal sighs.

"You know what," he begins, scratching at that bumfluff around his chin.

'How's this nigga twenty-six and still ain't got no beard?'

"Like, I'm happy you're going, my bro... But... I guess I'm a bit like you. I knew the day would come but never thought it would come so soon."

See, I knew my maximum tariff couldn't run over twelve years, so I worked out my release date a long time ago. I just never told anybody until last week. The way I figured was, what's the point of focusing on something you can't touch?

Nodding my head, I relax back into my chair. "I feel you," I say.

It would be nice to tell Jamal he'll be out soon, but boy, that would be like telling your best mate he stands a chance in a cage with a pack of hungry lions. Shooting a man in the head because you were 'banging for your block' tends to get you a long fucking time.

"What you gonna do? First day out and that?" Jamal asks.

Before I can respond, Scribbler comes running back into my cell. "How you mean?" he shouts, puffing his chest out. "He's gonna have a dark skin ting bent over on all fours," he says, grinding his body against the small wooden cupboard by the door like he's deep in the moment. Then, pretending to mimic someone having a seizure, he continues. "Then after about... Ten, twelve seconds, he's gonna seize up and drop pon floor," he says, his legs wobbling as he collapses on the ground.

Jamal shakes his head, and I laugh.

I watch Scribbler climb back to his feet like he's ascending a cliff edge. "Then him ah go say," Scribbler continues, deepening his voice to match mine. "Sorry babes... Usually, man lasts longer than that... But it's just... Obviously, you're mad peng and man's just come outta jail init, you get me?" he says, kissing each of his biceps one after the other.

7

The cell erupts into laughter as Scribbler then uses the extension cord like a lasso and flies it above his head like a mad cowboy.

"Fam, you need to put in a transfer to D-Wing 'cause you're off your fuckin' meds," I tell him.

His grin is infectious, and I smile back. That grin has helped me through many tough nights—I tell you that.

I swear, I love Scribbler like he was my brother. We used to share a cell, you see. It was about six years ago. Not in this prison, but in another one, further up north.

I had just moved to the place and hated it immediately. It was the middle of the winter, cold as ice, and I was surrounded by a bunch of weirdoes. Their lingo, their accent, their humour, just weren't what I was used to.

I was one of the only black guys on my wing, and some shit kicked off. Something about a white cop shooting a black boy in America. What's new, aye? Anyway, I overheard this one fool saying something about 'shoot all the niggers', so I confronted him. Long story short, I went back to my cell with a swollen knuckle, and he went off to healthcare, missing a couple of teeth.

Days passed, and I thought nothing of it. Screws hadn't approached me, no cell spin, no slip under my door, nothing, so naturally, I forgot about the whole incident.

Then, one afternoon when everyone was out on the yard, I decided to take a shower seeing that the shower room was empty. I was in there for no longer than five minutes when in slipped three fellas.

I turned, like you always do when you're half-naked and another man enters your vicinity. They were placing their towels on the bench, sorting their shower gels and whatnot, so I thought nothing of it. Then, from the corner of my eye, I saw one of these fellas nod at the screw by the door. The screw nodded back, then disappeared.

Next thing I know, something crashes over the side of my head, and I'm getting hit from all angles.

Now, if there's one place you don't want to fight in prison, it's the showers, I'm tellin' you. It's like having a boxing match on an ice rink. I managed to get my hands over my head and absorb some of the blows, and then I heard one of the men shout, 'shiv him.' In other words, somebody was trying to stab me.

The water was spraying everywhere as these three beefy Northerners backed me into a corner. I saw a razor blade swing towards me, narrowly missing my chest, and that's when it clicked—if I didn't do something, this lot would kill me right there.

Now, maybe I'd been a good Christian that week because out of nowhere came Scribbler, flying through the door.

He threw a solid fist into one of the guys and knocked him clean out. The fat prick dropped like a sack of potatoes, hitting the ground with a thud. It then became a two-on-two, and we fancied our chances.

I grappled the guy with the razor blade, forcing him to the tiled floor to unleash hell upon him. Then, seeing that me and Scribbler had the upper hand, the third guy grabbed his towel and pelted it out the door, literally with his tail, if you could call it that, between his legs.

I never mentioned it to anybody 'til this day, but after the third guy ran off, there were about eight to ten seconds where me and Scribbler were over this guy, who was cowered on the ground like a wounded animal. Of course, the other Northerner was there, but he was away with the fairies, fast asleep in La La Land.

Within that time, Scribbler picked up the blade I'd forced out of the guy's hand. Scribbler looked at me, and I'll never forget that look. There wasn't an ounce of bashfulness around his pupils. He pushed the guy's head to the side, pressed his knee over his arm, and held the blade an inch from his neck. The guy squealed like a pig, but Scribbler didn't even blink.

'Should I duppy him?' Scribbler asked, and I'll tell you this now, he wasn't messing around.

I've been around bullshitters and blaggers—prison is rife with them. No, that look in Scribbler's eye was as serious and as focused as I've ever seen in my entire life. From that moment, I knew Scribz was a real one. He was prepared to kill for me, and he barely even knew me. I'd only been there three months.

Scribbler never actually slit the guy's throat in the end. Whistles went, alarms rang, and before we knew it, we were being hauled down the block. Me and Scribbler were in that segregated part of the prison for two weeks before our hearing. It was a serious charge, as the Governor put it.

I remember Shanice went nuts. Imagine bringing your seven-year-old up to Yorkshire in the middle of January when it's snowing and freezing beyond belief. You turn up at the prison, only to find out your visit's been cancelled, and you have to tell your daughter that she can't see Daddy after a three, four-hour journey because 'Daddy had a fight.'

I mean, the officers could have at least had the courtesy of telling her beforehand; maybe, I would have been able to salvage something, but if I'm being honest, I genuinely think that was the last straw for Shanice.

That sealed it for her.

Scribbler and his silver tongue managed to get us into the same holding cell before we went for our hearing; the guy just had a way with words. Even in a racist jail like that, he would have a screw bending backwards to help him.

So, we were in this cell, and I was cussing myself about how stupid I was, how Shanice was going to go mental, how I was two days away from earning privileges on *Advanced,* reh teh teh. Not that I could have done much else, though, apart from allowing myself to be carved up like a Christmas turkey.

But all the while, Scribbler just watched me pace up and down, cursing and shouting my head off. I was sure we'd get extra time, but he was just poised on the bench, not saying a word.

Then, when I finally settled, the cell went silent. Nothing. We just sat together for two minutes, not sharing so much as a glance. Then, calmly as ever, Scribbler looked at me. We locked eyes and stayed like that for a few seconds.

I remember expecting some profound jailhouse wisdom, some advice on my problems, or at least a rehearsal before we sat in front of the Governor, but no. He opened his mouth and said, "Oi, Rakz... How can man's dick be so small, bruv?"

I thought, "What?"

Then he starts elaborating, pounding one fist on top of the other. "Nah, seriously, my man had a fucking micropenis," he continues. "Like, if my ting was that small, I'd fucking hang myself."

Now, we ain't no battymen, but these white guys in prison have a habit of showing their manhood. They don't care. They'll stand in the shower, stark-bollock naked, having a conversation about tonight's menu. All the while, they've got their cock out on show like a Broadway production.

I remember one of the screws opening that door and jolting back in astonishment. Seeing both of us emerge from that holding cell in fits of laughter must have bamboozled poor old Mr Dawson, the duty officer. Somehow, Scribbler had made me completely forget about Shanice, about going before the Governor, and anything other than our conversation regarding the unfortunate-prick-that-tried-to-slice-me-in-the-showers'-micropenis.

Some people just have a special gift—to see the light in the darkest and bleakest of situations. Scribbler was one of them. "Smile through the rain and laugh through the pain," he'd say.

"Last call—showers!" I hear.

After wishing me well, Devonte scurries off, a bag full of my leftovers in his hand.

"Jamal, my brother, I'ma miss you," I say.

He slips me his number and smiles at me. It's not a proper smile, more of a brave one than anything. "Anything you need, just shout me, you know," I call out.

With one hand on the door, he looks back at me. "Good luck out there, family; I'ma miss you too," he says and turns out of my line of vision.

That would be the last time I ever saw him.

My last few moments as a prisoner, I get up and share a warm embrace with Scribbler.

"Scribz," I say as I haul a plastic bag over my shoulder, like a workman carrying a sack of garbage. "It's been a journey. One that I'll never forget 'til the day I die. And one I wouldn't have shared with any other man on this planet, my brother." His grin sprouts up again around those hard cheeks that look like they've been carved from stone. "Forever, my bro, just don't come back. If you do, I swear I'll kill you myself."

And I know Scribbler is more than capable of that.

By now, Mr F is hovering outside my door like a wasp on a warm day. I see his little measly figure hopping from side to side behind Scribbler. He wants to speed this up, but he doesn't have anywhere near the required minerals to tell two certified generals to hurry up a goodbye. He's a baby in our world. One that Scribz and I will happily discipline, should he forget.

I reach into my pocket and, making sure Mr F isn't watching, slap a small wrap of the most potent weed to hit HMP Huntingley into Scribbler's hand. "My G, that's for you," I say.

Pulling him close, I whisper five words. "Light one for me tonight."

Scribz's smile returns. "My guy!" he shouts, his vibrancy well and truly back in the room. He picks up a pair of my old trainers and accompanies me out of the cell. And as my journey towards a new chapter of my life begins, he has to remain here.

I look back at him as Mr F closes the gate to the wing. I've never seen that look in Scribbler's eyes before—a genuine glint of sadness. And for the first time in over seven years, I feel a burning sensation in the corner of my eye. Leaving Scribbler there was the hardest thing I've done in almost a decade. He holds a fist up and throws me a signal that he'll be smoking tonight.

There's a cacophony of noise like any day, but today I realise a lot of it's for me. Men chanting, "Don't come back" and "Roll safe, bro," amongst other farewell wishes, all positive.

I think.

I guess I was well-respected and much-loved here. And in a place that's full of envy, hate, and pain where genuine heartfelt gestures are scarce, that's something I'm proud to say I achieved.

2

Every prisoner has these ideas about their first day out. Who they're gonna see, where they're gonna go, what they're gonna do.

Initially, it starts as a thought, but as months become weeks and the day draws closer, the idea transforms into a meticulous list of desires prioritised in order of importance. Covering everything from each person they hope to surprise, to what and where they're gonna eat, to every song they're gonna blast.

You're probably wondering what happened on my first day out. Well, let me just burst your bubble quickly because it wasn't all champagne over Rolls Royces and my *ride-or-dies* posting my return to the streets across their social media pages. Nah, nothing like that.

That stuff does occur, but only for a small percentage of prisoners and mostly all of them short timers. Don't believe me? Ask any man who's served over ten years about his release day. You'll be lucky to find one out of every hundred with that story.

You see, the thing is, it's not personal. You have to learn that the hard way when doing a long stretch. I can't stress that enough. The reason why everybody has forgotten about you isn't that you're a worthless piece of shit that nobody ever cared for. Not by a long shot, even though you may feel that way. It's more of a case that twelve years is just a long fucking time.

Think back to twelve years ago. How many of the people you spoke to then, do you talk to now? A lot? Okay. Do you see them often? Less than once a month, right?

14

I'm wrong? Okay, when was the last time you saw them? What are their kids into? When did they last go on holiday? Did you go with them? Are they with you right now?

By this point, if you've still got a finger up, hat's off to you. I'll concede you're one of the lucky ones. The point is, I wasn't.

Most of the people I knew when I was eighteen are long gone. Some had families and moved out of the area, some are dead, some are in establishments like the one I just left, and some, I reckon, are still drifting around like lost souls in purgatory, searching for a purpose in life.

My release day was nothing more than a casual affair. My sister, Leanne, came to pick me up in her Audi Q7. Not quite a Rolls, but it'll suffice. I gave her a warm hug, and she squeezed me back. Then I spent the entire three-hour journey to my local probation office, listening to Leanne update me on her husband's new projects and why the pair of them are contemplating visiting Monaco this summer instead of Switzerland.

I didn't say much back. I was more struck by the surrounding scenery. Until we reached London, where I saw more and more human robots plodding along with their earphones plugged in, oblivious to the rest of the world.

Once we got back to Mum's, Leanne and I spoke more in-depth.

It was strange. Growing up, we'd fight like cat and dog. Being three years older, Leanne always thought she knew what was best for me, and I hated it. It was only when I reached big old fourteen that she couldn't get away with trying to control me anymore.

I had a new family by then.

A family that took me in at a tender young age, rid me of my innocence, and harnessed my potential. And by that, I don't mean encouraged me to fulfil my dreams of playing for Chelsea. I mean, taught me how to rob, sell drugs, use guns, cheat, lie, manipulate, and every other wicked trait I learned from Squeeze and them man.

15

Don't get it twisted. I ain't complaining. Nah, I take full responsibility for everything I've ever done because I learned some pretty good lessons under the watchful eye of my olders, too. Loyalty, courage, and most of all, that unbreakable spirit.

Maybe that's what got me through the last twelve years, I think, as I recline my seat and let a gush of wind hit my face through the open car window.

My second day out now, and believe me, the novelties have worn off already. There was no hero's return or welcome home party. Just a handful of letters. Mostly unpaid bills and an empty house that I'm not sure I even want to be in.

The upside is, right now, Leanne's driving me back to hers, so I'll get to see my nephews, Nathan and Ricky. I've missed them bad.

"They were just babies when I went away, ya know," I say, my words floating around in the car like I'm half speaking to myself.

"Three and two are hardly what you would call babies," Leanne says.

I turn to her as her head bounces along to the music. "How you think they gonna react when they see me?"

She gives me this sort of condescending yet loving glance. "Rakim, the boys love you."

"Yeah, but d'you think they'd even remember me?"

"Of course. You know a child's mind is a lot stronger and more advanced than people give it credit for."

There it is. It hasn't taken long. You would've thought this girl was raised in a West London suburb, the way she talks, pronouncing every syllable. I tolerate it and continue. "Yeah, I hear that, but twelve years is a long time, though, Lee."

"Don't forget we visited you once. And they've spoken to you plenty of times on the phone, so...."

I nod my head. More to let her think I agree than because I actually do.

The car stops, and the whole thing goes to sleep, sounding like that noise you make after you take a long sip of water.

16

We get out of the car and walk towards the house.

"It's nice round 'ere," I say, noticing the wide pavements and the maple trees, evenly spaced along the street like its own private slice of serenity. "Doing well for yourself, sis," I say with a playful nudge.

Leanne smiles, lapping up the compliment. "You know, Taylor's firm has an opening for a junior position. You could—"

"—I'm good," I say, emphasising the word 'good' so we don't get any lines crossed.

'If you think I'm working for your man, you obviously forgot who your brother is... Sorry, I meant, was.'

I have to remind myself that those days are no more.

Leanne shakes her head, probably thinking about how ungrateful I am. As we reach the house, she opens the door. Before I ask if Taylor will be here, his freshly moisturised face greets me with a smile that I bet he's practised a dozen times in the mirror this morning.

"Hey, bro, it's good to have you home," he says, placing a patronising hand on my shoulder. "By God, you've put on some muscle," he adds uncomfortably. "Come in, come in."

He obviously doesn't know the code. Or doesn't give a damn about it enough to respect it. When a man's just done twelve years in prison, you don't just put your hand on him willy-nilly with no warning. That's very likely to get your wrist snapped in two. I guess he's lucky I'm one of the good ones. I give him the nod and carry on through.

Leanne takes my coat and hangs it up on the coat stand. That's right, I said coat stand. My black sister has come up in the world. The tour begins, and with Taylor as the guide, I know we're in for a long one. *'Rah boy,'* I think as I look around the place.

One thing that hit me as soon as I left prison was the sharpness of the colours. Green fields are proper green. Blue skies are proper blue, and the white lights that shower down upon me at this moment in time are proper white. All of it just seems to pierce my eyes like I need to refine my settings.

17

The amount of space there is in this house is mind-blowing. This living room alone could fit six or seven cells in it.

I think of all the ways I would've decorated this room had I had this much space in my cell.

'Tele there, photos on that wall, my table just below, then all that space to work out.'

I have to stop myself in my tracks as I realise Timmy, Taylor, or whatever he calls himself, is explaining how the granite mantlepiece was formed in the Bronze Age, blah, blah, blah.

'This nigga's so pompous, man.'

Leanne sees me roll my eyes and gives me the finger. That means behave yourself.

I cut Taylor short mid-sentence. "So, what? Where're my nephews at?" I ask, trying to hide my excitement.

Taylor pauses as if shocked that I'd interrupt one of his grandiose explanations.

'I know, bro. It's hard to believe that there're things in this world people care about more than the sound of your voice.'

I stare at him blankly. He knows I know this is all a façade. He knows I don't give a shit about the French Renaissance and the paintings he acquired while over in Paris. I just want to see my nephews so I can squeeze them, play footy with them, and see what type of people they've grown into.

Truth is, I don't even care if they're not keeping up with anything. I've met loads of people like that in the past twelve years. I just want to spend some time with them, and if I can enhance their lives in any way, shape, or form, then you can bet your life I'll try my best to do just that.

Taylor's mouth hangs open as his eyes flit towards my sister, who is pouring a glass of some 1967 Chateau blah blah blah. I'm sure old Taylor over here would have a story to tell you about that as well, but right now, I couldn't care less.

"Where're the boys?" I ask again.

18

There's an awkward silence before Taylor's dainty lips, the kind you should never find on any black man on this earth, come together to form a false smile. "They're away," he says.

"What?"

"They're away," chirps his parrot over there.

"What the fuck does 'away' mean? They ain't on a lad's holiday gettin' smashed in Ayia Napa, are they?"

Looking shocked and appalled by my language, Taylor blinks rapidly. "Well, you see, Rah-kim."

"It's Rakim, pronounced Ra-keem," I assert.

It's another reason I can't stand this nigger. He'll do dumb little things like that on purpose. He knows my name is Rakim. He's known it for eighteen years and knows how to pronounce it, yet he'll purposely mispronounce it to make me feel unimportant and inadequate.

"I beg your pardon. Well, when I say away, I mean they're at school. It's term time."

"It's a Saturday," I say, looking puzzled, no doubt.

"Yeah, they go to boarding school," Leanne says.

"What, since when, and why?" My face can't comprehend it any more than my brain can.

Taylor cracks that false smile again, and I swear if he does it once more, I'm gonna rearrange his smug little face.

"It's a brilliant school. The facilities they have and the programs on offer are absolutely second to none. I've known the Headteacher there for many—"

"—Last ting I remember, boarding school was for faggots," I cry, looking around the room to see if there's any black left in these imposters around me.

Answer is no, sadly, as they look at each other. "Rakim..." Leanne begins. "Boarding school's good for them. It's a chance—"

"—It's a chance for you to get rid of 'em," I say. "Come on, Leanne, what's all that about?" I say, throwing my arms out in front of me.

19

Leanne cuts an uncomfortable grimace before Supercoon steps in. "I think you'll find Rakim, a lot of things have changed since you last remember."

Wow. It's taken less than fifteen minutes for this punk to remind me of what I've missed. I feel myself raging inside, the adrenaline firing on all cylinders. I look at Leanne and ask, "why did you bring me here if you knew the boys wouldn't be here?"

She sips her wine but doesn't answer.

I look at Supercoon.

Usually, this pretentious piece of work has an answer for everything. But not right now, he just swirls his red around in his crystal wine glass.

"You know what, safe, you lot," I say before grabbing my coat and walking towards the door. I don't see him, but I feel like Supercoon is getting some kind of pleasure out of my disappointment, almost as if he orchestrated this little stunt on purpose.

I look back and feel a burning desire to knock this guy's head off or at least give him a piece of my mind. Instead, I find myself taking deep breaths and counting down from ten. *Five... Four...* By the time I get to three, the anger has simmered a tad. *'Rah, perhaps them Violence Reduction courses actually work after all,'* I hear myself thinking.

But I have to slow my roll.

'Easy. Don't think you're there just yet. There's gonna be a lot more tests than Supercoon.'

And believe me, there were, but we'll get to that later.

With my coat in my hand, I yank open the door. If I had to put my money on it, I'd bet Andy Peters over there has probably got his arms folded, shaking his head, 'horrified by my belligerence.'

'I've had enough. Fuck him. And her, too, for choosing that prick over me.'

I slam the door and head out.

No sooner than I do, I realise it was probably a stupid idea. I haven't a clue where I am.

Halfway across the driveway, I hear the door open behind me.

"Rakim, wait, don't go," Leanne cries.

I kiss my teeth and ignore her. But one thing about Leanne, she can be goddam persistent when she wants to be. Eventually, she catches up with me after jogging behind my marching legs for a hundred-odd yards. "What, Leanne, what d'you want?" I cave.

"Look, Rakz, I'm sorry. I should have told you about Nath and Ricky."

"Yeah, you should have. You led man here thinkin' I'm seeing them after all this time, for what?"

I notice a couple from across the road beam at me like I'm a foreign species, and I turn to face them. With one glance, they immediately surrender. The man pats his lapdog of a wife on the back as her face turns bright red, and they both hurry off.

I guess seeing a big black man raise his voice is like the Golden Fleece around these parts. Or maybe it's that old death stare creeping back into me.

"I know, I know. I'm sorry," Leanne says, holding one arm awkwardly as she shakes the locks of her jet-black hair from her face.

I relax, letting my hands drop to my side.

"I never told you because I knew you'd react like this," Leanne says.

'That old line.'

"Look, I can see it on your face now. You just think that I've abandoned my boys or something."

She's right, that's exactly what I think, but I stay silent. I've learned over the years that you tend to understand people a lot better when you just sit back and allow them to explain themselves.

"I know you think I don't give a shit about them boys, but you've been away a long, long time, Rakim," Leanne says as I notice a tear begin to form at the bottom of her eye. "You don't know what it was like to deal with everything by myself—raising two boys alone. Rakim, it was fucking hard. Mum was there, and I thank God every day that she was, because if she wasn't, I don't know what on earth I would have done without her."

I watch a solitary tear trickle down Leanne's face and reserve my judgement. This is all getting a bit embarrassing for her, I can tell. She wants to cry and let it all out, but that's not 'classy.' How dare she play the victim in this neighbourhood she's been accepted into. Whatever she's going through is nothing compared to the problems of this uppity lot around here; God forbid little Georgie doesn't eat his spaghetti hoops this evening.

No, she better suck it up, carry on with the fake smiles and be as grateful as a slave is to his master that she lives amongst these folks. Because as quickly as she got in, she could be thrown out. Then where does she find herself? I won't tell you where, but it ain't cooped up with Supercoon in a three-point-five-million-pound pad, that's for damn sure.

She brushes her eye with the back of her sleeve. "Sorry," she says as if she needs to apologise for feeling how she does. The mascara smears across her face, staining her beige sleeve, but she composes herself. Straightening her back, she puts her hand on my shoulder.

"Look, you've only been out a couple of days. I bet you haven't even eaten a proper good meal yet, have you? Why don't you just come back inside, and we can all sit down and eat together."

"Nah, I'm good," I say calmly.

If there's one thing I'm not about to do, it's take anything from that man. I did it once when he and Leanne were just friends, and I got bit hard. It was only a one'ner, but you'd think it was a kidney the way he went on. Knowing him, if I eat at his table, he'll probably bring it up ten years later when he wants a ride home or something, 'Oh, remember I made you dinner that time, though.' The type of petty shit I just can't get down with.

"Please," Leanne begs, squinting her eyes to exaggerate her sincerity. "Just stay for tea; Taylor's made a wonderful coq au vin."

"I bet he has," I scorn as I think of Jonesy and all the jokes he'd been running right now about Taylor and his coq au vin.

'He's probably taking some cock in a van, the fucking poofter. You sure he ain't behind on the rent on this gaff?' Jonesy's grainy, cockney accent plays in my head.

I look around and see the roads are beginning to get busier. Cars whizz by, and their fumes permeate the air. Children run by with their parents a little further along the pavement, and the mist of azure blue that the sky was an hour ago has begun to darken behind the curtain of grey clouds that linger above.

"Nah, I'm gonna head home, ya know," I reply.

Leanne sighs. She's disappointed, but I guess today, my stubbornness beats her persistence. "At least let me drop you, then," she says, trying to hold eye contact.

I swivel my head and give her a little something she's yearning for. "Of course, you're dropping me. You think man was taking bus?"

She smiles, satisfied she gets to play her part. It's that big sister in her, still feeling like she needs to protect me. Even though I'm stocky and scale the scarier side of six-feet, Leanne's maternal nature will never let up.

We walk in silence as we both kind of take in the atmosphere.

As we stroll, white petals from snowball bushes litter the pavement like confetti while birds sing mellifluously in the trees above, and I realise how much I've missed these early summer evenings. They used to feel so free to me before I went away. Like the world was my playground. A sense of weightlessness walked with me wherever I went, whatever I did. Nothing mattered.

I guess it's the case with most people before they get bogged down with the constraints of family and life in general. I never got that, though. My shackles were the ones that 'His Honourable' Judge Arun cast upon me. Twelve long years ago. And it wasn't no twelve-do-six or twelve-do-eight. The good old HMP staff made sure they set me up to do the full term, having me arrested for an alleged assault on a prison officer and activating my recall once I reached the reception.

That's right, I could've been out after eight summers but ended up doing another four. Twelve years and not a day less.

The Parole Board had no interest in my mitigation. Maybe they disliked my attitude, and perhaps I disliked theirs, or maybe it was six of one and half a dozen of the other. Either way, I lost those last truly free years of my life. The ones before expectations kick in, and you start measuring yourself by whatever parameters you've created to form your own ideas of failure and success.

To be honest, I don't really know what mine are. I guess I'm still trying to work that out, but I know what others think, and believe me, in their book of accomplishments, I'm right at the bottom. Shit, I'm lucky if they even gave me the time of day to write my name and put a big red cross next to it—an ex-con with barely any qualifications and even less money. I haven't even spoken to my fourteen-year-old daughter in over five years.

'Damn, when I say it like that.'

At least I had that going for me while I was banged up. I could have salvaged some pride by being a good dad, but I fucked that up and haven't even got that to boast about anymore. Life, eh?

We reach Leanne's car, and I get in.

"One minute," she says as she darts inside, her long grey overcoat flapping in her wake.

Minutes later, she returns carrying a plastic bag as she jumps in the car, looking a little rejuvenated, and starts the engine. When the drive's done, and we pull over, I check my phone.

One missed call.

I recognise the number and smile. I've used that tech so many times I could probably recall the number quicker than my own mother's date of birth.

"Scribz," I mutter.

I check the time and vow to call him later.

Leanne looks over at the three-bedroom house to her right that stands out like a black man in Cornwall. Not just because it's one of the only houses with a beautifully kept front garden. And I'm talking bushes trimmed neater than a gentleman's beard, flowers sprucing up now we're deep into spring and circular grey paving slabs like steppingstones in a lake of green, leading up to the door. Not just because of all of that. But because it's our house. Or at least it was. Leanne left a long time ago, and so did I, but life has a funny way of coming full circle, and now the house that we all shared together, me, Leanne, and Mum, has once again become my nesting spot.

"You looked after it well," I say.

Leanne glows like a pot of gold; she always loved a compliment. She's a Leo, and they revel in praise, in case you didn't know.

"You think?" she says, trying to sound humble.

Let me tell you. There isn't anything about my sister that's humble. Not since she shacked up with Mr Coq Au Vin, anyway. Whatever humility and sense of where she came from she once had, was discarded with the rest of us 'chaff' as soon as she entered the upper echelons of society.

I nod, thinking about what I want to do with mum's house. So much old junk needs removing, and I just don't have the motivation.

That's one thing about prison. Everything's done for you. Your food's cooked, you're given your clothes, your one hour to socialise, your TV, you know where you stand, and whatever you do to fill in the gaps is pretty much limited to reading or exercising (mentally or physically). I'd organise my cell with pride. That came naturally, but a six-by-eight-feet cell is much easier to maintain than a two-story, three-bed, if you catch my drift.

"We should get someone in there with you," Leanne says, probably hoping it will wind me up.

I bite.

"You're mad. Ain't nobody coming up in mum's house," I reply before opening the passenger door.

She giggles, and for a second, she reminds me of Keziah.

'Rah, that was weird,' I tell myself as I feel a hand on my arm.

With a little glint in her eye, Leanne hands me a plastic bag. "Here... It's good to have you back, Rakz," she says.

This time there's no sarcasm or hint that I'm not on her level. She's just my sister, and I'm just her brother. The way it's supposed to be.

3

I hate to admit it, but it turns out, Supercoon makes a pretty damn good coq au vin after all. Something about that makes me want to despise him even more, but I've never been a hater—*credit, where credit's due*—that went down a treat.

What he lacks in black culture he makes up for with fine dining; I'll give him that. It's definitely his lane.

But then I reckon we've all got our lanes in life. I think the best way is to find your lane and concentrate on whatever you're good at doing. Work hard, perfect your craft, and don't worry about what anybody else is doing because that's their lane, not yours.

Let me give you an example. I was about two years into my bid, and I was in this A Cat. For those who don't know, that's where they house the most hardened and dangerous criminals.

There were some violent guys in there. Serial killers, terrorists, hitmen. You name it. And upon my arrival at HMP Hellmarsh, its reputation as Britain's Guantanamo Bay had me edgy, to say the least.

But after a couple of weeks, I realised that although the inmates there were a different breed of prisoner, they weren't necessarily worse people than any other prisoners I'd met in other jails. In fact, I probably got along with those guys in Hellmarsh better than I got on with anyone else on my tour, bar Scribbler and Jamal.

Maybe deep down, I'm just one of them. I mean, the judge did send me there, after all.

Anyway, back to my story.

I was in Hellmarsh, and this guy was on my wing. An older fella, late thirties, in for murdering his friend over a stupid argument. You might remember it; it came on the news in late 0'12. They dubbed him the 'The Binbag Killer.'

And you can probably guess why they named him that. If you can't, I'll be brief. It involved a bathtub, a chainsaw, and a set of black bin bags. I'll let your imagination do the rest.

And to top it off, when they came for this guy, he hid in a wheelie bin in the back garden.

Not quite the ticket, I hear you say. You'd think that, but he nearly pulled it off. The police raided the whole house and never found him. Only when a neighbour alerted the police to the dustbin that seemed to have taken on a life of its own did they discover this guy.

His name was Dang-su, and he would perch himself on this table by the cafeteria doors with his chess board. And every day, he'd sit there, waiting.

Well, after a while, people got to know him as the 'chess guy.' Imagine you've cut your best friend up into big fleshy chunks with a chainsaw, and your reputation for being a chess genius is what precedes you. Crazy init? It just shows you how de-sensitised those bars and walls can make a man.

So, I ended up taking an interest in chess, you know, keep my mind occupied and all that, and I began to play against him daily, even though he was renowned for beating everyone he faced.

Every day I'd get better, but still nowhere near his level. He'd tell me I'd lost my queen three moves in advance. I'd do everything in my power to guard her, but he'd come along every time, just like he promised, and scoop her up.

As you can probably tell, I don't judge people by their crimes. I judge them by their character. For all you know, Dang-su may have discovered some kiddy porn on his friend's laptop. If that was why he murdered his friend, then he's a hero in my book and deserves a statue, not a sentence.

So, one day he gets this fascination with lifting weights, or maybe it had been stirring for some time, but I reckon most likely it was from

28

seeing how the lady screws blushed like little schoolgirls when the guys with enormous chests or biceps came along.

Now, this guy was Korean, Vietnamese, or some shit. And you know how those guys are built—noodle arms and bean sprout legs. But he kept talking about how he wanted to be big. 'Big and bad,' he called it, 'like Rambo.' I used to find it funny, to be honest, until one day, I returned from a visit, and the whole wing was on lockdown.

I was rushed back to my cell, and imagine what news greeted me? Apparently, Dang-su, the chess wizard, went to the gym and got some bad advice. He'd tried bench-pressing a hundred and sixty kilos straight off the rack, and the whole thing dropped straight on his neck, crushed his windpipe, and killed him. So yeah, I think it's fair to say I've learned a thing or two about staying in my lane.

Here we are now, it's been four weeks since my release, and I find I'm doing okay. "I'm adapting to modern society," my probation officer calls it. If you ask me, he should be the one in a chair taking advice from me. With one of the bedrooms clear now, I'm seriously considering taking up Leanne's offer and renting this place out.

And I know you may be shocked thinking about how ex-prisoners are exceptionally particular with who they let up in their business. Well, I'll let you in on another thing about ex-cons: many of us are broke, me included. So, if I have to tolerate someone for eight hundred pounds a month for a while, that's what I'll do. Hell, I've done it for free for over a third of my life, and that was much closer quarters.

So, it's around nine o'clock, and I'm at home with my rice, stew chicken, and a healthy side of callaloo.

Around this time, I usually find myself winding down. I've completed my five hundred press-ups, and I'm enjoying the cool evening breeze that floats through the open window when my phone rings.

I know it can only be a handful of people, and when I check the screen and find out it's Scribz, I instantly smile.

"Scribbler, my brudda," I say.

"What's going on? Every'ting straight?"

"Yeah, course, c'mon," I say.

Scribz knows I'd say that regardless, though. Even if I'd just had my leg ripped off by an alligator, he'd get the same response. Men like us have what some might consider a complex when dumping our emotions and problems on others. We're not 'bitches', so we're not allowed to complain. And that isn't me complaining. I think you'd agree if I told you I had something to complain about by this point in my story.

No?

Okay, wait a while.

"So, what, family good and that?" Scribz asks.

"Yeah, fam."

We wade through the small talk before Scribz pauses.

It's a long pause, so I know what's coming. It's something Scribbler genuinely doesn't want to ask me.

I cut the tension and save Scribbler the uncomfortable feeling of asking another man for a favour.

"How much, bro?" I ask.

He pauses and breathes deeply. "Four bills," he mumbles.

"Done."

"Rah, I should have asked for more init," he jokes.

"You would've got the same reply, my bro. What's mine is yours. 'Til the grave."

"My brudda," Scribz says.

It might sound pathetic at the grand old age of thirty, but that four hundred pounds will severely dent my pocket.

'I'm defo gonna have to find someone for that room. And sooner rather than later.'

A voice calls out from the background.

"Who's that?" I ask.

"It's Devonte, cuz."

"Wa gwarn, bro?" I laugh. "After all that bitchin', you man padded up anyway."

30

"Yeah, had to, that prick who was up on the top bunk, try bringing spice up in the cell, man fucked him up. And took his spice," Scribbler yells.

"Sell that and make some Ps."

"Of course. C'mon," Scribz says before going quiet again.

I feel another question coming.

"Rakz..." Scribz begins. This time he's got the serious voice on, though. "Listen, I know you're not on nothing right now, but I need a favour, bro. You know I'm not that guy to be—"

I feel the desperation in his voice, and it brings me no pleasure to listen to my friend drag this out, so I interject. "—Just tell me what it is, fam. I got you."

"My worker got nicked. I need the Ps quickly to switch up this phone."

He's talking, but he's still taking too long to get to the point, and it's making me a little nervous. I shift my body to the edge of the sofa. "Scribz, what d'you need man to do?" I ask, raising my voice.

"I need you to grab the food from the spot," he sighs.

"Ahhh, Scribz, man," I say, closing my eyes.

"Bro, I wouldn't ask if I weren't in need."

"I know you wouldn't, but bro, just listen to what you're asking me to do."

"Rakz, it's a quick ting, in and out, man."

'If I had a pound for every time I've heard that....'

"Your tellin' me your worker got nicked. That means the next ting gettin' raided is the spot," I say. "Feds have probably set up shop right opposite the yard and are just waiting for a doughnut to come up there."

"It's not an obbo ting, though. No one's watching the yard like that," he says as if that's supposed to put my mind at rest.

"How d'you know?"

"I just do," he booms.

"Just do... C'mon, you gotta do better than that, Scribz."

31

He pauses, knowing he can't argue with me.

"Ite let me find out. If Sally and Irish ain't been nicked, then there's no way feds are watching the place."

"Cool."

"The only thing is, though, as soon as I tell them the pattern, they're gonna know the yard's empty and all that food'll be gone."

I see his predicament. You can never trust crackheads. They'll steal money from their own kids, much less a load of drugs from a man locked away in a cell.

"How much you holding?" I ask.

"There's about a fours of each," he says.

I kiss my teeth. Loudly. Making sure my frustration's heard.

"Look, sleep on it, bro. I'll hit you first thing in the morning. But be ready for seven 'cause I'm gonna hit Irish, and you need to get there before him."

I haven't even said I'll do it yet. But I guess Scribz just knows me. I've never let him down in the six-odd years I've known him, why would I start now?

I take a deep breath. "Ite, ring me in the morning," I say.

"Soon come, my brudda," he shouts and hangs up.

I push the plastic carton of rice and chicken to one side and run my hand through my tiny afro, scratching hard at the crown of my head. "Fuck's sake," I curse, then quickly apologise as I look over at a photograph of Mum on the mantlepiece.

The clock reveals I've only got a couple more hours in me if I'm aiming to wake up at seven, but I don't think sleep is on the agenda tonight.

For the past fifteen years, the remedy for my sleepless nights has always been one thing—weed. But I haven't smoked since I've been out, which might sound like nothing to the average person, but to go from pretty much every day for half my life to nothing in nearly a month, is quite an achievement.

However, if I'm to help Scribz out then that achievement isn't about to last.

A few days ago, I came across some kids during one of my strolls. They weren't exactly kids. Probably, sixteen, seventeen—kids to me. Anyway, one of them reminded me of myself back in the day. It wasn't anything spectacular; it was just his tenacity.

I was waiting for my food in the Chinese shop, keeping a low profile, and this group of kids, about five of them, were messing around on their phones, hovering over their bikes, skylarking. But this one with the orange cap stood out, he was different from the rest.

How, you ask? Well, it's like this. There's a structure when you're a group of teenagers growing up around here. Or more like a hierarchy. Use a company, for example. You have the CEO, the guy right at the top, nobody ever sees him, but he calls the shots and makes the real money. Below him are directors, then maybe regional managers who oversee various individuals like site or store managers.

Forgive me if any of these details are not entirely accurate. Business studies were way back in 2007, and I failed miserably.

Well, right at the bottom of the pyramid are your everyday store assistants, waiters, receptionists, and what have you, the ones that directly serve Mr & Mrs Joe Bloggs.

The roads aren't much different, to be fair. Take Jonesy, for example. I told you about how he was in on a sixteen stretch. Now, before I continue any further, this is all 'alleged' I have to say. That's my disclaimer.

So, 'allegedly' Jonesy was a distributor for the southeast of London. His commitments were to adhere to his superiors who brought the merchandise off the ports at Dover, Felixstowe, or wherever it arrived. Jonesy was to collect the same amount of product each month from those above him in the chain of command. That way, his suppliers would never have to worry about doing business with anyone they don't know.

Jonesy's job was then to distribute the merchandise to lower-level dealers who would either break the stuff down and sell directly to users or move it on to smaller-time dealers at wholesale prices. Usually, the latter 'cause Jonesy only dealt in squares, not circles.

Lost? Well, I can't be telling you everything, word for word. You're just gonna have to get with the program. Otherwise, you'll get left behind.

Your turn to be the 'chaff.' Not nice, is it?

Anyway, back to Orange Baseball Cap. I watched him and his friends for a good fifteen minutes, and he pushed the most sales, approached the most people, and took the most numbers. Then he'd send one of his guys on the bikes to go and conduct the deals. It's pretty basic stuff when you've been around it your whole life.

Out of the collective, Orange Baseball Cap was the most organised. He had the most hunger. He was the one who had potential, and now he's the one I'm gonna get.

It sounds unscrupulous, I know, but I've realised you don't get anywhere in life by being squeaky clean. Then on the flip side, you only end up in two places when you're a downright dirty scumbag. So, I guess it comes down to that moral compass, which rules you can break, and which ones you can't, and somewhere in the middle, there're ones you can bend. But steer too much to the left, and you'll crash, and the same goes for the right.

I'd like to say I'm generally good, but then I've done many terrible things. Not to mention the one that got me put away for nearly half of my life. I'd also like to think I have a clean heart and good intentions. But then, you know what they say about good intentions, don't you?

So, if I am to get this young boy involved in something, I need to ensure that it's for the right reasons, not just for my own personal gain.

I know I'm not there yet, but even sitting here thinking about this, weighing up consequences for others is a massive step towards becoming a better man. Twelve years ago, I would have sent my mum into a burning building if I had something worth saving. Well, not my mum, but you catch my drift. Orange Baseball Cap would have been the first pawn I sacrificed.

Rest in Peace, Dang-su.

So how am I gonna get Orange Baseball Cap to my house by seven in the morning, you're wondering?

Well, I'm one step ahead of you lot. Remember I told you I picked up chess while on my 'tour behind the door.' Chess is all about strategies, seeing opportunities, and identifying threats. And that day I saw Orange Baseball Cap doing his thing, it was an opportunity I couldn't turn down.

I pull out my phone and dial the number I saved outside the Chinese shop. Straight away, it's answered.

"Yo, who's that?" a voice says that sounds like it's still clinging to childhood.

"I need a twenty," I say.

"Who is this? And where you get my number?"

So far, so good. He's passed the first test. Don't run for the money. Caution first. I could be anyone.

"I got your number off Jay."

"I know a hundred Jays, bro. Tell him phone me and shout man back," he says hurriedly. I hear scampering around in the background, under raucous motorbikes and the shouts of the high road before the line goes dead.

Orange Baseball Cap is living up to my assumptions. I ring him back and go through the same old process. He offers to send a worker to me, but I say I'll go to him instead.

My trainers on and coat zipped up, I hit the road.

The soft glimmer from the moonlight appeases me tonight. The sky is dotted with dazzling stars every so often as I look up above and go over Scribz's request in my head. Doing the maths, the merchandise sitting in that flat is probably worth about twenty-five grand when you break it all down.

And if you're at a loss to understand why a man needs twenty-five-grand when in prison, I'll fill you in. Just because you get sent away to prison, life doesn't stop there for everyone else, including your family. And Scribz isn't an exception. His motivation for all this is crystal clear—two children and a mother who's not in the best of health. Remember what I told you. When the odds are against you, you still try your best. Scribz earned my respect a long time ago.

I arrive at the same spot I saw the young bucks chilling at the other day, and in less than a minute of being there, a boy speeds up to me on a scooter. I tell him to take off the stupid ski mask he's got on, and hearing my tone, he quickly obeys.

'*Shit.*'

It's not Orange Baseball Cap. This yout' is clever.

But what he doesn't know about me is that this was my old life when he was probably still struggling at breaststroke inside his dad's ballbag. I ring him off another phone, and he answers straight away. "Oi, come out of the chicken shop," I tell him.

He goes silent, probably thinking how the hell I've clocked him.

"Say no more, man's coming," he cries like he's just charged his batteries.

Raindrops begin to hit the ground around me as a gush of wind snaps at my neck, and I turn to see four boys, all hoods up and wearing facemasks, walking towards me.

Honestly, I don't know whether to laugh or cry.

"What's good, big man?" one of them shouts, meandering through the oncoming traffic with a purposeful bounce in his step before finally reaching my side of the street.

The army of rugrats approaches, forming a semi-circle in front of me. One is bobbing up and down like he needs a piss, and another is talking some shit behind his mask.

"Take your mask off. I can't hear you," I say calmly.

This guy lifts his mask and manages to balls that up. Now it's folded over one of his eyes. I can tell he's not my guy by the shape of his mouth.

"What d'you want, bro? My guy just come to hit you. Do you want the ting or not? If not, keep it moving," he says.

I wave my index finger while my other hand remains in my pocket. "I like you," I say. "Keep that energy, I might need it soon."

He starts amping himself up as if he's been disrespected, and I hear shouts from his goons around him like these lot wanna get brave and attack me.

Now for some people, this is scary, and they get nervous; you see it in their movements, hear the quivers in their voices, or the gulping sound when their heart is working extra hard to pump oxygen around the body. But as you know, I've sat there and played chess with south London's answer to the Texas Chainsaw Massacre. I've shared cells with guys who have tortured people and told me all the gory details. I've fought with racist Northerners, seven-feet Latvians and showered with absolute nutters who will run a shaving blade across your throat just because Tuesday was supposed to be *Burger Day*. So, you can imagine these kids getting themselves worked up is the least of my concern.

One of them is shaking like a leaf as he opens his mouth. "Are you a fed or something, bruv?" this boy asks, evading the splash from a puddle.

I'm about to reply when Orange Baseball Cap lifts his mask and reveals himself.

"You," I say.

I extend my hand, which holds a fifty-pound note, and tell him to walk with me.

He looks at his cronies for confirmation, but he knows, and I know, I had him with that pink note.

"You good, bro?" one of his sidekicks calls out to him as Orange Baseball Cap and I walk off together. Orange Baseball Cap nods at his

37

friend and follows me until we reach a junction. "What do you want, bro?" he asks as the rain continues its assault on the road.

This guy must be perplexed. I would be if someone called me for some weed and did this whole song and dance before removing his hood theatrically like some Jedi Master. As I expose my face, Orange Baseball Cap just stares at me.

I lean in. "You wanna make some money?" I ask.

Wiping the rainwater from his nose, he moves his head away from me. Then I watch his shoulders drop as he seems to examine my face. "Oh, it's you from the other day. Why didn't you just say?" he says.

"You gotta pass the test first, bro... So, what you saying, you wanna make some money, then?"

"Course, bro," he says and holds out a fist.

I spud him as a mark of respect.

"Keep your phone on you. I'm gonna phone you first thing in the morning," I say. "And it's Rakz, by the way, yeah."

"I'm Deontay. Just call me D, though, bro."

"Say nuttin'. Tomorrow," I say, turning my body around and flicking my hood back up.

"Love," he calls.

I walk off back towards where I came from, take one glance across the road, and drag my top-heavy frame to the other side.

Seconds later, I feel a tap on my arm. It's the jumpy rugrat, and he's finally managed to get that mask off.

"There you go, big man," he squeaks, handing me a bag of weed. I tap his extended fist and stroll back home to set my plan in motion.

4

Scribz knew I wouldn't let him down. All that 'sleep on it, I hit you in the morning' shit; he knows me, I'm down. Whether that means cracking some punk's head open because he stole Scribz's burn from his pad or today's task of collecting a quarter kilo of the hard stuff from his stash house, I'm down.

Everything's in place. I managed to get Leanne to lend me the Audi for the day. She nearly jumped for joy when I told her I was gonna look for a job. I guess anything that brings me a tad closer to her world or leads me further away from mine is a reason for her to rejoice.

So, me and Deontay are sat in the Audi as we wait. This morning's air is crisp, only tainted by the overpowering smell of cement. Deontay turned up on time, courtesy of that scooter of his, no doubt. And although he wasn't the calmest soul when he arrived, he's learned quickly. No questions. Just how I like it.

Parked on the road adjacent to the block of flats Deontay will soon enter, I have a clear, unobstructed view and can see the whole estate from my seat. The streets aren't that busy. It's before the morning rush and only a couple of workmen in hard hats and steel toe capped boots linger around.

It's the perfect time.

Opposite me, a red plastic fence is erected around a gaping hole in the pavement, and a makeshift footpath occupies half the width of the road, which means if push comes to shove, it's a narrow escape, which can be a good thing or a bad thing.

I stroke the steering wheel softly, like I'm massaging oil into a beautiful woman—the way Shanice used to do my back in my old life.

I shelf that thought as my phone vibrates.

It's Scribz.

"Yo," I answer, feeling the hole that Deontay's eyes are boring through the side of my skull.

Scribz goes over our plan once more as I turn to face Deontay. "A step up from shottin' draws," I whisper to him, trying to calm his irrefutable nerves.

Deontay nods his head as I return to my conversation.

"Yeah... Yeah, yeah. Say no more," I say and put my phone away.

Deontay's eyes remain fixed on me, and I feel like a father who is about to send his child onto the football pitch for his first game. "Listen," I tell him. "You know what you gotta do. Just in and out, don't stop and chat to no one. Man's right here. I can see you the whole time."

"What should I do if I see someone?" he asks.

"Be calm, you're good, fam. I'm just here," I reassure him.

"Ite, bro," he replies with an overenthusiastic nod.

I think about dropping something a little more enigmatic, like, 'pressure makes diamonds, so if you wanna shine, you gotta handle the pressure,' but you know what it's like with today's youth. It'll just fly straight over his head.

Instead, I hand him one of them small Bluetooth headset things and let him connect it to his phone before dialling his number and sending him on his way.

This kind of thing is second nature to me, like my brushing my teeth, but I'm not sure how Deontay will cope. I've briefed him on what to do, so everything should run smoothly. I just hope he thinks like me and moves like me if he has to.

I watch him walk straight towards the block. Our way in is number twenty-eight, courtesy of Scribz. Any sign of police, though, and Deontay knows the rendezvous spot; we've been over this.

40

As Deontay enters the block, my mind drifts to the first time I was taken on a job like this. Me and some guy Risky, I think his name was. The funny thing is that it wasn't too far from here.

We had the task of robbing this stash house. Risky was tiny, so his role was to get through the open window round the back, then open the door and let me in. Spoiler alert: it didn't go to plan.

Risky got through the window as best he could, landing on a wash basin before crashing to the ground. Then I remember seeing the light go on and thinking, *'Shit, somebody's in the house.'*

That's the thing in this line of work; there aren't any guarantees or no ombudsmen to turn to if things go wrong. All that doesn't exist in the streets. If a man tells you that a house is empty, then it's up to you whether to believe him or not.

So anyway, Risky got through this window and... Wait...

"Shit, what's happened?" I say.

Deontay's walking like he's got a rocket up his arse.

"Wa gwarn, bro?" I ask.

"There's someone there, man; there's someone there."

"Chill out. What's up?"

I have to strain to make out the muffled words through this phone.

"Oi, bro, there's two men behind me," Deontay says.

I look, but I can't see anybody. Just blocks, an empty playground. "There's no one there, cuz."

"Two man just followed me down the stairs, bro; what do I do?" he panics.

"Just chill, keep walking towards me, there's nobody..." I go to say when I see the door of the block open and out step two men, looking dodgy as hell. Deontay's heard the creaking of the door behind him. I can tell—his legs are moving way faster.

"Yo, chill out, man," I warn him.

"Are they coming?" he asks.

From the side, these two don't look like police officers. I've been away a long time, but when you've built up a knack for it, sometimes you can just tell.

"Yo, where are they?" Deontay asks once again. He looks like he's in that ultimate panic mode. The one where you're so worried if the camera can see your face, you look directly at it.

"Don't turn around, just keep walking—look at me—keep walking towards me," I instruct him.

The gym bag he's carrying bounces around his waist like a kangaroo as he marches towards me.

'*Who the fuck are these guys?*' I think as I see one of the men, a sturdy Arab-looking guy, tap his lanky friend. For whatever reason, they're onto Deontay. And like two poachers, they begin to stalk him.

"Oi, bro. What should I do?" Deontay asks.

He's heard the footsteps.

The men are about thirty yards adrift; Deontay must feel them behind him as he clutches the strap across his shoulder. I know he wants to run, but it might not be necessary. He's over halfway back to the car. He may be able to outwalk them.

"Just be calm, keep walking, man," I say.

I notice the Arab-looking guy with the leather jacket behind him begin to speed up.

He's got that mean-muggin' face on–eyebrows, nostrils, and mouth all screwed up like someone's stomped on his clean white Air Forces.

'*He definitely ain't no fed.*'

The towering guy next to him has got the same look on his face. Something's pissed them off.

I gotta think quickly. I'm really not on this turning into a chase.

Firstly, I don't know if Deontay's got the legs on him. I've only seen him zip around on that scooter. I got no idea if he's the hare or the tortoise.

And secondly, I don't know who these men are. For all I know, they could have a Samurai sword and a sawn-off shotgun stuffed underneath those oversized jackets.

Farfetched?

You obviously didn't grow up where I did—I didn't get this hideous scar across my arm from peeling onions. Nor the one on my back.

'I gotta do suttin'.'

The men are less than five metres behind Deontay, and he looks like he's about to take off any second.

I open the car door and jump out. "Are you taking the piss, David? Hurry up! You got your Mum waiting 'ere," I shout, tapping my wrist where a watch would be.

The men freeze.

Deontay looks just as stunned as they do, though.

"Hurry up, or you ain't going football today," I yell, moving my arm swiftly to indicate he needs to run.

I wait for a second as the two men appear to be sizing me up. They're probably wondering if I'm old enough to be this boy's dad, and even if I am, can they take me on?

I can tell straight away that they're unsure. The uncertainty in the stocky guy's demeanour—a look I've seen many times on many landings.

When a man's looking for a chink in your armour, you either be the real deal or look the real deal. And sometimes, the latter's not even enough. Unluckily for this pair, though, I'm both.

While they're busy contemplating who the hell I am, Deontay takes the cue and jogs towards me just like a son would when summoned by his father. I turn my attention to Deontay as he approaches me.

"My bad, Dad," he says as the men watch on.

Deontay reaches my side, and I slap him round the head just for effect. "Get in the car, boy."

His eyes filled with terror, and his mouth wide open, he cowers and moves around to the passenger door.

I know he felt that one; I kept a little force in it.

I get in the car, start the engine, and spin the car around. The Audi roars and takes off like a missile.

"Rah."

If you've never floored a four-litre, twin-turbo V8 engine, let me tell you, it throws you back against the headrest like a body slam.

Once we're a safe distance away from those two goons, I slow the car as we approach a traffic light. Deontay's still sitting there in silence, looking a mixture of scared and confused. He's probably thinking about why he got a slap round the head and not a pat on the back.

"That was for your little badman act the other day in front of your friends," I say with two fingers pointed at him.

He holds my glare, then, after a few seconds, realises the playful tone behind my words and smiles as the light turns green, and we drive off.

"Oi, bro, who were them man there?" he asks, and I can almost feel the fear in his question.

"Don't worry 'bout that. You got the bag. That's all that matters."

Deontay removes the strap from his shoulder and places the bag on his lap. I can feel this yout' about to ask what's inside, but to my surprise, the words don't come out. That slap must still have his head ringing. That, or he's learned you don't ask questions above your pay grade.

We pass a long row of buildings on the right and a blur of a green field on the left before we stop at another traffic light.

"Oi, bro," Deontay begins, rubbing his hands together like a praying mantis. "How much you dropping me?" he says, squinting his eyes as he tilts his head to the side.

I glance over at this kid. Usually, I'd G-check a man for those types of questions, but he's young, and so far, he's done everything required of him.

I bury one hand in my pocket, and Deontay's eyes light up like a set of headlights when I pull out a small stack of twenties.

44

You would have thought the guy just won the lottery the way he grins as I hand him two hundred pounds. "Love, bro," he says, nodding along to some skippy drill flow on the radio. "Man did good, alie?"

"You did all right, cuz."

"C'mon, fam," he squeals with excitement.

With a whimsical shake of my head, I hit the accelerator, and we make our way back to familiar stomping ground.

By the time evening comes around, it's just the Audi and me.

The hush of blue from this morning has become an endearing deep black sky as souls light up the streets with their loud voices and endless jabber.

I pass hippy kids with flares and piercings, suits and uniforms unwinding outside pubs and bars, and all different creeds and colours, seemingly enjoying their night.

A bus to my right hisses, and I take in the fumes of the city.

It's the first time that I'm reminded that although many of the buildings and shops have been replaced or demolished since I was a young'un round here, the place is still very much the same.

I drive past a KFC that used to be a pizzeria when I was growing up. Now, there are six or seven teenagers taking selfies in there.

Fifteen years ago, that would have been me, Preddie, Hookz, Shaun, and FatMack. Not taking selfies but doing our thing.

'Rah, Shaun and Hookz are both doing life; Preddie's dead and FatMack was living in Jamaica the last I heard. Am I the last of a dying breed?' I wonder as I turn onto my street.

I'm about a hundred metres from my house when my attention's drawn to a set of wavy locks spiralling down the back of a satin-black jacket. I do what most men do and let my eyes wander down. The bum is my type of bum—weighty, but I can tell it's soft and juicy.

'Who is this?'

I've never seen her on this street.

Her black leggings cling to her loins, and on another night, I bet those sleek, dark heels would be on a dancefloor under a row of

45

promiscuous lights. I follow her legs back up and feel a flutter inside my stomach as my pulse goes off.

Cruising onwards, barely doing over ten mph, I spot two gold hoop earrings that twist and turn; you know the big old door-knockers Mary J was rocking in the nineties.

My eyes can't help but go back to that bum, though. God took his time when he created this one. The cheeks shake, taking turns, a tiny ripple at the bottom of them after each step as she continues her catwalk, drawing me in more and more. I can't see her face, but I just know this girl's a beauty queen: the body, the legs, the hair. Even the sexy side of her foot, visible under black leather straps, glistens an enticing shade of chocolate.

I'm not gonna lie; my body's gone a little hot. I unzip my jacket. I haven't felt something like this in years. My thoughts are so powerful that I have no control over them. *They're* guiding me.

My hand squeezes the steering wheel tighter as I shift about in my seat. Feeling the uncomfortable tightness my boxers are subjecting me to, I look down and notice a massive bulge in my tracksuit bottoms.

'*Boy.*'

I sort myself out and look straight back up.

As I do, my car draws level with this woman, and I'm met by her eyes. It's only a split second, but it feels like an eternity, that look could dwarf my whole sentence.

Remember, I told you she would be a beauty queen. Even better, she's a Goddess. Sent from an unreachable realm. Under the shimmer of the moonlight, that mocha-brown skin gleams in all its glory. Her half-moon-shaped cheeks show the signs of a tiny dimple.

'*Rah, she's beautiful.*'

You know those old clichés about taking your breath away—yeah, man, all of that.

Her beauty warrants my breathlessness, though—words can't suffice. She's like Kelly Rowland with Serena's thighs. She looks right at me, and immediately I'm taken back to my childhood—Erykah Badu's captivating caramel eyes on the TV. I could watch this girl forever.

Amidst her luscious coils cascading below her shoulders, she seems to be focused on me too. Her eyes appear to do that thing where they go thinner when you recognise somebody.

I don't want to stare too hard, so I soften my face before a sharp blast of a horn forces me to swerve an oncoming car.

'Rasclart.'

If she never knew she was a head-turner before, she knows now.

I steady the car and gather my thoughts as I look at her regal figure dwindle in the side mirror. I can't be sure, but I think she's still looking in my direction. My heart's thrashing against my rib cage as I go to pull over.

'Wait, nah, I can't let her know where I live.'

Now there's a thin line between paranoia and caution, but you don't get half a life sentence for manslaughter without making some enemies. And believe me, enemies come in all shapes and sizes.

After circling the block, I arrive back on my street, half-hoping she's still there, just to get another glimpse of her. Even though it'll mean a second trip around the block, she's worth it. Shit, she's worth fifty.

I drive down the road, feeling like a little kid.

'This is mad.'

I'm not the kind of guy that gets excited by girls, even after twelve years in the can.

See, I figure you can categorise most women. And by that, I mean no offence. It's just how I see myself in terms of whether I'm punching above my weight. There are 1-3s, 4-6s, 7-8s, 9s-9.5s. Then there's a straight-up ten. It's an exclusive club and not many make it as a ten.

Now, if I had to rate myself, it would be in two parts: Pre-jail and post-jail. I reckon I've gone from an eight or nine to a five or six, which I'm not mad about because I've seen prison completely destroy men. Hair loss, potbellies, tooth decay, acne, you name it. And that's just the physical effects.

47

I dodged those bullets, but one thing I'm definitely aware of is those twelve years whittled away at my confidence. It's not something the world ever sees, but we all have our secrets and every birthday I missed, every night I thought about my daughter and how I couldn't do anything for her, just told me I was worthless, no matter how much I tried to remain young and vibrant inside.

Shit, I'd be an empty shell if I never had Scribz and Jamal around me. No feelings, no aspirations, just a cold ex-con who'd probably find himself straight back in there if you looked at him the wrong way.

I reach my house, and I won't lie, I'm disappointed I didn't see her again.

Once inside, I find myself thinking about this woman all night. I wonder where she lives, what her name is, and what she is doing around here. Is she going home to a husband and kids, or is she single?

I don't know what it is. Something about her reminds me of my teenage years before prison. You know, before the world went and corrupted all of our women, bombarding them with that doctrine that natural beauty and needing a man were some sort of abominable crimes.

A text from Leanne pulls me from my daydream, asking about the job hunt and telling me I can hold on to the car for a couple of days because she's just put me on her insurance policy.

I'm sure Taylor will be over the moon about that, I text back as a joke, and she gives me the emoji version of the finger.

I'm about to put the phone on the side when it rings.

"Yo, Scribz."

He's straight to the point. "Love for the money. You do the ting, my bro?"

"Does it snow in the north pole?" I ask rhetorically.

"My guy," he says, sounding much more at ease. I feel the weight evaporate from his shoulders.

"You know me, broski," I say, and I think he picks up on the unusual buoyancy in my voice tonight.

"Oi Rakz..." he cries.

48

"What?"

"You got some pussy, init?"

"You joker."

"Yes, yes. Man like Rakz getting it in. What you saying, did you have her bawling out fi mercy, she ride pon di ting like a bike, you give her that angry backshot?"

"You're a disturbed guy, Scribz," I say, but truthfully that's all I've been thinking about since I got home.

"If it was that easy to get you smiling, I would've sent a couple badders' over there the day you left."

"Allow it, Scribz, you ain't got no badders, fam."

"Are you crazy?" Scribz shouts. "I'm the fucking man on POF, bruv. You should see man's getting fresh nudes every day—brown tings, white tings, Chiney tings."

"Make sure you go Friday prayers and repent for your sins, bro," I taunt him.

"About repent... The Imam's the one who got me on it, blood," he exclaims, and we both crack up.

You see, there are very few ways a man can get his sexual kicks in prison. And if pictures of naked women or dating sites, does it for Scribz, then who am I to judge?

"So, what's this ting saying? Tell man the details," Scribz persists.

"Don't be a stingy nigga," a voice shouts I'm guessing belongs to Devonte.

"There's nothing to tell, my bro."

After a short while of Scribz probing me to reveal the intricacies of my non-existent sex life, he hits me with a line that resonates more than any other.

"You know, whatever you're doing, just make sure you're stacking that paper, can't be a broke guy and keep a flyting these days... Nah, these women are about their business, they got their own money nowadays, and if you ain't gettin' it in, she'll find a next nigga who is, trust me."

49

I can't lie. That one deflated my spirit a little.

"I hear you," I mumble as the reality of being down to my last few hundred quid plays on my mind.

"Real talk... Stack them Ps. Popping bottles and pussy ain't gonna get you to The Gambia, my brudda."

I reach over to the bedside table and pluck my half-smoked spliff from the ashtray. As Scribz goes on about some guy kicking off on the wing because he had to have Goulash for dinner, I mull over his comment.

'If I'm gonna to get my life back on track, I'm gonna need money. And I'm gonna have to start somewhere, even if I don't wanna.' Squeeze always told me the best thing to do is the thing you know best. And as I weigh up my options right now, a light bulb comes on above my head.

"Oi Scribz, what you doin' with this work?" I ask.

He stops rambling.

"Gonna line up a next worker and maybe a next spot. Imagine, he's the second one to get nicked this month."

I sit up in my bed. "Bro, I'll move it for you."

"You?" Scribz cackles.

"Bruv, you're going on like I didn't have the ends on smash before I went away. You know about me in my town."

"Yeah... But that's ancient history, fam. And you were a weed guy, alie? This is a whole different kettle of fish."

"Brudda, food is food. Weed, white, sniff, b, pills, hash. The principle's the same, buy for a dollar, sell for two."

"Yeah, but bro, you ain't been in my world."

"Don't watch that," I say.

"So, what you're gonna be runnin' round lickin' shots, c'mon bro, we don't do the donkey work."

"Not me, you doughnut. I got someone. He's certy."

"I dunno 'bout all that, cuz."

I let the first one slide, but if Scribz thinks he's got a say in this, he doesn't know me as well as I thought he did.

"Don't make this a big ting. You need help; I need money. It's simple."

Unconvinced, Scribz starts umming and awwing, like he doesn't have faith in my capabilities, so I switch up the play.

"Listen, man went and got this ting today for you like you asked. I risked my freedom, and a good friend of mine nearly got battered by two bookey-looking bruddas on the block. So, when I'm telling you that I got this, all I need to hear is one word—done. You feel me?"

Scribz goes quiet, and I take another pull of my spliff.

He comes back onto the phone, a new man. "My bad, bro. If you say you got this, you got this init. Do your ting, hit me up tomorrow, and we'll pattern the details."

My words must have hit a nerve. And so, they should have. Loyalty works both ways. And if a man forgets that I make sure I remind him, no matter who he is.

Scribz tries to get off the phone, but a fire has been lit inside me. I know these roads and with all I've learned over the past decade of how police caught this one and how that one fucked up, I'm in a way better position to navigate this ship than I was as a yout'. And when I've got the desire for something, I don't just let it fizzle out.

"Nah, bro, chat to me now 'cause we're setting up tomorrow," I say.

I'm about to make things happen.

5

As you probably guessed, Deontay's my new apprentice. As soon as Scribz gets back to me, I'll have Deontay off the High Road, and fixed him up with somewhere to operate from. He still has his little weed thing for now, but when he sees the type of money he's about to make, I reckon he'll forget about that in a heartbeat.

Like I said, though, I'm not tryin' to corrupt this kid, so as much as I plan to get him involved, on the one hand, I'll keep him at bay with the other.

I've also got someone renting the bedroom at the end of the hallway, my old room. He's a slight Chinese guy. Leanne hooked it up. He's all right, I guess. As long as he keeps the place tidy and doesn't disrespect any of Mum's things, we should be fine.

The Audi's getting a good workout today too. After a trip to probation, I went to B&Q, took some of Mum's old junk over the dump, and now, I'm on my way to the graveyard.

Today is exactly three years to the day that Mum passed away.

'Rah.'

I take a deep breath, allowing a car to pull out in front of me as I lose my trail of thought in the traffic once again.

That's it, the reason I haven't mentioned Mum so far.

Woi, it's hard to even begin.

See, Mum died while I was in prison. Nine years into my sentence, to be precise. She wasn't even old. Sixty-two. Well, Mum was my Queen, the jewel of my heart. The best mum in the world, hands down, and when I say that I'm not just regurgitating the old cliché everyone uses to describe their mum.

Nah, my mum actually was.

If I had to describe her in one word, it would have to be 'perfect.' She always had the right level of love and discipline and always knew exactly what to say.

I remember when Leanne and I were kids, and Mum took us to this massive park. It was proper nice; I remember the three of us sitting under this giant oak tree, cotched on our little mat, the bees tirelessly buzzing around the place. The greenery was unfathomable at my young age. Scattered with dandelions and buttercups, it seemed to go on forever. I remember the little insects clicking between the blades of grass and dancing through the air as we admired the scenery.

Our picnic was lit as well, with crisps, ice lollies, strawberries, and even some chicken sandwiches. And I ain't talking about them cold slabs of processed chicken that Karen and Sally nibble at on their lunch break. Nah, this was the finest jerk chicken in south London.

So, we were having this picnic, and my empty crisp packet took off with a gust of wind. I thought nothing of it until Mum ordered me to fetch it and put it in the bin.

Being a naturally combative child, I asked why, and mum cussed me out. "And when did your likkle backside tink you can ask big people question, you is pickney, run go do as yuh told 'for me gwarn dash you inna di bin with it," she said with an extended kiss of her teeth.

I ran after the empty packet, but it had blown into the stream with the ducks. I told Mum, and we carried on our picnic. But a little while later, Mum stops and calls Leanne over like she's got news. It wasn't news, though—it was just the answer to my question.

You see, it had bothered Mum that I was even asking such a question to the point where she felt as if there was something I needed to learn. And the forthcoming lesson was so important that it warranted me stopping halfway through my ice lolly to listen. It pissed me off at the time, but Mum was one of those parents that were always teaching us something. Some parents just let their kids get on with it, not Mum, though.

She gathered us, gave me this peculiar look, and asked, "What did you mean when you asked why you should pick up your rubbish?"

I looked at Leanne, who shrugged, so I just went for it. "Well, like, won't the dustbin man just come and pick it up and put it in the bin? That's his job, right?" I said.

Mum pushed her bottom lip out and nodded almost sarcastically. "So, because the grave digger's job is fi dig grave, we should all go round and kill people, huh?" she said.

I looked at Leanne, and although Mum explained herself, we both never got it. Only a few years ago did it click for me.

One hot summer day, I was in the exercise yard, and a group of us were chilling.

Amongst all the traps and triceps, this guy, Danny, throws this crisp packet on the floor, and someone shouts, "Pick that up, man." Danny ignores the guy, and nothing happens. But just have a guess what Danny was in for. Yeah, murder. Went to rob this art dealer's place, and it went very wrong, very quickly, and Danny ended up caving the guy's skull in with a hammer. He left the scene in a haste and foolishly trusted his co-conspirator to make the whole thing appear like an accident.

When that man shouted at Danny to pick up his crisp packet, it took me right back to what mum was saying.

See, maybe Danny was just a kid in the park once upon a time with *his* mum and *his* sister. The only thing is when Danny's crisp packet blew away, *his* mum just laughed and said, 'don't worry, the dustmen'll clean it up.' And that's exactly what Danny did; spent the rest of his life expecting others to clear up his mess.

Now, I'm not saying I'm any better than Danny; after all, I killed a man too, but I do now understand the correlation between the gravedigger and the dustman. And the correlation was the whole point.

Mum wasn't saying let your rubbish blow away, and you'll end up killing someone; she was hyperbolising. What mum was saying was that just because somebody else will clean up the mess or get rid of the problem, it doesn't give you a free pass to go around and do whatever you want. You have to take accountability for your actions, so if that's your rubbish, you go and pick it up. It doesn't matter if somebody else will do it. It's yours. You deal with it.

Any problem you have in life, she was saying, take responsibility for, and fix it because it's *your* problem. Don't let the world and society allow you to think for one second that they'll fix it for you because there's a man for this or a man for that. You rely upon your damn self. And if you can't or won't be bothered to sort out your own mess, then don't create it in the first place.

I reach the graveyard and drive in. The first thing I notice is a half-dug grave amongst hundreds of headstones. I see a man in a long grey overall, wearing thick gloves, grasping a spade. Sweat drips down his brow as he wipes it with his sleeve, and I instantly have a great deal of respect for this man.

You see, he's the gravedigger, the one that clears up after all of our accumulation of mess and problems that we call life when it finally comes to an end.

After I park the car, I get out and walk the couple hundred metres to where Mum is buried. I spot Leanne, who's here early. But she's not alone.

I sigh as I see the figure of her beloved Taylor by her side. I thought this was supposed to be a *family* thing.

Shoving my hand in my pocket, I join them around the grave.

Now, I know I slate Supercoon a lot, but in all fairness, he paid for the headstone, funeral, and everything. My sister and my other relatives never even had to open their wallets. So, for that reason alone, he gets a pass today.

I put an arm around Leanne, who takes the bunch of flowers from me, kneels, and places them by the headstone. I check my phone, hoping for the go-ahead from Scribz. Still nothing.

Supercoon looks over at the two of us. I give him the nod, and he returns the gesture. Good to see he knows his lane today because this ain't the time or place for any bickering or snide remarks. And I swear

55

to God right here, if he forgets that, he'll be forking out for his own headstone.

"You like them?" I ask Leanne.

"They're beautiful," she says with a wry smile.

I notice the pale line down her face, a shade lighter than her skin. She's been crying already.

She stands back up, and I let her return to the comfort underneath my arm.

'This is strange. Mum died three years ago, and it's my first time here.'

"You miss her?" I ask Leanne and see I'm about to set her off again.

"Every day," Leanne says, her voice as light as a feather.

Three years and the pain's just as raw as the day I found out.

I look to the skies above. Clear sea-blue that runs for miles and miles without the occlude of a single cloud.

From my peripheral, Taylor's stood, with hands in pockets, staring at the headstone that's well decorated with bright blues, deep yellows, vivid reds, and coral pinks.

"What did she think of you, then?" I ask Taylor, turning my head towards him.

He pauses, and for the first time in my life, I see a genuine smile form on his face. "You know, I couldn't tell you what she thought about me," he begins.

I'm surprised. Hot Shot Tesla Driver's turning down an opportunity to blow smoke up his arse.

"But I can tell you what I thought about her," he continues.

"What's that?" I ask, actually intrigued by what he has to say for once.

He looks at Leanne and me and says, "Anthea loved you both more than anything in the world. It was so obvious by the way she spoke about you both. And I know as sure as the sun will rise tomorrow, she would have gone to the ends of the earth to help either of you out, no questions asked. You both were her world, and now *our* world is that much bleaker without her love and warmth in it."

56

To be honest, it sounds like a well-rehearsed speech, but I'll give him his props. My eyes return to the flowers, and Taylor's back to the false smile. All lips and no teeth. "I'll be in the car, dear," he says, looking past me at Leanne. "Nice to see you, Rakim," he adds as he raises a hand, grandiloquently bows his head, and walks away.

'I knew he could get my name right all this time.'

I don't sweat it, though. I just say, "Later." Then I turn my focus back to Mum.

Leanne sighs, and there's a silence we both fill by just kinda reflecting on life.

"You know what, Lee," I say. "I feel like if I'd got out earlier, she wouldn't have been so sick and got so ill, and she might—"

"—Don't say that stuff, Rakz. It's not your fault. Mum was sick. There's nothing you could have done about it."

"Yeah, but I'm saying, me being in prison didn't help, did it?" My tone, a bit sharper this time.

"Well, obviously not, but that doesn't mean it's your fault, you could have been the most successful person in the world, and the same fate could have fallen upon Mum."

I smile. One of embarrassment mostly. She's basically stated, in other words, that I'm a fuck up. It's cool, though, I know what I am, so I don't retaliate.

"I just wish I could've been there to see her off. Or at least her last days. I mean, how's her last memory of me in an orange netball bib, in some visiting hall in Yorkshire."

That's right. When Supercoon said she would go to the ends of the earth to help us, he wasn't bullshitting.

Even when I got shipped up north, every month without fail, Mum would journey from south London to Yorkshire, and she was secretly ill all this time. Shanice came once, and that was the time she didn't make it through the gates. I've never seen her since. (A message to you lot who treat your little girlfriends better than your mum).

"Rakim, don't," Leanne says. "Mum doesn't remember you like that."

"How d'you know?" I ask.

"Because none of us do," she says, putting her hands out in front of her.

I look around, trying to do anything that will keep my eyes from welling up. The lines of graves go on for hundreds of metres. Some look well-kept, and some look abandoned. There's a little pathway behind us lined on either side with trees, and I feel like we're the only people in this place.

"How did she see me then? 'Cause I know how the rest of the family see me—like I'm the one who caused it. Like she should have stopped wasting her prayers on me and cut ties with her no-good murderer of a son a long time ago."

"Forget them, though. Who cares about Uncle Jonathon or Aunty Sylvia? Seriously?" Leanne says.

Yeah, those are the words they actually used to describe their own flesh and blood.

I know Leanne's tryin' to stick up for my name, but she knows, and I know, Mum's unending love for me was killing her seeing me caged up like an animal.

"You don't know, Lee. Mum rode every single second of that bird with me. Never once did she miss a visit or a phone call. Even in my darkest hours. When that judge told me to rise and said, 'twelve,' I saw mum's reaction. I swear a tiny part of her died that day, and after them eight long years to catch another four, that must have just done it for her."

I check my phone again to divert from the inevitable as a rush of emotion warms my throat. Still nothing from Scribz.

Leanne puts her hand on me as I drop the phone back in my pocket. "Rakz, it's not your fault. They denied you compassionate leave. What were you supposed to do, break out?"

58

"You don't get it. It's the fact I went in the first place, Lee. I come out, and I've lost everyone and everything that mattered to me. Keziah's gone, Mum's gone, Shanice is gone, and the boys have gone. What have I got? Mum's left-over furniture that just reminds me of how much I fucked my life up every time I look at it."

"Rakim!" Leanne shouts. "Don't swear by Mum's grave. What's wrong with you?"

"Sorry, Mum," I say.

There's a minute or so of silence between us. And although we're stood a metre apart, the gap could be a canyon. Leanne will never admit that her precious little baby brother was the cause of his own mother's death.

As I stand here, I feel my nose quaking. It's not cold, but my lips are wavering, and my body's shivering.

I put a hand over my eyes as Leanne clears her throat. "You've got me, Rakz," she says before pausing for effect.

A good old trick she probably learned from Taylor, hoping that her words will soothe me.

She rubs my back as I take my hand away from my face and stand up straight.

"You know, usually I say a little word," she says. "You wanna do the honours this time?"

I look at her hopeful face and lift my arm for her. "Yeah, cool," I say.

She rests her head on my shoulder and wraps her arm around my waist.

I close my eyes, take a deep breath, and compose myself as I picture being present at Mum's funeral on that little stand with all those black suits watching me.

Then with my chin up like Mum always taught me, I let my heart express just a smidgen of what I've kept locked away for over three years.

"Mum, I don't know if you're still here or if you can still hear me, but if you are and you can, I just wanna say I'm sorry. I'm sorry that I left you. I'm sorry for all the stress I must have caused you. I swear,

Mum, I never meant to. I guess I was just too stubborn to hear your words and see that your love for me was way more real than everything else around me. I'm sorry for putting you through the things I put youthrough, and I hope wherever you are, you know you did the best job ever. You were the best Mum. Tell that to Auntie Cynthia if she's up there with you," I say as Leanne's teary face cracks a reminiscent smile.

"I loved you... Love you, more than anyone or anything in this world. I wish I could go back and be there for you," I continue, trying to keep a steady face. The wind around me whistles as I carry on.

"Even though we didn't always see eye to eye, Mum, you were my best friend. The one who taught me everything I know, how to work hard, how to treat people with respect, and most importantly, how to always strive to be a better person. *'None of us put on this earth are perfect in God's eyes, but we can all try to be,'* you'd say. Thank you for never giving up on me, regardless of what I did. One day, we'll meet again, Mum, in this life or the next, and I swear I'll be a much better son. On my life."

I sign off, and it feels good to give Mum my own personal send-off.

I can't lie; my chest is rattling, and I'm parched like a man stranded in the desert, but I'm holding it down. I pull out my phone. "One for Mum?"

Surprisingly, Leanne agrees.

I hand Leanne the phone, and she lets the raw vocals of a hero in our household begin to bless the whole cemetery with his pure, soulful spirit. The lyrics blast out of my phone with enough power to penetrate our souls and resurrect the ones who were loved and lost like our Queen as Buju Banton roars like a lion in the heart of Africa and one of Mum's favourites touches me for the last time.

By the end of the song, Leanne's in bits and I'm just about hanging in there when my phone beeps. *'Saved by the bell,'* I think as I wipe my nose with my sleeve.

I check my phone to see Scribz's name written across the screen and open the text.

We're set, make sure your guy's ready. It's about to pop off.

6

Forty-eight, forty-nine, fifty. I roll over onto my back and let out a sigh of relief.

'I'm slacking.'

On the days in prison when I didn't go to the gym, it was six sets of fifty press-ups morning and night, but I haven't done a single one since I visited Mum's grave, and that was over a week ago. Still, that little workout felt satisfying.

"I go now. Bye," Ping, the lodger, says as he passes the door of my room.

"Later," I call out.

Ping's a quiet character, which suits me fine. Besides uni, work, and playing computer games, I have no idea what the hell he does.

Lying on the floor, I gaze at the ceiling as I listen to the rhythmic rise and fall of my chest.

'I need to drop Deontay some more of this food.'

He's already called me twice this morning, saying his soldiers have nearly run out.

'That little bit of authority, and now they're his 'soldiers'.'

I roll my eyes, but his determination, drive, and organisation have impressed me so far, I can't lie. I've also put a nice little four thousand pounds away, which will continue to accumulate as the weeks pass.

I put my vest on, go downstairs, and pick up the two bags of rubbish resting by the old mahogany grandfather clock in the hallway. As I open the front door, the sun's brightness stabs at my eyes.

Throwing an arm across my face, I hurry down the concrete steps and dump the bin bags in the wheelie bin before attending to a couple of weeds that have dared to usurp the roots of Mum's bush lilies.

Bent down on my knees, I hear a voice.

"Excuse me, do you live here?"

It's the voice of a woman.

I rise to my feet, turn around, and there she is.

Stood just on the other side of the brown picket fence; it's the woman from the other week. She's poised there, looking like an embodiment of beauty once again.

A grey nylon vest top hugs her golden-brown skin revealing her bare shoulders that look like some sexy chocolate liquor. Her belly's all chiselled with every smooth curve, defined and delicate.

My eyes come back up to meet her face, quick enough for her to still feel comfortable. The confusion in those pools of vivid hazel is evident as her perfectly-shaped eyebrows stoop ever so slightly.

My body's doing that thing again; my heart's driving beyond its limits as air zooms up my windpipe, clogging the pathway for a response to her question. 'Her eyes, though,' like two perfectly crafted smoky quartz crystals, captivatingly drawing me in with a hypnotic charm.

If I've got the death stare, then she's most certainly got the life stare because that's precisely how I feel as I stand here and look at this ebony queen—alive. Striking chords in my body, she wakes up every inch of my psyche. Maybe a few too many inches.

I quickly clear my throat. "Why?" I ask.

My baritone voice seems to have the usual effect. I see the subtle recoil in her head as she brings an arm across her body towards the opposite shoulder as if she's just felt a sudden chill.

She studies me carefully as I shake a few remaining petals from my hand.

A narrow gap emerges between those ripe, sultry lips. Her hand moves towards her face, and she slides a finger in between one of her oil-infused ringlets, leaving it there, fiddling, fondling like she's thinking of what to say.

'Is she checking man out?' I wonder.

Remember I told you about how I assess if I'm punching above my weight? Well, there's no assessment needed with her; she's a straight ten. And out of my league.

She scans me from head to toe like she's unsure, and I feel like a Mandingo fresh off the ship, being examined for any flaws. The only difference is I wouldn't mind being *her* slave.

Her other arm relaxes again as she continues rolling those carmine-red nails around that lonesome strand that hangs in front of her ear.

"It's just because," she halts to clear her throat. "Excuse me," she cries. "It's just because I didn't know it was being rented out?"

'Rented out? Has this girl been watching man or suttin'?'

My heart starts pumping harder.

'You're not on the yard no more, Rakz. Chill out.'

A glimpse of those electrifying teeth catches my eye, wizard white, as each millisecond reveals more of what I know will be the most enthralling smile ever.

My stomach refuses to settle, and this vest feels tight around my neck. I gotta think of how to respond.

'Come on, man, what's wrong with you?'

"It's not gettin' rented out just yet; I'm just tidying up the place. How about you, you from round here?" I say, appearing like I've regained my composure.

She sucks in her luscious bottom lip, and I swear my big man downstairs is on his own mission.

'Lucky these shorts are the baggy kind.'

"Yeah, I live just down the road," she replies, pointing to her left.

Her finger remains amidst the few spools of hair that didn't make it to the bun as she swallows a deep gulp of air, and I watch the slender movement of her throat.

Her eyes flit around a bit before they return to me.

"So, did you know the lady who lived here well, then?" she asks.

She's still hanging around and instigating conversation. It's a good sign that she's interested to some level, at least.

Finding comfort in the ambiguity halfway between a lie and the truth, I answer. "A little," I say.

"How come I've never seen you?"

'Shit.' It's the question I was hoping she wouldn't ask.

See, it's not a good idea to reveal your past immediately when you've just come out of prison. Some may disagree but hear me out.

Say you've been away for a year; well, that doesn't really separate you from the rest of society—not much changes in a year. But say you've been away for five years. Now we all know you don't do five years for swearing at somebody because they pulled out in front of you at a junction.

The longer you tell a person you've been away, the slimmer the margin for interpreting what put you there becomes. So, if I explain that I've been incarcerated for the past twelve years, I've essentially pitched myself as either a high-level drug dealer, a murderer, a rapist, a terrorist, or an armed robber.

Then once that's been ascertained, what woman in her right mind will say, 'Oh nice,' and continue talking like normal? I'll tell you who, no woman. From here on, all we become is raised eyebrows and polite hellos.

'I can't tell her the truth...'

I know I'm not a liar. I know my intention isn't to deceive. It's just this crime that I committed; I did it when I was a fucking kid, and up until this day, it still hitches a ride on my conscience, following me around wherever I go. I shouldn't have to wear my criminal history like a badge of shame. I've done my time, and I'm tryin' to put that part of my life behind me.

I'm already reminded every time I wake up in the middle of the night wondering where the hell I am or thinking the sound of the letterbox in the morning is an army of police banging off my door. I'm reminded by my bank balance, by everybody and everything moving so fast around me, by not knowing how to operate Amazon Prime, by the subtle wrinkles that have emerged around the corners of Leanne's eyes–the reminders are non-stop.

And now this stunning woman is here, having a conversation with me, offering a glimmer of hope that she could be my freedom one day, a getaway from my past, and this one question could shut everything down before it's even begun.

I know what I have to do—swerve it as best and tactically as possible.

"I knew the lady who lived here from back in the day," I say.

"Oh, I see. She was a real character," the woman in front of me says, and I notice a fondness in her voice.

"You knew her well?" I ask.

"Erm… Pretty well, I'd say. She was always cooking up these huge pots of oxtail, soups, and mutton. She even taught me a thing or two right up in that kitchen," she says as we both turn our heads to look through the open door.

She draws in her bottom lip again, and we both pause as I imagine Mum standing over the stove in that kitchen with her wooden spoon, big old Dutch pot, and an array of herbs and spices by her side.

I turn to face this woman and realise she's clocked my smile and maybe a bit more. "You watchin' me hard there?" I say as I summon a bit of confidence from somewhere.

A dimple forms on her face, and an angelic smile displays her sparkling calcite-white teeth. It's the smile of a movie star. A smile I could never get tired of seeing.

Her bottom lip disappears again before swiftly reemerging.

'Behave,' I have to warn the big guy downstairs.

It's no use, though; this woman's set me off, and standing there with that enticing look on her face, I think she knows.

"Is that what you think?" she asks inquisitively.

"I see your eyes."

"Oh, right, and why would I be watching you?"

I hold my smile back this time. "You tell me."

66

Seeing her trying to figure me out is doing everything for me right now; I want to savour this moment. No woman has looked at me with this degree of interest in years. Like I'm her prey, sizing me up to see if she can deal with all this weight.

'Forget all that 'good things come in small packages,' shit, this is a big package, and if you can't handle it, don't try, 'cause you're liable to hurt yourself.'

I'm even gassing myself up right now.

'Calm down, Rakz. Chill. Don't get carried away.'

"I'm Rakim, by the way," I say, reeling in my ego. "I would shake your hand, but I don't wanna get you dirty," I add, showing her my muddy palms as I think about what I just said.

'Get you dirty, ya know, c'mon Rakz.'

"It's fine," she says. "I'm Nia."

"That's a nice name. So, you like running then, yeah, Nia?"

"Looks like I'm not the only one who's watchin' hard," she says with a beguiling tenor of sarcasm in her response.

"Ite, I deserved that one," I say, wagging my finger.

"You did," she winks.

Maybe, I'm just desperate for her to quench my thirst right now, but I swear that wink was the most seductive wink I've ever seen.

"How about you, you work out?" she asks.

"I try look after myself, still."

She nods her head, still not in any hurry to go anywhere.

This is going better than I could have ever imagined. My old confidence is flowing through me again like a roaring wave. It's like she's brought me back from the dead—resurrecting that part of me that's been locked away for over a decade since prison squeezed every drop of optimism out of me.

I knew there was something different about this girl. The fire she lit when I saw her walking down the street that day has become a blaze of smouldering flames that have spread throughout my entire body.

Prison teaches you how to read a person well. The shifting of your body weight to the other foot, the sudden eye movements—they all spell anxiety. And as I look past the veneer of togetherness on the frontier of this girl—between those languid shadow black lashes, I sense a vulnerable soul.

'Be a man,' I tell myself. 'Take the lead.'

"Ya know, I'm still clearing out one of the rooms upstairs. I know you said you knew Anthea. So... erm, if there's anything you want, anything she said you would like or whatnot, feel free to come over and help yourself."

Nia shakes her head. "Oh nah, I'm not trying to get my hands on anything, don't think that's why I—"

"—I know," I say calmly, attempting to put her mind at ease. "You're more than welcome to; that's all I'm saying."

"Oh. Okay, well maybe, if you're sure she wouldn't mind. I mean, won't her daughter want to go through it?"

"Not if Supercoon has anything to say about it," I hear myself say.

"Supercoon?" she says, looking confused.

'Shit.'

The conversation was flowing so smoothly that one just kind of slipped out.

"You know... Leanne's husband."

"Ohhh." Her head moves back like the words have just slotted into their rightful position. "Him!" she asserts with a look of disdain across her face. "I can't stand that guy."

As the words leave her mouth, I swear I could get down on one knee and marry this girl right now.

'Finally, someone gets it.'

"Yeah, you get what I'm saying," I say.

"Oh, don't worry, I hear you loud and clear," she replies as those wafer-thin brows curve into a playful frown.

The birds chirp around us, sharing a delightful love song that both of us seem content to listen to.

"Well, Rakim," Nia says with squinted eyes, unsure if she's got it right. "It was nice to meet you. I'm going to take off now..." she states, bringing those elegant hands together with the softness of a feathered pillow.

Her hands move closer to her chest, and I feel there's more coming.

"If there's some stuff you're going to get rid of, I wouldn't just want it to go to waste so I could come over this evening... If you're okay with that?"

"Course I'm okay with that," I say, not allowing those hopeful eyes to feel a shred of anxiety for a second longer than necessary. "Listen, any enemy of Taylor is a friend of mine," I say and up shoot those crescent cheeks as she giggles.

I smile, even showing a couple of teeth myself this time.

"Well, I'll see you later then," she says in that dulcet whisper.

"Yeah, yeah."

"Worse case, if there's nothing of use to me, I can always help you carry some things out, you know, you look like you'll struggle with those arms," she cries as she turns her body to saunter off.

"You got jokes, Nia," I say. "I'll see you later," I call.

She strolls away, and step after step, I gaze like a child at a window on a summer day, pining over the departing ice cream van.

But this isn't that type of yearning, though. My desire is driven by something way more powerful. The most potent force on this planet—love. Or is it lust?

Or is it a perfect blend of both?

I'm unsure, but my uncertainty doesn't stop me from fantasising about kissing the back of Nia's bare neck just under the lines of loose hair that sway in the wind. My eyes drop further down to her decanter waist that rocks from side to side without skipping a beat as she crosses the road.

Those skin-tight leggings use all their might to carry her bum before she finally disappears behind a hedge to my right.

I desperately want to walk to the end of the gate and see which house she enters, but I remain cool.

Still, in a daze, I wonder if I'm in a vivid dream or if that really just happened.

I look at my hands. They're still dirty, which means I'm not dreaming.

I walk back inside like a proud colonel returning from an arduous conquest, and I imagine this is how I would've felt had that foreman in the courtroom stood up and said, 'not guilty.'

Well, things didn't go that way, and that feeling never erupted in me. Not until now, that is. I switch the kettle on and grab a mug from the cupboard when I realise what's just happened.

"Shit, Nia's coming over here... Tonight... Boy, I gotta get a move on."

I scan the room, making a mental list of all my tasks while the kettle climaxes with a dull click, and I drop a teabag in the mug.

'Lemme drink this quickly and then go get ready, man.'

Then once I finish, I head upstairs to do just that.

7

The Grandfather Clock in the hallway tells me the time is 7.55.

It's evening, and my list of tasks has been ticked off one by one. I've dropped Deontay half of the remaining product for his 'soldiers' to sell, cleared Leanne's old room, pleased my new probation worker, Lauren, with my 'punctuality' and 'drive to succeed' and sorted Scribz's sister with some money.

It's all been done on autopilot to tell the truth. Since my conversation with Nia earlier, everything has been a sort of blur. I couldn't tell you what Scribz's sister was wearing, what Deontay said, or even which route I took back to the house from probation. It's as if my body has been conducting what needs to be done, but my mind is still lost in that feeling that gripped me this morning.

You see, all men have secrets, shameful and disparaging, that stultify their capacity to feel worthy. You may not see them at first glance but look close enough behind the lenses of politeness and banality, and you'll find them. Lurking like a scolded child petrified of the playground.

I know this more than most; I've lived with my demons for years. But when Nia looked at me, those demons disappeared. The way she smiled at me like she was actually interested, like she actually cared, I felt ten-feet tall. All the worries I had about life, seemed to fade like a midday dream.

I wasn't just a surname on a clipboard or a number in a system. To her, I actually mean something. I know it. I felt it. And that feeling is indescribable.

71

As the feeling rises within me again like a tide at the mercy of a whirlwind's wrath, wild, feral thoughts submerge my tranquility. They torment me as I wonder what it would feel like to taste those plump, velvet-soft lips and work my way down her neck while she throws her head back, defenceless to my dominion.

My thoughts drift once again and I have to slow my roll. *'Chill, fam. She's only coming over to look through some stuff. She's probably not even interested in your broke-just-come-out-of-jail-fiending-for-some-pussy-self.'*

To distract me from what looms, I give downstairs a once over, brushing any dust off the living room table, before spraying and wiping down the kitchen surfaces.

An unexpected chill sneaks through the open window and I light the coals inside the fireplace just like Mum used to and it feels like she's here, watching over me, as if she orchestrated this from her high seat in heaven.

I check my reflection in the glass cabinet next to the small dining table. The light hits the glass at a favourable angle and does just enough to boost my confidence.

Since being released, I've mostly rotated between a few outfits, but I've gone for the best of the bunch today.

It's a pair of slim-fit Dolce & Gabbana joggers in jet black, with a black fitted Gucci t-shirt, courtesy of Leanne, of course.

'You're looking suave, cuz,' I tell myself.

Nia obviously noticed my thick, robust arms earlier, so I ditched the idea of wearing the matching tracksuit top and left them on display for her to examine once again. It's crucial to know your lane in life, as I've explained, and right now, I know mine. I'm not about to shower her with expensive gifts, send her flowers, or whisk her away to Bali for three weeks anytime soon. I can't afford to do any of that, anyway.

So, for now, I gotta give her what I'm confident she likes, and my colossal presence is what I got going for me. Granted, I've been out of the game a while, but I figure some things don't change. I've never met a woman who could resist a man she knows who could sweep her off her feet and carry her to the bedroom without a single stutter.

A quick glass of water cools me when there's a knock at the door. It's a gentle, *ter... ta-ta-ter* knock. You know, the one a friendly neighbour gives to return your jump leads you lent him the other day. Although, I know what waits on the other side of that door ain't no rasclart jump leads.

It's the spark that lights the ignition of my soul.

'I wonder what she's wearing. I bet she's in a black dress with those sexy legs out...'

I have to remind myself to relax as I move into first gear and walk over to the front door.

I've never been one for surprises, but right now, I'm like an overzealous teenager as I ponder whether to peep through the keyhole.

'Chill out, Rakz. What's wrong with you?'

Once I'm done fiddling with my collar, I pull the door back, and I'm greeted with a portrait of true beauty. A tumble of thick, spinning hair sparkles like the crystal kiss of the ocean down Nia's face. Just below, her eyes are an effervescent Eden, two cinnamon-brown portals to a soul that I can't wait to acquaint. *'I knew it,'* I tell myself proudly as if guessing which colour dress she'd be sporting strengthens our bond or something.

Her orbit-round eyes focus on me, closing in just a tiny bit, producing a look as mysterious as the cosmos itself. Even though I barely know her, I'm convinced they hold all the wonders of the universe behind them.

"Hey, how are you?" Nia says as she hugs me. Her lips are so close to my skin, her words sail melodiously through my ears, and I feel a tingle that nearly makes me dance an unintended groove. Her honey-sweet voice instantly shifts me into second gear.

My eyes inspect her cotton jumper-dress that rests on her body perfectly. There's not one crease out of place. It curves where it should and curtails where it needs to, stopping just above her knees. I try to

73

focus on the whole picture, but I find my mind journeying down along those slender cocoa limbs.

"I'm good. Come in," I say, eager to close this door.

One of Nia's legs is slightly crossed over the other, displaying a lean calf that could battle through any terrain. A sparkling pair of black flip-flops is at the bottom of the coffee-skinned seductress. A thin strip of rubber separates her nimble toes that shift around. She has a small beauty spot on the top of her foot, just beside the middle strip of the flip-flop, that holds a row of dazzling diamantes, all as close-knit and exuberant as her.

One thing about me—I'm a man who loves a woman's feet. Not in a weird fetish type of way, like them weirdoes who suck toes, dress in leather masks, and all that freaky business. Nah, it's just I've learned how to appreciate every part of a woman.

The blood-red tips of Nia's toes are cleanly polished and point towards me as if keen to come inside. They move around which can only mean she's a tad nervous too. Her feet are as radiant as every other part of her, and I'm once again blown away by how effortlessly amazing she looks.

"Should I take these off?" Nia asks, and for the first time in over a decade, I feel empowered. I have a home that somebody as fine as Nia can respect.

"Nah, it's cool. Go on through," I say, holding my arm out towards the living room.

Her sparkling Havianas catch my eye again taking me back to those times in the visiting hall with Leanne and Mum. It was there I learned how to tell a lot about a woman from the appearance of her feet. I'll give you an example.

Every man who's ever been incarcerated for long enough to understand that God's greatest gift to us men is women, knows that the visiting hall serves many purposes. Not only does it provide a reprieve from the tedious, repetitive nature of prison life, but it's also an opportunity to check out a wide variety of women.

Now, these women may look average at best to any free man, but surround yourself with potbellies, facial hair, and the unrelenting stench of body odour for a few years, then a harried mother of four will look like a supermodel to you.

I'd scan that hall, and amongst all the women who'd clearly taken extra time to glue down their hairpieces, exfoliate their faces, get their nails done, apply their mascara, wax their legs, shave their armpits, and all the rest of it, I noticed what separated the women from the girls. You see, while Leanne nattered away about how Supercoon was 'diversifying his portfolio,' I'd be checking out every nook and cranny of a woman a few seats away.

I remember the face would be nice, the body would suffice, the legs would entice, then I'd reach the feet and see this white, chaffing crust around the heel as it bounced up and down against the sole of a flip-flop.

I'm not saying that unkept feet were a deal-breaker by any means. Shit, I'd have jumped on a woman with athlete's foot after about two years had passed, so you can imagine how I was when I entered the latter years of my sentence.

However, I'm saying that certain women take care of what they think a man takes notice of. Nine times out of ten, those women are trying to attract a man and only concentrate on their main assets. But a woman like Nia, as I can see by the smoothness of her whole foot, takes care of herself as a lifestyle—man or no man. There's not one piece of her entire body that looks even slightly neglected or abandoned. She's a ten from head to toe and doesn't need a single bit of make-up or surgery to reinforce that belief.

"Thanks," Nia says as I close the door.

A flutter occurs in my chest as I allow her obsidian-black hair to pass me. The enticing aroma of clary-sage hangs in the air, filling my nostrils and creeping between my lips. It's sweet and floral and reminds me of those lavender bushes in the front garden.

75

I follow behind her midnight-black dress as we pass the stairs. "Wow. It's been so long since I've been in here. It still looks just the same, though," she says, her voice climbing as it harbours excitement, happiness, or some other positive emotion.

'Her and Mum must have been pretty tight.'

I respond to keep things flowing. "Yeah, I've tidied up a bit, ya know, these arms are capable of some work after all."

Her body half-twisted to face me, she shows off that flawless heavenly smile, displaying those pearly whites that look like the gates to Olympus. "Oh, I brought this for you, by the way," she says, holding out a bottle of wine.

"Thanks," I reply, focusing solely on her eyes. My heart slowly settles as she strolls into the living room, her hands angling by her side. "You want a glass?" I shout from the kitchen.

"I wouldn't say no," she calls.

I search for a bottle opener and eventually find one stuffed away with some cutlery. I've never drunk red wine before in my life. Before I went away, I was more of a Hennessy or Courvoisier man. I can't say I've ever had to open a bottle that required a corkscrew, and I certainly wasn't counting on her bringing one tonight.

I fiddle around with it, frustrating myself in the process. "How d'you work this ting, man?" I say under my breath. I'm aware she's waiting all alone in the living room, and I suspect a woman like Nia doesn't like to be kept waiting.

"You all right in there?" she calls.

"Yeah, one sec," I reply.

Eventually, I get the thing open, pour a modest amount into each of our glasses, and return to the living room. I'm not about to be rude and let Nia drink alone.

A gentleman first. Always.

"There you go," I say, handing her a glass of swirling burgundy liquid.

"Thank you."

I find myself a comfortable spot on the sofa and go to take a sip of my drink, but Nia stops me in my tracks. "No, not yet," she says, placing her left hand on my arm. "Come on, we have to toast."

"Toast? To what?"

I can tell she didn't think that far ahead, and to be honest, I'm more drawn to her hand on my arm. Her touch is a dominant-delicate squeeze, making my blood pump harder and faster.

"I don't know. Anything. To life, to health, to family. You just always have to toast before you drink, to show gratitude," she says, calming herself as the words begin to come out slower. I look at her, and I'm at a loss for answers. The only thing to celebrate now is my freedom and what it's given me. But I ain't about to suggest that. Luckily, Nia saves my blushes. "How about... To Anthea?" she says with a satisfied smile.

I look at the four boxes in front of us and nod. "Yeah, that can work," I say, and we both hold our glasses up, touch them together and look into each other's eyes. "To Anthea," we chant in unison before we both take a big sip.

I get why Mum liked Nia. She's humble, just like Mum.

I drag a box closer towards us. Nia's sitting a metre or so to my right on the sofa, and all I can smell is the intoxicating tropical fragrances that flirt with my senses. "Your perfume smells nice," I say.

"Thank you," she replies before clearing her throat. "So, how long you been doing this kinda thing then?"

I don't want to lie, so I keep my answer vague and change the subject back to her. "Not that long. What about you? What d'you do?" I ask.

"Well, I used to work as an operations manager for a shipping company, but I left that."

'Thank God for that.' Those corporate types are the most judgmental. Whether it's about lags living up at the taxpayers' expense or black men being too lazy to work. Those suits just can't help their conditioning, regardless of their race. That could have been the end of things before they even started.

"What do you do now?" I ask.

"Now, I'm a yoga instructor," Nia says with a beaming smile and proud head tilt.

"Swear down? You teach yoga, yeah?"

"Yeah, why? You thinking about getting involved?" she asks, taking another sip of her wine.

"Me, do yoga...?" I smile.

"Why not?" Nia asks, trying to test my resolve.

"Nah, I don't think I'm built for that kind of stuff."

"Rubbish. You're strong, right?"

I take a while to respond. I don't want to come across as self-obsessed, so I try to be modest. "Kinda, yeah," I say.

She rolls her eyes.

'She's read me.'

"I'm strong, yeah," I rephrase.

"Okay, well, that's exactly what yoga's about, building strength, muscle and becoming in sync with your body—physically and mentally."

"Interesting," I say, nodding slowly.

"You should give it a try one day," she says, and I can tell it's something she's passionate about, the persistence in her voice. It reminds me of Leanne.

I take another sip of my wine, and believe it or not, I can feel it in my system. I stretch my arm out across the headrest of the sofa. "So, you're telling me, if I was to take one of your lessons, you'd have me doing backbends and stretching in all these mad positions?" I ask.

"I wouldn't go that far. Let's start off with some baby steps first, yeah?"

I smile as she switches up the way she talks. It goes from well-spoken and soft to blunt and cheeky in a split second.

'Mum always said I needed a woman who could keep me on my toes.'

Nia's ruby red lips are perched elegantly over the rim of her glass as the wine flows into her mouth, and thoughts about her in lacy thong are coming back. And with a vengeance. "Who knows, I might even outshine you," I say.

78

"I'd love to see you try, Mr 'How d'you even open this?'" she says, mocking the deepness of my voice.

My face changes.

'Is she tryin' to take the piss?' I look at her laughing innocently, and I'm glad her eyes are elsewhere because, for a strange moment, I'm reminded of being on B Wing, and Thomas McGregor mocking my shot at the pool table.

I'm taken back to whacking the cue over his head, then hearing the dull rattle as it hits the floor while I unload a flurry of punches to leave him in a crumbled heap by the laundry room.

I snap out of it and settle back into my seat before Nia turns to face me.

Deep breath.

"Umm... Listen," I start. "I've never been a wine man, ya know."

Her eyes gaze at me in bewilderment as she sucks her bottom lip inwards and shakes her hair. "You're what...? Mid-thirties, right? How d'you go through nearly twenty years of being legally allowed to drink and never opened a bottle of wine?"

'They don't have Merlot on the canteen sheet,' I feel to say, but I take my time and play it cool.

"I'm thirty, actually," I state, wagging my finger like she's in trouble.

She immediately submits. "Sorry, I never meant no offence."

"I'm playing," I say, regaining my composure after that weird little episode. "To be honest, I've always been more of a Henny or a Voss man, you feel me?"

She rolls her eyes. "Ahhh, you black men and your Hennessy..." she cries.

"If you're all about this red wine business, I'm sure you could fly over to Taylor's house. He'll be more than happy to tell you all about how it originates from the black grape family in the Bordeaux region of southwest France," I say.

A vivacious chuckle comes from Nia's mouth. "No, thank you, I think I'll stay here with you. Let you educate me on something."

The wine is kicking in now.

I focus my attention, telling myself I'm not merry. "You sure? I thought you and Taylor would've got on like a house on fire."

"Please, my eight-pound bottle of wine wouldn't even make it through his front door, let alone his wine cellar," she sneers.

She's got him down to tee. "Not your type, nah?"

"Not by a long shot."

The room falls into silence.

Refusing to allow her to drift away, I re-assert myself.

"So, what is your type?" I ask, sliding my body ever so slightly closer to her.

"My type, you know... Ooooohh," she says as her enthusiasm overflows. Those mouthwatering lips pout as she makes me wait in anguish. Now I'm even more intrigued. "My type... My type?" she repeats.

My movements are discreet enough, but I know she doesn't mind if she does see me move closer.

I think about her wrapping those supermodel legs around me while I slide one hand up the back of that dress over her supple frame 'til I reach the back of her neck and pull her up close to me.

'Cool nuh,' I tell myself. The big guy's hanging in there, and I'm hanging in with him. Her neat brow rises as she thinks carefully.

"I got all day," I whisper.

Her dimples ascend on those cheeks, smoother than melted Lindt. Then she smiles. It's a smile from deep within. Her cheek shows the most diminutive sign of blushing, like she's missed these conversations and I sense she hasn't spoken like this with a man for a long time. But I don't say anything, I just mark it in my head.

Turning towards me, she puts a hand over her mouth before removing it and answering. "So, right. Firstly, looks-wise, I like a man who's strong, big, and bulky. I like being wrapped up next to my man, all safe and warm," she begins.

Her eyes check my reaction, but I'm poker-faced. I'm not giving anything away just yet. "Erm..." she continues. "Nice eyes, nice smile, short hair. Maybe a little beard, not too long though," she says, nodding contently like she's done an excellent job.

"And personality-wise?" I ask as she notices the subtle grin I'm trying to hold back from spreading across my face.

"Well, you've gotta be loyal, trustworthy, erm... Good with your hands, can do stuff around the house, reserved, not all hype, into fitness or some sort of exercise or sport, and, oh yeah, can make me smile and laugh. That's key, I swear. I've met so many people who look good but have no personality. That's just not for me," she says, shaking her head.

I continue to listen.

"Erm... Yeah, that's mainly it," Nia states before jumping in to add something. "Oh, and you've gotta be able to teach me something, anything interesting about the world, life, existence, just be smart and wise, challenge my brain."

'That was good.'

"What's got you smirking like you just won the lottery?" Nia asks.

"Nothing," I say, but it only makes my smile grow. I can't help it. Nia's basically just described me. "That was a good list," I tell her.

She bows her head with elegance. "It was *my* list," she says, comforted by my approval.

I rest my hands behind my head as my chest pushes out, threatening to burst out of my t-shirt. I'm in my element right now, feeling confident that Nia likes me. I am her type.

'She went through all those specific little things, and not one time did she mention anything about money, fame, clout, or anything to do with that lifestyle.'

Perhaps I was sold a dream about the outside world. Maybe there are some real women left out here, after all.

I never assumed Nia would be arrogant, but her humility has taken me by surprise. She's an out-and-out 'ten', you see. She could have any man she wants with a snap of her fingers. She could do a 'Leanne' and

81

be with a millionaire tomorrow and not have to worry about a damn thing if she wanted to. But instead, she's sat here with me.

I look over at the glowing flames of the fireplace as they dance hypnotically, swaying from side to side, bright orange waves of untamed passion. The King of my castle, I turn to look at my soon-to-be queen.

She clears her throat. "So, what's your type then?" Her tentative words just about overcome the sound of my thoughts.

Nia starts talking again, but the words aren't registering. I'm locked onto those strawberry-red lips, moist and full of everything I desire. She's looking back into my eyes as she adjusts the collar of her dress. The heating in the room has shot through the roof.

I feel it.

She feels it.

Her smile emerges again, but my face is as straight as an arrow.

'This ain't playtime.'

The big guy swells, and a blatant bulge appears in my tracksuit bottoms.

'Yeah, take note... You think this hunk of dark chocolate just stops at the waist, think again.'

I see Nia glance ever so quickly and subtly, but I don't take my eyes off her. Locked in an intense gaze, she knows what I'm thinking. I know she's thinking the same. She wants me, and I want her. She reaches for her glass to escape my gaze.

I can feel the uncontrollable urges rushing through her body. She fidgets, knowing I've got her where I want her. But by now, it's too late. They've reached between her thighs. I'm guessing, but I bet I'm right.

I see her body taking over her thoughts. She raises her empty glass and welcomes the tiniest drip of wine.

It's illogical.

An impulsive governed by those nerves inside.

She puts the glass down, and I lick my lips.

'Should I make a move now?'

The big guy is fully swole, and I ain't trying to hide it. To do that would mean I'm embarrassed.

Nia blushes again, and against every urge in my body, I free her from the captivity of my command. "My type...?" I say delicately.

She nods, barely able to muster a word. "Umm-hmm," she says as she gulps.

My hand is right by her head, and I want to pull her close, let her feel what I can tell she ain't had in a while, but I don't want to rush this. If I do it, I want her to know I'm serious. That I'm in it for the long run. That I'm all those things she said because when it's time to reveal the truth, she needs to know I ain't no random fuckboy who lied to get into them lacy drawers. I'm the real deal. And she won't find another man like me.

Sat here, her mouth hanging open, she raises her eyebrows with a mixture of expectancy and caution.

"My type... Black and beautiful, from head to toe, inside and outside."

She smiles a full set of teeth, and I give her a half-one in return.

'Can't be giving the whole game away just yet.'

But she's read me once again. She knows those words were only meant for one person—her.

"You want another drink?" I ask.

She nods quickly and continuously as if I've starved her the whole night. But it's not that. It's just the chemistry in our bodies is rife. The heat of it has her parched.

Rising from my seat like a titan going to battle, I head off to satisfy her request.

We spend the next half an hour talking and going through the boxes we forgot were even there until she requests another top-up.

I go off to the kitchen and fulfil my duties once again.

When I return, she's holding a photograph in her hand. "Awww, who's this guy?" she asks.

"Let me see," I say.

She hands me the photograph.

It's a picture of me, Mum, and Leanne. I'm thirteen, standing in the park, wearing white shorts and a navy-blue windbreaker, with a football underneath my arm. I've got the corniest grin a boy could have, but I look genuinely happy.

'Rah,' I think as I look at a younger version of myself, a little boy full of hopes, aspirations and dreams that he had no idea he'd never get to fulfil.

I feel Nia's eyes piercing the side of my head, and I quickly snap out of my daze. "I used to know him... A long time ago."

She gives me this discreet look like she's unsure of my response, so I briskly change the subject.

"You want those bits, yeah?" I ask, pointing my head towards a set of books, a Dutch pot, and a quaint old lamp piled together on their own.

"Yeah, I love this little lamp," she says before lifting the Dutch pot and smiling. "And there's no way I'm letting this go... Uh-uh."

"Take it all. She'd be happy it was going to you."

"You think?" Nia says as if she's measuring the level of sincerity behind my compliment.

"Of course," I say assertively.

I pour myself another glass of wine, and we continue to talk about Mum. She tells me stories that bring a smile to my face. It pains me that I have to behave like I don't know half of the things she's telling me, but that's the price you pay when you get locked up for twelve years. People know your own mother better than you, or at least they get to feel like they do.

Deep into the evening, I feel myself winding down. Nia rises to her feet, clutching her Dutch pot, which is big enough to house the lamp and the books. "I better get home," she says with a disheartened look.

I stand up, seeing she's ready to leave. I don't want her to go, but like I said, I'm a gentleman first. We stroll towards the hallway, neither of us in any hurry.

84

But that look has bothered me. *'Is she disappointed I didn't make a move?'*

"So, you staying here while you fix up the place then or are you going home tonight?" I hear her ask.

I scratch my unshaven beard like it's something I need to think about. "I'm staying here. I got a bit more work to do to get that room ready to let. Probably be here another week," I say.

She nods, pushing out her bottom lip. She doesn't say anything, but I feel a shrewd sadness in her expression. Maybe she doesn't want me to leave.

We reach the door, and she's stood with the Dutch pot and the other bits locked underneath her arm. Her lips look ravishing. And those sculpted cheeks look as if they've never seen a blemish in all their days.

She moves her head to the side a little. "Well, catch me before you do go, and I'll put this to good use," she says, tapping the Dutch pot.

I catch a waft of that exotic perfume, and it takes hold of me.

When she moves to step over the threshold, I assert myself. "Wait," I say. Looming over her, I take the pot from her hands and place it on the ground in one swift motion, almost taking her by surprise. Looking helplessly into my eyes, like she's back on that sofa, I take her by hand and pull her up against my chest. She sinks into me as her breasts squeeze up against me, soft and satisfying.

My hand supports her back as she becomes a feather in my palm. I slide my other hand to the back of her neck and hold her head as if it's the most precious artefact on earth. I lean in, and our lips connect.

And for all the times I've fantasised about kissing Nia since I met her, it has nothing on the real thing.

Fireworks go off through my body as my manhood expands and presses into her thighs.

She moans as the residue of our lips merge.

Her tongue enters and I follow Nia's lead without hesitation. I've wanted this since the moment I met her. Now she's in my grasp, I'm never letting her go. Our tongues swirl around, moving in tandem, slipping and sliding to each other's rhythm. She moans again as I get become lost in her quintessential allure.

Intwined, nothing around us exists.

Time stops, and it's just the two of us.

She rolls her head passionately as my hand moves lower, squeezing a handful of her bum, which only turns me on even more. She kisses me harder and faster, her tongue showing no mercy. The squishing of our lips has me ready to throw her over my shoulder and take her upstairs when I feel her slow the pace. Her kiss becomes soft and sensual. Her hands come together behind my neck, giving me a few more seconds of euphoria. Then, with pure loving tenderness, she kisses me on the lips, squashing them before pulling away.

"I gotta get home," she says, knowing she doesn't want to get carried away.

I sigh, followed by a smile as my hand quickly sorts out the mess she's left me in.

She sucks in that bottom lip.

She knows what I want and feels content having me there. I count down from ten in my head. Seeing me take a deep breath, she giggles as she picks up the Dutch pot and everything in it. "You want me to walk you home?" I ask.

She squints her eyes, wondering if I've got an ulterior motive.

"I'm okay," she says.

"All right then, cool," I say as I open the door for her. "Look after yourself, yeah, and I'll see you later," I say, watching her walk down the pathway like she's back on that catwalk.

She opens the gate and turns back to look at me. Her scorching hot eyes burn holes in my chest. "Not if I see you first," she says cheekily. I shake my head and watch her move underneath the majestic glow of the stars. I walk down the pathway, and as she reaches her front door, I raise my hand.

8

I was once told by this old man, something that would stick with me forever. It was near the start of my sentence, and I was probably only nineteen or twenty. The man had been a soldier of the Irish Republican Army and fought against the British in the seventies. He was in for murder, a pub brawl that had resulted in a man being killed.

Well, me and this old codger were locked in a holding cell together as we waited to be taken to another wing. Sat metres apart on this built-in bench that ran the perimeter of the pale walls, we both adhered to the code of silence you obey when you don't know somebody. Nobody in prison wants to come across like a beg-friend. It's a sign of inferiority, and the weak get preyed upon inside. After about ten minutes or so, the man looked up, and a set of chilling rapture-blue eyes shot through me.

He stared at me for a couple of seconds before finally speaking. "It never leaves yer, ya know?" he said.

I ignored him, thinking the old man was probably off his meds, but he continued gawking at me like I owed him a response.

Pretty sure he wanted to spark a conversation; it left me with two options. Either I made it into an altercation, or I entertained his ramblings. I figured we would be locked in there for a while, so I opted for the latter.

"What's that, then?" I asked, hoping he'd shut up after getting whatever he needed off his chest.

Then, as slow as the sunrise, he lifted his hands and turned his palms to face me. "The blood," he said.

I glanced at his coarse skin, which looked like all it had ever done was mix concrete and lay bricks.

"What you on about?" I asked.

A frown came down his face before he dropped the line that's stayed with me all these years.

"Yer nor when yer kill a man, it never leaves yer."

I remember simply nodding my head at the time, thinking this guy's off his rocker.

We were eventually taken to another wing, and I only saw him a handful of times after that, but his words never left me.

From that evening onwards, I've thought about the man I killed every time I laid my head down on my pillow at night. Whether I'd had the best day and gone to bed laughing or had the worst of days and gone to bed raging, the thought of what I had done always resurfaced. And when the nightmares intensified a couple of years before my release, I put it down to the karmic ways of the universe, telling me that my time would soon be coming.

For over ten years, the fear of how I may die has played on my mind constantly, hanging over my head like the sword of Damocles.

It must be my punishment for taking a man's life.

See, what old Paddy was talking about that day, was guilt. And the worst kind. The kind that no amount of repentance can extinguish.

I had condemned myself to believe it would never leave me; that the dreadful night terrors were my penalty, and that the rest of my nights would be spent reliving the incident that robbed me of half my life.

Until last night that is. The evening I spent with Nia has done something to me. Holding her as she kissed me like I was the only person on earth that mattered. I was a man. Not a prisoner, not a failure, and not an unremorseful savage killer.

Nia's warmth has altered the fabric of my being from within. I couldn't tell you precisely what or how, but I find it no coincidence that the same night I spend with her is the same night I go to sleep without so much as a single thought about the young man I murdered or about what kind of retribution lies in store for me.

I can't explain how good it feels to wake up from a peaceful sleep to the melodious lyrics of the birds outside instead of halfway to hell, sweating buckets.

Once I finish my morning workout, I go to the kitchen to make myself a cup of tea when my phone rings.

"Yes, yes D, what's happening?" I say, my voice as fresh and crisp as the morning breeze.

"Yo, where are you?" Deontay cries.

"My yard man, what's up?"

"Bruv, I tried calling you last night..."

He probably did. I was gone, though. Nothing was pulling me out of that sleep.

"... Couple man try run up on me, bro," he cries.

"Run up on you? What, where?"

"I dunno, fam. Two youts just approached man when I came out the alley by the barbers."

"What'd they want?"

"Bro, I dunno. One of them tried bang man in the face, and the other backed out a shank, so I ran off."

Baffled, I sit on the sofa, trying to make sense of what Deontay's telling me.

'The barbers is less than a mile down the high road. Deontay's from these parts. He knows these ends. Why would somebody just randomly try to attack him like that in his own hood?'

"Have you told anyone about our movements?" I ask.

"Nah, course not, man."

It doesn't make sense.

'Scribz set us up with the traphouse to operate from and it's only really us and Deontay who know about the inner workings of this operation... Other than the crackhead's flats we use. But they wouldn't set us up, as long as they keep gettin' free gear they're not a problem.'

The phone to my ear, I hear a few rowdy voices in the background.

"You all right?" I ask.

89

"Yeah, man's good."

"What did these youts look like?"

"I dunno, Turkish, Greek or something," he squeals as the shouting around him gets louder.

"Turkish?"

"Yeah, I don't know, one was fat, and the other one had a beard."

I can tell he's irate. The octaves in his voice are jumping all over the place. "What, and they didn't say anything, nah?"

"Dunno. Just asked where I'm from, I think—I can't remember—I didn't hear them properly."

"You good, though? No one touched you, right?"

"Nah, they tried to. Man just bucked up with my niggas, still. I'm gonna go back there now."

"Nah, don't do that. Just chill, man," I say, rising to my feet.

"Fuck that, I'm going there now, bro. Man can't just try move to me in my ends."

I kiss my teeth. "Listen, chill out, man. Relax," I tell him.

"They got my fuckin' hat. It dropped when I ran off. Plus, they violated man, blood."

I can hear the chants in the background, and I figure it's those same rugrats, pumping him up, fuelling his anger.

"Don't watch that," I say calmly, but I feel my frustration growing.

"Nah, I'ma show them man what time it is. Man ain't no pussy," he cries. "Oi Ribz, come man."

He must be rallying one of his troops.

I squeeze the phone, and my forearm becomes as stiff as a post. "You ain't going nowhere, are you fuckin' dumb?" His voice stops completely, and I can just picture him standing there with that same look on his face when I slapped him around the head. "You don't even know who these man are. What... You really think they're gonna still be there waiting for you? Use your brain, man."

"But—"

"—But nothing. All that's gonna happen if you go there is you, and those dickheads you're with are gonna buck up with the first person who looks at you wrong and end up stabbin' someone up."

Deontay remains quiet.

I think he's listening. He better be, anyway. I carry on to make sure he's got that phone right up against his ear.

"Did they hurt you?"

"No," he mumbles.

"Did they take anything from you?"

"My hat."

"Forget your fuckin' hat! Anything like your phone, keys, or any of that?"

"No."

"Exactly. You still got money in your pocket, and you still got the food."

I hear a deflated sigh and pause for a moment as I count backwards from ten. "Look, go send them rugrats to work, don't worry, I'ma check you later, init."

"Cool," he says with a distinct whiff of disappointment.

I grit my teeth as I hear the reluctance in his voice. "I hit you later, man," I tell him.

"Cool," he says before hanging up the phone.

I toss the phone back onto the sofa and shake my head.

Deontay knows I'm right, but I also know his pride is dented, and his ego's desperate to reassert itself. I know this all too well because I was once that kid myself, but like I said, I didn't get him involved in this life to follow in my footsteps.

Deontay doesn't know it at the moment, but I'm saving him. As long as he adheres to my instructions, we'll continue to get this money. And for me, every week is a step closer to getting out this place.

I stare out of the window and beyond the outstretched arms of the Callistemon, that's recently begun to boast luscious pink flower heads.

91

They sway elegantly as I think about who would have tried to attack Deontay.

'He told me he's lived round here for years. He ain't got no problems with anybody.'

I stroll into the kitchen and flick the switch on the kettle as I rack my brain for the most logical answer to my question. The thing rumbles violently as the steam curls towards the ceiling.

'It must have been someone who's got a problem with one of his friends,' I conclude. *'Them lot are fools. I can just imagine them running their mouths and causing problems. Maybe they got into suttin' with a couple of Turks, and now Deontay's got caught up in it... I'll chat to him properly later.'*

Just as I go to pour my tea, my phone rings again.

'What now, man?'

I answer the call.

"Yo," I say, my frustration seeping through my larynx.

But when I hear the woman's voice on the other end of the phone, my head lowers, and my neck bends forward slightly.

"Hey."

"Yo," I say. I'm about to ask who it is when she identifies herself.

"It's me, Nia. I hope I haven't caught you at a bad time."

I quickly clear my throat. "Nah, not even," I reply. Then just before I can ask her how she is, she swiftly interjects.

"Good. Right then," Nia says, switching her tempo. "Go get a t-shirt, grab a bottle of water, get your trainers on, and be outside in five."

'What?'

"Oh, and Rakim," she continues.

"Yeah."

"Bring your smile."

It's as if there's a timely disconnect between the words coming from the phone and what I'm hearing. Confused, I go to respond to her instruction, but the line goes dead before I can.

'Wait, what...? She's gonna be outside... In five minutes. And what the hell does bring my smile mean?'

"What's this girl got planned?" I ask myself.

I rush to the window as if Jamal's just given me the heads up that the screws are spinning cells. I move the thin netting out of the way and crane my head around the side of it to peer out into the street. I see a lady pushing a pram and a couple getting out of a car, but there's no sign of Nia.

I take a deep breath and put the netting back in its rightful position. That psychiatrist back in Huntingley told me it was customary to suffer these episodes. She called it PTSD. I played that shit down, but maybe she was right.

'Calm down. She said five minutes. Let me just get ready.'

After jetting upstairs, I replay her instructions in my head. I put on a t-shirt, hurry back downstairs into the kitchen to grab a bottle of water from the fridge, and then slip on my trainers.

Seeking appraisal from my reflection in the hallway mirror, I crack a smile.

'Nah, nah, nah.' It's been a while since I practised one, and it shows. *'No smile, fam, you look creepy.'*

Wondering what this girl's got in store for us today, I propel myself up and down on my toes. I take a sip of my water, then put the cap back on when I hear movement outside. I peer through the spyhole and open the door.

9

Radiant as ever, stands Nia, her skin looking like she belongs on the beaches of Barbados. She raises a hand, and her smile hits me. It's that of a real Caribbean goddess as pure and untouched as the golden shores of an island paradise.

She wiggles her fingers as she waves, tilting her head teasingly to the side.

Squinting her eyes to evade the striking sunshine, she says, "So you ready then, Mister?"

The smile she asked for forms across my face. I'm powerless to resist it. She's in her running gear, tight in all the right places. "I was born ready," I say, closing the door behind me.

I walk down the steps and greet her with a strong yet gentle hug.

"I'm not going easy on you," she says, releasing herself from my arms.

"I don't like easy, anyway."

"You sure you don't wanna warm up? Perhaps do a little one-two stretch?" she asks, twisting her hips from side to side.

Press-ups, sit-ups, and squats completed this morning; I'm already warmed up. I put a reassuring hand on her shoulder. "I'm good, don't worry."

She gives a smile that says she's unconvinced.

Either she's not confident in my running abilities, or she rates herself highly. Whichever one it is, she's the one who's about to be surprised.

"Okay," she concedes.

"Which way we going then?" I say, looking towards the left. It's a subtle gesture, but thankfully, she picks up on it. There's no way I'm jogging down the high road.

We set off at a steady pace, and straight away, I can feel her sizing me up, checking me out. We pass the newly built flats on the left and stop at the junction at the end of our street.

She's bouncing up and down like a Duracell bunny as we wait for a car to glide past. The car turns right, and off we go again.

"So, you do this every morning, yeah?" I ask.

"Well," she says, pausing for a breath. "Not every morning, but most mornings."

We continue on for roughly another twenty minutes, passing white picket fences and quiet backroads. The morning air is cool, and I catch the whiff of freshly trimmed grass as I pass a hedge on my left. Birds chirp excitedly, cantillating in the treetops above, as we exchange mostly small talk.

Nia's eyes remain straight ahead the whole time, though. I can tell she's focused. Maybe she's got a point to prove, or maybe she didn't think I'd even keep up this far.

I peer over at Nia once again. "You hanging in there, yeah?" she says.

"C'mon, of course."

We turn right, passing a string of terraced houses as a dog goes berserk from behind a garden fence. I graciously manoeuvre past a lamppost, lending Nia the space to navigate the gap, and she takes the lead.

A couple minutes later she comes to an abrupt stop. She places her hands on her thighs and looks up above. Taking a deep breathe, she turns towards me.

By now, my shins are feeling a little strained. If the running's over right now, I'd be grateful. The tank isn't empty, but I could do with a break. I puff deeply as I catch up to her. "What? You done, already?" I say, pretending I've still got a million miles in me.

Giving me that look as if she's taking it as a challenge, she shakes her head. "Just getting started," she smirks. We both sip from our bottles of water, keeping eye contact with one another.

'This girl's actually competing with me.'

95

"Let's go then," she says.

I duly obey, screw the cap back on the bottle and follow her down a narrow pathway. The world is thrown into darkness but for the glowing white daylight at the end of the footpath. Three-storey houses and large ash trees block out the sunlight from both sides, and I find myself just following Nia's bum as it moves up and down, each cheek knowing its place.

'That bum though, mmm.'

"You tryin' to kidnap me or suttin', Nia?"

I can't see her face from behind, but I can tell she's smiling from the pitch of her voice.

"You wish that were true, don't you?"

We exit the alleyway, and I'm hit with a blast of sunlight.

Back to reality.

We go on for a short while, and Nia glances over at me once again. She smiles before increasing her pace a little. By now, I can't lie. I'm starting to feel a bit drained. My heart is going off like a jackhammer against my chest, and my throat is pleading to be quenched. Even my back is beginning to feel tense, but there's no way I'm letting her leave me lagging behind.

Never that.

As I speed up to match her intensity, I can tell she's feeling the burn too. The lack of speech, the look of determination like she's fighting hard to go on.

"You... enjoying... this?" she asks.

And although she says it with tongue-in-cheek, she knows I'm passing her fitness test so far. She ain't messing with an unfit old man. Nah, she got the full package right here—big, strong, and fit.

After we clock up what must be more than forty minutes of running, we reach Diamond Palace Park.

A few paces in front of me, the rhythmic tap of her soles against the pavement cease. I follow suit, and although I'll never admit it, I'm relieved. With her hands on her hips, she turns towards me. Nodding, like I've earned her approval, she holds up a palm. "Well done," she says.

I give her a high-five and finish off the water in my bottle. "So, that's your secret then, yeah?" I ask, feeling a cheeky grin emerge on my face.

"Secret?" Nia says.

"For how you look so good," I say, examining the hour-glass physique God has presented in front of me. My eyes come back up to meet hers, and I note a tinge of redness around her cheeks.

'She blushing?'

"I try," she says, being sure to sound humble.

A sweet chorus from the sparrows that flit from one tree to the next fills the silence. I notice how Nia holds one arm, twisting from side to side, as strands of her hair escape her bun and plunge over her shoulders.

Silently, I scan the area. It's still quiet. There are other joggers around, a few families scattered across the vast abyss of green across from us, and a small queue by an ice-cream van stationed near the park entrance.

As Nia stands a few metres away from me, the tweeting of the blackbirds and starlings provides a soothing touch of familiarity. She pulls out her phone and begins to scroll as her breathing finally settles. I sense she's in no hurry to go anywhere.

Despite the two of us kissing yesterday, I'm still unaware if she feels anything for me. I'm not naïve to think she's fallen in love after one night, but I think I'm picking up a few signals.

Then again, I've been inactive for over a decade, and my receiver could easily be a bit dodgy. This could all be a bit of fun for her. She may play this game with numerous men. And although she doesn't seem like that sort of girl, the truth is, I barely know her.

'Be the man. Take the lead,'

I stand up tall and go for it. "Aye Nia, you want some ice-cream?" I ask.

Her phone makes a clicking sound, and those iridescent brown eyes look directly at me.

"Sure," she replies, and I lead her across the road towards the ice-cream van.

"What you having?" I ask.

She puts a hand on her chin and appears like she's deep in consideration as she examines all the different flavours on offer. "Hmmm," she says as I wait patiently.

I look at the lady in the van, whose eyes pierce through me like she's looking into my soul. I look at Nia, and an urge to tell her to hurry up rises within me. From my sternum to my jaw feels all tense again.

'Calm down.'

In prison, it was simply, go in the cafeteria, collect your slop, get out, and fuck off back to your cell. There *were* no choices or changing your mind. And when somebody did hold up the line, violence was nearly always the answer.

I have to remind myself that Nia is not a prisoner, and neither am I anymore. She's oblivious to my way of life, which is evident as she innocently stands there going back and forth between a 99 flake and a Twister like she's a tourist on Copacabana Beach.

"Erm, I'll have a twin cone, one scoop of chocolate, and one scoop of vanilla, please," she says with a smile.

The woman disappears behind the counter, and I feel my body relax. "You thinkin' hard about that one?" I joke in order to regain some normality within me.

"You know what, I felt like a change this time. But then, chocolate's always been my favourite," she says, raising her eyes from my barrel-chest up towards my face.

"Chocolate's your favourite, yeah?"

"Definitely," she says, narrowly opening her mouth to give me the slightest glimpse of the tip of her tongue in between those porcelain white teeth.

'I swear this girl wants me.'

The thought sends sensations shooting throughout my body.

We hold each other's stare for a moment, and my pulse fires up again, triggering an abundance of sexual cravings. The intensity between us absorbs me as it increases with every passing moment. The sound from lawnmower engines and sprinkling hoses fades away into the distance as I tower over Nia. She's a picture of perfection. I wish I could take her back home this second.

"There you go, sir. Strawberry for you and a double for the lady," croaks a voice, bringing us both back to the world of smells and sounds. Nia notices my delayed reaction and points her head to the expectant lady beside me.

"My bad," I say as I hand the woman the money and follow Nia into the park.

"You were a bit looking lost there," she says as her tongue delicately ladles a scoop of chocolate ice-cream.

"What can I say? It's those eyes. They can have an effect on a man."

"Mr Smooth, yeah?" Nia says with a playful nudge.

Once again, I flash a smile. There's something about this woman. She brings out my confidence, then at the same time, makes me nervous. Just being around her wraps me in comfort but she knows how to keep me on my toes.

Under the unfathomable drape of blue above, we amble along a path that's beset with trees on either side, their sprawling limbs clothed in petal robes. The air is daisy-fresh, but for the redolence of sweet nougat that dispels the further we walk.

"So gwarn Nia, tell me more about you," I say as I attack the tantalising strawberry ice-cream atop my cone.

"What do you wanna know?" she says, her reply carrying an air of mystery.

"Well, I know you live just down the road from where I'm staying, I know you're quite a private person, and I know you're into the fitness ting."

She exaggerates her nod, dipping her neck forward slowly. "Yup."

"Oh, and you love your yoga."

"That's right," she says, looking at me, seemingly proud that I remembered.

"Yeah," I say, letting my words hang as I look into those virility-brown eyes. "I bet you do a proper good Downward Dog, init?"

She turns her head away. "Behave," she says impishly.

"Seriously though, how d'you get into it?"

She tilts her head back, and I get the sense she's glad I asked.

"Well, I used to work in this office, doing all of that office-y type stuff, and after a few years, I kinda realised that it just wasn't fulfilling me. Don't get me wrong, it was a good job, and the pay was good, but the more I went there, the more I felt like I was just wasting my time. I don't know how to explain it. One day, I just looked around and thought, urgghh, I don't wanna be like any of these people when I'm older, just sitting at their computers, gossiping about the management, then begging friends with them when they come around. Then they go out for their cigarette breaks and come back in to moan about how the day is dragging out," she says as she looks over at me.

Seeing I'm still invested, she continues. "Like, have you ever had that feeling that you're just being trapped, like you're in a prison?"

The words reverberate through me to the very core of my soul. She looks back over at me, and I swear to God, I want to scream out to let this whole park hear, 'Yes, Nia, I had it for twelve long years,' but I know I can't.

"Yeah, I hear you," I say and let her carry on.

"Well, that's how it was making me feel, like I was trapped and couldn't do anything without my job. Like, if I quit, then I couldn't pay my bills, if I wanted to go on holiday, I have to ask for time off almost a year in advance, and I just questioned myself about loads of things," she continues before taking a bite of her ice-cream. "After a little while longer, it just got me feeling depressed and down. I knew I couldn't carry on doing the same meaningless stuff day in, day out. I don't care what anyone says. Nothing about sending emails, creating spreadsheets, and answering phone calls all day does anything to uplift your soul."

"I hear you on that," I say as I smile, remembering my conversations with my mum when she'd bang on about getting a job, 'just any job.' "It never appealed to me either to allow some company to control my life, where I go, what I do and when I can do it, just for a pay slip," I reply.

"Exactly," Nia says passionately as we reach a fork in the pavement and veer off towards the right. Arrows of sunlight thrust through the canopy of the greenery overhead, creating splashes of saffron-gold beams on the ground. The shadows of branches shimmy around in the light breeze as we continue deeper into the eternity of the park.

"Nah, you gotta be doing something that invigorates you. Could be painting, music, building, teaching, whatever it is, it's gotta stimulate not just your body and your mind but your soul too, otherwise your desire for it won't last, trust me."

Nia smiles, raising one hand in the air. "Thank you," she says as if I've just freed her from some kind of mental bondage. "That was me with yoga. I started it about four years ago, and I just instantly felt free when I was doing it," she says, one hand theatrically moving through the air as she explains, and her vitality exudes from the pores of her skin once again. "You know that feeling when you just know." She squints her eyes as she looks at me. "You don't know how, but you just know, what you're doing right now, feels right. You know that you should have been doing this all along—"

"—Yeah, and you know no matter what, you could never go back to doing what you were doing before," I interrupt.

"Yes! I was literally just about to say that," she says, covering her mouth to stop laughing.

"Great minds think alike, you feel me?" I say, holding my hand out for a high-five.

She takes the cue and continues. "Yoga was that for me. I feel like it kinda saved me."

"From what?"

101

She opens her eyes wide and jerks her head to the side. "From ending up like all ah dem dry prunes that still work up inna that office 'til this day." The words roll off her tongue so eloquently she sounds like the most well-spoken Caribbean I've ever come across.

"I feel you," I say humbly.

In the distance, an endless line of astral blue knitted with silver glimmers as I spot the lake on the far end of the park. From the higher ground we currently occupy, I can catch its mesmerising sparkle that glitters underneath the arcing gulls that use the sky as their playground.

"Come, let's go this way," I say, and Nia follows my lead.

We walk downhill, passing children on scooters and couples enjoying picnics as I embrace the mesmeric beauty around me.

We get a bit further along, and Nia turns to me, narrowing her eyelids once again. "You know, you never even asked me if I'm single, Rakim?" she says.

I quickly dissect her expression and note the spirited undertone. "Do I need to?" I ask.

She licks the last of her ice-cream that's feeling the effects of the sun. "You can't answer a question with a question."

I roll my eyes.

"What? You can't."

"But that wasn't a question, was it? That was a statement," I say, shaking my finger as we stroll along.

I see her eyes look upwards as if she's recanting her words. "Fair enough. Let me rephrase. *Why* did you never ask if I was single?"

I study her face. "Well, after you kissed me yesterday, I assumed that you—"

"—No, I mean before that, when we were going through Anthea's things."

My lips retract as I think of a response. "I dunno. I guess I'm a man that just goes with the flow when it comes to all of that."

She nods her head. "Okay, so does that mean you would cheat on your girlfriend then?"

"Whoa, where you pull that one from?"

She smiles and lifts a palm in apology. "No, I'm not saying you would. I'm asking. Hypothetically speaking, let's say you had a girlfriend and you happened to meet another woman while you were out, clubbing, having a good time, the music's pumping, the drinks are flowing, and you're talking with this girl. You and her are getting on, and there's chemistry between you. You're all looking in each other's eyes, sitting close together, and you know you both feel something. Would you 'go with the flow' then?" she asks.

It's a trick question. 'Yes,' means I'm a cheat, and 'no,' means I've contradicted myself. I let the silence between us linger for a few seconds as indistinguishable chatter mixes with the murmuring of the wind, noticing Nia's expectant eyes from my peripheral.

"I don't go clubbing," I say.

"You know what I mean," she cries.

"I'm messing with you. But to answer your question, no I wouldn't."

"So, you don't always go with the flow. You pick and choose?"

This time I can't refrain from cracking a smile. The reason being, I knew that one was coming. I'd already planned four questions ahead. *Dang-su may have taught me chess, but I apply those skills to real life.*

"That's not it, nah. It's more of the case that I wouldn't betray someone like that. I'm not a snake."

"Hmmm," Nia says, slowly dabbing her lips with a tissue. I let her finish, then take the tissue from her and place it in a bin to my left as we carry on.

I shake my head, and she instantly responds. "What?" she asks.

"Nothing."

"No, go on. Feel free to say whatever you want. I'm a big girl. I can take it," she says, regally lifting her chin.

I look at her. "Ite, cool. Let me take a guess, yeah, and please correct me if I'm wrong."

She stops her stride, and we both turn to look at each other. She seems intrigued as she opens her arms to signal for me to proceed. I'm

103

not sure how she'll take it, but if she says she's a big girl, then it's only right I test the waters. "All right, so you've been cheated on in the past, yeah? And since then, you're now of the opinion that all men cheat, right?"

She pushes her bottom lip out and slants her head to the side. "You could say that."

"Then that's the problem right there."

"Care to elaborate?"

"Well, look. Mind follows matter, yeah. So, from you assuming that there's not a man out there that's capable of being faithful, then what you're effectively doing is limiting the possibility of meeting such a man."

Nia looks as if she's contemplating my words, so I go on. "Now, when you continuously repeat that idea in your head, that all mean cheat, it then becomes a mantra, which you speak into existence, and what started as an ideology becomes a cornerstone for the reality you experience. It's like if a person keeps saying, 'I'll never lose weight, I'll never lose weight,' it doesn't matter how much they diet or exercise, it ain't gonna happen, you feel me?"

Crossing her arms, Nia appears deep in thought. Perhaps, she doesn't agree, or maybe she's conjuring a reply.

"Interesting."

"Like I said, mind follows matter, so your thoughts will always manifest your reality. The stronger your emotional connection is with the thought, the more power it has over what you experience."

She nods, seemingly still in deliberation.

Sensing a bit of scepticism behind her eyes, I come from another angle. "Believe me, I ain't saying that men only cheat because women think they will, nah not at all. I'm just saying that if you ain't *open-minded* to the *possibility* of something, it makes it nearly impossible for you to experience it."

There's a short pause while Nia digests my words. I can only hope they resonate with her and that she's not the ignorant type to dismiss me straight away.

"I get you," she says. "Maybe I shouldn't be so cynical then. What do you reckon?" she asks mischievously.

"I reckon no matter what I tell you, you're gonna make up your mind anyway, init?"

She points a finger at me, winks, and clicks her tongue. "You're damn right, Rakim."

Glad to have taught her a little something, I laugh as we continue along.

The cerulean-blue sky looks down upon us, and I catch a fragrance of mint as we saunter by a few pine trees. Their thistles waver with an enticing welcome. We're much closer to the lake by now. I can taste the salty particles that drift through the air. In the near distance, specs of light jump and dance off its argent-silver surface as the sun hits the idle water at a perfect angle.

I'm reminded of the life I've missed out on all these years. All the small things I took for granted. Taking a walk in the park, the sunshine on my skin, the mystic beauty of the natural world, and of course, the company of a beautiful woman.

I look over at Nia, who catches my glance in perfect timing. "So how come you're single then, Rakim?" she asks.

I'd love to tell her the truth, but I'm nowhere near that level of comfort within myself yet. "Who said I am?" I say teasingly instead.

Nia stops to throw a look of derision my way. "Please," she says. "A woman knows these things."

"Ite, cool. I deserved that one."

"Yeah, you did."

"Nah, to be honest, I don't know. Maybe I just ain't come across the right woman yet," I shrug.

She raises an eyebrow. "Okay."

I sense she's yearning for a deeper explanation, but the problem is I can't just turn around and say, *because I was locked away for the past twelve years*. I can't tell her my experience, which only leaves me with my current feelings to go with.

I let a few more seconds drag out before I elaborate.

"To be real, if I'm in a relationship, it's gotta be serious. All or nothing. I'm looking to get out of this country one day soon. That's a big step. So, for me to be with someone, our energies have gotta match on all levels, you feel me."

She puts her hands together. "Hmmm. Explain what you mean," she says.

"I ain't no relationship counsellor yeah, but I know, in every relationship, the energies from both people should match. So, say you're with someone, yeah?"

"Yeah."

"If you're stimulating them in a way that they desire, then they should be able to stimulate you in a way that you desire. For example, if you're someone who likes your thoughts and opinions challenged or needs help with her fitness goals and I'm doing that, then you gotta be helping me grow as a person—mentally, physically, spiritually, or emotionally. Otherwise, the energy is out of balance and I'm gonna feel exhausted init? One person can't be giving, giving, giving, and the other ain't providing nothing. All that does is leaves the giver feeling drained."

"I feel you," agrees Nia surprisingly.

"And to go live in a next country with a woman, that foundation has to be there."

"You're right. I agree," Nia says.

It sounds like it's more of a line to comfort herself than to praise me, but I don't mind. I like Nia, and if I can give her even a slither of advice that may benefit her life, then I'm satisfied.

"So, have your relationships left *you* feeling drained?" Nia asks.

I smile. "Nah, but we all know them people who have been... And moretime, that's why."

"It's true. Energy is vital. That's why I love teaching yoga. It's helped me raise my Kundalini, so if I can help someone else, then I feel blessed... If you know what I'm saying," Nia says.

As she looks over at me, I sense her seeking my approval.

"Well, you know you could probably help me raise mine then, init?" I say, and as I lick my lips, I see a smile appear.

"Yeah, and how would I do that, then?" she asks.

I stop walking and take her by the hand.

Gently, I pull her close to my chest, to which she puts up no resistance. Inches from each other, we're back outside that ice cream van.

Those eyes, a-lit with hazel stardust, stare at me longingly as her windfall sweet essence engulfs me, almost throwing me into a trance.

"Nia." My voice rumbles. "You don't know how sexy you are. There ain't a man alive who sees you the way I do, I swear."

Those perfectly threaded eyebrows don't move an inch. Nia sucks in her lip and blushes.

"You sure?" Nia whispers and her words float like a stream of rose petals down my ear canal. I lean in, and just as I expect to feel the sorbet-sweet touch of those pilgrim-pink lips, her finger intercepts. "Behave," she says, and I'm totally at her mercy. She kisses me softly, and my shorts bulge with eagerness, begging for my thirst to be quenched.

'This girl knows how to work man,'

Nia turns away with a seductive smile.

We reach the shimmering lake that sits tranquil like a river lost in the embers of time. Hours pass as we talk about everything from relationships to food to my yearning to travel to The Gambia; even the existence of alternate realities and past lives make the cut.

Before we both know it, evening is beginning to settle in as the leaves of the ancient pines around us flicker like candle lights.

"Rah, is that the time?" I exclaim.

My joints click, and my calves thank me as I rise up from the wooden bench we've warmed for the past few hours. Seeing my hasty reaction, Nia looks over at my phone.

"Remember, Rakim... Time's just an illusion," she says with a wink as she stands up to stretch her arms.

I'm unsure if she knows, but her jovial side is quickly becoming my kryptonite.

Once we arrive back on our street, we both slow our pace, letting the chaos of the world around us pass by.

"You not cold?" she asks, hugging herself as a gust of wind rushes by.

"Nah, not even. I'm a soldier," I say and put my arm around her goose-pimpled shoulders.

She rests her head against me as we walk along, and I catch various glances from ordinary civilians. Usually, I'd glance back, or my mind would go off on its own mission, exploring every possible explanation of where this person may know me from or what they're thinking about me. But as we approach Nia's front garden, none of that matters. The only thought that passes through my mind is how lucky I am to have met such a beautiful soul like Nia.

10

"Just here, bossman," I tell the cab driver as I look at my phone. He slows to a gradual stop at the side of the road and switches off the engine. "Wait here. I'll be back in five," I say, handing him a ten-pound note to appease the worry written across his face.

The concrete jungle around me is filled with tower blocks that range in colour from clay-grey to a dull brick-brown, some recently constructed, and others corroded by decades of acid rain. Dozens of satellite dishes shoot off from the exterior of the unloved structures, their cables dangling in the midst of the night sky.

I pass a damaged lamppost that once stood upright. It sprouts from the grimy pavements and bends at an awkward angle like a stem-thin gymnast poised in a stretch.

Squares of luminosity reach far into the distance until they become nothing but dots of light. I walk further into the estate underneath the teetering glow of numerous streetlights and past a toppled silver dustbin that leaks the remnants of old waste. The stench shoots up my nostrils as I turn right through a narrow alleyway.

I come to a long road that's as quiet as a coffin. An eerie chill snaps at the bare skin around my neck as I hear the faintest of echoes, a laugh or cackle of some sort, too far away for me to make out any meaning. I pass a kid's playground and hastily navigate through this maze of run-down buildings and graffiti-covered garages before I reach my destination. A group of around ten teenagers is huddled in a circle around a black VW Golf. It's impossible to distinguish Deontay from any of them, the dark clothing conveniently camouflaging every frame under the black of the night.

A chilling memory resurfaces as I look at the block on my left.

'Rah... It was right there, the first time I see somebody get stabbed.'

I'm reminded of the small pools of blood that got thicker and deeper in colour, the further they ran into the hallway and up the stairs. I peer at the cracked glass panel on the block door and shake my head.

'Fuck this place, man.'

As I get closer to the group of boys, heads and hoods flick up, alerted by my footsteps. I recognise some of the boys, and after a quick scan, I locate Deontay. "Yo," I call, drawing the attention of the entire collective. I continue marching towards them, and they begin to separate, spreading like a drop of ink in water.

I give a couple of familiar faces the nod before putting my arm around Deontay's shoulder. "You good?" I ask him.

Barely acknowledging my question, he seems just how he sounded earlier, deflated and void of his usual exuberance.

"What's going on then?" I say as I lead him away from the chatter of his friends.

"Nothing," he says.

"Bruv, chat to man. You look like your best friend just died, wa gwarn?"

He remains silent, his face unmoved.

"If it's about earlier, don't even watch that. I got a cab waiting," I say.

Some life returns to his face.

"You got the dough, yeah?" I ask.

"Yeah, I got that still," he says.

"Cool, leave it in the yard and then come back. We gonna fly over to the barbers."

"What now?"

"Of course, now. Hurry up."

Deontay's eyes light up. "Ite, bro," he says as I hand him a rucksack full of more product and watch him hurry off.

"Yo," I shout, bringing a host of eyes back on me. "Leave anything you got on you up in the yard."

110

He disappears into a block of flats with one of his friends, and minutes later, the two of them re-emerge.

I watch as Deontay boasts to his friends, and they encourage his bravado. He catches up to me, looking rejuvenated. "What you saying, bro? We rolling there now, yeah?"

"Yeah, man."

Deontay tightens the drawstrings around his hoody as we approach the white Toyota Prius that waits patiently. Before he can open the door, I stop him in his tracks with a firm grip on his shoulder. "In the back."

As we pull out of the estate, Deontay's energy changes; he begins looking around, and I hear his breathing.

We enter a new world of neon lights, roaring engines, and unruly conversation that all blend together to create the buzzing heartbeat of the community.

It's gone ten o'clock, but the streets are still amok with hipsters, locals carrying shopping bags, and cars and scooters buzzing around like sets of worker bees around their hive.

Pools of intoxicated partygoers spill into the road, and as the traffic light turns green, the cab takes off, leaving them to their night. The driver rapidly accelerates, and the buildings on either side of the car become a colourful blur intercepted with flashes of glass and brilliance.

I turn around to Deontay. "You ain't got nothing on you, right?"

He shakes his head vigorously. "Nah, I left my flicky back at the spot."

Within five minutes, we arrive at our destination. Slickz, the barbershop, is on a much quieter section of the high road, but the atmosphere is still relatively buoyant. "Just turn down this road and spin the car around," I order the driver. I can tell he's eager to get on with his evening shift, so I ease his nerves and hand him another tenner. "Take that," I say.

He thanks me and obeys my command.

"Yo, Rakz, you got the drop on these man or suttin'?" Deontay asks.

"Just chill. We're waiting here."

Deontay settles into his seat, and we share a perfect view of the barbershop and alleyway next to it through the windscreen. The only occasional obstructions are the bodies that cross the road at the junction ahead.

The cab driver places his hands on his lap and appears to take a vow of silence, which suits me fine. Now isn't the time for twenty-one questions.

"You sure you'll recognise these youts if you see them?" I mutter to Deontay, barely turning my head.

"Yeah, a hundred, one of them had a red hoody on, he was fat, and he was the one that—"

"—Cool yourself," I warn him.

He's talking too much. His trepidation is filtering through into the musty air in this enclosed space. I lower the window to let the smell of foreign spices escape.

Beneath the sound of growling engines, boisterous screams go back and forth as Deontay's head sits poked above the centre console, like a mole emerging from a tunnel.

"What, bro, how long we staying here?" he asks.

"Jus' chill," I mumble.

I'm looking straight ahead, but I can feel Deontay fidgeting. He's tapping his fingers against the driver's seat, and I can sense his uneasiness.

I let it lie and keep my attention fixed on the barbershop.

"Boss, put the radio on," Deontay squeals.

"Leave it," I say, stopping the driver before he even moves.

"My bad," Deontay says before he starts tapping his foot this time.

About five more minutes pass as I study each individual that I see. I silently guess where a person is off to or where he or she has just come from. A little game me and Leanne used to play as kids.

Scores of people cross my sight as I think about all the different lives everyone around here must live.

As they move around, oblivious to my existence, it gives me a feeling of comfort. For I know that whatever they're doing with their lives, however great or however terrible things are, at this moment, right now, we're all the same. We're all just trying to get where we're going, moving through life at different speeds and on our own terms. The only guarantee for all of us is that we all die at the end of it. It's a somber yet reassuring feeling; no matter what each of us does or doesn't do with our time on this earth, it all ends with the same result.

I feel relaxed, until Deontay's voice, once again, penetrates my space. "I don't think these man are here, broski. Should we just turn back?" he asks.

I take a deep breath.

At my grand old age of thirty, I've come to understand that some people can tolerate the silence and wait while others can't. For those that can, they are able to tap into a higher level of consciousness. Their minds are able to occupy themselves by just entering deeper and deeper into their own thoughts. They don't require external things like technology or conversation to stimulate them. They can just simply *be*.

I'm aware that mastering this ability involves years and years of training and practice or, in some cases, even lifetimes. Still, it is paramount that a man tries, especially in the hectic world, we live in. Otherwise, he risks getting pulled from pillar to post every time his mind conjures a thought.

Now, I'm far from a Xiaolin Monk or a seasoned Yogi, but I know that my twelve years in prison weren't completely spent in vain. You see, it taught me how to play the long game. How to be patient. How to focus on nothing yet take in everything, gaining control over my thoughts and allowing me more influence over the events in my life.

From time to time, I backslide. I'm not perfect, but with somebody like Deontay, whose mind is undeniably scattered and will not allow him to go two minutes without moving around or opening his mouth, it's imperative that he's first stripped of who he *thinks* he is.

113

If he thought he was coming with me today to have a look for the two boys that made off with his hat, then he's got me all wrong.

I look over at the cab driver. "Yo bossman, here's another fifty. I got you for the hour, yeah?"

The cab driver peers over his spectacles as if I've just handed him a cheque for a million pounds. "Yes, my friend," he cries and stuffs the note deep into his trouser pocket.

I order Deontay out of the vehicle, and as I predicted, I see his body become tense. "Where we going?" he asks.

"Follow me," I say, closing the door.

He pulls the drawstrings on his hoody until his face is barely visible. "Did you see someone, bro?" Deontay asks.

I lead the way as we cross the road and a car zooms by behind us. Now he's next to me, I can almost hear Deontay's heart stomping away in his chest. He looks from left to right, all jumpy, like a fugitive on the run.

We could be ghosts for all the attention we receive from the pedestrians around, though.

I knock on the door of the barbershop, and Deontay looks at me in bewilderment. "What's going on?" he asks, bobbing up and down on his toes.

"Chill out, man."

After a couple of seconds, the door is pulled back. In front of us stands a short but stocky, well-groomed fifty-something-year-old named Clinton.

From well beneath me, Clinton's bald head glistens in the streetlight as he combs his salt-and-pepper beard with his fingers. "Weh you want, big man? We closed," Clinton says in a traditional thick Jamaican accent.

I step forward, making him straighten up. "Even for me, Likkle C?"

He opens the door further, and I watch his face do that thing where it screws itself up. I literally witness him scroll through the archives of

114

his brain as if trying to locate a time and place within all of the memories that would lead him to the buzzword I just dropped.

His shoulders drop. His arms fall against his sides, and his mouth opens as wide as a barn door.

"No way... Bloodclart," he says, the words dragging out at a snail's pace. Then, frozen to the spot in utter astonishment, he stares into my eyes.

"It's me, brudda," I say, and within seconds, Clinton springs to life.

"Rakz, Rakim?"

"Yeah, cuz. It's me."

"Bloodfire!" he screams from the top of his lungs. "Bloodclart Rakim, mi breddah!"

His voice thunders through the whole neighbourhood like a claxon, turning heads towards this little, burly ball of life. Before I know it, he's got his solid arms wrapped around my neck, almost headlocking the life out of me.

"Rakim," he yells.

"It's me, cuz, it's me," I say, wanting to get him off me but allowing him to feel the adulation of seeing someone he hasn't seen for over twelve years.

"Mi breddah, mi breddah!" he cries as he finally allows me to compose myself. He grabs a hold of my arms and shakes me with the pride of a father who's just seen his prodigal son return.

Looking me up and down, his grin is one of pure happiness. Not a single bad thought lives in his mind—just an abundance of sheer joy.

I catch the amazement on Deontay's face as Clinton ushers both of us inside his establishment. "Come, come," he says before locking the door behind us.

"Mi was just finished fi the day, breddah, but mi could'a never wish fi suttin' like this," Clinton says, staring at me, still shaking his head with incredulity.

"Man's back, bro."

He grabs a hold of my palm and pulls me close once again. We separate, and I introduce him to Deontay. "Yo, this is my likkle cousin," I tell Clinton.

"Yes, king," Clinton says as he spuds Deontay, who takes a seat on one of the plastic chairs that sit by the front window.

The shop is decorated with posters of handsome black men with suave haircuts. The waves in their cobalt-black hair all precisely positioned and smoother than silk. The faded posters belong to the nineties, the days when men all hoped a new haircut would have them looking like Mekhi Phifer, Omar Epps or Michael Jai White.

The facial shots of the women in some of the posters wear everything from short Nia Long hairstyles to long thin braids. The worn black and dull gold italics against the purple backdrop of the pictures advertise products you probably couldn't find anywhere anymore.

I recall sitting down in this very room, scanning some of these same posters as a child. The stools are new, though. They're a tough black leather, and there are four of them now, not three. I see all the bottles and cans, scissors and combs, and business cards prodded in the bottom corners of the mirrors to my left before I notice something that catches my eye, transporting me through time and space.

"Don't lie," I say. "You still got this?"

Pinned to the wall is a photo of Clinton alongside former world heavyweight champion boxer Lennox Lewis somewhere in Los Angeles.

"C'mon, mi breddah," Clinton cries, still a-lit with excitement.

A laugh from the depths of my belly erupts as Clinton begins to retell the story of how he nearly beat *the* Lennox Lewis in an arm wrestle in the summer of '99.

"Oi C, allow it, my man would've fucked you up," I cry.

"How you mean? Nuh listen to him, my Lord," Clinton shouts, swivelling his body to face Deontay, who still appears to be deeply bamboozled.

116

Clinton's energetic soul begins to delve into pastimes as he reaches into one of his drawers before returning with a bottle of Wray & Nephew in his grasp.

Rum was never really my thing, but Clinton's a true Jamaican, which means he doesn't take no for an answer, and by the time I've opened my mouth to accept his offer, he's already shoving a glass at my chest.

He then turns his sights to Deontay and hands him a shot glass of the 63% volume rum.

Raising his glass, he instigates a toast. "To the return of a true warrior of the Most High himself, Rakim!" he bellows, forcing me into a submissive smile.

Then in unison, the three of us take a shot.

The clear liquid feels like an arrow of fire has been let off straight through my chest. "Shit," I say, before turning to Deontay who's having his own coughing fit, curled forward, beating his chest like King Kong.

Clinton chuckles as he puts his glass on the side, seeming to digest it like its water. He signals me over, and I follow. "Mi cyah let you leave here like that," he says, pressing the pads of his thumbs around my forehead as he examines my hairline. "Nah man, come sit down," he orders.

"Ah bro, I didn't come for a haircut, ya know, I just—"

"—Nah man, sidung," he yells.

As I said, trying to refuse an offer from Clinton is pointless, and within minutes, there's a black apron over me bearing the gold logo of the shop, and I'm being suffocated by a cinnamon-sweet fragrance that takes me back years. A clicking sound introduces the deafening roar of a set of clippers that rattles my eardrum, and my haircut begins.

Any black barbershop always has the latest news, and as tufts of hair fall around me, Clinton wastes no time filling me in on twelve years of missed gossip. The next twenty minutes he spends telling me about how Kelly, a former love interest of mine, now has three children and he regularly cuts her two boys' hair, and how Squeeze, the man who first

117

taught me how to hold a gun, was murdered last year in a drive-by shooting in Miami.

It doesn't surprise me to hear that Squeeze died of a gunshot, and even though, in hindsight, I'd refer to Squeeze as a wicked man, a part of me still feels a certain sadness.

By the end of my trim, Deontay looks just about recovered from his shot of absolute poison.

Clinton hands me a small black mirror which I hold like a massive lollipop and examine my reflection. Seeing my reaction, Clinton grins. "Mi look after mi people dem," he says.

The man looking back at me is unrecognisable. His skin is more radiant, his beard is sharper than a blacksmith's axe, and all in all, I look about ten years younger.

"My guy," I say as I rise to my feet and brush myself down.

"What 'bout likkle man?" he says, pointing his head towards Deontay.

"Ah nah man," Deontay says, all flustered. "Man's good still."

"Your cousin always used to come here round mi shop at this time, ya nuh?" Clinton tells Deontay, while drenching the blade of his clipper with disinfectant.

"For real?" Deontay replies.

"Yeah, man. That's when mi always know say somebody or somewhere just get robbed, because him want haircut before the police come looking fi him in the morning."

Deontay chuckles. "Swear down?"

"Yeah, man. All ten, eleven o'clock mi ah trim him, FatMack, Preddie, the whole a' them. And mi trim them so good, police can't identify them when time them ah stand up inna' ID parade."

Deontay shakes his head and laughs. "So how come you don't trim him no more then?" he asks.

Clinton's smile gradually returns to a blank face as he turns to look at me.

118

I notice Deontay's eyes flitting between the both of us, aware his question has just changed the mood in the room.

"Go check the cabman. Make sure he's still there," I say.

"Ite, bro," Deontay says before turning to Clinton. "Safe for the drink, fam," he shouts as he exits the shop.

I sweep the hair on the floor as Clinton packs some boxes of supplies into the back room. After a short while, he returns and places his hand firmly on the black countertop below the mirror. He stands still and just watches me for a moment.

"Mi nuh know what kind of people them tink they are fi cast judgement pon another man," he says.

I shrug my shoulders. "That's life, bro."

"How long you spend there, what, ten, eleven years?"

"Twelve."

He kisses his teeth and shakes his head. "Mi couldn't believe it when mi heard the news breddah. And I know you ask for mi to come... mi sorry mi never come visit the I—"

"—Come on, bro. Don't watch that." My reflexes swiftly kick in, repelling any shred of pity that threatens to come my way.

"Nah man, mi should'a come see you—"

"—Fam, don't—"

"—Let me speak, man!" Clinton yells, slamming his fist against the countertop.

I take a deep breath and fold my arms.

"Mi should a' come see you, and I know mi never had to, but mi should a' come same way."

He looks straight into my eyes.

"Mi sorry fi that, man," he finishes, and I feel his candour words.

"It's cool, bro. On the level. It's cool."

Silence befalls the shop for a few moments when I decide to get something that's been niggling away at me off my chest.

"C, you seen or heard anything about Shanice and Kez?" I ask.

119

I know I shouldn't. I know the memory of them only holds pain and torment, and I know legally I'm not allowed to pursue this line of enquiry, but it's a chance to find something out about my daughter, and I can't let it go.

He pauses.

Then after a couple of seconds, he shakes his head. "You nuh see her no more?" he asks, his words much softer.

"Nah, man. Not for a while."

The noise of speeding cars combined with the hustle and bustle of the street pierces the melancholic atmosphere in the shop as Deontay re-enters sounding a ringing bell by the doorway. Slowing his step, Deontay quickly acclimatises.

As Clinton opens his mouth, the wisdom of his years senses the sadness and the guilt I still cling to regarding not being there for my daughter.

"Nuh be too harsh pon yourself king, you is a good person. Mi know that from the bottom ah mi heart. And the Most High never forsake you yet. One day through the powers of The Almighty, you ah go see di likkle princess again," he says.

I lift my head and bite down hard to tighten my jaw as Clinton walks over towards me. "And anything you need, jus' come check me, anytime, you see it?" he says, putting a hand on my shoulder.

"Course, my brother," I say as I inhale deeply.

He turns around to continue tidying as I signal for Deontay to step outside.

Deontay leaves, and just before I follow him, I call out to Clinton. "C, watch out for my man, yeah. He had a little problem with some Turks from round 'ere. You see any of them, dial me ASAP."

"No problem, anything fi the I," he says.

He reads out his phone number, and I input the digits into my phone.

"How much for the trim?" I ask.

With a look of something halfway between disgust and shock, he says, "It on the house, man!"

"Respect, my bro. I'll come by soon, we'll reason."

"Yeah, man. It good to see you, man. Look after unuh self. Blessings, king," he calls, and I leave the shop.

Once outside, the breeze bites at my freshly shaven head.

"You hungry?" I ask Deontay.

He nods, and we make our way over to a *Burritos*, a quaint little Mexican takeaway shop that's outlasted my sentence. I sit down on the stool that looks out towards the street while Deontay orders.

He returns to sit next to me, spinning on his circular stool as he fiddles with the receipt. "We still gonna go catch these man then?" he asks.

As his body swings to face me, I put a firm hand on his shoulder, causing his rotation to stop abruptly.

"Listen," I begin. "Don't ever let anybody make you feel like you have to prove something, you understand?"

Deontay looks at me, puzzled.

"You heard back there, init?" I say.

"Heard what?" he says.

"Who I am?"

"Nah, I didn't," he utters, and I can almost see the cogs functioning in his head as he puts the pieces of the puzzle together.

Bound to silence by his apprehension, I put him out of his misery. "I killed a man, D. And I didn't stab him or shoot him, I done it with my bare hands," I say as I raise both of my boulder fists and watch the chill in Deontay's eyes absorb my words. "The judge hit me with a twelve, and I done every single second of every single year."

Deontay swallows hard as he nods his head.

I'm close enough to feel his warm breath now. He's probably petrified, realising how much I dwarf him in size, but I must get my message across.

"You wanna know what happened before I went away?" I say.

"What?"

"I had a bagga man round me, just like them youts you chill with every day. And you know what?"

"What?"

"Everyone was screaming 'bredrins for life' and all that shit, and after eighteen months, I didn't get a single visit from any of 'em."

Deontay stares at me, like my words are filling him with the fear they should do.

I keep my eyes locked on him, as I go on. "And you heard 'bout my daughter?"

He nods.

"Not one of them so called 'ride-or-dies' sent her mum a single penny in all the years I spent banged up, until one day apparently, she couldn't take it no more, and put my little girl into care."

He stares at the brown wood flooring as the grill hisses away in the background. I squeeze his shoulder, and his head shoots right back up until our eyes are level again.

"Believe what I'm tellin' you, D. Respect don't come from living up to other people's opinions of you. Respect comes from knowing yourself and never breaking or bending your morals for nobody. Me? I had respect before I went away, and I have respect now, from the fools on the street to wise old men like my man back there. And that's 'cause there ain't a fake bone in my body. I ain't out here for clout, and I ain't out here for recognition."

I see Deontay's eyes slowly well up as my words hit home.

"There ain't no one who loves you like family, trust me. And if you wanna be out 'ere tryin' to prove you're a badman, then be prepared to lose them forever."

Deontay's lip quivers like he's fighting against the lies he's fed himself for as long as he can remember. As if he's struggling to battle his emotions, trying to bury them deep down like he's learned all men should do, but I put a strong palm around the back of his head, and holding him tightly, I tell him straight from the heart. "You ain't ever gotta prove nuttin' to me, bro, you understand. You got a problem; you come straight to me. I got you."

He runs the back of his hands across his eyes, blinking heavily.

"I hear you, fam," he snivels, and I see the scared little boy within come to the surface.

Our conversation is interrupted by the smell of garlic, peppers, onions, and tomato as a tray full of tacos is presented. "Enjoy," the waiter says.

We devour our food, and as we approach the cab, I hear the driver through the open window, deep in conversation on his phone.

I look at Deontay, who strolls sluggishly after filling his belly. "Pop the boot," I tell the driver.

Seconds later, the boot clicks, and I lift it. "Look inside," I say, turning towards Deontay.

Confused, he delves his hand inside the only bag in the boot. "What for me?" he shouts, his eyes like two giant footballs.

"C'mon."

His hand reappears, holding a limited edition DSquared tracksuit. "Nah, this is wavey," he says with a huge grin. The price tag alone shocks him as he covers his mouth. £705.

"Check the bottom," I say.

Startled, he pauses, like he can't believe there's more.

"Go on."

He rummages through the packaging and reveals the matching baseball cap. "Oi, G, this is cold, man."

"No more orange hats, bro. That shit's too bait."

Deontay laughs. "Nah, you got taste still," he says, waving his hand playfully. "Love, my bro."

"Don't watch that. I told you; I got you, fam."

He puts an arm around me and thanks me again.

"Come, let's go make this money," I say, and we get in the cab to return to the estate.

11

Nearly a week has passed since I last saw Nia. We've spoken on the phone a couple of times, and I get the sense it's been a busy week for her. She always seems to be either getting ready to teach a yoga class or just coming back from one. Several times I've wondered whether I should walk over there and knock on the door, even if only to check if she's okay. But I'm apprehensive about it. I'm not sure we're on those kind of terms yet. And I know about the consequences of overstepping boundaries, trust me.

Twelve years ago, when I stepped off that Serco van with a host of other unlucky souls who were also soon-to-be prisoners, the first thing I noticed were the towering ancient walls and the cold solidarity of my new lifeless home. After being searched, questioned, stripped of my clothes and any sense of dignity and individuality that remained, I was placed in a cell on the induction wing, where every new prisoner spends their first couple of nights.

There, I learned the consequences of walking into another man's cell unannounced. You see that six-by-eight-foot alcove is a man's only true sanctuary when locked away. It is his home. His refuge. And even though most people share a cell with somebody they've just met, you quickly determine whether the two of you are compatible. If you are, he stays, and you become friends. If you're not, one of you has to go one way or another.

On my second day, I saw this stout man with a hefty beard attempt to play a practical joke on this eastern European lad we called Polak. I don't know exactly what the bushy-beard man was planning, but I picked up on the vibe from the sniggering and pointing amongst him and his companions just beforehand.

The Viking look-alike crept across the landing and approached Polak's cell, and that's when he broke that all-important rule. He entered Polak's cell unannounced. The next thing I heard was an incensed scream and a blaring crash. Seconds later, an enormous thud commanded my attention as if a body had just been dropped off a balcony.

The sneering around the bearded man's so-called friends just carried on as they witnessed him get literally knocked out cold.

Polak was later put before the governor because of the altercation, in which he had caused the man a broken nose and a fractured eye socket. Polak's explanation, however, was simple. He had acted in self-defence for fear of being robbed or assaulted.

Now, you might think Polak overreacted, but you have to understand that every prisoner has been detained for a reason. The last time some of them entered a house without an invitation, they wore ski masks and held a crowbar while demanding the combination of a wealthy couple's safe.

How was Polak to know the man who entered his cell wasn't of that ilk?

Of course, I'm not saying that Nia is anything like Polak, and if I turn up at her door unannounced, she'll end up trying split my skull open. (Although I can't lie, it would be funny to see her try). However, I am saying that, when you approach somebody unexpectantly, you can surprise them and cause them to feel uneasy or awkward, especially if right on their doorstep.

When caught off guard or backed into a corner, people often react entirely differently from their usual selves. And the last thing I would ever wish to do is make Nia feel uncomfortable.

So, it's back to playing the long game.

Sat on a chair in my front garden, I sip my tea. The wind puffs by my naked calves as shafts of light pour all across the street. I listen to the coal tits, and the song thrushes, exchange their fervent trills, and think of how the world is my oyster this fine day.

The wind whistles across the rustling grass as I revel in the sense of freedom that has dared to sneak into my psyche this morning. I'm starting to feel like this is my home again as I watch people pass by, unbothered by my presence.

Slowly but surely, I'm blending back into my neighbourhood.

The door behind me opens, and I see Ping emerge. "I go now, bye," he says as he hurries down the garden path.

I raise a hand. "You're a good tenant, you know, fam. You ever need a reference, just let me know."

"Thank you, bye," he chuckles, probably more out of conformability than understanding my spirited praise before he disappears past the hedge to my right.

I shut my eyes and take in the sunshine from God's golden eye. My vision becomes a vivid orange canvas as the rays still fight to penetrate my closed eyelids.

"You enjoying yourself there?" a voice says, and I recognise the frisky tone immediately.

The front two feet of my chair hit the ground, and my soul comes alive. I open one eye with a squint. "You make a habit of creeping up on people like this, Nia?" I ask.

She smiles, standing there looking like a film star. "Nope. Just the ones that need keeping an eye on."

"You know, if you miss me, all you gotta do is pick up that phone. You ain't gotta stalk me."

"Oh, please."

I laugh. "I'm messing with you."

"I think you're the one that misses me, anyway."

"Yeeaah...?"

"Don't think I didn't see you, walking past my house the other day, trying to gaze through my window."

"Who me?" I say, but the prim falsetto of my voice gives me away.

126

"Yeah, you," she mimics with her own high-pitched sound.

"Looking through windows, nah, that wasn't me," I say, shaking my head and avoiding eye contact.

"Ummm. I bet."

"You must have got me mixed up with someone else," I say, trying to hold back my guilty smile.

"Rakim... I could never get you mixed up with someone else."

She pauses, sucking me in with those vermilion-brown portals to another world as she remains inconceivably beautiful in her stillness. I suspect she shared those words in the hope of me knowing that for her, I'm not just any other man.

"Ite, you got me," I confess. "Just wanted to make sure you were all right. You seemed a likkle stressed on the phone the other night."

"Aww, ain't you sweet."

"So, what you doing today, then?" I ask.

"Hmmm, I'm gonna go home and give my house a proper tidy. Then I might treat myself, get my nails done before I visit my little brother tomorrow, then it's back home to cook."

"Where's he live?" I ask.

"Far," she says.

'Visit... Far...? I wonder if he's doing bird in prison.'

"What about you? You got anything planned, or you just gonna stare at the sun all day, out here in your vest trying to attract all the ladies."

"Is it working?"

There's a slight blush around Nia's cheeks as she points behind me towards the house. "Have you finished all your work, then?"

"Yeah, mostly all done." The words kind of roll off my tongue without any real thought.

She clutches at the golden strap of her handbag that rests over her shoulder as one heel slightly raises off the ground. "Well, in that case, seeing that you might be off tomorrow, why don't you come over to my house this evening? That way, I don't have to dine alone."

"Tonight, yeah?"

"This evening, yeah. Unless you've got something planned. I can tell... You're a busy man and all that," she says, scanning my casual attire and the mug in my hand.

"I'll be there."

"Good. Well, I see you around eight o'clock, yeah?"

"Yeah, yeah, definitely."

"Okay. Enjoy your little sunbathe, and I'll see you tonight."

"Yeah, I'll see you later," I say as she walks off.

After a few steps, she swivels that supple body, turns back to face me, and we lock eyes. With a polished tip of one of her sparkling nails pointed at me, she says, "Oh and Rakim—"

But before she can finish, I'm in there straight away. "—Yeah Nia, I'ma bring my smile, don't worry."

Smiling with a sense of satisfaction, her face glows as she turns away and moves out of sight.

Back inside, I analyse several different outfits that lay sprawled across my bed. A cream jumper that looks like it was knitted by my gran has me shaking my head. I know Leanne meant well when she bought this stuff, but this jumper has Supercoon written all over it. How, whoever sold this item, had the audacity to charge three hundred pounds for this monstrosity is beyond me. I inspect the rest of my wardrobe, and my immediate thought is, '*I need to go shopping.*'

I eventually settle on a black fitted jumper and black jeans, which I sauce up with a black leather Hermes belt that's spent its last two years curled up inside a plastic storage box underneath my prison bunk.

In the shower, I begin to envisage the events of tonight. I see myself turning up at Nia's door, and straight away, we're all over each other, kissing passionately. She wraps her arms around me, and I pick her up and march her up the stairs as she devours my neck.

'*Cool yourself, that ain't happening,*' I think as I turn off the tap and step onto the bathmat.

Once dressed, I go downstairs to pour myself a Henny & Coke. I take a prolonged sip while the thought of being alone with Nia in her house replays on my mind.

'She thinks I'm leaving this place tomorrow. She doesn't know I live here. She just thinks I'm staying and now I've told her I've completed my work, she must think I'm going. Maybe that's why she invited me over, to say goodbye.'

A sort of heavy churning feeling starts inside me.

"I gotta tell her man," I say as I take another sip of my liquor.

'I know she's gonna think, 'why did you lie?', but I got my reasons. Even if she doesn't accept what I'm saying, at least man kept it real with her.'

I sigh as I think of the best possible way to tell her that this isn't just a place of work. This is my house.

I start thinking of all the possible inquiries my admission could lead to. *'Why didn't you tell me before?', 'Why haven't I ever seen you?' 'Where have you been all this time?' 'Why didn't you look after your mum when she was sick?' 'Why have you just come around now after she's died?'*

So many things bombard my brain as I try to prepare my answers without revealing where I've been for the past twelve years. I want to be truthful with Nia. She's been sincere with me, and it's only fitting that the sincerity she's shown is repaid. I go over her words, recalling how she values honesty.

'Maybe I should just tell her everything. About why I went away, about my time in prison.'

But my demons swiftly return to cast doubt in my head.

'Don't tell her, you'll fuck it up.'

The headlines of that night flash across my mind.

SAVAGE TEEN BEATS MAN TO DEATH IN FRONT OF HORRIFIED PARTYGOERS.

I pour another shot of Hennessy and fill the glass with Coke. While I start on my second drink, another thought hits me. It's a lot more enticing but a lot more daunting.

129

'Wait, if she thinks I'm leaving tomorrow and she's inviting me over, in the evening... After dark... Just us two, she might be expecting me to have sex with her. Fuck...'

I'm reminded of Scribz's comment about me lasting ten seconds on the morning of my release.

'What if she's expecting some two-hour session, and all I got is thirty seconds in me?'

The thought alone gets my heart racing. Maybe it's the alcohol, nerves, or a combination of both, but I find myself starting to panic as my forehead becomes damp with sweat.

It's a distinct possibility. I haven't been with a girl in over twelve years. And even then, it was Shanice, the mother of my child. We'd known each other for years and were so comfortable together that sex was more of an activity we enjoyed rather than the pinnacle of our courtship. There was never so much riding on it.

'This is mad. What happens if I'm done after two minutes. Every time I see her on this road, I'll have to do that walk of shame, knowing I couldn't even please her. What will she think of me then...?'

I swear I never even felt this anxious when I was on trial.

I look at the time. Five past six.

I take out my phone. Even though there could be a screw by Scribz's cell right now, and my phone call could jeopardise him, it's a risk I must take—this is urgent business.

On the third ring, he picks up.

"Yo," he says.

"Scribbler, my brudda, wa gwarn?"

"Who's that?" Scribbler says.

"Bruv, it's me."

"Who's me?"

"Stop being stupid, man."

"Who's me? This ain't Scribbler, bro." I listen carefully, as I hear the difference in the sound of the voice.

It's not Scribbler.

"It's Rakz, who's this?"

"Rakz?" the voice shouts. "Why didn't you say bro, it's Jamal."

"Wait, Jamal. Wa gwarn, my brother? What, where you? How come you got the tizz?"

"Scribz let me have it for the night. He's cool, but what about you, though?" he yells. "You been ghost. I haven't spoken to you since you touched road."

"I know, my brudda. I'm just out here ya know, tryin' to pattern one, two things."

"Come like you forgot 'bout man."

"Not even, man."

"It's good to hear your voice though, fam. Man's been tellin' Scribz to say bless up from me."

"Yeah, yeah, he told me, what you saying though, you good? Still hittin' gym and that?"

"Yeah, c'mon, always. I need to get that likkle Gym Orderly job, and then I be going every day."

"For real, that's the one. You still in the same cell up on the threes, next to Sammy?

"Yeah, yeah."

"He still moving mad with them wild noises in the middle of the night?"

"Yeah, man," Jamal says. "Man was thinkin' he was a flipping wolf last night. The prick wouldn't stop howling."

I laugh. "Fuckin 'ell."

"One sec, bro," Jamal says.

The conversation goes quiet, and I contemplate whether to seek Jamal's advice on my dilemma regarding Nia. Then just as I go to do so, he returns to the phone, filled with enthusiasm.

"Rakz, you know why I've really got the phone, fam?"

"Go on."

"Bro, my girl's coming to see me tomorrow, and she got news from my solicitor."

"What about your appeal and ting?"

"Yeah, bro. She said she wants to tell me in person, init."

I sigh.

"That's good, man."

There's a short silence.

"Wa gwarn?" Jamal asks, picking up on the change in my energy.

I want to warn Jamal not to get his hopes up too much. I've seen so many people go through years of trying to appeal their sentence, but the percentage of those who are actually granted a re-trial or given a reduced sentence is so marginal that it's not something I encourage. To build up all that hope just to have it destroyed again, that shit can break a man. "Yo, Rakz," Jamal says as I ponder whether to be the voice of reason. The words are on the tip of my tongue, but I'm wary of raining on his parade. Jamal seemed so downcast when I left; I just can't bring myself to do it.

You see, he's only twenty-four, and three years ago, he was recommended to serve a minimum of thirty-two years, so I guess even if he can get his sentence decreased by ten years, it's a reason to cling to hope.

I opt to talk about his girlfriend instead. "Yeah, well, it's gonna be good to see your girl," I say.

"Truss. It's been a while man," he replies, and for the next fifteen minutes or so, he informs me about the new evidence that's come to light that can prove that he deserves a re-trial.

I go along with his newfound fervour, just to refrain from throwing a dampener on him, but when he tells me the battery on his phone is about to die, I can't lie, I'm relieved. I don't like having to hold my tongue. It's just not me.

However, sometimes you've got to let a man come to his own conclusions.

"Listen, if there's anything you need bro, just shout me. I got you," I tell him.

"I'm good, family. I hit you up tomorrow and let you know wa gwarn with my girl."

"Yeah, bro, do that. Keep your head up," I say before signing off.

I look at the time and realise I've got over an hour to kill before Nia will be expecting me, so I roll a spliff and take a walk to the corner shop.

12

'*I should've told her from the start, man.*'

The thought weighs on my conscience more and more with every step closer I get to Nia's front door. It seems like such a simple thing to do, to tell her that Anthea was my mum and I'm her son that's just come out of prison.

But that's hindsight for you. Everything seems simpler, looking back on it.

'*You fucked up,*' I tell myself. '*You've gotta put it right.*'

As I reflect upon how I've gone about things, I feel a sense of shame hovering over me like a raincloud, and I vow that come what may, I will get everything off my chest tonight. No hiding anything about my past. About Mum, about being in prison, about having a daughter. Nia deserves to know the truth about who I am, and if she likes me the way I hope she does, then maybe, just maybe, she might understand.

The swaying of the leaves and the gentle murmur of the wind casts its medley behind me as I approach the doorway to a new world of possibility, one that was nothing more than a fleeting fantasy just a few months ago.

I knock on the door and wait. Looking from side to side, I tell myself that once I'm settled, I'll find the right time, sit Nia down and get everything off my chest.

It's not long until the door opens, and I'm met by a plethora of smells. A heavenly whiff of perfume swirls before my nose, followed by a lush exotic aroma.

"Hey, Rakim," Nia says, dazzling me with her polar white smile, as delicate and pure as settled snow. She looks exquisite in her silk-soft carrion-black dress that feels like velvet on my skin as I greet her with a hug.

"You good?" I ask, stepping into the hallway to allow Nia to close the door behind me.

"Yeah, look at you all on time. I knew you missed me," Nia says as the door eases shut.

I smile as Nia turns to face me. I can tell she's tried today. Her strong afro sits atop her head like the crown of Queen Nandi, looking majestic in all its regality. Her hair shimmers and shines brightly as the light in the hallway meets it with a mutual grace.

I note her lips, elegant and glimmering like they've been sprinkled with stardust. They're shaped like a strawberry-red oxbow and look ripe enough to feast upon.

'I could kiss you right now.' The words nearly come out of my mouth, but I control myself.

A pair of Solomon-gold hoops hang from her scrolled ears, rotating and refracting the illumination from above us, remaining resplendent as she looks at me.

"Come through. Let me show you around," Nia says as I take my trainers off and leave them by the doorway.

I thank God for the slender hallway as her voluptuous bum finesses by me, and I feel the paper-thin veil that separates her precious body from my pelvis.

"Excuse me," she says, putting a graceful hand on my chest as she slithers across.

I watch her bare calves move through the harsh light of the corridor and onto a luxurious sea of rich grey that feels like sand beneath my feet as I step onto it.

"So, this is my living room," she says, proudly bending her knees like she's introducing royalty.

"It's nice," I say, taking a quick look around.

It's well-kept, from what I can see. There's a thick raven-black rug in front of a built-in fireplace. Above that runs a marble mantlepiece that displays two photographs, a pot of fragrance sticks, and, in the centre, a black Buddha statue.

Across the walls are various African artefacts. A depiction of a tribal woman draped in a mixture of yolk gold and beaded jewellery takes centre stage above a black leather sofa. To the left, there's a dining table that's been prepared already, and a large mirror with a glossy silver frame hangs on the far wall.

I follow Nia out of the living room as she leads me into the kitchen.

"Suttin' smells good," I say as I'm hit with a carousel of smells. A concoction of time and effort emanates from the stew that bubbles away on the stove.

"Yeah, well, it's nearly ready. So, you can go and wait in the living room," Nia says, shooing me with her hand.

I watch her reach for a glass in the cosy magma-red glow of the kitchen, quickly getting a full shot of her waist. She's already got my mouth-watering, and with the alcohol streaming through my system now, my tension eases.

"So, does this tour include upstairs, then?"

"Behave, Rakim," she orders, pointing a wooden spoon my way. I lick my lips as her eyebrows curve so seductively.

"Oh, I got this for you, by the way," I say and reveal the box of Ferrero Rocher's that have been stuffed under my arm the entire time.

"Oh, thank you, I love these," she says.

Her dimples sprout up on her flawless bronzed complexion as she places the box of chocolates on the side. Then she plucks a bottle of Remy Martin out of her cupboard and turns back towards me.

"I remembered, you're more of a 'brown liquor' man, right?" she says.

It's exactly what I need right now. "You're like the perfect woman, sent to me to appease my every desire, init?"

I don't know where the hell the words come from, but they roll off my tongue pretty damn smooth, I gotta say. Shit, I'd probably even fall for me if I heard that line.

Nia looks at me, and those bronze cheeks display a reddish glow. "I don't know about that," she says, trying to remain humble.

The fridge makes a clicking sound, then, with a rumble and a clink, three cubes of ice drop into the whiskey glass Nia holds in her left hand. She pours in the cognac and hands it to me.

The urge to wrap my arms around Nia's sexy body and squeeze up next to her is overwhelming. She's juicy and thick, and her tight dress against that brandy-coloured skin doesn't leave much for my imagination. My blood races through my body as I pull at the collar of my jumper.

With a glass full of red wine, she turns to me. "To a good evening, good vibes, good food—"

"—And good company," I say.

She smiles, and we bring our glasses together with a clank.

As I sip my drink, my exhilaration is brought crashing back down when I notice Mum's old Dutch pot on the stove, and I'm instantly reminded of what I have to tell Nia tonight.

I leave her in the kitchen and sit down in the living room, stretching my feet across the rug. "Maybe I should wait until after I eat. Or maybe I should leave it right before I'm about to go," I mutter as the feeling of hollowness in my gut widens.

"Rakim," Nia calls.

"What's up?"

"Put some music on. The remote control should be just on the table there."

I switch on the TV, and an array of different apps pop up on the screen, imposing themselves like they're counting down the seconds until I select one. I stare at the monitor in front of me.

'What is all this?'

Everything might as well be written in Japanese.

I'm used to the standard Freeview channels but playing music from a TV seems just about as sci-fi as all these people paying for their groceries by tapping their phones against a card reader.

137

There's a long list from Now TV to Rakuten to Disney+, and as I look down at the remote control, I just begin to get even more confused.

'What the fuck do I press? Which one should I choose?'

My brain starts going off on its own anxious trail.

'I can't keep her waiting. She's gonna think I don't know how to use this ting.'

And although I could ask her, I'm aware that'll lead to more questions than answers.

"I know these two ain't for music," I say as I scroll past Netflix and Amazon Prime.

I come across a green and black thumbnail that I half-recognise. I remember Leanne saying something about Spotify a couple of years ago, and if my memory serves me correctly, she was talking about playing music at the time.

I select Spotify and press the 'OK' button. The screen transforms into a list of words, pictures, album covers, and a variety of options. Now, I'm even more confused and beginning to get frustrated.

'Why is this so difficult?'

I randomly start pressing a few buttons, and seconds later, the speakers burst into life.

The beat booms across the room and takes me back in time for a moment as I immediately feel myself immersed in the rhythm.

'I know this tune... This is Tupac, man – Hit 'em up.'

The bass bangs on, and it's only when I fail to hear Tupac's voice cussing Biggie in the intro, I start to second-guess myself. Moments later, I hear the melodies of an old smoothie, making noises that are halfway between a yawn and a roar.

"Who the fuck is this?" I ask myself.

'She gonna think I'm some weirdo, how do I change this?'

I'm about to violently start pressing buttons when Nia enters the room, carrying two plates of something that smells almost spellbinding, followed by a trail of vapour.

"Aaaye, what you know about these tunes, Rakim?" Nia screams.

I finish my drink in one swift gulp and look at the names on the screen.

Dennis Edwards ft. Seidah Garrett – Don't Look Any Further.

The answer to her question is, 'absolutely nothing,' but judging by her reaction, I've impressed her, so I sit back and appear as casual as possible.

She begins to sing along, and I have to say her voice matches her beauty—impeccable, and I can tell she's not even trying. She sees the look of amazement on my face and quickly stops.

"Nah don't stop. You got a banging voice."

"Thanks," Nia says.

"Where you learn to sing like that?"

She shrugs. "I didn't learn anywhere. I just like singing."

"You're proper good, still."

She chuckles before quickly changing the subject. "Come over here. Let's eat."

I rise from the sofa and sit at the dining table opposite Nia.

"I hope you're not fussy with food," she says, her knife and fork clanging in her grasp.

"Fussy, me? Nah."

I look down at the plump dark cuts of oxtail stacked in a small heap next to a portion of fluffy white rice. There's plantain, callaloo, carrots, and soft cabbage drizzled in some sort of dressing.

I stare at the hours of attention and warmth put into my dinner. The oxtail's peppery scent and earthy hue remind me of Sundays with Mum as a child. It's something I've missed for so long. My mouth waters, and to be honest, I don't even know where to start.

This is nothing like canned tuna cooked from a prison kettle.

I look across at Nia, who's already started eating, and I feel a hint of sadness, knowing that she'll never appreciate this moment as much as I will.

She looks up, her eyes a-dazzle with wonder. "Is it okay?" she asks, seeing I'm still holding my cutlery.

"Yeah, yeah, I was just—"

"—I know you're probably accustomed to way better, but I tried to just—"

"—Nah, this is banging. Don't be silly," I say, touching her hand. "Thanks."

"Good. Well, tuck in and enjoy. There's more if you're still hungry."

I obey her instructions, and I'm not disappointed. The spice from the scotch bonnet scorches my mouth, and the tender chunks of meat dissolve effortlessly as I chew and take in the sumptuous salty flavours.

This beats Burritos, and it beats Supercoon's coq au vin, hands down.

I finish first and notice Nia's watchful eyes on me. "You were hungry?"

"Yeah, for real, that was banging. Thank you."

She smiles and sips her wine. "I'm glad you enjoyed it."

I relax into my chair, allowing my belly to settle. "You hit the spot," I say, hoping she'll say, 'Well now follow me upstairs and return the favour.'

"Well, I aim to please," she says instead.

"When was the last time you cooked for someone?"

"Hmm," Nia says as she swallows a portion of food. "It must have been over a year ago, my brother, I think."

"He's a lucky guy."

"That's what happens when you got an older sister. They can't help but look after you."

I want to tell her I know exactly what she means, but I'm still angling for the right time to unload everything.

"You and your brother close then?" I ask.

"Not really anymore. He went to prison, and now we just don't get on. I'll visit him once in a while, but he wanted to live a life I can't condone, not in my house."

'She knows about this prison life then.'

It's a relief, but a tiny one. Whatever Nia's brother has done, I doubt it's anything like twelve years for taking a life.

"I hear you," I say, sensing the guilt behind her eyes as she pushes her food around with her fork. "It's not a bad thing, ya know, Ni. Boys need that discipline, especially if their dad ain't around."

She takes another sip of her wine.

"Hmm, perhaps. I still wonder why all these boys wanna choose a life of crime over just getting a job though. Why would you wanna spend your days in prison just wasting away?"

'Ouch.'

Her words hit home, kicking me in the gut.

I have to swiftly adapt and realise it's not a dig at me. She doesn't even know my past. I pour another glass of Remy and regain my composure. "It's not that simple, though," I say.

"How is it not?"

"Well, look. See how you used to work in that office?"

"Yeah."

"Well, after a while, you said it was just depressing and that. You couldn't stand it no longer."

"Yeah."

"Well, that's exactly how nuff young men feel about doing a nine to five, but we still gotta live in a world where you need money to survive. We still got bills to pay and families to support, you feel me?"

"No, I get you, but you can always find an avenue in life. Like, I didn't turn to crime, I took up yoga, and I'm not saying everyone should follow me, but there are so many ways you can use your talent to work for you."

"True, but same way, not everybody has people around them advising them correctly. Check this—most black youts round 'ere probably don't even know their dad, and if they do, most don't live with them. Now you see when a likkle boy's growing up, he seeks approval. He needs to be respected in his family, amongst his bredrins, and in his community. And that approval and guidance needs to come from a man. Not a woman, a man."

"Why?"

"'Cause you women; sisters, mothers, aunties, and that, nurture and mould a boy emotionally. But teaching him how to have the confidence to go out in the world and showcase his gift or his talent and not be swayed by the fast life that's consuming all of his friends around him. That strength can only come from a man setting an example."

"Hmm... Maybe, but why've you gotta sell drugs to be 'respected...' Or 'accepted?'"

"You don't, but the thing is, nobody says anything when Superdrug and Boots be selling thousands and thousands of different pills and tablets, but when a young boy starts hustling to get by, he gets arrested and thrown into prison."

"Yeah, but that's because he's selling drugs."

"And so are they."

"How?"

"It's called Superdrug... Super-Drug."

"I get you, but they're not the same things, though."

"What's the difference between Ibuprofen and weed?"

My words bring a smile to Nia's face. "Well, Ibuprofen gets rid of headaches."

"So does weed."

"Yeah, fair enough. But Ibuprofen doesn't make you get all paranoid and go mad."

"Nor does weed."

"No, there's a lot of people I've come across over the years who've just turned mad over smoking that stuff."

"Yeah, that's skunk, not weed. Two different tings."

"That's true. However, the majority of people smoke skunk, wouldn't you agree?"

"Yeah, well paranoia can be a side effect of skunk, but Ibuprofen's got its own side effects, just like every single drug these places sell. They put it on the box, clear as day for you to see. And just like those side effects don't impact every single person who takes the tablet, nor does skunk. Some people smoke it for forty years, and they're fine."

"Hmmm," Nia says as I watch her sit there and ponder.

"You know there's a drug called Baclofen that doctors prescribe people who suffer from multiple sclerosis. It's supposed to ease the stiffness of a patient's limbs, but all the while, it erodes muscle tissue and causes it to waste away. Now, if that ain't a mad side effect, I dunno what is."

"Yeah, that's crazy."

"That's the system, though. It will twist your mind until you don't question what you're being told anymore. You just accept it without even thinking for yourself. How's it legal to sell cigarettes that cause lung cancer and kill bare people every year, but I can't smoke my plant in peace?"

"True."

"You know how many people died from weed last year?"

"No, how many?"

"None," I say, my eyebrows raised and mouth wide open.

Laughing at my expression, Nia shakes her head. "I suppose you're right."

"The way the system's designed, it's either, 'be our slave for minimum wage and make us millionaires' or 'fend for yourself.' Sometimes, the only option you're left with is one that may risk your freedom, but a man's gotta do what a man's gotta do, even when the odds are bleak, you feel me?"

Nia nods her head as I take a swig of Remy.

"Do you smoke weed, then?" she asks.

"Yeah, not as much recently, but yeah."

"Does it help you...? Because my dad always told me that it helps with anxiety, stress, glaucoma, arthritis, and stuff, but to be honest, I just thought it was typical Caribbean-man-jargon trying to justify everything they do."

I smile.

"Your dad sounds like a smart man, but it doesn't *just* do that."

"What else does it do?"

"It opens your pineal gland and allows you to tap into higher frequencies. It increases your clairvoyance, allowing you to perceive time and space not as a linear experience but more like an archive of moments that are happening all at once."

"So, you kinda get drawn to whatever moment you're thinking about at the time?"

"Yeah, that's why sometimes people look like they're daydreaming an' ting."

"I get you... I still think it turns people crazy, though."

"A lot of that's got to do with their own mind."

"What do you mean?"

"Well, when you smoke weed, it amplifies your thoughts. It reveals things that've been stored away deep down in your subconscious mind for years and years. A lot of people lock their traumas there, and that's why people say they go mad, because when they're smoking weed, their subconscious mind is being revealed to them, and they're not ready or prepared to deal with what it is that it's showing them, you feel me?"

"I feel you. I never looked at it like that, but I understand," Nia says, raising a hand. "One time, long ago, I was smoking weed with my friend, and you know when you're young, you wanna impress people and those kind of things," she says, and I already feel the outset of a laugh in my throat.

"What?" she asks, noticing the grin I'm struggling to hold down.

"—Nah, my bad, go on," I insist.

She puts her glass down. "What?" she asks, a half-smile on her face.

"I'm just tryin' to imagine you in a lotus position with a big old spliff hanging out your mouth."

She covers her smile with one hand. "Listen, it was a long time ago, don't judge me."

"Nah, go on, you've got my attention."

"Where was I? That's it, smoking weed. So, this guy was smoking away, and I'm sat next to him on the sofa. He looks and me and says,

144

'You smoke a lot, yeah?' So, me trying to front, I say 'Yeah, all the time, let me hit that.'"

I burst into laughter. "Wait, wait, wait, *you* actually said, 'let me hit that?'"

"Yes, Rakim, I was young, and I was in uni, and I was trying to impress this guy."

"Who was this guy... Snoop Dogg? About let me hit that."

Her dimples shoot up as she starts to laugh. "You're messing up my story Rakim. Let me just tell you what happened?"

"My bad, my bad, go on."

"Right, so I was smoking with this guy, then after about half an hour or something, I just feel myself start floating outside of my body. I'm looking all around the room, and I'm freaked out. I want to get up, but my body won't move. Then this ringing starts in my ears, so I think I'm going deaf and start calling out to myself saying, 'Nia, Nia, Nia.' The guy I'm with sees I've got tears in my eyes, and I'm totally out of it, and runs off to get me a glass of water. Eventually, it wears off, and once I'm calm, he orders me a cab, and I go home and get straight into bed."

I'm shaking my head as my laugh turns into a cough. "Yeah, I don't know what you smoked, but weed ain't for everybody," I say.

"Well, I never saw him again after that, and I've never smoked weed since."

"I'm not surprised."

I notice Nia's cheeks brighten as she puts her hand across her face. "Oh my God, I can't believe I just told you that. That's so embarrassing."

I remove her hand from her face and keep it entombed in my palm.

"You can tell me anything, Ni."

She looks at me, and for a split second, everything fades away. But then, she gives me this strange look. Her eyes squint a little, and it feels like there's something she's not telling me like she wants to say something, but she's holding back.

The moment passes, and she finishes the rest of her wine and stands up. "I'll be back in a minute," she tells me as she heads towards the kitchen, and I'm left to figure out what the hell that strange look was about.

Moments later, she returns with a full glass of red wine that swirls around with every step she takes. She slopes back into her seat and smiles.

"So, when was the last time a woman cooked for you, then?" Nia asks as the song changes, and one that I recognise comes on.

Still concerned by that strange look just a moment ago, I'm hesitant with my response as Luther Vandross sings away in the background.

"And you can tell me anything as well, Rakim."

'What's she tryin' to say?'

The speed of my heartbeat increases as my eyes lose their affability. I feel a coldness about my glare coming on as I try to arrange my emotions and thoughts, what I should show and what I should hold back.

Nia looks at me, and I feel that rumbling in my stomach. I need to get this off my chest.

Her words have opened up the floor. Now it's my turn to be the vulnerable one.

I lean back in my seat and try to rehearse my lines in my head. "I can tell you anything, yeah?"

"Of course," Nia says, trying to appear more comfortable than she really is.

My stomach trembles insanely.

"All right... Cool."

I take a deep breath.

"... I ain't doing work across the road. I live there. And I ain't no family friend of Anthea... I'm her son."

I can hear my breathing, even with the music banging away. My jaw clenches shut, and my face tightens like a bowstring.

146

Then Nia strikes a soft smile and shakes her head. I look at her perplexed, wondering what she's doing.

"I know, Rakim," she says calmly.

'What?'

"I've known all along. From the moment I saw you in your front garden."

"For real?"

"Well, I suspected, but when we were in your house, and I saw that photo, it just made me even more certain. You and your mum have exactly the same eyes."

I'm startled.

'What else does she know? Does she know about me being in prison? Does she know what I done, who I killed? What did Mum tell her about me?'

I keep my poker face on. You don't go through all my years of trials and police interviews without learning how to remain calm under questioning.

"It all clicked for me when I realised you were the same man I saw in your sister's car that night, you remember...? That night when you swerved in the middle of the road."

I lift my head up, noting a tenor of apprehension in Nia's words. Maybe my silence is scaring her.

I allow a long pause before speaking.

"Why didn't you say anything?" I ask.

"Why didn't *you*?"

She's right. I can't argue with that. I swig the last of my Remy that's had me feeling blissful up until now. "If Mum never mentioned it, I have a daughter as well."

I look towards the table, then back up into Nia's eyes.

She puts her glass on the table and her mouth opens slightly as I do my best to keep my face stiff.

"Oh right. How old is she?" Nia asks.

"She's fourteen."

"What's her name?"

"Keziah."

"Oh, that's a pretty name... I take it you don't really—"

"—Nah, not for a while."

Nia nods her head with a cultured refinement. "That's a shame," she says. "Maybe one day things will change."

Nia comes across so calm and understanding but the look in her eye when she mentions Keziah fills me with sadness.

Deep within, she knows my failure to reveal my own seed can only mean we aren't close. A fact that's put a black mark against my name and given her rating of me a hefty blow. She doesn't say it, and I know she never would, but I can sense it, and it hurts my pride, badly.

Reaching out, I take hold of Nia's hand.

"Sorry. I don't know why I never told you from the jump. I should have," I say.

A courageous smile forms across Nia's face, and I reckon she's probably fighting against her inner worries.

'Maybe I'm not the man I came across as, maybe I'm full of shit like the rest.'

Then she responds. "Look, Rakim, it's up to you. I mean, you can tell me now why you didn't say anything initially if you want to, or another time. I'm always here to listen, but you don't have to if you don't feel to."

Her words feel like pity, something I avoid like a plague, but there's nowhere to run right now.

"I get it," she continues. "Family's complicated, yours is, mine is, and you've obviously got your reasons why you never told me. I waited to see if you would tell me about your mum, and you did. It may have taken you a while, but I understand it's a sensitive topic. I'm not trying to unload all my family dramas onto you when we've just met, and I don't expect you to do the same."

She stands up, and I watch as her body mystifies me with its movement.

The alcohol is definitely in my bloodstream by now. She looks like a black Baywatch model the way she glides over towards me.

I study her tender neck all the way up across her beautiful face. She looks ravishing, and every urge in my body agrees.

I spread my legs as she takes a seat on my thigh and wraps my arm around her like she's yearned for my touch. My hand strokes the side of her thigh, playing to her rhythm as she gets closer to me.

Her eyes gleaming with a deadly focus, she leans in. "I've been wanting to do this all night," she whispers and kisses me.

She kisses me, and through her syrup-sweet lips, I feel the power of thousand volcanoes erupt throughout my body. A fusillade of force explodes within me, travelling from the tips of my toes, through my ankles, my body, my fingers, my chest, and every crevice of my being at lightning speed before it shoots back downstairs and sparks the big fella into life.

I sit up like a Titan as Nia's tongue meets mine, sending shockwaves through my psyche that cause an earthquake to threaten my stability.

But I remain sturdy.

As she pulls away, I feel like I'm falling from a tightrope. She runs her hand across my shaven head. "You look much better like this," she says, her fingers settling on the back of my earlobe and her other hand on my cheek.

Halfway between buzzing euphoria and hazy intoxication, I strum my fingers along Nia's waist, exploring the mild curve of her back, and down to rest on her bum. "You look sexy. Every time I see you."

"Is that right?"

"Yeah, you should invite me round more often."

"Maybe, I will," she says, breathing life into my ear.

My neck tingles as sensations zoom through my body, and I move in to kiss her again. This time she plants a sultry finger on my lips.

"You know, you telling me the truth wasn't the only reason I invited you over tonight," she says, her words a magnetic hum, drawing me closer.

149

"Yeah? Why d'you invite me, then?"

She rises from my lap. Then moving with the assurance of a diva on a catwalk, she drifts to the centre of the room. Seductive with every step, she switches the light off along the way. If this is New York Fashion Week, she's the main attraction as she stands there looking immaculate. The only light in the room, the warm glow of the TV, she gives me her answer.

"To show you this," she says.

She raises her shoulder and slips off her dress. It slides down her torso and falls gracefully to the floor as I witness the sexiest woman I've ever seen standing before me, waiting for me to take charge.

I lick my lips and rise like a Spartan taking to the battlefield.

"Come here," I say and take hold of my Empress.

13

I'm not a kiss-and-tell kinda man. We caused the heavens to fall and stars to collide, yeah, but a gentleman keeps his woman as sacred as his word. Long story short—Nia is now my Queen, and I won't share her with anyone.

I wouldn't have always referred to myself as a gentleman if I'm being honest. The neighbourhood I'm from is more accustomed to spitting out violent thugs than producing noblemen of upstanding morality, but as I said, I do my best, no matter the odds.

It's almost feeling strange this morning, waking up in my own bed. Other than yesterday, the last couple of nights has been spent in the embrace of my woman.

'My woman, ya know.'

I seriously doubted myself when it came to charming any woman, let alone one like Nia. I thought she was way out of my league, but she's shown me that there's no such thing as 'leagues.' Just good people with clean hearts and clear consciences. And if two such people share a special connection, as we undeniably do, then the external factors that make up the circumstances of their lives need not matter.

I sit up and shift my bedcovers from my chest as the only thought that imperils my peace of mind returns—I never told Nia where I'd spent the last twelve years. I know I should have seized my opportunity when we spoke freely at the dining table but put yourself in my shoes for a moment.

Twelve years without feeling the touch of a woman, then I'm presented with Miss Universe herself, stripped down to her lingerie,

151

offering herself to me. I think I speak for most men when I say it slipped my mind.

It must be late morning, judging by the sunshine that snakes its way through my curtains as I put my clothes on. After demolishing my breakfast, I phone Deontay.

"Yes, yes, big bro," he answers.

"Every'ting good?"

"Yeah, broski. I need more food, though. There's hardly any dark left, and the white's finished."

"For real?"

"Yeah, bro."

At this rate, I'm going to have to tell Scribz to arrange another batch.

As I think of Scribz, I'm reminded of Jamal.

'I wonder what happened with his girl and his appeal. He said he was gonna call me two days ago.'

"Rakz?" Deontay cries, dragging me back to the present moment.

"Yeah."

"The food's nearly gone, I said."

"Ite, don't watch. I'ma come drop you the key for the spot. You can grab what's left yourself," I say.

"Calm. When you coming?"

I tell him I'll be there shortly, disconnect the call, and phone for a cab.

It's not long before I'm sailing down the high road watching men and women go about their busy lives. The cab turns into Tunwell Estate, pulls over at the side of the road, and I tell the driver to wait for me.

The short walk through the mountains of flats triggers memoirs of a past life. They pluck at my heartstrings as I recall both good and bad days spent around here.

I navigate further through this labyrinth of distasteful buildings that even fail to appease the eye when bequeathed with the sun's glory this morning. A couple more corners traversed, and I reach a dead-end road to see Deontay standing in the distance.

152

He seems to have taken my advice. No ten-man legion today, just him and this joker who looks like he's let the sun get to his head.

The kid Deontay is with has his bare chest out, flexing his muscles as Deontay laughs.

This guy looks more like an advert for Feed the Children than any sort of imposing figure.

"Oi Ribz, allow it, bro," Deontay cries, still oblivious to my presence.

'Ribz?'

His name pretty much sums him up.

I get closer to the pair of them, and when Deontay notices me, he immediately starts towards me.

"Yes, yes, bro," he calls.

"What's going on?"

"I'm good. Man's just waiting on you," he says.

There's an air of arrogance in Deontay's aura today, which I can't help but like.

I nod at the half-naked Ribz and throw an arm around Deontay.

"Listen, my bro. Hold this key, yeah. You know the spot."

"Yeah, yeah, calm."

"Take Dwayne Johnson over there with you, separate the wraps and get to work."

"Say less," Deontay says.

I shake him. Powerfully, like I'm playing with my own son. "Man like Deontay, ya know."

He looks at me, folding his arms all comically like he's posing for a picture, and I can't help but grin. "You're doing well, my bro, but it doesn't count for nothing if you let that work rate slip. You feel me? So, keep doing your ting, all right?" I tell him.

"Nah, a hundred. I feel you."

"Good."

"Oi, Rakz, you ain't heard nuttin' 'bout that Turkish brudda, alie?"

I shake my head. "Nah."

Deontay hands me a small black shoulder bag, and we touch fists. I tell him to ring me later before leaving him and his number two to get on with their task.

Once back in the cab, the driver whizzes back towards my house, and the fragile breeze from the open window brushes against my face. I settle my head against the headrest and gaze up into the celestial-blue skies as the orchestra of the high road withers, and I sink further into my thoughts.

'I used to pray for days like these. All those summers I was out on the yard, freedom just beyond those walls.'

A deep sense of gratitude warms me. It's no longer an aspirant illusion. I'm actually a free man.

I arrive home, find a relaxing spot on my sofa, and empty the bundles of cash from the bag Deontay gave me. After a few minutes of counting, I surpass eight thousand pounds when I'm interrupted by a violent vibration as my phone dances along the wooden coffee table next to me.

"Yo," I say, answering the call.

"Hey, darling," Nia says.

"What, man's been upgraded to darling now, yeah?" I reply, the phone pressed between my ear and shoulder.

"Looks like you have."

I smile, still trying to focus on my count, even though I know I'm fighting a losing battle. "You, okay?" I ask.

"Yeah, I'm fine. What you doing with yourself?"

"I just got home, chilling right now. What you up to?"

"Not much, I had a class this morning, and now I'm back home."

"Good?"

"Yeah, it was. It was a small turnout, so I got to focus on this one elderly lady. She's been coming for months. She's so cute, and I got her doing a handstand, imagine?"

"Swear down?"

"Yeah, she was so happy. I'm well proud of myself, I must say."

"If anyone can do it, it's you. I've seen how flexible you are."

"I know, you should come along to one of my classes. If you're not scared us girls will embarrass you, that is."

"Nah, I'ma hold out for a private class still."

"Private class, that's intense."

"That's cool. You still owe me a downward dog, remember?"

"Hmm... I don't know if you're ready for that yet, though, Rakim."

I laugh.

"Oi, don't play with me, Nia," I say, my words vibrating in my chest.

"Don't play with you? I thought you liked when I do that, though," she says so innocently.

Adjusting the heavy machinery under my boxers, I say, "I think you like it even more, though."

"I've forgotten what it feels like. It's been so long."

"Is that your way of saying you miss me and want me to come over?"

"Rakim, we both know it's you who misses me, but don't worry, my door is always open to you. You know this."

"Good answer."

There's a momentary pause—nothing awkward, just perfect silence.

"I'm doing ackee and saltfish and fried dumplings later, so if you get bored *chilling*, feel free bring to that big old chest of yours my way," Nia says.

"Just the chest, yeah?"

"What, did you think I actually liked you all this time? Come on, Rakim, you're smarter than that," Nia says, and I just envisage her teasing smile.

"You got jokes, but you know what happens when you put your hands on my chest, init?"

"I do."

By now, my count is sabotaged, and Nia wins yet again. Tossing a large handful of cash on the table, I admit defeat. "Listen, I'll be over in a bit, all right. Keep them fried dumplings warm for me."

"That's not the only thing I'm keeping warm for you."

"Yeah?"

"I've just come out of the shower, and this bed's way too big for just me, so... you know..."

I don't need no further invitations. I end the call, and it takes me all of two minutes and thirty-seven seconds to find myself in what has swiftly become one of my favourite places on planet earth, Nia's bedroom.

Sacrosanct energy embeds this place like it's her own personal tabernacle. Entirely different from the rest of the house, the walls are an understated lilac that looks like they never grew out of those teenage years. Not in a bad way. In fact, to the contrary. They're dated, but they've got character. Not that plain, modern grey lifeless-but-sleek-looking stuff, Supercoon and Leanne have all over the place.

I'm not from that world, and neither is Nia.

A medallion cornice runs the perimeter of the ceiling, and the floral rose carpet reminds me of a simpler time. A time when women openly embraced the natural feminine energy that flows through their bodies. A time when it wasn't frowned upon for a woman to be soft and gentle.

Underneath the radiance of four spotlights that constantly remain on the lowest setting, a shaggy white rug lies at the foot of a queen-sized bed. The frame is strong, probably oak. It's a perfect white, decorated with coral-pink sheets and pillows.

In the corner of the room, there's a small dressing table with a vanity mirror attached. Subtle fairy lights adorn the edge of the mirror, and I imagine Nia has spent many nights getting ready under its mellow flame.

Enveloped within the security of my arm, Nia's head rises and falls in cohesion with my chest as I look to the ceiling and recuperate.

She runs her finger across my belly in small circular motions, orbiting my naval. Our passion-induced breathing emits the symphony of the room as the world ticks by out there, and Nia puts her palm flat on my belly.

"You know this is your sacral chakra, right here?" she says.

I look down at her hand. "Yeah?"

"Yours is all warm."

She says it like she wishes to elaborate.

"What does that mean?" I ask.

"Well, you know about chakras, right?"

"Of course, not in-depth, but I know the basics."

"Okay, well, in yoga, we call this chakra svadhisthana, which, to make it easier, we split into two words. 'Sva' and 'adhisthana.'

"Yeah?"

"Sva means one's own or self, while adhisthana means dwelling or residence."

"Never knew that."

"You see this part of your body right here? It's where your true feelings and your carnal desires lie—one's self-dwelling."

"Okay, so what does it mean when it's hot?"

"Well, it can mean that your desire is being fulfilled, or maybe there's a strong urge to fill it."

My eyes focus on Nia's lips as my hand slides down her outer thigh and takes a grip on a handful of that special gift that God reserved for the black queens of the world.

"Behave," she purrs, and moving her hand from my belly, she interlocks my fingers with hers and takes control of my hand.

"You know that chakra specifically deals with sensual pleasures, like eating, drinking, and having sex."

"That's probably why it's hot, then. You've been fulfilling my desires for the past hour."

She kisses my chest.

Gently.

The way you kiss someone you care about.

"What's more important to you then, being stimulated physically, like sex and looks, or being stimulated mentally?"

"That's easy. Mentally," I say without hesitation.

"Really?" she says.

"Yeah. You're saying it like you sound surprised."

"I am a little bit."

"Why?"

"I don't know."

"Well, what would make you think I prefer the physical over the mental?"

Her eyes open wide, and she brushes my naked chest with her hand as she scans herself with a face that says, 'well, what do you think?'

"Oh, what, 'cause we're all up on each other all the time?"

"Well, kinda... Like for me, this is something completely new, trust me."

"How d'you mean?"

"First of all, I've only known you a couple of weeks, and you're already in my bed, then secondly, like, how you sometimes look at me. When you catch my eyes and stare deep into them."

I'm not sure if Nia's words are supposed to be encouraging or condemning. She tries to gauge my reaction, but my face doesn't move a muscle.

"Go on," I say.

"I'm just saying, the way you look at me sometimes, it's like you wanna get right inside of my soul."

"Maybe I do," I say, focusing on Nia's eyes.

"See, look, there again," she cries.

"Don't you like how I look at you or suttin'?"

"No, no, it's not that at all. It's actually the opposite... That's why it scares me."

"Scares you?"

"Yeah, it scares me, but not in a bad way."

"How then?"

"It's hard to explain. It's like, it makes me feel like you really, really want me, as if you don't just want me, but you *need* me. My body takes over, and I get this rush of energy when I look at you. It's weird. I swear I've never had this before in my life."

Nia's words not only massage my ego. They praise it and exalt it to the heavens. I can't lie. She's turning me on. I want her to continue singing this sweet melody, but I'm intrigued now.

"Why's that scary? That's a good thing, right?"

"It can be, but it can be dangerous too, to be that intense with someone you've just kinda met, don't you think?"

I remain silent, an encrypted book, as Nia squints her eyes suspiciously.

"I bet you're like this all the time," she says, and the tinge of some negative emotion behind her statement hits me.

I hesitate as I feel my heart sinking.

"Nah, not all," I say.

"All right."

Somehow, she's got the total wrong end of the stick and I realise maybe it's reciprocation that she's seeking. It's not my forte, but to put to Nia's mind at rest, I'll give it a go.

I lift her chin, bringing it closer to my face until we're inches apart. "You're way more than just beautiful to me, Nia. I look at you like that because I've never been attracted to a woman like I am to you."

She nods her head, her response somewhere between 'thank you, that's sweet,' and 'please nigga, I've heard it all before.'

It makes me wonder if she's questioning my genuineness. Or perhaps it's the cogency of my explanation, I haven't been close with a woman in a long time. And the last time I was... Well, let's not talk about that.

The faint humming from the dryer in the hallway fills the silence before Nia lifts my arm from her. She pulls herself onto me, using my shoulder as a climbing frame. Her breasts are now pushing up against my chest, and the entirety of our naked bodies are touching. She focuses those captivating chestnut-brown eyes on me. They perforate my being, exploring my inner thoughts, my fears, and desires.

I focus on her back, which looks like an immaculate, unblemished slope dipping before rising like a chocolate mountain, accentuating her bum.

159

Her eyes still trying to examine the secrets of my soul, she says, "Can I ask you something?"

"Gwarn."

"Okay, so... If this was to end right now, and I was to go away, would you miss me?"

Her question throws me off. It's the type of question a man asks a woman before his upcoming court date arrives. Not the kind I'd expect from a yoga teacher.

"Why, you about to go away or suttin'?" I ask.

"Just answer. And you don't have to be a man about it and be all 'I don't miss people ya know; it is what it is,' reh teh teh."

"I am a man, though. All I can be is a man."

"Whatever. Would you miss me or not?"

"It depends where you're going. How long you'll be away and that, I guess."

"No, it's a simple question. Yes, or no?" Nia asks, her face moving closer to mine like she's trying to govern this exchange.

"Why do you women love this tactic?"

"What tactic?" She smiles.

"Always leaving the deeper questions for just after sex."

I've been deprived for a while, but I know Nia's motive. She's trying to weaken me.

"Just tell me the truth, yes or no?"

I stare at Nia as she places her palms on my cheeks. "Maybe a little piece," I say.

Nia smiles and shakes her head. "You're such a man."

"What d'you mean?"

"Men and their emotions... Or lack of them." Nia sighs as she rolls her eyes.

"What about them?"

"It's like you're incapable of expressing anything deeper than a two-sentence compliment. Anything that threatens to reveal how you truly feel or makes you appear vulnerable you avoid like a bad disease."

I shake my head slowly, although I know Nia can sense it's a disapproval lacquered with uncertainty like I'm bound by that guy code no matter what I really think or feel. *Never bend, never break.*

"Look," I say, putting two firm hands on the curvature of Nia's lower back. "Men and women are just wired differently. Men are more logical; women are more emotional. Ain't nothin' wrong with that."

"Sometimes, though, a woman can get bored with waiting for the man to catch up to how she's feeling."

'Is it me, or is this moving faster than I expected?'

"You do know that, right?" Nia asks.

"Yeah, I hear you, but just because men don't show feelings like that doesn't mean they're not at the same level as their girl. They might be, but they might just show it differently." And even I can sense my defensive undertone.

"How would I, as a woman, know that if my man doesn't communicate it to me, though? Am I just supposed to read his mind?"

"That's why you get to know your man, init, the way he shows how he's feeling."

As the words come out of my mouth, I wonder if *I* really believe them. It's such an automatic response programmed into my mind from a teen. It has me second-guessing myself.

"So, it's on the woman to pick up the cues?" Nia asks.

I shrug and wait for her to continue. She manoeuvres herself to rest her folded arms just below my chin while the distorted sound of children playing outside whittles away.

"That's why us women ask questions. Sometimes we get things misconstrued, granted. But mostly, it's because men just don't know how to talk about things properly. Or they just refuse to because they don't want to be labelled as bitches," she says with a shudder. "I hate that word... But it's the truth. Even a basic question like what I just asked you, you've gotta be Mr. Super-machoman and not answer."

There's sarcasm in her words, but I sense a more profound concern hiding behind her playful tone.

The room falls back into silence. Children outside laugh and scream without a care in the world as I mourn a part of myself that's been lost for so long I can't recapture it.

Nia must notice the change in my demeanour because she weighs in.

"I'm not trying to stress you, I'm just saying, I'm invested Rakim, I'm too grown to front. I like you. And I don't need you to be where I'm at right now or require you to tell me every little thing you're feeling, but I just need to know if this is just something physical for you?"

Her eyes drop to my chest.

I squeeze her bum to bring her attention back to me. "Listen, this ain't just suttin' physical for me, I'm tellin' you."

My chest rumbles as I make sure the conviction in my words runs strong. Nia looks into my eyes and the essence of her gaze confess what I'd hoped for. She's falling for me. But still the fear of her feelings not being reciprocated flickers behind her pupils.

All the qualms I ever had. All my insecurities about not being good enough for this girl instantly evaporate. I wrap my arms around Nia to let her know she's safe. If ever she questioned my motives, my embrace settles her queries like a verdict.

"Don't think for a second that's this is just physical for me. Never. You feel me?"

"Good, because I don't just want your chest or your arms or your dick, Rakim. I want all of you, but if you don't want all of me, then that's cool. We can go our separate ways."

I don't listen to her doubt us for a second longer. Supporting her body, I turn over, lay her on her back, and take my place as her protector and provider.

I hear a slight gasp underneath me as she succumbs to the swiftness of my strength that takes her breath away momentarily.

Her chest expands, then drops as she, once again, gets lost in my eyes. She quivers like we're a pair of teenagers about to do it for the first time before she submits to me, the man she craves.

162

I look down at this woman I've wanted all my life and tell her. "All I want is you. All of you. And I'm here for the long run, Ni. I ain't going nowhere."

She wriggles into position for my indelible arrival. We're back in our own utopia of passion and pleasure within seconds. And right now, right here, nothing else matters.

14

I stretch my arm across the bed, trying to reach for Nia, but I don't feel her.

In prison, when something is out of the ordinary in your pad, it instantly puts you on high alert, and for a second, I'm back in HMP Wrydown. I spring up like a meerkat, sensing danger.

"Nia," I call out, but there's no response. I jump out of bed like I'm going into battle, enamour myself in tracksuit bottoms, and hurry towards the bedroom door.

As soon as I open it, I'm met with the smell of salty fish and frying oil.

Music gets louder as I descend the stairs and my eyes adjust to the lighting. I turn the corner of the hallway, and as I see Nia from the kitchen doorway, my shoulders relax.

Swamped in humidity, Nia's draped in my t-shirt and a pair of fluffy pink slippers, skating from station to station as saucepans bubble away. Heat engulfs the sauna slash kitchen as Earth, Wind & Fire sing about a Boogie Wonderland.

So in her element, Nia doesn't even notice me spectating as she uses a wooden spoon for her microphone and belts out a number that Maurice White himself would have been proud of. "... *Boogie Wonderland*," she cries.

She sings her heart out like she's on Broadway, and a complete stillness comes over me. I smile, knowing this fragment of time and space is one that only I'll ever see or know.

While I embrace a moment, I know I'll cherish forever, Nia turns around.

"Oh my God, Rakim, you frightened me. What are you doing just standing there?" she gasps.

Grinning like a man who literally has it all, I walk over to her slowly, take the mixing bowl out of her hands, and place it on the worktop.

"My bad," I say, taking her in my arms. I kiss her softly, lighter than the touch of a feather, and she comes back at me, meeting my slow, sensual pace. For a minute, we stand together, her body resting in my arms as we lose all sense of our surroundings.

"You woke me up," I say as I slowly pull away.

"Well, you put me to sleep, so I'd say we're even, right?"

Nia's words make me chuckle. "Fair enough."

She spins around and returns to the countertop to begin kneading dough for the dumplings as I lean against the fridge and look around the room. Amongst the canvases and pictures on the wall, my favourite displays the silhouette of a Masai warrior.

Spear in hand, he walks in the blood-orange sunset of the plains of Africa that stretch far out behind him. I stare at the picture, and after a while, it reminds me of an old friend of mine—Kazim.

Kazim was a couple of years older than me. The calmest person I've ever known. His motto was 'see no evil, hear no evil, do no evil, and you will never be miserable.' Judging by his constant grin, I'd say he was a man of his word. He used to tell me stories of his life in The Gambia, and on those frosty winter nights, picturing those scorched orange skies and rich sandy beaches, his tales would literally warm me up. A few months after his release, I received a postcard from Banjul, The Gambia. Kazim hadn't forgotten about me, and I hadn't forgotten about his stories.

"I wanna go to The Gambia, ya know," I say.

Nia turns to face me. "Gambia?" she says, surprised by my outburst.

"Yeah."

"That was random. Where did that come from?" Nia says, turning back to attend to the mixture in her bowl.

165

"I've always felt like I had a calling for another way of life in a next country."

"Have you been there before?"

"Nah, I ain't been anywhere apart from Jamaica and St. Lucia."

"Really?"

'Yeah, really, Nia. They don't arrange all-inclusive getaways for prisoners,' I feel to say, but instead, I nod and absorb her amazement.

She starts listing the countries she's visited. Spain, Egypt, Morocco, France, Barbados, Antigua, and Mexico. I begin to think of the years of my life I've wasted.

'Thirty years old, and I've only ever left the country twice. If I never went to jail, we could've travelled all these places together.'

It's a kick in the teeth that I don't need to torment myself with right now, so I swiftly revert to my Gambia ambitions.

"Africa's the one, though, trust."

"You said you've never been," Nia replies.

"Nah, I ain't."

"So how do you know?"

"It just is, trust me. It's where every black person originates from. Ain't no repatriation in the plantation islands of the Caribbean, you feel me?"

"Oh, are you talking about to live?" she smiles.

"Holiday or to live, either."

"I don't wanna live in England, but I don't know about Africa. I'm a Caribbean girl at heart," she says proudly.

"All us Caribbeans say that, but when you check it out, that place is just another slave yard, just like America."

"How?"

"That land don't originally belong to black people. Arawak Indians, they're the natives of them islands. Europeans went there and slaughtered off them Arawak mandem just like they did with the Native Americans. That's the only reason the plantation owners came to own

166

the land in the first place. Then obviously, they brought black people from Africa to work there."

"That's peak."

"You know what else is peak...? The house prices there. They're crazy, just like the western world. In The Gambia, you gettin' a big six-bedroom house for eighty-thousand and ting. Try taking that to Jamaica or St. Lucia, you'll be lucky to get a likkle board house."

"Yeah, true, my mum lives in Barbados, and she's always telling me how expensive house prices are there."

"You see The Gambia, the people there, they welcome black people with open arms, anyone who's been there will tell you. And not just that, they've kept their culture, and the country actually cares for its people, not like Jamaica. The people who run that island won't even let a hungry little yout' pick a mango off a tree because it's on Government Yard. Yet they'll let the Chinese and them man come and dig up the same land, build a whole heap of hotels and businesses while the people of the island live in squalor. Then we wonder why all those islands be getting licked with hurricane after hurricane. All the bloodshed and wickedness that's happened on that land come like God's way of telling us that place is cursed."

Nia listens intently, digesting everything. "Why you so sure about The Gambia specifically, then?" she asks.

I don't tell her about Kazim. Instead, I answer in a way I know will appeal to her. "They call it The Smiling Coast, Ni, so if there's anywhere you ever wanna bring your smile, Gambia's the place.

I tell her how the minds of Jamaican men have been polluted and indoctrinated to respect nothing other than money and violence and how the women are encouraged to be as promiscuous as possible from a young age, breeding before they should even be having sex.

She nods in agreement as the lid of a saucepan rattles and the contents inside bubble viciously.

"I never really thought about it like that. I've just always been raised to know Caribbean and nothing else. My mum would've beat me if I ever even mentioned fancying an African boy, let alone wanting to live there. But when you explain it like that, compared to Jamaica, Gambia kinda sounds like a paradise," Nia says.

"For real."

"Hmmm... I never looked at it like that."

"I'm telling you, Africa, Gambia—that's where it's at."

"So, when you taking me, then?" Nia asks.

"Taking you...? Who said you were invited?"

Nia's mouth hangs, making my shoulders bounce as I laugh at her reaction.

I look away, and within seconds I feel something slap against my head. It sounds like skin clapping together as something damp strikes my temple and falls to the ground leaving a sticky, uncomfortable trace.

Instantly, my face drops, and my jaw tenses.

My frown lowers, my nostrils flare, and Nia's laughing abruptly stops. She nervously clears her throat as she feels the death stare on her.

I'm instantly transported to E-Wing in HMP Dutton. I've just approached the pool table, and I ask the guy opposite me if he wants to choose which of my hands contains the white ball to settle who will break. He stares at me, or through me, to be precise, his face white like he's seen a ghost. Only then do I notice several other faces giving me the same glare. Reason being, I've just taken the place of a steroid-induced skinhead at the table. Before I can apologise, a stiff fist clatters into my jaw, and it feels like a bulldozer's hit me.

"Are you okay? I was just joking, sorry," Nia says, her powdery palms showing her submission.

I throw myself at this muscle maniac, and as whistles blast across the landing, I twitch and snap out of the melee in my head.

A soggy ball of dough sits on the floor, and as I realise it's just a dumpling, my face slowly relaxes.

"I'm sorry. Are you okay, Rakim?" Nia asks.

My heart thumps away as I see the anguish strewn across Nia's face, and I nearly die of embarrassment.

168

Still frozen in the same spot, Nia waits for a response to free her from her angst.

"I'm good," I say, although I'm clearly not.

Panicking, I reach inside my pocket for my phone. "I'll be back in a minute."

I leave Nia standing in the kitchen, probably wondering what the hell just happened, and head outside to phone Scribz.

'You idiot. Why did you just bug out like that? She's gonna think you're some psycho woman-beater now, man... Fuck's sake!'

I'm not even finished berating my actions when Scribz answers the phone. Flustered, I spill the beans all at once.

"Yo Scribz, I gotta chat to you, man. Listen, I'm with this girl. I've been seeing her for a while, and she certy, proper good girl, everything man needs. She might even be falling for man, but I think I just fucked it up. I was in the kitchen when—"

It suddenly hits me that Scribz hasn't even said a word. And that isn't like him, especially when I'm talking about a girl.

"Yo," I call out.

I'm met with the most dejected-sounding Scribz I've ever heard. "Yo," he mumbles.

Immediately, I know something's wrong. Scribz never lacks enthusiasm like this.

"Wa gwarn?" I ask as a thousand thoughts fire through my brain. "What's going on, Scribz? Is it your mum?"

"Nah, man," he sniffs.

I'm puzzled—first Nia, now Scribz. I try to count back from ten, but it doesn't help at all.

Frustrated, I raise my voice. "What is it then?"

"It's Jamal, fam..."

"What about him?"

"He's dead."

Scribz pauses, and I fail to comprehend what he's saying for a second. The world around me goes mute as my ears question what their hearing. "What, what d'you mean he's dead?"

As I ask the question, the words pierce my chest like an icepick stabbing my heart.

Scribz sounds choked up. He sniffs. Hard. "They found him this afternoon in his cell."

I freeze as seconds pass.

"What... what happened?"

"He fucking hanged himself." I hear Scribz's voice quiver like a nervous child, and I'm rocked to my core.

My stomach feels like it's just been hit with a sledgehammer, and my head is on its own merry-go-round, spinning, getting lighter and lighter with every orbit. Time completely stops, and I have to channel my inner strength to muster a sentence.

"But... I just spoke to him the other day. He was gassed. He couldn't stop talking about seeing his girl. She had some news about his appeal."

"I know."

"So, wa gwarn, what happened?"

"Apparently, the visit went left." Scribz pauses to blow his nose. "She's a fucking bitch, I swear," he curses.

I allow him a moment to compose himself and hear my heavy breathing.

"The visit went bad, bro. His girl told him the CCRC won't take his appeal."

'Why didn't I just say suttin'?'

"Then the bitch said she can't do it no more. Came all this way to tell him it's over," Scribz continues.

I plant my face in my palm as everything falls into darkness.

"He told me things went bad, and then yesterday, he didn't come out on the yard. I knew I should'a gone and checked him. I fucking knew. I should'a gone, man. I should'a fucking gone," Scribz cries.

Scribz goes to talk again, but he breaks down.

The phone disconnects, and I'm left standing in the front garden with my phone in my hand, staring into a world that doesn't even seem to matter no more. The trees, the cars, the one or two passers-by, and even the chaos of the high street in the distance all feel insignificant.

I look to the heavens, and an overwhelming rage within me threatens to erupt. I just want to smash someone or something into a million pieces.

'What the fuck? Jamal, my brudda, why? Why didn't you just call me?'

From nowhere, I feel a hand on my shoulder.

"Rakim, are you okay?" Nia asks.

I don't say anything.

I hardly move.

My eyes stay focused on the wonder of the unknown above me. Somewhere up there is Jamal.

Nia takes a few steps until she's directly in front of me. I must have annoyed her because she's frowning. Her mouth is moving, but I can barely hear the words coming out. My mind's in a different realm.

It's telling me this isn't true.

That this is just a dream.

'It's just a dream. It feels real, but don't worry, it's just a dream. It don't matter I didn't call Jamal back 'cause he ain't even dead. This ain't real. I'll wake up in a minute... It's just a dream, Rakz. It's just a dream.'

15

I'm still in a sort of daze sitting at Nia's dining table.

She hurries into the living room with a glass of water in one hand and a half-empty bottle of Remy Martin in the other. "I'm so sorry, Rakim." she says.

"It's cool," I mumble.

"I don't know what to say. Are you okay?" Nia asks again, pacing around.

This time I nod.

"Why did he do it...? If... if you don't mind me asking."

I reach for the bottle of Remy, pluck the cork from it, and put the rim straight to my lips.

"Sorry," she says. "I'm just shocked. I can't believe somebody would do that."

I think of Jamal hanging in his cell. That green bedsheet wrapped around his neck as his lifeless body dangles like a flimsy cord of cotton.

I pity Nia. She probably thinks Jamal was just a civilian who couldn't take the pressures of life or perhaps a poor chap with some mental illness that got the better of him. She doesn't know he was a kind-hearted young man who had just been denied the chance of freedom for the next twenty-nine years.

She doesn't know that the one person Jamal thought would be his rock during his years confined to the cold, dark loneliness of a prison cesspit had suddenly cut all ties with him just like that. Thank you for our time together. Good luck and all the best.

It hit Jamal like it does everybody when they hear that news.

Life gone. The part of it that matters away.

No chance of redemption.

Nobody to share late-night phone calls with on those arduous nights when your mind torments you, denying you any comfort. Nobody to miss or tell you they love and miss you too.

Some learn to adjust to a life sentence. But not everybody.

People forget that prisoners are human beings too, even the ones who commit the most heinous crimes. We were the same type of men, just like your brothers, sons, fathers, and uncles once upon a time. We played happily with our children in the past, we shed tears, shared jokes, and cracked up in front of a TV screen with our loved ones around Christmas while stuffing our bellies.

And just because we were thrown into prison doesn't mean we somehow change overnight.

Sometimes people overlook the fact that we, too, have feelings.

But I guess you're just supposed to accept you don't deserve feelings anymore once you're convicted of a crime, right?

"Nia?" I say, my emptiness secreting through my tone.

"What's the matter, Rakim?"

My eyes unfocus, and I must look like I'm either deep in meditation or I'm going crazy. Like a plug's been taken out of my body, the burning rage that threatened to consume me just minutes ago has drained from me.

"Are you okay? What is it, Rakim? Talk to me."

"I don't *feel* anything."

"What do you mean?"

"I mean right now... I dunno why, but I don't feel nuttin'."

Our eyes meet, and Nia catches the coldness in my stare.

"Rakim, maybe you're just in shock. It takes time to process these things."

I feel sorry for Nia, she means well, but she's out of her depth with this one. She doesn't know what to say or do, so she's just saying things she thinks she should. Regurgitating things she's probably heard on TV, things she thinks I need to hear.

I reach for the bottle of *Remy* and let the liquor flow down my throat. As soon as I'm finished, Nia copies. She pokes her tongue out and pulls an uncomfortable grimace before continuing to try and comfort me.

I zone out, though, as I start questioning myself.

'Why don't I feel sad? Jamal just died, and I'm just sitting here chillin'?'

My anger, my sadness, they've both ceased.

I'm not happy, I'm not content, I'm not angry or upset, I'm just numb. I don't feel anything.

Nia finally realises I'm not in the room with her and stops talking. She sits on the chair next to me, puts a hand on my leg, and I look up at her.

She goes to speak, but I get there first. "Yo, I'm gonna go home tonight."

Her eyes stay fixed on me, holding an equal measure of sympathy and fear.

"I don't think you should be alone right now, Rakim," she says.

I stand up, grab the black bottle on the table, and head for the exit.

"Wait," Nia says, rising to her feet.

She reaches for my hand, and I turn to face her. She wraps her arms around me and squeezes me until I feel the tips of her fingers dig into my sides.

Tilting her head back to look up to me, she asks, "Rakim, are you sure you're okay?"

I kiss her on the forehead as the aroma of oud and sandalwood hits me.

Nia wants me to stay. She wants to be the cure for my pain, the remedy for my ailment, but she's realised I'm not the usual kind of guy she's used to.

After twelve years in prison, I barely know my emotions or if I'm even capable of revealing them. They're imposters in my body, strangers to me. We meet occasionally, size each other up, seeing who will get the better of the other, but we always retire into our comfortable space. That place where we hide from the world.

Nia's eyes cling to me, and I reckon she's figured that getting to the depths of my soul will be the most challenging task she ever took on.

"Sorry about the food," I say.

"Rakim, I don't care about some wasted ackee and saltfish. I care about you."

I release myself from her arms and head towards the front door. "Rakim, please don't go," calls Nia.

"I have to. I'll call you in the morning."

Her arms hang helplessly by her side as she lets out a sigh. "Make sure."

I don't remember anything about the short walk back home, but I find myself fully clothed, sitting on my bed as the wind whispers to me through the open window. I take another swig of this sweet poison. It's smooth and warm in my chest.

I go through the next hour or so, depleting what remains of the bottle next to me as I wonder if Jamal's death is partly down to my dereliction.

I feel the Remy in my blood doing its job, slowly dragging me away from the despair of this night. I lay down and fold my arms behind my head, staring up at the ceiling, wishing I was in another universe, but my guilt anchors me to this world.

'I knew his appeal wouldn't go through. Why didn't I just tell him not to get his hopes up? I should've just hollered him. I could've talked to him, at least. I knew there was suttin' up when he didn't phone me yesterday.'

Memories of Jamal flash before me. How he would always be the first to have the new boxsets and hating lending them out. How he complained about them being returned with fingerprints on the disc because it made the DVD skip, and he couldn't stand it. I recall him kicking off at Scribz over the condition of his Peaky Blinders DVD and the two of them nearly coming to blows about it which made me chuckle. But my joy lasts no more than a few seconds before I fall back in into a hebetude of guilt.

I hear Mum's sweet little Jamaican accent as one of her lines plays in my head. 'The only ting we're promised in life is death,' she used to say. Even though Mum lived here for so long, her accent never abandoned her. Neither did her wisdom.

I look over at a photograph of Mum, and she stares back at me. I'm a toddler, and she's holding me as I smile like I've just had the best day of my life.

'She'd know exactly what to say right now. She'd come with some magical bowl of soup or a wicked hot drink, hold my hand, and chant a Psalms.'

And when Mum sang those verses, heavens moved, and mountains shook. She carried more power in her soul than any preacher or pastor I've ever seen.

'Damn, I miss Mum.'

That drunk, light-headed feeling gradually merges into a heavy burden.

'Why does everyone close to me always get taken away? First dad, then Shanice, Keziah, Mum, now Jamal.'

My thoughts run on until my phone rings.

Reaching inside my pocket, I pull it out and answer the call. "Yo," I say.

"Oi Rakz, where are you?"

It's Deontay. And he sounds frightened.

Fuzzy stars waltz around me as I sit upright and shake my head. "I'm at my yard, what's going on?"

"Man's in some garden. I just got chased, bruv."

"What... what d'you mean?"

"Fam, some next youts pulled up on a bike when I was hitting a shot. I just dust out, hopped some fence."

"Wait, slow down. What happened?"

"I just told you, I got chased."

"Where are you?"

"I don't know," Deontay cries.

Adrenaline shoots through me as Deontay rattles on.

"Oi Rakz, man. What do I do? I think the guy in the yard heard me... Ah shit!"

I shake my head vigorously and force myself back into a focused trance.

"Calm down. Chill out. Where are you?"

"I don't know. I just jumped one fence. Now I'm in some bush in some next man's garden."

"Where was the shot?"

"I dunno, man."

"Think!"

"I dunno, Rakz, these man just pulled up—"

"—Forget them. Who did you meet?"

"Erm... What's his name...? Bertie."

"Where d'you buck him?"

"Erm, just past the church, you know that one just after the barbers."

"What way you turn right, left, what?"

"Right, right!"

I strain my memory, trying to picture the name of the road. Moments ago, alcohol was my trusty companion. Now it's become my enemy—the blockade between my 'trying-to-remember face' and the words on the tip of my tongue.

"Rakz, what do I do? If I go out, them man—"

"—Chill, man. Wait."

I silence Deontay as I try to picture the road sign.

My brain doesn't play ball, though.

Then just as I go to curse furiously, I remember what Nia showed me the other day.

"Rakz?"

"One second, fam." I swipe along to the maps app on my phone, tap the icon and scroll across until I locate the church. Moving my fingers apart, I zoom in. "Boom, there it is, Malvern Drive."

"What?"

"You're on Malvern Drive."

"Yeah, what do I do?"

"Don't worry. Man's coming now. Just stay there."

"What...but..."

"Stay there!" I shout.

Deontay realises this isn't up for discussion. "I beg you be quick, bro. Please."

"I'm coming right now, fam."

16

Curious glances and strange looks follow me as I power through the streets in an undersized hoodie and a pair of shorts. Blinking repeatedly, I battle against the wind, determined to maintain control over my trajectory.

Neon lights from the signs of shops shower me with a brightness that seems even harsher this particular night. Heads and bodies from windows beside me flash by like pages in a flipbook as I catch snippets of conversations about football and clothes.

I push on towards Deontay, my chest now beginning to burn a little. I feel it tightening the further I go on, but my lungs fight on until I finally reach the church Deontay was referring to.

The spire on top of the roof tapers high. Reaching towards the heavens, it pierces the shroud of grey that separates the night sky from the diminishing nightlife below.

I check my phone to see three missed calls from Deontay.

"Shit."

'I must've not heard it ringing.'

I look at the maps app on my phone.

"This is the road."

A glance at the sign opposite me validates my assumption.

I cross the road evading a cab driver whose abuse whizzes away with him as quickly as it came. The road sign displaying Malvern Drive is to my left, along a low brick wall that acts as a barrier between the church car park and the pavement.

That state of intoxication when a man becomes a philosopher kicks in, and I stop for a moment, wondering what side of the wall I belong on.

The church represents righteousness, faith, and loving thy neighbour. I'm a convicted murderer, so I've already broken God's holiest commandment. I've sought forgiveness from within, but surely that doesn't mean much now I'm standing back on the same streets, searching for a young boy I've enticed into a similar life that led me to my demise.

I've always labelled Squeeze, the man who lured me into a life of crime and violence, a wicked man, but am I really any different?

I know the dangers that come with this line of work. Men will kill you for selling on their turf, and addicts will rob you for even less, given a chance. And that's if the police don't catch you and send you to prison first. I want to convince myself why I should be on the other side of the wall with the holier-than-thou, God-fearing Christians who can boast about their lives every Sunday while they parley with their pastor. But I know deep down I don't belong there, and if I'm being honest, I don't think I ever have.

I snap out of my daze and call Deontay. The phone goes straight to voicemail.

"C'mon, man, what you on? Answer the phone."

I call again. Same outcome.

Either he's on the phone, or his battery has died.

"Shit, how am I gonna get him now?" I say, assuming the latter.

I walk further down the road. Slowly.

"He said he bust a right, so that means he's definitely on this road."

I examine every house I pass. "He said that he thought someone was coming. That means somebody's in the house, so it's got to be one with lights on," I mutter as I stalk each window.

To my surprise, most of the houses I pass are beset with complete darkness from within. Not a single bulb emits any luminance whatsoever.

"He said he hopped a fence, so it's gotta be one that's got a fence. At the side, maybe."

So far, I've only seen one house with a side gate, but all the lights were off.

I'm roughly two-hundred yards into Malvern Drive, and the discord of the high road has become a distant memory.

Beneath the pearly moon that hangs in the sky, playing hide and seek with the flint-grey clouds that amble along, I hear the nocturnal cries of foxes and cats as they break the eerie tranquility around me.

"Where could he be?" I ask myself.

I look around, thinking I may have missed a house with a gate along the way when I'm alerted to the rattle of an engine. Before I even turn, I know it's a moped. That annoying buzz, like the intoning of a swarm of bees, snaps through the mild air.

I turn around, and on the adjoining street, I see two figures seated on a moped, getting closer. I crouch down and peer through a car window in front of me.

A Honda Scorpion Serket comes into view as it slows to pull over at the side of the road. From my position, I'm not sure if they've noticed me or not, but it only takes a couple of seconds for me to know that these are the two boys Deontay was talking about.

The young man sitting pillion removes his ski mask and reveals a beige-coloured face with a jungle of facial hair. I watch as he speaks in some foreign language with his friend. He throws his arms in the air as he gets off the saddle like he's complaining and approaches a brown wooden fence.

'These man are looking for Deontay, fam.'

I quickly switch on.

From the cover of a parked car, I watch as the yout' still seated appears to order his companion to peer over the fence.

The guy wearing the ski mask on the top of his head like a woolly crown seems reluctant to follow orders. He looks from side to side before executing a poor attempt to get over into the garden. Clinging onto the fence panels, he demonstrates his lack of upper body strength as he struggles to lift his chin over the summit of the rough wood.

181

I keep a close eye on him as his legs dangle a couple of feet above the pavement while I try Deontay again.

Voicemail.

I kiss my teeth.

'Deontay might be over that fence... I gotta do suttin'.'

Seeing the pair are at their most vulnerable as one hangs onto the fence and the other with his feet attached to the pavement and hands glued to the handlebars, I make my move.

Bursting into life, I rush towards the two of them like a charging buffalo. I hear one of the boys' cry as two heads swivel towards me.

"Hadi gidelim," the leader shouts.

The guy with the ski mask jumps off the fence and hits the ground with a thud.

"He there, man," the bearded guy on the bike yells.

The alcohol tells me I'm moving like an NFL quarterback, but in reality, I'm dragging along a two-hundred-and-forty-pound deadweight with tired legs.

The moped's headlights flash, illuminating the road with a whitish-yellow dazzle as the bike's resurrection lets off a juvenile roar. I stop abruptly and nearly topple over as I decide whether to go after the guy on the bike or his friend. The driver takes no chances. He whips the handlebars to the right and spins around to face the opposite direction.

"Pussyhole," I hear myself shout.

There's hollering coming from somewhere, but I can't identify who or where. I reach the other side of the road, and by now, the guy with the ski mask has clambered back to his feet.

He looks up to see his friend racing down the road, circling his arm as a signal for him to follow. Ski Mask shouts something in his language at the friend who has seemingly abandoned him.

'You ain't gettin' away too, no way.'

Only empty pavement stands between me and this chunky youth. He looks from left to right, panting as one hand forms a fist and the other has no idea what it's doing. His friend beeps the horn, but it's irrelevant. Fear has already sunk its claws deep into Ski Mask's flesh. It's oozing through his bloodstream.

This ain't flight.

This ain't fight.

This is fright.

He's mine now—he knows it. I know it. The chill in his eyes knows it.

He turns his head to search for his friend as the moped still squeaks its getaway cry from way up ahead. He's too late, though. "Come here," I bellow.

His belly flaps a he rotates his body in a last-ditch bid to get away. Too slow and sluggish, I pounce on him. Throwing my two palms on the back of his shoulders, I rip him from the pavement like I'm uprooting a weed.

"Where you think you're going?" I cry, hurling him to the ground. He skids across the concrete and collides with the tyre of a parked car.

"Allow me, brother, allow me," he pleads.

"Brother? Shut up," I say, my face tightening as the thought of stomping down on the boy's skull passes through my head. I listen to him beg for mercy behind his cowering hands. As he peers through his fingers, they shake like a feather caught in an updraft. "Put your hands down, man," I command, and he gradually lowers them.

I tear the black ski mask off of his face to reveal the image of a young man. He's not my age, but he's not a teenager either. His beard and his moustache are a dead giveaway.

There's some chatter from across the road, but I don't even care right now.

I use one arm and yank him to his feet. "What you doing round here?" I ask him.

He crouches his head as his shoulders come up. "I sorry, I sorry, man," he says.

Gripping his collar, I drag him closer. "I don't care about your fuckin' 'sorry'—and put your bloodclart hands down," I thunder.

183

"Sorry. I just get order to come with my friend, brother. Please, allow me," he cries in his foreign accent.

I hate cowards. I want to punch his head off, but I need to know who sent him after Deontay and why.

"Order to do what? Who you here for? Who are you?" I say.

"Sorry, brother."

"Fuck your 'sorry,' you were a badman two minutes ago."

"Please, brother."

"What you doing trying get over next man's fence? You ain't no fucking gardener."

The rage is taking over my body. My arms are shaking, and I'm about to lose it any second. "Tell me now, or I'ma go on wicked wid you, you little prick. Why you here?" I scream.

The young man cowers further, then just as I go to unleash a decapitating blow, I hear a voice.

"Rakz!"

I turn to my left and see Deontay. He's covered in twigs and undergrowth as he emerges from the corner of the street. Around him, lights are now shining from houses that I'm sure were dark as cellars minutes ago.

I spot a man at an upstairs window with the netting pulled to one side. He's looking directly at me. But it's too late to worry about that.

"What you doing, where you come from?" I ask Deontay.

Deontay brushes himself down. "Rakz, man, I was in that garden over—"

He sees the boy on the other end of my arm, and his adulation quickly turns to anger.

"You fuckin' prick," he shouts.

Without hesitation, Deontay flies across the pavement and swings a thunderous blow that smashes into the foreigner's face.

The Turk lets out a painful cry as his head snaps back, and he reaches to protect his nose.

If the neighbourhood wasn't aware of what was happening before, they are now. "Allow me, please, brother," the young man cries from behind his hands.

"You pussyhole. Come, what you saying now?" Deontay shouts, ready to assault him further as leaves and hedge trimmings fall to the ground around him.

"Relax," I warn Deontay, throwing an arm in front of him.

"Nah, Rakz, he tried to come for man."

"Sorry, brother. I don't mean no harm. I just get told to come for you," the Turk cries.

"For the last time, who told you?" I shout.

"It just come from inside. Please. Please. Allow me, my brother. I'm sorry."

"Come from inside? Inside where?" I yell as Deontay bounces up and down on his toes like an animal waiting to be unleashed.

"I don't know, please, I just—"

"—Who?" I shout.

I await the response through the sobbing and pleading of this blood-and-snot-nosed ball of wretchedness when I hear a cry from a voice across the street.

"I'm calling the police," the voice of a good Samaritan shouts. There's always that neighbour who just has to ruin the moment.

"Fuck off," Deontay cries, which only attracts more attention to us.

By now, several sets of eyes are on us. Bedroom lights switch on, curtains slide across, and blinds rise.

'If you lot actually bothered to find out what this little prick's been up to before tryin' to defend him, maybe you would see why man's got him held up against this car like this... He's lucky.'

Another cry comes from the same window, and I sense that the goon on the end of my mighty hand has suddenly found his balls. He spits a pool of bloody saliva onto the ground and grits his teeth as I strengthen my grasp on him.

"One more time I'ma ask you, why you come for my likkle bro. Who sent you? Who's inside?"

"They tell me to come for you, and I come," he says.

His words carry an air of arrogance as if somehow the cries about police have given him a feeling of security, and now, he's gained a little bravery.

I signal for Deontay to deliver another blow to remind this wasteman that he was begging for his life a minute ago.

Deontay hits him with a stiff right in his belly, and I watch the fight drain from the Turk's body right before my eyes. I shove him up against the car behind him when another shout about police catches my attention.

Infuriated, I can't listen to these fools' chants. To leave this lad to go about his business would be an injustice. Not just to me but to every real man out there who has taken a beating and lived to fight another day. *I've* paid for my crimes and then some. I've been held accountable for my actions by a court of law and had to spend twelve years ruing my behaviour that night. I've been shot at, stabbed, beaten up, and robbed, and not once did I beg for mercy or cry like a little bitch.

Nobody shouted out the window to come to my rescue, so why should this little punk escape punishment?

He raises his head, exhaling heavily. "You... Dee and Rakz."

I look at Deontay, then back at the Turk. "How d'you know my name?"

He shows me an overconfident set of teeth, and my rage resurfaces.

"Who told you my fuckin' name?" I cry.

'Who is this guy?'

I shake him by his shoulders. Then, he makes the mistake of all mistakes.

"Fuck you," he says, and all my rationalising flies out of the window.

Deontay looks at me with that 'you-just-gonna-let-him-cuss-you-like-that?' face, and I'm a hot-heated teenager back on the battlefield again. The old Rakz rushes right back through my body with a vengeance. The

186

energy surges from my toes to my legs, to my hips, and right through my forearms and fists, contracting every muscle along the way. This prick has violated for the last time.

My fist becomes rock solid, and I lock in the power of a million men.

"Fuck me, yeah?"

"What?" he says, his head sagging over his lethargic torso.

I turn my body like Tyson before a left hook. Then, twisting my hip, it's Frazier, Foreman, and Holyfield all in one. All seventeen stone of me comes round, fast and wicked, as my knuckles crash into the jaw in front of me, and I instantly know I've hit a home run. The man drops like a rag doll. There's a thunderous cracking sound as the car breaks his fall before he slams against the pavement.

"Ooh shit!" Deontay shouts as I stare at the unconscious body before me. "That was a bang," he yells.

Deafening screams pierce one ear and fly out the other.

'What did I just do?'

I look around and see dozens of eyes focused on me, staring through windows like they've just witnessed a wild animal attack an innocent cub.

Deontay tugs at my arm, and I hear the faint wail of sirens as instant regret fills my head.

"Oi, come, bro, we gotta move," Deontay says.

There's now a noose around my neck, and with every familiar screech, the rope tightens.

"Shit, man."

The man slumped across the pavement before me is out cold. I'm not sure if he's dead, but I'm sure if I stay around, it's straight back to prison. And there's no way I'm going back there.

"Rakz, let's go," Deontay shouts.

I pull my hood up, and with Deontay alongside me, I disappear into the darkness of the night.

17

I flick through news channel after news channel, like I've been doing for the past hour and a half since Deontay and I arrived at my house.

"Bro, d'you think he's dead?" Deontay asks.

I look over at him, spread out on the living room floor with two pillows underneath his head. He asks so casually as if he wouldn't believe it, even if it were the case.

I guess it's easy to talk about killing another human being when you've never done it. It's all just words. No realer than the movies. You can say it so blasé to another man because you've never experienced the gravity of such a situation.

That's the luxury afforded to those who are virgins when it comes to being a killer. When you've killed before and paid for it with half your life, you never want to hear, see, or talk about killing again, trust me.

One of Deontay's scrawny legs sticks out from the sleeping bag I've provided him for the night as his drowsy eyes struggle to remain open. Both hands behind his head like he's lapping up the comfort of a hammock, he rolls his neck to look back at me.

I stare at him for a couple of seconds, shake my head and turn my attention back towards the TV.

No breaking news about a man found dead.

So far, so good.

After knocking that Turk out cold and bolting through those desolate backstreets, I haven't thought of anything else.

I hadn't planned a sleepover with Deontay, but I wasn't about to abandon the kid. He's already vulnerable as it is, with these Turks looking for him, and I'm sure my actions have just exacerbated that.

As Deontay breathes steadily, I ask, "You sure you didn't mention my name to any of your little friends?"

"Nah, man."

"You sure?"

He notices the seriousness in my eyes and sits up, resting on one elbow. "I swear, bro, I told you when we were on the way back, I got no idea how them man know your name... Or mine."

I settle back onto the sofa with a sigh.

'I could do with a fat spliff right now.'

I picture myself twisting the end of the rolling paper, crowning it, then hearing that click from a lighter as a hypnotic flame shoots up, carrying her ghostly blue tint, ready to take my mind far away from my problems. I close my eyes and imagine the sound you hear when you take that first pull and listen to the paper sizzle and burn. I can almost feel the immediate relaxation that comes straight after until Deontay opens his mouth again.

"Do you think them man are gonna come back for us?" he asks.

"Not if they know what's good for them."

My response has the desired effect. Deontay chuckles and relaxes back into his makeshift bed.

I have no idea who and why these people have been sent after Deontay or how they know our names, but Deontay is the apprentice here, and I'm the leader. That means he mirrors my energy, and I'm not about to show him I'm paranoid and overwhelmed with anxiety before I send him back into the world in the morning.

I'm pretty sure the guys who came for Deontay are affiliated with the two who tried to attack him outside the barbershop, but the more pertinent matter of why, is the thing that's eluding me right now.

When your enemy knows more about you than you know about him, it makes it ten times harder to go to war.

I spend the next forty minutes or so asking myself hundreds of questions.

'Who would want to hurt Deontay? Who have I wronged that would come for me after all this time? What beef have these Turks got with D? Is this about us selling food round 'ere? Are they running things now? Have they got beef with Scribbler? Or has it got something to do with someone when I was in jail? Maybe some little punk who didn't like me? The yout' mentioned the order came from inside... Maybe someone I boxed up is still holding a grudge? And maybe he's seen me with Deontay, and he's using him to get to me.'

When I try to filter through all the possibilities, it leaves me with more questions than answers.

In the end, it tires me enough for me to lie down and rest my head on the arm of the sofa.

I check the news channels one more time. To my relief, there's nothing about a dead Turk.

I switch the TV off, and the room falls into complete blackness.

I'm only reminded that Deontay is still here when he opens his mouth.

"Rakz," he says with that fatigued voice.

He pauses like he's mulling over his next few words, then spits it out.

"I'm sorry I drew you out and got you involved in this beef, fam, like... Seriously on the level... My mum and my sister always told me I drag other people into my bullshit." I hear him moving around before he continues. "On my life, I called all the rest of the mandem before I phoned you, 'cause them man are always local, but none of them came through, bruv. Only two of them answered, but I didn't see them when I got out of that garden. I know you got your own things to deal with, bro but like, if you didn't come, I don't know what would've happened, I swear... So, yeah, I'm sorry, g. Thanks for coming bro... I know you didn't have to, init."

All I hear in his admission is guilt, like he's to blame for all of this.

"D, my brudda," I say, sitting up to get my point across. "Don't be chattin' that shit. You done the right thing. I told you before, I got you. Any problem, just ring me. You rang me, and I came through. We're in this for the money, yeah, but that don't mean you can't call on me for anything else."

"Yeah, I know, it's just I wasn't trying to get you involved in—"

"—From you're involved, *I'm involved*," I say, commanding Deontay's attention as I raise my voice. "I don't know about your sis and your mum, they probably love you and just want the best for you, but either way, like I told you, I got you. Whenever things get sticky, and you're in a jam, just call me. I'm there. I told you that, and I meant it. Believe me. 'Cause if a man don't keep his word, he ain't a real man, you feel me?"

"I feel you, bro," Deontay says, and I feel the reverence in his words.

"Good."

The cessation of our voices gives way to a ringing ambience for a few seconds until, once again, it's interrupted by Deontay's mouth.

But this time he keeps it short and sweet.

"Goodnight, bro," he says.

18

There's a knock at the door.

Jerking out of my snooze, I jump to my feet and peer over at Deontay. That space he's called 'bed' for the night might as well be a coffin. He's dead to the world. I reach for my phone when I hear the knocking again.

Three steady taps.

Light.

Rhythmic.

They don't sound like police knocks, they're not loud, and there's no voice identifying who they belong to. I refuse to allow myself the comfort of ruling it out, though. The curtains are drawn, so the old peep-from-behind-the-netting-trick is out of the question unless I want to risk revealing I'm home.

I see two missed calls from Leanne across my phone screen, and my heart settles a bit.

Only *she* turns up unannounced and uninvited at these unsociable hours. I rub my eyes and walk towards the doorway when I remember.

'Shit, Deontay. Leanne can't find him sleeping on the floor. She'll probably think I've turned Mum's into a B&B for the local chaff.'

I pull the pillow from over Deontay's head as I wonder how people sleep like him without suffocating. I shake him vigorously, and after a few seconds, his soul returns to his body.

"Get up," I order him as I drag him from the floor and usher this dark-skin zombie through the hallway and onto the staircase as quickly and quietly as possible.

The smell of a body that's had the best sleep it's had in years drifts through the air in his wake as he carries his pillow and his sleeping bag upstairs. Mumbling to himself, he turns out of my sight.

I take a look through the upstairs banister, and once the coast is clear, I peer through the keyhole. Leanne's hair looks thicker and darker than I've ever seen, or maybe it's just the time of day, and my eyes haven't properly adjusted yet. Either way, for once in my life, I'm grateful it's her.

Rubbing the corner of my eyes, I open the door.

"Rakim."

"Nia?"

"You okay?"

Caught by surprise, I look behind me, making sure Deontay's totally out of sight before I shimmy out into the front garden and pull the door behind me, leaving it narrowly ajar.

"I'm good. You just woke me up," I say.

"Yeah, well, I had to come over and check you were okay after what happened last night," she says as she touches my arm softly.

She takes me straight back to Jamal, and my head throbs as I feel my body become heavy. The brightness of the morning sun catches me like a sharp thorn, prodding at my forehead.

"I'm cool, Nia."

"Are you sure?"

"Yeah, I'm good. Last night I was just..."

It's only when I'm halfway through my sentence that I realise I don't have an explanation for my behaviour.

"... It was just... A bit mad for me," I say, regaining equanimity.

I put my hands together as I watch Nia linger in anguish.

Running her hand over her ear and combing her hair back, she responds, "I'm really sorry about your friend."

"It's okay," I say.

"I know it's not the easiest thing to talk about, but if you want to talk at any time, I'm here," she says.

I know Nia's seeking something more, perhaps for me to expose my vulnerabilities. I want to give her that. I want to unload my pain and sadness for once. I want to tell her what a cool bruddah Jamal was and how I keep thinking about his family, but that means revealing my past.

'I can't be doing that right now.'

I feel the touch of Nia's velvety skin against my hand, and I draw her closer. "Sorry 'bout yesterday."

"It's fine. I understand, Rakim."

I hug her tightly, offering her the warmth and security of my body.

"You look nice, by the way," I say.

"Thank you."

"Don't worry, you ain't gotta return the compliment."

"I mean I would, but... you know," she says with that mischievous smile as she looks me up and down.

I smile, thankful for Nia's understanding.

"Look there it is, that beautiful smile," Nia says.

"You know I was pissed I missed out on that food last night. I went to bed all hungry and that."

"Aww, poor you," Nia says.

I tighten my grip around her waist, making her jolt and giggle at the same time.

"So, are you gonna invite me in then or...?" she asks.

I turn my head towards the door.

'Deontay.'

Nia notices my reaction, and she narrows her eyes.

"Everything okay?" she asks.

"Yeah, yeah. Just not the best time right now. How about I come over to yours later?"

Nia's dimples rise, and I lean in to taste those succulent lips.

"Uh-uh," she says as she evades my head. "Not before you go and brush your teeth. I know you just got up, and I can smell the alcohol on you."

I smile. "We're gonna get over this, ya know."

194

"Maybe, but not today," she says as she eases out of my grasp.

Stood on the steps of my front garden, the thundering sound of an engine seizes bout of our attention.

Nia's head swivels, and mine follows.

Seconds later, a familiar vehicle appears. As white as snow and as clean as a whistle. "Is that your...?" Nia asks.

'Shit, that's all I need right now.'

I watch Leanne pull up outside the front gate, and instantly, I feel my shoulders tense up, and my throat turn dry.

'She better not mention anything about prison, I swear.'

Leanne's hair flows behind her as she steps out of her car and opens the front gate.

"Hey darling," she says to Nia, raising her Chanel sunglasses and resting them on her forehead.

"Hi, how are you?" Nia says, doing her best to mask the awkwardness in her voice.

"I'm fine, thank you," Leanne says as she hugs Nia. "It's been such a long time. How have you been?"

Already she's talking like the two of them are best friends out on a bougie brunch, and I feel my annoyance growing.

After returning the hug, Nia fixes her vest top.

"I've been good, just busy with work and family. Same old, same old," she says.

"Tell me about it. Taylor's got a convention tomorrow, a big one. The number of times I've had to listen to his presentation, by God, I swear I could probably conduct it myself," Leanne says with a high-society chuckle.

Nia cracks an awkward smile as Leanne turns her attention to me. "Hey bro," she says.

"Wa gwarn, you all right?"

"Yes, I'm fine," Leanne replies as she removes her sunglasses and places the end of one of the arms between her teeth. "I never knew the pair of you were... acquainted."

'Here we go.'

Leanne looks back and forth between Nia and me.

Seeing Nia's uncomfortable smile return, I step in.

"Yeah, we are acquainted. Nia's a friendly face. She knew Mum. That's how we got to talking."

"Well, I knew that Sherlock," Leanne says trying showcase her humourous side and I can't help but cringe. "So, you two are...?"

"I told you Nia's a friendly face, she's helped me settle a lot."

"Ooh, interesting," Leanne says like the three of us are kids back in the school playground.

I run my hand across my forehead. "What you doing here this early anyway, Lee?"

"Excuse me, this isn't early, the time is actually—"

"—Look, this ain't the best time, Lee."

I note Nia's reaction to my bluntness and wonder if I should tone it down a bit.

"Oh well sor-ree Mr Too-busy-for-your-sister," Leanne says.

I shake my head. "What did you want? I'm just kinda busy, init," I say.

"I actually had something to tell you if you're ever gonna invite me inside," Leanne replies.

I look at Nia, and thankfully she reads my mind. "Erm, I think I'll leave you both to it. I've gotta be going, anyway. Rakim, I'll give you a call later," she says, leaning over to hug me.

"And Leanne," Nia says, turning towards my intrusive sister. "It was nice seeing you again. Take care and tell Taylor and the boys I said hello."

"Oh, no problem. Nice seeing you too," Leanne says as she waves Nia off.

"See you later," I call.

The light breeze passes by, gently blowing Leanne's curls to the side as she turns to face me, and without even looking directly at her, I feel her mischievous grin.

196

"So Rakim, making friends, are we?" she says.

"Allow it, Lee."

"Come on, you can tell me."

"I just did. I told you to leave it."

"No, I want to know all about it."

"There's nothing to know," I say sharply.

"Hmm... Well, it's good to see you talking to people instead of being cooped up in that house all day. It's a good way to rebuild confidence and begin to integrate yourself back into society.

This is blatantly Taylor talking.

"Is that right, yeah?" I say.

"It is. I read it in an online forum about ex-prisoners, it was—"

"—Yo, look Leanne, I know you didn't drive all this way over here to give me a lesson in rehabilitation, so get to the point."

I watch Leanne's mouth drop.

"Wow, sometimes, Rakim, you can be so rude. How does a nice girl like Nia put up with such a vulgar attitude?"

I roll my eyes.

"What d'you want? I told you I'm busy."

"Well, am I not at least allowed inside my own mother's house to sit down and have a coffee?"

"I told you it's not a good time," I say as I remain posted between Leanne and the door like a bouncer outside a nightclub.

Finally getting the message, Leanne shakes her head and replaces her sunglasses. "Seeing as you're in a hurry to get rid of me, I'll just get straight to the point."

'Thank God.'

She pauses for a moment as I hold my arms out, awaiting what was so important she had to interrupt my conversation with Nia.

"I came over to tell you that Ricky and Nathan will be coming home this weekend, and you're invited for dinner."

"For real?"

"Yes, that's why I came over here. To deliver you some good news, and all you've tried to do is get rid of me."

"My bad. I'll be there."

"Don't sound too happy. Gosh," Leanne says.

"What day?"

"Saturday, come for around three. I haven't told them either, so it's going to be a nice surprise."

"All right, cool."

"Bring your 'friend' along too, if you like, it's about time you spent some time with a woman."

"Please... I been a ladies-magnet since the day I could talk."

Leanne rolls her eyes.

"Ladies-magnet? I wouldn't exactly call your past escapades 'ladies,' but whatever floats your boat."

"I'll see you on Saturday."

"No coffee, no catch-up?" Leanne says, her arms wide apart like I've done her the worst injustice imaginable.

I know it's all a ploy to get all up in my business, and I ain't fooling for it.

"This ain't Starbucks. And like I told you three times already, I'm busy."

Shaking her head, Leanne turns and walks towards the gate. She places a hand on the gate, then spinning back towards me, she says, "Rakim," with a serious face.

"Yeah."

She pauses as she looks at me for a moment and gives me that concerned sister's face.

"I don't know what you're hiding up in that house, but whatever you're up to, look after Nia, please. She's a lovely girl. Mum liked her a lot, and she was always there to help out, so make sure you don't get her caught up in anything."

Its why I didn't want her turning up; Leanne knows me too well.

Ninety per cent of the time, her patronising tone irks me, but I know when her words come from a genuine place of concern. And right now, she's just a worried sister.

"I won't," I say.

"Good, because I don't want to lose you again either."

"You won't."

"Okay. I'll see you Saturday. Let me know if you need anything, okay?"

"I'm good."

"Just asking. Jesus, I can't do right by you, can I?"

"Later, Lee."

I close the door, and to my surprise, Deontay is standing at the top of the stairs.

"Wa gwarn," I yell.

"Man was looking for the bathroom," he calls.

I give him a conspicuous look. "Down the hall, to the right."

He trods off while I call a cab.

About ten minutes later, I hear the toilet flush before footsteps descend the staircase, and I meet him at the bottom of the steps.

"Yo, you gotta get going, man's called a cab for you still," I tell him.

"Who was at the door?" Deontay says, appearing to look over my shoulder as if he's trying to see what's outside.

"None of your rasclart business."

"Nah, it's just 'cause I didn't realise where we were. We came in over the back fence last night. I know this road, I used to—"

"—Brudda, the cabs here, go put your fuckin' clothes on man."

"My bad, I heard a girl's voice init. I was wondering if—"

"—Are you deaf? Ain't no pussy out there for you. Go upstairs and get ready. You gotta go open the trap so you man can get to work."

I watch Deontay's shoulders drop.

He huffs as he spins around and stomps upstairs. I shake my head. "You love to talk, but you hate to listen."

Moments later, he sprints down the stairs and straight past me.

"Yo," I call.

My voice, like a fishing rod, reeling him back.

"Don't mention anything about last night to your bredrins, all right?"

"Cool," Deontay nods.

'I need to find out why that Turk came for us and how he knows our names.'

"Oi, Rakz, by the end of today, all the food's gonna be done."

'More money, more problems.'

"Don't worry. Let *me* deal with that," I say.

"Ite, cool," Deontay shrugs.I hold a fist out and spud him before he flicks his hood up and leaves my house.

19

A few days have passed since the incident with the Deontay and the Turkish yout'. I haven't heard anything about it, which from my experience, is a good thing.

Sat on the steps of my front garden watching the cars travel up and down my road, I recall the Turk saying that his orders came from inside. Which means somebody in prison was behind the ambush on Deontay. I know that when it comes to prison gossip and rumours, my best bet is Scribbler.

I try to call him, but yet again, I'm met with the automated voicemail I've been hearing since yesterday.

'Wa gwarn with Scribz, man?'

I wonder if he's still grieving over Jamal. Or if he's been caught with the phone. The thing about being on the other side of those walls is that you just don't know.

My phone vibrates in my hand, and for a split second, I get excited.

I look at the screen and see the text message.

'Yo G, wen u gtn the re-up?'

It's Deontay. And he's eager for more product to sell.

He's not the only one. A customer calling when you have no product hurts any real hustler. That phone he carries has probably rang over a hundred times since last night. That's a few thousand pound we've already missed out on. If I allow this to continue any longer, all of our clientele will find other dealers, and then it's back to square one for him and me.

It's all the more reason I need to get hold of Scribz.

Today.

I shelve my concerns for a moment as my cab arrives.

As I get in, I reach underneath the front passenger seat and slide it back as far as it will go.

Within twenty minutes, we're entering a leafy suburb.

High steel gates, decorated in colours from black to gold, stand tall like Poseidon's trident, pointing towards the sky. I catch glimpses of front doors with large golden knobs, double garages bigger than my living room, and mammoth driveways embellished with exotic plants, CCTV cameras, and basketball hoops.

It's just what I need. A getaway from my life. Something to take my mind off Jamal and these Turks.

We continue deeper into this wonderland.

Luxury cars are the norm here.

As my cab steers by, I see them all. Range Rover. Aston Martin. Lamborghini. Tesla. McClaren.

'Leanne really hit the jackpot.'

But as much as I admire it all, one overriding thought plays on my mind—it's still the same England.

Still the same woeful weather for most of the year, the same cold dog-eat-dog culture, the same authorities hell-bent on oppressing people like me, crushing our rebellious spirit until we conform to the ideologues of their system.

I pass a driveway that boasts a Range Rover Sport, Mercedes C63, and a Bentley Continental, and I can't help but think the money spent on just one of those cars could buy a six-bedroom house on the golden shores of The Gambia and still have a nice bit of change left over.

The driver indicates to turn left, and I'm yanked from my daydream. "Slow down, boss," I say, tapping his shoulder. Leanne's house is about a hundred metres ahead, but this is supposed to be a surprise. I can't let the boys see me pull up.

I order the driver to pull over, and I call Leanne. She gives me the all-clear, so I pay the fare and exit the cab. The rumbling in my stomach increases as I walk underneath the dancing shadows of giant conifers and cedar trees. *'What if they don't wanna spend time with me? What if they don't even remember me?'*

I approach the driveway of Leanne's fortress and have to check myself.

"Yo, they'll remember you, man. You're their uncle. And you're the man here, so fix up. What's wrong with you?" I mumble to myself, looking like I've lost my sanity to any bystanders.

I knock on the door, and seconds later, it opens.

The door moves backwards, and before me stands a glossy bald head that tilts forward to greet me. "Hey, big guy, how's tricks?"

It's Leanne's benefactor, with his best cultural welcome. I hold my fist out, momentarily forgetting where I am. Taylor quickly reminds me, though, as he awkwardly shakes my fist like it's an open palm.

"I'm good," I state as I walk past Mr Coq Au Vin and enter the palatial area ahead of me.

'At least this time, he didn't put a hand on my shoulder.'

I move further into this room that just reeks of wealth. The smell of shallots, butter, and white wine mingles with the aroma of peony and rose from the Jo Malone candle that flickers away on the mantlepiece.

I turn to my right to see Leanne emerge from the hallway. She greets me with a kiss as I whisper to her, "Where're the boys?"

Her champagne tangos in her glass as she turns around. "Ricky, Nath, come downstairs. Someone's here to see you," she shouts.

"Who?" I hear a voice call from upstairs, and for a second, I pause. The voice sounds like that of a grown man. I was half-expecting the cry of a little toddler. I have to remind myself these boys are fully-fledged teenagers now. The sound of rubber slapping against the granite staircase disrupts the silence in the living room until, eventually, the footsteps stop.

I catch a glimpse of Leanne beaming the way she used to when we were kids.

Then, from the hallway, I see a brown-skinned teenager appear, his eyes deep into his phone.

It's Nathan.

Or at least an adolescent version of Nathan. He's dressed in a black cardigan and a pair of dark ripped jeans. His afro springs out on top, with the sides and back of his head shaven. He looks up and straight away catches my eyes.

He freezes.

His head moves back, and he narrows his focus.

Raising a finger, he says, "Wait—is that?"

His eyes flit from me to Leanne, to Taylor, then back at his jubilant mother, who's ditched the champagne glass and now has two palms covering her mouth like her pride is about to force her to tears.

"It's me, bro," I say, unable to hold back a massive cheesy grin.

"Uncle Rakim?"

Leanne nods as Nathan's arms drop. His phone doesn't matter anymore.

"What, for real? Uncle Rakim, what... how?" he says, looking at the adults in the room for answers.

"I'm home," I say as I walk up to him with my arms wide open.

It must finally register in his brain as he bursts into life.

"Ricky, come! Uncle Rakim's here," Nathan shouts, and within moments I hear footsteps thundering down the stairs.

I grab hold of Nathan.

"Fam, how you get so big?"

"What the hell?" Nathan says.

I'm about to respond when I see another familiar face. It's just way too mature and on the wrong body.

"Uncle Rakim, oh my days. No way," Ricky shouts, holding his phone out to capture the moment. "Fresh home and that!"

"Put that away and come here," I order him.

He strides towards me and holds out a fist.

"Erm Ricky, manners," Taylor says.

I take one look at Ricky's fist and feel my eyebrows knit together.

"Come here, man," I say as I force him into my huddle with Nathan. "About you're gonna try spud me, I'm your uncle," I say as I squeeze both of them tightly like they're the two little kids I left a long time ago.

Laughter fills the room as both boys struggle to get free.

"Are you mad? Nah, you ain't going nowhere," I shout as I squeeze harder.

They plead for mercy until I let them overpower me, and together, the three of us hit the floor.

Leanne's laughter governs the room as Ricky complains. "Arrgghhh, Uncle Rakim, you broke my back, man," he moans.

"What are you, a man or a mouse?" I say as I sit on the floor, watching both boys climb to their feet.

"I guess I'll leave you all to it," Taylor says as he heads for the kitchen.

As Nathan turns towards Leanne, Ricky attempts to pull out his phone and video me for a second time.

"Mum, how did you pull the wool over our eyes like that?" Nathan asks, his smile still bright and infectious.

"That's mummy, darling. Full of surprises," Leanne says with a wink.

"Yeah, don't underestimate your mum, ya know," I say as I climb to my feet.

Ricky gets closer to me, filming me like I'm an endangered species. "Tell 'em you're fresh home, Uncle Rakim," he says.

"What?" I snatch the phone from him and watch his jaw drop like I've committed the worse crime in human history. "Leave that ting, man," I say.

"Give me my phone back," Ricky shouts.

I laugh and turn to Leanne. "You hear how my man said that with his chest?" I say.

"Ooh Rakim, just give him his phone," Leanne says.

"Yeah, give me my phone," Ricky says, once again, as he jumps to reach the device I hold high above my head.

I use my free hand to usher him aside as he tries again.

"Nah, ain't nothing in life free, ya know, you gotta earn it," I say, as it turns into a juvenile game.

Leanne shakes her head as Nathan comes over to join in. I laugh as I fend them off, taunting them all the while.

"Come on, you man, what you playing at? Is this what you do if someone takes your tings at school?"

Ricky launches himself at me, but I swat him away. "Come on, you man," I say taunting both my nephews.

"Careful," Leanne shouts.

"Give me the phone," Ricky yells. Somewhere halfway between frustration and playful he comes at me again, his dreadlocks waving like plants in a cornfield.

I back away, crouching low as Nathan tries to flank me. "What you gonna—"

I feel my shoulder touch something behind me. Then a heart-stopping crash, instantly followed by a high-pitched shriek, pierces my ear, and I see the horror on Leanne's face as Nathan and Ricky stop in their tracks.

"Oh no!" Nathan shouts as Ricky lets out a gasp.

I turn around to see what used to be a beautiful vase shattered across the dark stone flooring. Dozens of crystal fragments litter the floor as I glance at Leanne, who looks like she's just witnessed a murder.

"What's the rumpus?" Taylor cries as he comes running in from the kitchen like there's a fire.

It takes less than a second before he soon realises the answer to his own question.

"Oh, my goodness! What on earth happened?" he shouts, turning to look at Leanne. "Who did this?" Taylor yells.

His eyes turn to Ricky and Nathan, who seem to know the code well, and both remain silent.

"It was me. My bad, bro," I say as I raise my hands.

"Goddammit, Rakim, it's like having a third child in the house," Taylor squawks.

"I was messing about with the boys, and I accidentally knocked it over. My bad," I say calmly.

"You're damn right it's your bad. How does a grown man like you manage to destroy ornaments within minutes of entering an accommodation?" Taylor says.

"It was just an accident," Ricky says.

"Be quiet, Ricky. I'm speaking with your uncle," Taylor snaps.

Turning back to face Leanne, who looks terrified, Taylor shakes his head, placing his hands on his hips. "How does something like this happen? Please enlighten me?" he asks.

His undertone of frustration is slipping into disrespect now. His first comment, I let slide since it was my fault, but one thing I'll never stand for is Taylor, or anyone for that matter, disrespecting my sister with their passive-aggressive bullshit, especially in front of her children.

"Yo, chill out now. I told you it was an accident. It wasn't her fault or the boys' fault. It was my fault," I say, letting Taylor hear the bass in my voice. It's an untamed warning, a cue to let him know I'm the alpha male in the room and I'm putting this situation to bed.

I hand Ricky his phone as Taylor appears to get the message. The veins in his forearms bulging, Taylor raises his eyebrows as he strolls over to the broken remains of the vase and kneels down to assess the damage.

"It's irreparable," he mumbles to himself.

I watch him cradle a large shard as if it's a sick child and with each passing moment, he looks increasingly mortified.

"How?" Taylor mutters.

I need to step in. "Look, if it means that much to you, I'll pay for it."

"I highly doubt that," Taylor scoffs, avoiding eye contact with me.

"There you go," I say, offering a hand holding two hundred pounds.

He barely acknowledges the money.

"There's two bills there. Take it," I say.

207

"Two hundred pounds? This is a hand-crafted Lalique. Try two thousand, then we *might* just be nearing halfway," he says, trying his utmost to contain the aggression behind his words.

I can feel Ricky and Nathan from the corner of my eye.

They're watching.

Waiting to see how this turns out.

And as much as I wish to punch Taylor in his face for his impertinence and be done with him already, I know that's not an option.

"Ite, cool," I say, delving into my pocket. I pull out two wads of cash, each containing a thousand pounds, neatly stacked, and secured within a rubber band. "There you go, take that."

Taylor looks at me like he's lost for words, but anything to wipe that arrogant sense of superiority off his face is money well spent in my book. His eyes find Leanne, and I feel the energy in the room shift.

"No, Rakim, you can't—" Leanne says.

"—It's cool, take it. I'll give you the rest tomorrow," I say, raising my voice and almost forcing the cash into Taylor's face as he mourns the death of his beautiful 'Lalikwee' or whatever the hell it is.

"You gonna take it or not?" I ask, and he knows from my tone I'm not playing around.

Taylor looks at Leanne for a hopeful intervention, but she has no words for him. He turns to face me with the ignominy of defeat stamped across his face. His attempt to humiliate has failed.

"No, keep your money," he says, waving me away.

"Nah, man, take it init," I say. Louder this time.

"No, no, I can't, Rakim," Taylor says as if suddenly he's all humble and merciful.

"So, what was the big fuss about, then? I broke it. I'm offering to pay for a new one. Take the Ps, fam."

I hear a snigger, and I guess it's Ricky, seeing the embarrassment on his stepdad's face as Taylor rises to his feet.

"It's okay, I... I'm sorry," Taylor stutters, offering his hand for me to shake.

I suck my teeth and stuff the cash back into my pocket.

"Lee, I'm taking the boys to the park."

She nods, sensing I need to cool down. However, it seems Supercoon hasn't received the memo.

"We're going to have dinner, though," Taylor says, now begging to be my best friend.

"Listen, go back into the kitchen and see to your lobster bisque. We're going out," I say.

Taylor swiftly retreats, and I turn to my nephews.

"Rick, you still on this football ting, yeah?" I ask.

"Course," Ricky replies.

"Good. Go grab a ball and put your trainers on. You too, Nath."

Both boys disappear as Leanne ambles over to me.

"You want the car?" she whispers.

"Cool."

She touches my shoulder gently.

"Don't worry about the vase," she says, her words as soft as her face.

"Believe me, I ain't worried."

My frown eases as Supercoon finally takes the hint and disappears into the kitchen.

Seconds later, the boys emerge together, say their goodbyes, and I'm grateful as the three of us head off to the park.

20

Taking in the scenery, I pass wooden benches, lilac shrubs, and dozens of other soaring bushes.

"Mum never lets us come round here," Ricky says as me and Nathan walk either side of him through the greenery of Hortiman Park.

"That's because it's dangerous over here," Nathan says, sounding like a miniature Taylor.

"Dangerous? Why d'you say that?" I ask.

"Just because..." Nathan says.

"Because what?"

Nathan looks at the ground.

"Who told you it's dangerous?" I ask.

"Who do you think?" Ricky says, rolling his eyes.

I shake my head in disbelief as Nathan avoids my eyes.

"Listen, you two. The world ain't like that bubble you live in over there. As much as your mum and Taylor might pretend it is. It's not all private school and croquet lessons." I say, making Ricky laugh. "This is your home. This is where you man were born. I used to take you here all the time when you were young."

"For real?" Ricky says.

"Yeah, you don't remember me, Preddie, FatMack?"

"Nah," Ricky says, shaking his head.

I look at Nathan, who shrugs.

"Rah, you man really don't remember?"

"Nope," Ricky says as he dribbles along with his ball.

Dogs dart around, and families bathe in the heat of this boundless green paradise that stretches her beauty far beyond the parameters of my vision. The grass glistens as the sun hits, causing it to sparkle like the floor of an enchanted forest.

We divert from the winding pathway, and Ricky runs off, lost in his own imaginary football match.

"Come," I tell Nathan.

He doesn't look particularly enthusiastic but follows my lead, nonetheless.

We spend the next hour or so basically chasing Ricky, trying to get the ball off him. I let the two of them play against each other while impersonating a goalkeeper, but it's no challenge. Ricky's flair and guile are way too much for Nathan to compete with, and Ricky comes out victorious in just about every game we play.

After a final round of penalties, which Ricky wins once again, we sit together on the grass. I wipe the sweat from my forehead as Ricky continues to show off his talent, doing kick-ups while seated.

"You're a proper baller, init," I say to Ricky.

"Yeah, course. Man's Mbappe in the making," he says, keeping his rhythm as he continues showcasing his skills.

"Your mum told me, but I never knew you were this good," I say. "Stick with that, ya know."

He doesn't appear to be listening until the ball eventually hits the ground, and I grab hold of it.

"I'm telling you, Rick, talent's nothing without application. You gotta go out there and put the work in. Trust me, I've seen nuff man who are talented but got caught up in the wrong things and ended up wasting their lives."

"Nah, I'm gonna play for PSG. Watch," Ricky says.

I smile. "You will, but you gotta stay focused and put the work in. Nothing comes easy in life, you feel me?"

Ricky nods as I turn towards Nathan, who silently picks at the grass.

"What about you?" I ask, throwing the ball at Nathan to get his attention.

"What about me?" Nathan asks.

"Well, what d'you wanna be when you're older?"

"Dunno," Nathan says.

"What d'you mean, you don't know?"

"I dunno."

"Yes, you do, man," Ricky interrupts.

"Ah, shut up, nobody's talking to you," Nathan says.

"You shut up," Ricky says.

"Nah, on the level. What d'you wanna do with yourself, Nath?" I ask.

Nathan looks up, and just as he goes to speak, we're interrupted by my phone. Thinking it might be Scribz, I rush to answer. "One sec, Nath."

I get up and take the phone from my pocket to discover it's not Scribz.

"What's going on, Ni?" I ask.

"Hey, stranger. How are you?" Nia says.

As soon as I hear her voice, I think about being back in her bedroom, lying there, her head resting on me.

"I'm good. Sorry I didn't call you back the other day, just had a lot on my plate. I meant to call you tonight."

"Well, you're lucky that I've just finished teaching my yin yoga class, and I'm in a very forgiving mood, otherwise...."

"Otherwise, what?"

"Otherwise, you might have to—"

"—One sec," I say, turning to see Ricky and Nathan about to come to blows. "I gotta go, Ni. Sorry. I call you later."

I stuff the phone back in my pocket and rush over to my nephews to intervene. "Yo, what you doing?" I say as I pull Nathan off his younger brother.

"This boy's too rude," Nathan says.

"Shut up before I knock you out," Ricky cries as his black face reddens with anger.

"What's going on with you two?" I shout, stepping between them.

Nathan straightens his back as Ricky punches the palm of his hand.

"It's him," Ricky complains.

"You started it," Nathan says.

"How?" Ricky says.

I hold my arms out as I wait for Nathan to elaborate.

"All I said is I wanted to be a doctor, and then he goes, 'Are you gay? Why d'you wanna be a doctor?'" Nathan explains.

I look at Ricky, who stands there trying to hold back the wicked temper I see brewing.

"What's gay about being a doctor?" I ask Ricky.

He shrugs his shoulders as he rolls the ball back and forth with his foot.

"So, when you're this big-time footballer playing for PSG, and you get an injury, who d'you think's gonna be the one helping you to recover?"

Ricky stays silent as he looks down at the ground, probably realising how stupid and immature his comment was.

"Exactly," Nathan cries.

"Shut up, man," Ricky moans.

"And you, why you lettin' these little names draw you out? Are you some emotional little girl or suttin'?" I say, turning to Nathan.

He moves his head from side to side, trying to put on a brave face, but I see right through it.

"Listen, if someone calls you a name, laugh that shit off. Life's too short to be fighting over name-calling, especially when you man are brothers, you feel me?" I exclaim, placing a firm hand on both boys' shoulders. "The world's already against you both. You don't need to be fighting each other as well."

Ricky's eyes threaten to stream, and I see myself for a split second while I look at him. A young, confused boy, out here trying to prove something to the world. I see that old demon. Anger. Lying deep within him. Silent. But all the while, festering; getting ready to strike like a venomous cobra.

213

'Ricky's only a few years younger than Deontay. And I've got Deontay running the streets selling crack and buj.'

Just like Squeeze had me doing.

And although my nephews are from a totally different walk of life, Ricky looks just as angry as I used to and just as confused about himself as Deontay.

While I'm here for Ricky and Nathan, watching over them, I can't help but feel guilty about Deontay. I know he already had one foot in this life, but I can't deny I've contributed to firmly planting his other foot in it.

Nathan continues his stubbornness, looking anywhere but at his brother until I order the pair of them to shake hands, and reluctantly, they do. But I sense there's more to this than meets the eye.

"What's going on with you two, man?" I yell.

I look at Nathan, then at Ricky.

"Gwarn, talk, 'cause we ain't movin' until we sort this once and for all."

After another few seconds of silence, Ricky opens his mouth.

"It's him, man. He just thinks he's better than me," Ricky says.

"That's rubbish," Nathan says.

"He's a nerd, and he licks Taylor's arse," Ricky says.

"You're just an idiot. I don't mind being smart. It's better than being reckless."

"I ain't reckless."

"Did you just see what happened? Or are you blind? You were jumping around the place because you want to video Uncle Rakim and put him on your Snap, and then you make the vase smash."

"That wasn't my fault," Ricky shouts.

"That's another thing. You don't take no responsibility for your actions either. You think life's just about enjoying yourself and messing about. The reason I'm smarter than you is because I study hard. You don't take anything seriously," Nathan replies.

Clearly frustrated, Ricky holds out an arm. "See, even the way he speaks, like he's some posh little snob. You're black, not white."

"Being black has nothing to do with how you speak. You're so immature. That's exactly why Dad wants *me* to come and work with him and not you."

I listen intently as both boys unload God knows how many years of pent-up anger.

"Why do you keep calling him Dad? He ain't even our real dad. He doesn't care about us. He can't wait for us to be back at that stupid school so he can have Mum all to himself," Ricky cries.

Nathan goes to respond, but it's time to finish this. This is going nowhere.

"Yo, dead this, man! Come here, you two," I say as I put an arm around both boys.

I crouch until all of our eyes meet.

"Listen, let me tell you suttin'," I begin. "'Cause you man both seem to think you got life all figured out. First of all, Ricky, there ain't nothing wrong with wanting to be a doctor or work for Taylor. He's smart, and so is your brother. You should be proud of Nath. He can put his brain to use and make lots of money. Not everyone's a gifted baller like you. You feel me? And just because he can articulate himself well, that doesn't make him any less black than you, d'you understand?"

"Yeah, but..." Ricky says.

"Do you understand what I'm saying? Yes or no?"

"Yes, Uncle Rakim," Ricky groans.

"And you, Nathan, don't be jealous of your little brother. Jealousy's a weak emotion. Real men don't get bitter, they get better. So just because he likes to live life, have fun, and probably gets more girls than you, don't be standing there being a hater. Let him live his life. Being more successful, intelligent, or well-spoken don't make you any better than Ricky. D'you understand?"

Nathan nods his head.

"What was that? I didn't hear you," I say, leaning closer to Nathan's mouth.

"Yes, Uncle Rakim, I understand," Nathan says.

"Good," I say before letting go of both boys.

There's an awkward pause as I shake my head. I certainly wasn't expecting this after not seeing these boys for over six years.

The three of us walk back towards the pathway, and I notice Ricky checking out an older girl.

"Is that you, yeah?" I ask.

"I like older girls, init," Ricky declares.

"Yeah?"

He nods with enthusiasm, and I smile.

"What colour?" I ask.

"Black, obviously," he says as if I'm silly for even asking.

"What about you?" I say, turning towards Nathan.

His downcast face barely acknowledges my question as he shrugs his shoulders and keeps walking.

"What's wrong?" I ask.

He stops walking, tilts his head back, and puts his hands together.

"... Why don't you like Dad?" he asks.

I stare at him for a moment and have to remind myself these are sensitive teenagers I'm dealing with, not hardened criminals and not the toddlers I left twelve years ago.

"Look," I begin. "I've always told you lot to respect your elders, especially your mum and Taylor, but with Taylor and me, it's a different dynamic," I explain.

"How so?" Nathan asks.

"Well, we're both grown men, and I know I've always told you boys to be respectful to people, but don't think for a single second that it means you've gotta be submissive to another man. Just because he might have more money than you, a nicer house or a better car or job, that don't mean nothing, you feel me? You carry yourself with pride and dignity and don't let no man, ever, ever talk down to you like you're below them, 'cause once you let one person treat you like that, everyone will... If a man doesn't respect you, you force him to respect you, you understand?"

I put an arm around Nathan, who seems to agree with me.

"That's what happened with Taylor earlier, that's all. He just forgot who he was talking to, so I kept him in check to remind him he *has* to respect me."

Ricky sniggers and runs off ahead with the ball at his feet as me and Nathan wade wistfully along the path.

"So why d'you wanna be a doctor, anyway?" I ask Nathan.

He scrunches his lips into a tight ball before answering.

"I just want to save people... If I was older, and I was a doctor years ago, then maybe I could have saved Granny."

I sigh as the sky looks down upon us. If Mum's up there in that perfect blue right now, I know she'll be proud of her two little soldiers.

"You're a good boy, Nath, and you gotta kind soul, but nobody could have saved Granny. When God says it's our time to go, it's our time, you feel me?"

He doesn't respond, but I see a glimmer of light in his eye and feel maybe I've restored some positivity into this boy. "You'll go on to save loads of people when you finally become a doctor, anyway, don't worry," I say.

We walk the rest of the short distance in silence before catching up to Ricky and leaving the park.

I notice Ricky's stopped dribbling. He's clutching at his ball, and he looks tense. As I look up ahead, I see a group of young men, probably early to mid-twenties, all dressed in black. Three of them are standing by a car smoking while the other sits, his legs hanging out of the wide-open passenger door. There's a steady base coming from the vehicle that masks their voices.

Ricky waits until I'm right beside him before he continues to walk. As we get closer to the group of boys, I notice the distinct smell of weed. It sails through the air, and although it smells pleasant to me, Nathan

217

squeezes his nostrils like it's the most hideous odour he's ever come across.

"Why are they looking at you, Uncle Rakim?" Nathan whispers, and I feel the tension behind his words.

I'm a big guy, I'm used to people staring at me. I scan the collective of young men. There's no animosity in any of their glances, but they're far from friendly faces, either.

I turn my head away and continue walking.

Then a few more steps and I hear a voice. "Oi, fam."

Ricky swivels around like a startled rabbit, dropping his ball.

"Keep walking, man," I instruct Nathan and Ricky, who seem almost petrified.

Young black men wearing durags, tracksuits, and baseball caps aren't the norm in their neck of the woods.

I ignore the call and usher the boys along.

Seconds later, I hear the voice again.

"Oi, fam."

Now, I know somebody wants my attention.

"Carry on towards the car," I tell the boys as they look at each other. "Gwarn man, I be there in two seconds," I say calmly.

They begin to walk off, still with their heads facing me.

I kiss my teeth, turn around, and casually stroll towards the gang. "What's good?" I ask.

The guy who I suspect tried to get my attention takes a long pull of his spliff before blowing smoke in my direction.

"Where you from?" he asks, his thick eyebrows forming a frown as he tilts his head back. He's well-built and roughly my height, with a trim beard. As I study his face, I can just about make out a scar across his forehead that's partly concealed by his durag.

"From round here," I say, waving the smoke out of my face. "Why?"

His friend smiles as he leans forward from the car, his hands stuffed in his pockets. "Your face just looks familiar, init," he says.

His breath stinks of rum, forcing my head back.

218

"Is that it?" I say, looking at each man individually.

The guy with the durag, who appears to be the leader, waves his finger. "I swear I know your face though, akh," he says.

"Nah, you don't. And I don't know what kind of game you man got going on between you, but I'm with my nephews init, so I'ma keep it moving. Have a good day, yeah," I say as I turn to walk away.

"Wait, where you going?" I hear in a much less friendly tone. The guy who was seated stands up. He's a lot taller than I expected. Skinny. But lanky. To the point where his tracksuit stops way above the white socks around his ankles.

"Listen, none of you man know me, trust me," I say.

"Take the bass out your voice," the guy with the durag says like he's trying to assert dominion over me.

'Why has everyone gotta think they're a badman these days?'

I clench my fist tightly as I step closer to the guy with the durag, letting him and my nephews know that Rakim Morrison isn't just full of chat. He doesn't ever back down from a fight, no matter the odds stacked against him.

'If this kicks off, I know who I'm knocking out first.'

The four men surround me as if trying to intimidate me when I hear my name.

"Rakz?"

I turn my head to my left as the quartet in front of me mirrors my action.

An enormous unit of a man comes jogging towards me, and I see the guy with the durag begin to go inside himself like someone just punctured his inflated ego.

As this giant draped in a black tracksuit and pitch-black sunglasses approaches, a smile beams out from his crooked mouth.

"What the fuck, when you come home?" he says.

"I'm good, bro," I mumble, still unsure who this guy is.

219

"These man try a ting?" he cries as his expression swiftly changes. "What you man saying?" he says, turning towards the group of men who all seem to have changed their demeanour drastically.

"Nothing man was just—" begins the guy with the durag.

"—Do you know who this is?" the giant shouts as the guy with the durag looks at the floor.

Now I'm completely baffled.

The giant reads the confused look on my face and lifts his shades. "What, bro, you don't recognise me?"

I stare at him, trying to sort through the files in my memory.

He smiles as he holds a palm out. "It's Darkos. B-Wing, Tollesley Bay."

'Tollesely, Tollesely, Tollesely...' Then, finally, it clicks. "Oh shit! Darkos. Man didn't clock you without the plaits."

We share a hug as the group around me appears collectively embarrassed. Quickly, Darkos turns towards them. "Oi, you man, pay some respect. This is my nigga. Held man down when we were doing bird together years back."

And just like that, I'm flavour of the month as all the group greet me like I'm their new favourite companion.

"My man giving you problems?" Darkos asks me as he points at the guy with the durag.

I note the anxious look on the guy's face and take pity on him.

You see, I've witnessed Darkos' violent side. When I met him in prison, he was two years into an eight-stretch for three separate stabbings, and believe me, those three chaps weren't the last he used a knife on.

"Nah, he's cool," I say as I see all that bravado evaporate from Black Durag and he becomes a little boy outside the headteacher's office.

Darkos takes one look at him.

"Go shop and get me a drink, man," Darkos says, to which the boy duly obeys, before turning to me. "Youts nowadays, no manners, no respect," Darkos continues as we amble away from the gang.

I look up and see Nathan and Ricky standing by the car, frozen.

This must be like a Hollywood movie to them, American Gangster, Training Day, or something. I know I'll have to explain this to them later, but for now, I am catching up with an old friend.

"When you get out?" Darkos asks.

"Couple months ago, still."

"Boy-yoi! They're mad letting you out," he says as we both laugh.

"Member that Nigerian you smacked over the head in the gym, fam," he says as he begins cackling even harder.

"Mate..."

"All 'cause he wouldn't let you use the squat rack. You remember? You licked him with a dumbbell," he says, reminding me of something I had totally forgotten about.

We wade through old jail stories, who's back inside, who's dead, and who's got stinking rich, for a couple of minutes before I tell him I need to leave, which seems to spark some interest in him.

"What you doing with yourself now?" he asks.

"Not much, ya know, this and that."

"I'm doing rentals now, plus I got loose there as well. Best price around. You need anything, hit me up, my nigga."

"Who you working with?" I ask.

"I'm plugged in with the Albo's, my G. And my business is up and running," he says as he hands me a business card and puts his number in my phone.

'Darkos is a lot of things, but he's not a liar. If he's linked up with the Albanians like he says, he must be doing well.'

I glimpse the rose gold Rolex Daytona on his wrist and figure it must be worth thirty, thirty-five grand easy.

"That's good, my bro. I member you tellin' man about the rental ting, you made it happen. Long way from Bully Beef Sundays, alie?" I say with a smile as I pull him close for an embrace.

He laughs, and his mouth stretches wide open.

221

"For real. But on the real, anything you need my G, hit me on that number. I got you. Any car you need, I sort you at cost price, no problem. Lambo, Merc, Audi, anything you need, my G."

I nod my head as I examine the business card in my hand. "Love, my bro."

We hug once more before I go to walk off.

"Hit me up, fam," Darkos says as he backs off, beating his chest, before waving to my nephews.

I raise my hand when a thought comes to my head.

"Oi, Darkos," I say signalling for him to come back over.

"What's good?" he whispers.

"You know anything about some Turkish gang around these sides?"

He scratches his head as his shades drop back over his eyes.

"I know a couple of them still. One of their main guys just got birded off. Judge hit him with a 'twenty.' Couple others might be going down as well."

"Swear?"

"I don't know them personally like that, but I know they're all fighting to be the boss right now," Darkos shrugs. "Why, you got problems with 'em?"

"Nah, just asking."

Darkos smiles, punching me in the arm.

He sees through my lies.

"Listen, if you need machines, man can sort that too. Japanese Star Nine, 9-mills, 32s, G-locks, whatever, my bro," he says before backing away. "I'm out. Hit me up, Rakz. Good to see you, fam."

"Yeah, I'ma shout you for definite," I call as we go our separate ways.

I approach Leanne's car, and Ricky and Nathan's starstruck eyes follow me like I'm a celebrity. I just know I'm in for a journey full of questions.

But Darkos' words have given me food thought.

21

"Yo, listen, when we go inside, no talk about my bredrin outside the park, all right?"

"Yeah, yeah," Ricky says.

Nathan nods and gets out of the car as Ricky reaches for the football in the backseat. As he holds it in his hands, Ricky looks at me with an impish grin. "Uncle Rakim, you're a gangster, init?" he says.

"What, say that again?"

"You're a gangster, like, you got bare money, and you catch bodies."

As the words come out of Ricky's mouth, it shows me how detached from reality this boy really is.

"I ain't no gangster, Rick. I ain't got bare money, and I don't go around 'catching bodies.'"

He throws me a conspicuous glance.

"What'chu know about 'catching bodies' anyway? You're fourteen, fam. You need to be more worried about catching an STD."

The seriousness on my face soon wipes away his smile.

"Go inside, Nath. We're coming in a minute," I call from the window before turning back towards Ricky.

"I dunno what kinda stuff you been listening to, Rick, but take it from me, there ain't nothing cool about catching a body, yeah? All these little kids you listen to with their drill rap and all that shit, not one percent of them have even had a fight, let alone killed a man and caught a body."

I pause as I watch Ricky digest my words.

"Most of these fools are just scared little boys who've got no one around them to teach them how to be a man, so they think the way to do that is by going around tryin' to make everyone fear them. They're

223

not bad boys. They never were, and they never will be. They're just shook to be themselves in case nobody likes them. They think they need to be accepted, and the only way they know how to achieve that is by following in the footsteps of the clowns before them."

Ricky looks uneasy. I think I'm getting through to him.

"I'm tellin' you this 'cause you need to understand, being a murderer ain't nothing to boast about. There's nothing glamourous about prison. You live a good life with your fancy little en-suite up there. Imagine sharing a cell where loads of crackheads have bled, shit, and pissed, where you can hear the cockroaches and rats at night. Just because you wanted to 'catch a body.'"

Ricky's eyes expand as he moves his head away from me. He squeezes his football, clutching it like a reminder of his fortunate reality, and I feel satisfied that I've got the message across.

"You're a good boy, Rick," I say, softening my voice. "You're funny, and you got a fire in you, and one day you'll be playing in the Champions League, not spending twelve years of your life wasting away in a cell, unable to do anything for anyone. 'Cause that's where thinking that catching a body is cool gets you, you feel me?"

"Yeah, I get you," Ricky says, looking a little humiliated that he even brought it up in the first place.

"Good."

We look into each other's eyes for a moment, and then I hear my belly rumble.

"Come, man, let's go eat," I say.

We go inside, and I watch Ricky shoot upstairs as Leanne strides towards me like she's on a catwalk.

"Taylor recovered yet?" I ask, standing where the broken vase lay hours ago.

Leanne smiles and hits my chest. I can tell by her eyes she's a little tipsy. "How was your afternoon with the boys?" she asks.

"All good, man. They've grown so much. It's mad. I can't believe I've missed all these years," I say as I fall onto the sofa, and Leanne settles beside me.

"You know, Rakz. I never apologised for Taylor refusing to let us—"

"—Leave it, Lee," I say. "It's not your apology to give."

Leanne puts a hand on my shoulder.

"Well, you're here now. That's all that matters," she says.

We chat away until dinner is placed on the table. A delicious feast of seared scallops and baby spinach in a pomegranate glaze, lobster tails with chive butter, and chicken chasseur hit the spot.

I hate to admit it, but once again, Taylor pulls out his party trick.

"Thanks, that was banging," Ricky says as Taylor raises his glass like he's accepting an award before taking the plates out to the kitchen.

Leanne, Nathan, and I find comfort spread out on the U-shaped sofa, followed by Taylor, who brings over a bottle of champagne. As Taylor and Leanne snuggle up, Ricky goes off to wash his hands.

"How did you find the chicken, Rakim? To your liking?" Taylor asks.

I raise a thumb as Nathan hands me the remote control.

Scrolling through the channels, I come to The Chase. An old cellmate of mine, Leon, springs to mind, and how we used to watch this program every evening.

I put it on and sit back while Nathan taps away on his phone, and the lovebirds in the other corner treat themselves to a glass of champers.

'These lot better not start flirting in front of me, or I swear I'm gone.'

I turn up the volume to distract me from the juvenile giggling.

"Which sport is featured in the 2003 film Seabiscuit?" Bradley Walsh, the quiz show host reads.

"Horseracing," I say without hesitation.

I suck my teeth as the contestant answers incorrectly. "How d'you not know that?" I mumble.

Two more questions and I answer both correctly.

"You're actually quite good at this, Uncle Rakim," Nathan says as Ricky comes along and plonks himself next to me.

"Come on. Of course," I reply.

"What happened?" Ricky asks.

"Uncle Rakim just got three right in a row," Nathan says as Ricky gives me a congratulatory fist bump.

"Don't think your uncle's some dunce old man, ya know," I say, casting an eye over Ricky.

My words seem to have attracted the attention of Supercoon. He's seated upright now and has that conspicuous look on his face like he's intrigued.

"Three in a row, impressive," he squeaks with his pious approval.

I ignore his comment as I focus on the seventy-inch plasma on the wall that beams the final stage of the game show.

"Look, Uncle Rakim's in the zone now," Leanne says, trying to mock my concentration as she nudges Nathan with her foot.

Nathan looks at me, and I feel like I'm on a stage, as if I'm about to perform and everyone around me are the judges.

"Dad got five in a row before," Nathan goads.

"Is that right, yeah?" I say.

"Yes, I'm afraid it is," Taylor says, returning to his snarky self, brimming with arrogance.

"Don't worry. I'll set a new record," I say.

Taylor lets out an uncomfortable laugh. "No, Rakim. You won't," he says.

"You think?" I say, sizing him up with my eyes.

"Three is luck, four is form, but five... That's pure class," he says like he's quoting some spiritual guru.

I shake my head. "Whatever, man."

Leanne laughs, and Taylor's head swivels towards her. She covers her mouth in a poor attempt to conceal her sniggering as Taylor turns back to face me.

"How about we place a gentleman's bet?" Taylor asks.

'This guy's ego is insane... But fuck it, let me play along.'

"Gwarn, what you tellin' me?" I ask.

"Erm... Well, how about we say the loser washes up," Taylor says.

I kiss my teeth. "I'm not one of the boys, be serious when you're betting with me," I say.

Ricky laughs, and it automatically ups the ante.

Taylor tilts his head back and finishes the last of his drink.

"Okay, well, let's hear your proposal then."

"Let's bet on the vase," I say.

I watch the smugness drain from Taylor's face as the painful reminder of the word *vase* unsettles him.

He looks at Leanne, but all eyes are on him now. "Rah-kim," he says.

"It's Rakim."

"Apologies. I told you, forget about the vase, it's a—"

"—Five-thousand-pound Lalique. Yeah, I done the math earlier," I interject.

"Well, exactly. How could you possibly bet on—"

"—Listen, don't worry about it. I'm good for the money and suspect you are. So cut the chat. Let's do this ting. You win, I buy you a brand new one. I win, you owe me five grand."

"Yeah, that's good," Ricky shouts. "Go on, do it," he yells, egging Taylor on.

"Are you sure, Rakim? I mean, five thousand pounds is a lot of—"

"—I'm sure," I say and reach out a hand to seal the bet.

Taylor scans the room as Nathan and Ricky liven up to encourage him.

"Go on, Dad," Nathan shouts.

"I guess I'm going to have to take your money then," Taylor says as Ricky jumps up from his seat in excitement, and Taylor and I shake hands.

The game is on.

"Ite, it's two minutes each to get as many questions right as you can," I say, being clear to inform everybody of the rules.

Taylor nods as he sits back, seemingly comfortable, with one leg crossed over the other.

His arrogance offends me, but I keep my cool.

"You first," I tell him as the timer on the screen begins.

"Go on, darling," Taylor's one and only fan cheers.

"Nath, you keep scores," I say.

The room goes silent.

'Time... Starts... Now,' Bradley Walsh cries as he kicks off with an easy one.

What are birds of a feather said to do?

"Flock together," Taylor answers, getting off to a good start.

The Great British athlete, Linford Christie, was what age when he became the oldest man to win an Olympic Gold Medal in the 100 metres?

"Thirty-two, I believe," Taylor replies.

It's correct.

The third question comes quick, and Taylor answers before it's even finished being read.

'Shit.'

I watch this machine answer the following two perfectly, sending Leanne into a frenzy. By the time a minute has passed, he's already into double figures, and I begin to feel the hole in my pocket the cost of this vase is going to burn.

There are thirty seconds left when he's asked the surname of the singer, Adele.

"Atkinson," he shouts.

It's close, but it's incorrect.

"Yes," Ricky cheers discreetly, and I regain some confidence. I've got support here.

Taylor's form begins to falter as the end of his time nears. He answers the last question incorrectly, and I look at Nathan for the result.

"Time's up," the game show host cries.

"Eighteen," Nathan says as Leanne kisses Taylor on the cheek.

"Eighteen, babe, that's amazing," Leanne says.

It's an impressive score considering the three contestants on the screen managed to get only two more between them.

Taylor does his best impersonation of being humble as he slowly sips from Leanne's glass.

"You know Rakim, it's not too late to—"

"—Never that," I say, without even glancing at him.

It might be the wise thing to do, but there's no way I'm backing down now. A man always tries his best, no matter the odds.

Nathan sends me a doubtful look, but I don't let it affect me.

"Just count," I say as I prepare for my turn.

'Concentrate, man. Don't worry 'bout the score. Just keep answering.'

"Are you ready?" Bradley Walsh asks.

I feel like he's asking me directly as he turns towards the quizmaster on the screen, and I realise I've got the more onerous task of answering before the chaser does.

Seconds later, we're underway.

I make a decent start, getting the first two right, but the questions start coming thick and fast.

What is the first animal named in Webster's dictionary?

"Anteater," I call before listening to the chaser say, aardvark.

I struggle through the next six or seven questions, probably getting one or two at best.

A few more fly by, and I look at Nathan's hand next to me.

Six fingers.

That means six answers right.

With seventy seconds to go, I can feel the flatness amongst my nephews. I see Taylor reclined in his seat, studying my face. I imagine him laughing at me, telling my nephews some rubbish like, 'This is what happens if you don't go and get a job, you turn out to be a stupid criminal,' in his whiny, condescending tone.

'Nah, I ain't losing this.'

I hear the word 'snails' as I come out of my daze and call out the first word that comes to mind.

"France."

To my surprise, it's correct.

Halfway through the next question, I'm confident I know the answer. "Robert De Niro," I shout as I start to find my groove.

Again, it's correct.

I go on a decent run before getting beaten to the answer by the chaser. I look at Nathan. He's got three digits up, which must mean I'm on thirteen.

I look at the timer.

'Twenty seconds?'

I now need six correct answers in twenty seconds. The next three correct answers come and go like a race car. The words roll off my tongue, and I hear Ricky cheer again.

Five on the bounce, I'm on a roll. The momentum's with me.

Taylor suddenly moves to the edge of his chair.

'Come on, give me suttin' I know.'

My prayers are answered.

Michael Owen scored over 100 goals for which—

In unison, me and the chaser both shout, "Liverpool!"

It's correct.

"Come on," I say, unable to hide my excitement. Eight seconds remain on the clock as the next question comes.

A poult is the young of what flightless bird?

I hear 'flightless bird' and claw at something from the depths of my memory.

"Turkey," I yell.

The chaser procrastinates, and I wish I could jump inside the TV and slap him.

With four seconds left, he answers.

It's right.

Ricky's up out of his seat as I sense the fear in Taylor. Leanne puts a hand on him, but he brushes it away. He's as focused on these last four seconds as I am. It's him or me. Last chance saloon. Dying embers of the World Cup Final.

'*Please, God, let me get this one right.*' For some reason, I feel God's on my side.

The question comes.

"How many people sit on a jury in a UK crown court trial?"

I nearly freeze.

All those days spent on trial, standing in that dock; the loneliest place on earth, avoiding the cold glares of those jury members as they analysed my every move, and now here I am, being asked how many people sat together and decided my fate over a decade ago.

"Twelve," I cry just before the chaser can answer.

The time runs out, and I turn to Nathan.

"You won, man, you won," he cries as he gives me a high-five.

"Wait, how many I get?" I ask.

"Nineteen," an ecstatic Nathan says.

I look at Taylor, who looks utterly shocked. I swear to God you could land a Boeing 747 between his open jaw. Leanne rubs his back as if nursing a wound.

The only thing hurting him right now, though, is his pride.

"Nah, Uncle Rakim, you went in," Ricky says as he pats my shoulder.

I stand up and walk over to Taylor. Anybody would've thought he'd just lost his mother, not a little quiz.

"Unlucky, big man."

Taylor puffs his cheeks out and shakes his head.

"I accept cash, cheques, and all major credit and debit cards," I say with a wink as I almost watch the steam hiss out of his ears.

Leanne sucks in her lips, trying to hide her urge to laugh, and I sense it's about to be a frosty evening for the pair of them.

Still, I just can't ignore the opportunity to rub it in.

"Expensive night for you, aye T? Lost a vase, lost five grand, and now you've lost to a criminal. Can't get much worse for you, can it?"

He cracks the falsest smile I've ever seen as Ricky laughs his heart out.

"Ah, Dad, man, what happened?" Nathan asks.

Taylor sighs as he rises to his feet.

"The better man won," he says reluctantly.

I turn my head at such speed I nearly sprain my neck.

'Did he just say 'the better man?'

I never thought the day would come when Taylor admitted someone was better than him, especially a thug like me.

"Well played, Rakim," he says, offering me his hand. We stand opposite each other, and finally, after all these years, I genuinely feel like I've earned this man's respect.

"Don't mention it," I say.

I shake his hand and walk past him, still being applauded by my nephews.

"Lee, I'll take this as a down payment," I say, reaching over and helping myself to the near-full bottle of champagne.

"Ooh, Rakim, go on then. Well done," Leanne concedes. I give her a wink and turn towards my nephews. "Boys, I'm gonna keep it movin'. Remember what I told you, man, yeah?"

Nathan and Ricky both look at me like I'm speaking a foreign language.

"Brothers stick together, you feel me?"

"Oh yeah, that, yeah we will," Ricky says as Nathan nods his head.

"And you, Rick, keep kicking ball, yeah?" I tell him as I head for the front door, passing Supercoon, who stands with his hands in his pockets like a lost soul in his own house.

I guess he thought us prisoners just spend our time living it up at the taxpayers' expense and not learning anything.

'Oh well, making assumptions about things you don't know is a sure way to remain ignorant.'

The words are on the tip of my tongue, but I refrain—no need to kick a man while he's down.

"You want the car?" Leanne asks, and I gladly accept.

"Drive safe, Rakz," she says to me as she hands me the keys, then gives me a tight hug.

"Course."

"Oh, and tell Nia I said Hiiii," Leanne calls childishly as I put a hand on the doorknob.

One final goodbye, and I close the door, much happier and a little wealthier than I was this morning.

22

Sitting in Leanne's car with a bottle of champagne in my hand, I think about my victory over Taylor.

It may seem insignificant to most people, but you must understand that all the men in my family are considered failures, me included. Whereas Taylor is the complete opposite. A black man just a few years older than me. He's professional, and educated, runs his own software company, and is also a successful property developer.

So, when he and Leanne finally got together, it was like the arrival of the Messiah. Sent to emancipate our family from the wretchedness that life had in store for us.

Taylor and Leanne had known each other from schooldays, and he'd always had a thing for her. However, their lives took very different trajectories. They always kept in contact, but by the time they rekindled, I was already a couple of years into my sentence. And coming from a life where people settle arguments with emails, Taylor was sickened to learn of my crime.

Every visit Leanne dragged him along to, he looked at me like I was less than a piece of shit on his shoe until one day, he made the executive decision that his family would no longer be visiting me. And for all these years, I've tolerated him, for Leanne's sake.

But after defeating the one thing he holds dear, his intellect, I know, and he knows that I know, that being a prisoner, or a murderer doesn't make you any less of a man. Not in any way, shape, or form.

A text comes through from Deontay, and for the third or fourth time today, he reminds me we need more product.

I phone Scribz.

To my surprise, the phone rings.

234

It's not long until he answers.

"Yo, Scribz," I say, turning the music down in the car.

"Yo," Scribz says.

"Wa gwarn, my bro. Man's been tryin' to get hold of you for the longest while."

"Yeah, it's been mad in here still."

"Wa gwarn?"

Scribz sucks his teeth.

"Chat to me, fam."

"Man had to kick that wasteman Devonte out the cell, init."

"Kick him out? Why? What happened?"

"Cuz... Imagine, couple weeks back, I clocked some of my things had gone missing. One of my jumpers, a CD, then a vape, then a couple tins of mackerel."

"What, and you think Devonte teef'ed your tings?"

"Bro, I was like you—surprised. He confessed about the mackerel; said he ate it when I was sleeping and said he'd put it back when canteen comes. But then I asked him about man's CD, the jumper, and my vape, and he said he didn't know, so I allowed him again. He replaced the fish, so I thought, cool. Maybe I lent the CD out and forgot, and maybe my jumper's still with the laundry man, minor, they'll turn up. Then imagine..."

"What?"

"Man came back to the cell one day and find this Devonte yout' going through my things."

"Swear down. What did he say?"

Scribz voice shoots up a few octaves.

"He didn't say anything. Man got it cracking with him on site."

"Like that? So, where's he now?"

"Bro, he moved wing like a pussy."

'Rah, man. I thought I knew Devonte... But then I thought I knew Jamal.'

235

Maybe those years in prison have given me a warped sense of reality, taking people at face value, forgetting their past that ultimately led them to being behind bars in the first place.

Scribz continues deploring Devonte's actions for a while before we get to the reason for my call, the product.

"I need more, asap, Scribz. This ting's going well. Man's got my worker running through it like water."

Scribz exhales, and I imagine him puffing out his cheeks as he drops a bombshell.

"Bro, I can't even get no more," he says.

"What d'you mean?"

"My connect's dry."

"Well, when's he getting more?"

"I don't know. It's peak right now."

"Ain't you got no one else?" I ask.

"C'mon. If I did, I'd hook you up straight away."

"Man need that like yesterday. Nitties are gonna go cop elsewhere."

"Chill, Rakz. Man will sort something," Scribbler says, but his words do little to ease my concerns.

"Just do it soon as. I beg you. If your guy needs the cash up front, I got that," I tell Scribz.

"What... You got eighteen bags to put down for a half?"

'With Taylor's five grand and the money I've saved so far, I can probably just about scrape that together, and if I can, I know man's seeing over thirty grand profit off that, easy.'

"Yeah, I just need the food," I say.

"Yeah...? Okay," Scribz replies, sounding surprised. "I'ma try sort suttin', init."

"Asap, my bro," I urge him.

"Yeah, yeah. You good otherwise, though?"

I relax back into the leather headrest.

"Man's straight. I was just kickin' ball with my nephews and that."

"I hear you," Scribz says before pausing.

"My bad about the other day. The Jamal thing threw me off still."

"Don't watch it, man. It threw me off, too. I bugged out. Backed a whole bottle of Remy."

"I hear you."

"It's mad knowing he's gone."

"Trust me," Scribz mumbles.

The conversation goes silent while we both silently mourn.

Then in true Scribz fashion, he brightens the mood.

"What you saying though, did you pattern things with your girl, yeah? Lay her down and give her that sexual healing?"

"I'm about to find out now."

"Ah yeah, what you gonna Facetime man, introduce me to this likkle spice?"

"Wa'am for you, easy yourself."

"You shook I'm gonna take your Mrs?"

"Brudda, you couldn't if you tried."

"What, no pics?"

"Oi, brudda, chill out."

Scribz lets out a deafening cackle, and I know exactly why.

"You proper like this one, init," he says before laughing some more. "Rah, man like Rakz all boo'd up and that."

I shake my head. "Listen, put yourself to use and go sort some grub for man, you feel me?"

"Say no more," Scribz says before letting his laugh simmer.

I'm just about to disconnect the call when I remember something else. "Yo Scribz, you know anything about some Turks from round these sides."

There's no reply for a couple of seconds, but when Scribz comes to the phone, I sense his energy shift.

"Not too tight. Wa gwarn?" he asks.

"They causing problems for our business. I need some info on them. I thought you might have heard something."

"Nah, not even, but if you need me to put in some work on anyone, just say the word, you know me, cuz. I'll stab a man up, lightwork," he says.

"Not yet. Just look out for any Turks on the wing and let me know if you hear anything."

"Say no more, fam."

"Ite. I'm gone. Soon come, my brother. Oh, and I beg you get us some food by tomorrow."

"I'm on it, man."

I disconnect the call, pick up the bottle of champagne, and exit the car.

The evening mist casts a scenic backdrop across the sky as the sandstone orange sunset blends with the night's grey and dark blue hues, and two moments in time merge into one.

It's that time in the late evening when the body synchronises with mother nature and slowly unwinds. My only craving for the next few hours is to relax and get close to Nia.

As I approach her front gate, I think of all the nights I've spent laying in those rigid bunks in those nasty cells, picturing this kind of evening.

I'm grateful I'm free to have these nights, but as I reflect, I feel sad for Scribbler. Through all his banter and jokes about Nia, I know deep down how he wishes he could do what I'm about to do tonight. I know what he'd give to cosy up for just one night with a girl he cared about.

Nia's gate screeches as I close it behind me and walk up to the front door. I knock on the door, and after a few seconds, Nia answers.

As soon as I see her standing in the doorway, I smile.

Her coffee-coloured skin glows like stardust as she plants one hand on her hip and the other rests on the frame of the door. She leans her head to the side, and the silky pink headscarf that covers her hair moves with her.

"You not lettin' me in?" I ask.

"I thought this is what we do now, isn't it? Stand and talk on doorsteps, right?" she says as her eyes narrow.

My smile turns to a laugh. "You for real?"

She doesn't answer.

"Oh, you for real, for real?"

She remains silent.

"So, what, we gonna stand here all night?"

"Maybe," she shrugs.

I nod my head slowly with a purposeful pinch of sarcasm. "Okay. I guess you're not gonna want this, then?" I say as I reveal the bottle of Dom Pérignon from behind my back.

I see the edges of her mouth creep up. Then a little dimple. "We still doing this on-the-doorstep ting then?" I say.

She leans in to kiss me, and I put a hand on her hip, just above the red low-cut shorts she wears to bed. They leave little for the imagination, and I'm already away with my thoughts when she snatches the bottle from my hand.

"If you think I'm that easy, you really don't know me," she whispers in my ear before returning to her stance in the doorway.

"Ah, what's up?" I ask.

Right now, I just want to kiss her.

"You have to ask... Really?" she says.

I sigh.

"What, when you called earlier? I was in the park with the boys. They were about..."

From the blank expression on Nia's face, I can tell she's not interested in my *excuse*. "There's nothing wrong with calling me back to tell me that, you know," she says softly.

Her words seem more like advice than unnecessary admonishment, so I take hold of Nia's hand.

"Ite, look. I'm sorry I hung up on you. My bad. Please, can I come in?"

She looks me up and down as if to evaluate the sincerity of my apology. Then, seeing she's undecided, I gently cup her chin and meet her eyes. "I'm sorry I hanged up the phone on you."

Satisfied, she steps aside and allows me to enter.

She closes the door behind me and directs me into the living room, where I lie down and feel at home right away.

Minutes later, Nia enters the room holding two glasses containing champagne. "There you go," she says as she hands me a glass.

"Thanks."

My eyes follow her to the armchair adjacent to the sofa, and I study her as she takes a sip.

"What, no toast tonight, nah?"

She shakes her head.

I place my glass on the table behind my head and sit up straight. "What's wrong, Ni?"

"Nothing."

"Nah, I ain't buyin' that. What's wrong?"

I slide across the sofa to get a little closer to her.

"This ain't because I had to cut our chat short earlier, alie?" I say, leaning forward.

Nia runs her finger around the rim of her glass as her lips move to the side.

"No, it's not that, Rakim."

"Then what?" I ask. "You know you can tell me anything, Ni."

She looks up at me.

"You sure?" she says, and now she really has my mind running.

'What if she's found out about me being in prison...?'

I want to reach for my drink, but I refrain. "Yeah, you know you can," I say, trying to appear casual.

She nods her head.

"Well, it is kind of about earlier," she begins.

"Wa gwarn?" I ask as my mind settles a bit.

She flicks her hair and takes another gulp of champagne, sounding her approval. "You see when I called you."

"Yeah."

"When you hanged up?"

"Yeah."

"Well, you kinda didn't."

"What d'you mean?"

"I mean, you forgot to hang up. You didn't end the call."

I pause for a second.

My brain does that thing where it goes into panic mode, trying to frantically scramble around for any information that could land me in hot water.

'What was I saying earlier when she called? Come on, man. Think.'

"Go on," I say.

"Well, I know I shouldn't have, but I'll admit, I listened to your conversation."

I sense Nia's shame, but as her eyes remain on me, I can't help but think she's sizing me up, examining my reaction, hoping I give something away.

I remain poker-faced. She breaks eye contact with me, and I can see she feels as guilty as she sounds. As she bites her lip, I feel the energy in the room shift.

I'm now in control.

"You spied pon man?" I say.

Nia rolls her eyes.

"I wouldn't call it spying as such, but yes, I kind of... Slightly... Maybe... Just a little bit, heard you talking."

I shake my head. "Already, you don't trust man?"

Nia denounces my words with one look. "No, nothing like that, Rakim."

I sit back and get comfortable, realising I have nothing to worry about.

"Well, you were listening to my private conversation, alie? I mean, I don't know about you, but I'd call that eavesdropping."

Nia puts out a hand as if to try to rebut my accusation. "No, I wouldn't say eavesdropping... I'd more call it—"

"—Call it what?" I say as I watch Nia crack an awkward smile.

241

"Okay, I was eavesdropping. I apologise," Nia says, bowing her head.

"I didn't hear you. I beg you say that again?"

"Don't push it. You got your apology."

All smiles, I sample my drink, and I'm hit with a hint of cream and coffee. "So, what part of my conversation was so interesting you had to eavesdrop on me?" I ask as the champagne gives me a taste of the life Supercoon lives.

"I just heard you talking to Leanne's boys. Giving them a little speech," Nia says.

She brings her knees to her chest as she interlocks her fingers just below her kneecaps.

"Oh yeah, they were fighting. I swear they beef over anything. I don't know why they can't just get on. I would've loved to have a brother, growing up, one year apart as well. Instead, I get an older sister. Imagine when we were beefing, all the—"

It's only when I look up, I notice Nia's lost in her own world.

"Yo, what's up?" I ask, reaching to touch her leg.

"I never told you about my brother, did I?" she says.

"Yeah, you're little brother. You said you and him don't get along no more."

"Not him."

"You got another brother?"

"Had..."

"Oh..."

There's an awkward pause.

I'm unsure how to respond. Slowly I sip my champagne awaiting an invitation to provide Nia some solace.

"What happened to him?" I ask tentatively.

Nia breathes deeply.

"He died," she says. "Car crash."

I shake my head.

'Life, man.'

"He was my older brother," she goes on. "His name was Trevan. He was two years older than me, and today's exactly three years since he died," Nia says as she appears to fight that choked-up feeling.

'There was me thinking she was just being petty... I'm so stupid.' I put my glass down and run my palm across Nia's leg cosseting her with my undivided attention.

"Excuse me," she says before continuing. "He loved motorbikes, especially that Ninja Kawasaki, I think it's called. Anyhoo, one day, just like any other, he was out on his bike, and I don't know what he was doing, probably up to no good, but I got a call saying he had a crash."

"Rah," I say to fill the pause.

"He died at the scene."

"Sorry," I say.

"It's okay. It was his fault. He was to blame. He was going well over the limit, and a driver pulled out and didn't see him. Then just like that, he crashed and flew off his bike, hit his head, and died instantly."

Just as I thought I was shredding my guilt, a reminder of Jamal hits me like a sucker punch.

Nia takes another sip of her drink, and as much as she portrays herself to be over her brother's death, I see her pain. That pain of losing someone close never truly goes away. It's always there, niggling at the back of your brain. You may think you've forgotten about it, or you've moved on and come to terms with things, but then one conversation, one song, one smell, and you're right back where you were the day you got the news.

"Were you two close?" I ask.

"Erm... Sort of. But not like Trevan and Daniel."

"Daniel, your likkle brother, yeah?"

"Yeah. Those two were like best friends, always winding each other up and messing around. Trevan was like a God to Daniel," Nia says as she shows me a picture of her two brothers together on her phone.

"This is when Daniel was four."

"He's big for four."

"Yeah, when Trevan died, though, he took it hard," Nia says, pausing to compose herself.

"I hear you."

"To be honest, he just started to go off the rails. Starting going out all the time, not coming home until the morning, not answering my calls, getting into fights at school, and things just escalated."

It's a story I've heard a thousand times. The story of so many teenagers. A story that hits home way more than Nia can ever imagine.

"Me and my mum tried to talk to him, put him into classes like swimming and boxing, but he just wasn't interested. He wouldn't listen to anyone. He just became so angry all the time. All he wanted to do was hang around with his friends, smoke weed and get into trouble," she continues.

Nia shakes her head as she pulls a sleeve over her hand.

"When we moved here, like five years ago, when Mum went back to Barbados, I thought things would be so different from how they turned out. I thought we'd all just live together and everything would be fun. I'd cook meals for both of them, Trevan would do up the house a bit, put in a new bathroom for me, maybe build a little gym in the shed outside, but none of that transpired. Instead, Trevan ended up dead, and Daniel ended up in prison."

Nia dabs her sleeve against her eye, and I take her hand, caressing my thumb back and forth across her delicate skin. As I do, the heartache she percolates reignites my own traumas and I'm taken back to my first prison visit, sitting on remand awaiting trial.

Mum and Leanne sat across the table from me. They brought some clothes, and we discussed what the future would hold. Mum was strong, steadfast in her belief that God would grant mercy upon me, but Leanne...? Leanne crumbled. She couldn't bear to see her little brother in such a place. She tried her best to keep it together, but I guess the reality sunk in near the end of the visit that this could well be my life for the next twenty years because she broke down and sobbed like a baby.

"It ain't your fault Ni," I say. "Your brother's had a hard time, but *you* didn't force him to do anything that would send him to prison. We all make our choices in life, and, good or bad, we gotta live with them."

"I know, Rakim. I do. It's just when I heard you earlier on the phone, the way you spoke with your nephews, you just reminded me of how Trevan used to speak to Daniel. What you said was exactly what they needed to hear. I know them boys love you. I bet they hang on to every word you say and believe anything you tell them...."

Nia sees my discomfort at accepting her approbation.

"You don't even need to tell me, Rakim. I know they do. Because in their eyes, you're exactly who they wanna be. You're strong, funny, caring, humble, and wise, and they're lucky to have you."

'Rah.' That's the most compliments I've heard about myself since I was a child.

"I try, init," I say, wanting to allow Nia's praise to saturate my soul, but she only knows half the story. She doesn't know what I'm capable of... What I've done.

Nia wipes a tear that's sneaked out the corner of her eye. "That's the only reason I listened to your conversation earlier, Rakim. I'm not crazy or anything. You just reminded me of my big brother. He always had the best advice for Daniel."

"I know, Ni," I say, gently squeezing her hand as she takes another sip of her champagne.

"You said your brother's just a teenager. That means there's still time for him to change." My words do little to change Nia's doubtful expression, but I persist. "Trust me, Ni. Loads of boys go through this likkle stage. He's still got time to turn his life around."

"But how? He won't even talk to me."

"When was the last time you spoke properly?"

"Ages ago. He was getting into too much trouble, so I said he couldn't stay here anymore. We had an argument, and he packed his stuff and left. The next thing I know, I get a phone call saying he's in

245

prison. I tried the tough love approach and told him, 'You made your bed now lie in it,' and 'til this day, I wish I never."

"How long did he get?" I say, hoping this kid still has a chance. "It couldn't have been that bad, right?"

"It's not that, Rakim."

"What is it then?"

"He hates me."

"Why you say that?"

"He does."

"How d'you know if you ain't spoken to him?"

Nia laughs, but it's far from a joyous one. Tears begin to fall down her face as she breaks away from my hand to stop the streaming. "It's not like I haven't tried. I called up the prison to visit him weeks ago."

"Yeah?"

"He's out... He's out, and he didn't even tell me!"

I search for a comforting response. "Maybe, he just needs some time, Ni. Prison's not the easiest place."

Nia looks at me, and I realise that came out way too casually.

"No, he's been out for months. I found out where he was staying, and I went there. Rakim, it was some nasty, run-down flat. It was disgusting. I brought him food, I apologised, I even begged him to come home, and he just slammed the door in my face. He would rather stay there than come back home with me."

Grateful, my comment went over Nia's head, I keep quiet.

She shakes her head. "I wish I had never told him that."

"You can't change what's happened," I sigh.

"I wish I could, though. I wish I could just blink and have him back here. He doesn't belong in that horrible place. It's not for him."

I take Nia by the hand and gently pull her towards me. She sits across my lap, and I wrap my arms around her waist, holding her tight like the trophy she is. I lift her chin and look deep into her eyes, trying my best to soothe her pain.

"Look, Ni. All those things you said about me, about me being wise, caring, humble, you're all of that and more. Daniel's lucky to have a sister like you, trust me. That ain't just coming from your man. That's coming from a man who knows about having a big sister."

I wipe a tear from Nia's face as she sniffs hard. A smile emerges, and combined with her blushing cheeks, it brings a whole new radiance to her.

"My man, yeah?" she says.

"Yeah, *your man*."

Laughter bubbles from her throat like someone who has landed her biggest crush. "So, do I get a say in this?" she asks.

I lean my head back, securing my grip around her waist. "Hmmm, not really. No."

Her laughter bursts out as she leans towards me, and I finally get a proper kiss.

It's worth the wait. She just tastes so good.

She pulls away slowly to reach for her glass, and I continue. "Sometimes, Ni, you just gotta let a man make his own mistakes. I know you love your brother, and I know right now, you might not think it, but trust me, he loves you too. He's probably just hurting. Probably just wants to prove you wrong. Prove that he can make it on his own. Us men are stupid like that sometimes. Give him time. He'll come round, you feel me?"

Nia cleans her face with her sleeve, and even on her worst day, she's still a clear ten.

"Maybe you're right," she says.

"I mean, come on. Who can resist your charm, anyway?" I say, leaning in to kiss her once again.

23

Nia's zest for early escapades has given me the house to myself for the morning, and after a shower and a generous portion of cornmeal porridge, I spend the next few hours waiting for a call from Scribz.

'I need to get back on this.'

Sitting around not making any money isn't gonna get me to The Gambia.

By the time it reaches one o'clock, the anxiety starts to kick in. Deontay's already called me twice this morning. His eagerness to get to work is usually a welcome trait, but when we have no product, his name flashing on my phone screen annoys me.

Another half an hour passes, and I decide I can't wait any longer for Scribz's call. I text Nia telling her I've left and to let her brother sort his own life out before making my way back to my house. Engrossed in my phone, I barely even look up as the sun wraps me in her invisible blanket of warmth.

"C'mon Scribz, tell me you sorted something," I say with my phone pressed against my ear.

The phone rings and rings, but nobody answers.

I try again, but I'm met with the same result.

'Fuck's sake.'

Just as I'm about to cross the road, I hear my name.

"Yo, Rakz, where you been?"

I look up and see Deontay. "Man's been belling you, broski. You cool?" he says.

"What you doing here?" I say as I cross the road.

"I couldn't get through to you, so I rolled by to make sure you're good after the other night."

I spud him as I scan the vicinity like a burglar's lookout. "You can't be coming round 'ere out of the blue. This is my yard, not some rasclart youth centre."

"Fam, these are my ends. I used to—"

"—Are you fuckin' listenin'?" I say, raising my voice.

Deontay instantly closes his mouth.

"I don't care if these are your ends. You can't be comin' round 'ere unannounced, d'you understand?"

"My bad," Deontay mumbles as he looks at the ground. I see his scooter parked by my gate, and now the excitement in him seems to have disappeared, I relax a little.

'I hope he didn't see me come out of Nia's.'

Deontay's a wanted man. The last thing I want is anyone following him to this road. If they find out where I live, it won't be long until they discover where Nia rests her head. And I'll die before I allow anything to happen her.

Moping around like he's just been grounded, Deontay reaches for his scooter. "Hit me when you got the re-up init," he mutters, barely bothering to look in my direction, let alone make eye contact.

He's about to leave when I put a hand on his shoulder. "Oi, listen. Look a man in the face when you talk to him, especially when you say goodbye. You never know. It might be the last time you see him," I say, repeating a line a wise old man once told me a long time ago.

"My bad for just showing up randomly, broski."

I study Deontay from head to toe, and a smile comes to my face.

"Tracky looks good, fam," I say.

"You think?"

I nod my head. "Yeah, the cap, too," I say, tugging at the brim. "It's cold. Man's got good taste, alie?"

Deontay laughs. "It's all right still, I won't lie."

"*About all right.*" I suck my teeth. "You hungry?" I ask Deontay, who's still hovering over his scooter like he's in some sort of hurry to leave.

"I'm not gonna lie. I ain't even eaten today."

249

"You can't keep doing that. You gotta eat, man," I say, knowing this won't be the last time I repeat myself. "Go shop and get suttin' to eat, yeah," I say, handing him a twenty-pound note.

"Ite, broski."

"And grab me a couple fried dumplings too."

Deontay flicks up his hood and whizzes off to collect our food.

Once back in my house, I make a green tea and try Scribz again.

Still, there's no answer.

I sit down on my sofa and empty my pockets. As I take out my phone, I feel a small piece of card. I pull it out and read the writing on it.

Prestige Car Hire.

"Darkos."

'*He said he's got the best product in town. Maybe he's the solution to my problems.*'

Now, I know Darkos, but I don't know him if that makes sense. I mean, we spent time together in prison, but that was years ago, and I didn't even know he existed before I met him in HMP Tollesley Bay. One thing I can say is that he's always been a stand-up guy, but lately, my confidence in judging people's character has taken a few blows.

I sit there for the next few minutes, fiddling with the business card, typing the phone number into my phone, then deleting it.

'*Scribz is gonna think I went behind his back if I get product off Darkos. And how do I know Darkos' product is any good? He says it is, but then he ain't gonna say it's shit, is he? What about if he tries to bump me? That's gonna cause a whole new set of dramas.*'

Thoughts galore run through my brain until I eventually decide to call Darkos. There's not much general chit-chat. I tell him what I need, and he gives me a time and location. I end the call and look at the time on my phone. I've got an hour to make the journey to a café on the other side of south London.

I wait for Deontay to return before breaking the good news to him. "We're getting the re-up, so hurry up, cab will be here soon."

"Swear down? Finally, man," he says as he punches the air.

We sit down together while we devour our food, and I can almost see Deontay calculating his impending wages in his head.

I finish the last of my dumplings and order Deontay to wash his hands before we leave.

'I hope this runs smoothly.'

Darkos spoke genuine enough on the phone, but just one thing bothers me as I put my trainers on. He told me to be sure to take a cab or come on foot. Maybe it's just a cautious approach, maybe he's wary of me, or maybe it's just how he does business, but it's an unusual request. And unfamiliarity in my line of work breeds suspicion, which is far from the feeling you want when you're carrying nearly twenty grand in cash and meeting a seriously violent, unstable man.

Ping comes down the stairs, and as I wave goodbye, a part of me feels envious of his life. Not jealous in an evil way, where I want what he's got, but more a deep sense of curiosity.

'My man lives a proper simple life. Just goes to uni, work, comes home, and plays computer games.'

I stand in the hallway, wondering what kind of person I would be had I chosen a similar life to Ping instead of dodging death and meeting up with bookey youts to do drug deals.

A text from Darkos brings my mind back to the task at hand. 'Come alone,' it reads.

I tighten the shoulder straps on my rucksack and take one last look in the mirror. I can't deny I have a bad feeling about this, but it's too late to back out now. I need product, and I need it today. Caution's a luxury I can't afford right now.

Deontay returns from the bathroom, and as he comes down the stairs, I shelve my worries. "You ready?" I ask.

"Yeah, yeah."

"Cool, let's go," I say, and we make our way to the cab together.

24

I arrive at Sunrise Café ten minutes early.

Deontay and I get out of the cab, and I tell him to wait across the road at a bus stop.

This area is teeming with life. Pedestrians fill the streets while cars and vans sit tightly congested on the opposite side of the road like a neatly stacked set of dominoes. Bicycles fly past me, and the smell of raw fish clogs the air as I scan the dozens of shops, from fishmongers to supermarkets to clothes shops to bookmakers and funeral directors.

With my hands gripping the straps of my rucksack, I cross the road. Sandwiched between an off licence and a hardware store, Sunrise Cafe is a small humble establishment.

As I enter the café, I feel a little more relaxed. This doesn't feel like the setting for a robbery or an ambush. It's far too busy.

I walk across the laminated flooring, passing unsuspecting diners as I look around for Darkos. He's not here, so I take a seat and wait.

I study the artwork on the wall. Some framed watercolour paintings of London in the early 1900s. I'm there for about five minutes, seeing if I can work out what area each one is depicting when I sense someone next to me.

I look up, and to my surprise, it's Mr Durag from outside the park yesterday. No attitude today, he sits down and signals for me to hand him the rucksack.

This isn't how I usually do business, handing over the money before even seeing the product, but when in Rome, do as the Romans do.

Keeping my eyes firmly locked on this guy, I take a plastic bag out of my rucksack and pass it over.

He slides a set of car keys across the table.

"Wait five minutes, then come out, turn right, then first right again," he says.

Then as quickly as he arrived, he vanishes.

I call Deontay, who is keeping watch from across the road. He confirms the guy got in a vehicle and left in a hurry, which has my heart doing somersaults.

I wait five minutes and not a second longer before following the directions. On the second right turn, the reason Darkos told me to come by foot or cab becomes apparent.

A Porsche Panamera sits twenty metres ahead of me. By the logo on the keys, I know it's for me. It's the only Porsche on the road.

I press the key button, and its lights spring to life. I open the car and, on the backseat, lies a duffle bag.

I open it, and instantly I thank God.

It turns out, Darkos is more than a man of his word. There's double the amount of product that I requested.

As I bask in the smell of new leather, I open the glove compartment and read the front page of the handbook. Porsche Panamera Sport Turismo V8 GTS. Now I'm not gonna lie. I have no idea what the letters and numbers at the end of this car's description mean. My guess is that they're something to do with the engine, but either way, I'm unbothered... This car is bad!

The next few days, I spend grafting customers with deals and bargains while roaring around with Deontay in the passenger seat, listening to all my old favourite rappers. Juelz Santana, Tupac, Stacks Bundles, and Cormega, all blast from the speakers, but one, in particular, has me feeling like I'm truly back in my zone.

Styles P comes on, and I'm transported back through time to the Rakim I was before I went away. The old Rakim, a figurehead in this neighbourhood, was a confident young man loved by those who knew him and feared by those who didn't.

Darkos' product proves to be a revelation, and within three days, Deontay and I are selling more crack and heroin than we ever have. As we fly around in this racecar, making good money at the cost of a few hundred pounds a week, it feels like a bargain only a man who has lost his freedom can truly appreciate.

I can tell Deontay feels like a star, but to tell the truth, the main reason I'm grateful for this car isn't even for my benefit or his.

While I was alone in Nia's bedroom the other morning, I took the liberty of going through one of her drawers. Not in a creepy way, far from that, but since she eavesdropped on my conversation, I thought it was only appropriate that I made things equal.

Amongst a few keepsake photos of her grandparents and some old jewellery, I found a provisional licence which showed her date of birth— 26th July 1993, which means it's her birthday on Saturday.

As I wait at a traffic light, I text Leanne who confirms she's handled the reservation I asked her to make this morning. She also says she's transferred my winnings from her husband. Nia will be in for a surprise when she's driven in style to a plush restaurant in central London this weekend, and once she's blown away by my efforts, I'll find a convenient time to slip in my past.

I ease off the accelerator as I turn the car into a side road that branches off the High Road. Deontay raps along to his new favourite song, My Life, thinking he's the modern-day Styles P as he puts it on repeat for the fourth time.

"Tune's cold, alie," I say, happy to have educated him about music after he tried to play some millennial drill rubbish.

I park the car, and we take a short walk to my beloved taco place.

"Rah, sun's hella bright, fam," I say, squinting against the rays.

"That's why you need stunners like this, my guy," Deontay says, pointing at the jet-black sunglasses that conceal his eyes.

I shake my head. "Why you always got the badman look on?"

"What you talking about?" Deontay smirks.

"Brudda, you know what I'm talking about. You're always in black this, black that, black every'ting, like you're going to war. Now you got them black Yardie shades on lookin' like Morpheus from Matrix."

"Don't hate. Man looks suave, cuz," he says, pretending to swipe some dirt off his shoulder.

I roll my eyes.

We turn the corner and nearly bump into two young women.

"Woah, woah, easy," I say as I narrowly evade one of the girls, brushing her handbag as I do.

One of them gasps as she brings her hands to her chest.

"Sorry, I never saw you there," I say, catching a glimpse of her slicked baby hairs. Her eyes hide behind a pair of Fendi sunglasses that rest under two meticulously threaded eyebrows.

"It's okay," she says as her nose stud sparkles in the light.

Her friend giggles, and they both continue along.

"Oh my days, she's peng," Deontay mutters.

From the back of the two girls, I can see they both have good figures. One is wrapped in a zesty orange dress that hugs her skin like it's never letting go.

The other looks older from behind, she's more rounded, and her high ponytail plummets far down, boasting sunset-golden accents amongst the curtain of luscious ebony-black curls that bounce against her shoulder blades. I follow her body past a shapely waistline to her rich ochre-coloured legs that look richened by today's sunshine.

"Which one you talkin' 'bout?" I ask.

"The one in the orange, she's peng," Deontay says.

"Gwarn, talk to her then, bro."

I glint at a window across the road like I always do when I pass the barbershop, checking for Clinton.

"Nah, it's cool," Deontay says.

"What...? You scared or suttin'?"

"Nah, not even," he cries.

But it's no use. He knows I see through him.

I burst into laughter, which probably doesn't help his cause as it draws more attention to us, skylarking like two idle tourists on the pavement, letting dozens of folks pass us by.

"Just go holler at her," I encourage him.

Deontay scans the vicinity, and I won't lie, he looks slightly rattled.

"Yo, babes," he calls out, and I swear I nearly die.

The girls don't even flinch, let alone turn around.

I put a palm over my face and shake my head. "Brudda, seriously?"

"What?" he says.

"Is that how you approach women?"

Deontay smirks, doing his utmost to hide his embarrassment. "What's wrong with that?" he shrugs.

I suck my teeth.

"You can't approach women like that and think you're gonna get somewhere, cuz."

"They're just stoosh lighteys, man."

"Nah, it's you, bro. Shoutin' at them like they're your bredrins on the block. You can't talk to women like that."

"Ah, allow it. You sound like my sister, man."

I reach down to grab a tube of lip gloss from the ground. "Yeah? Well, your sister sounds wise. Maybe you should listen to her."

"Whatever. All of a sudden, you're Aunty Rakim, yeah?" Deontay says, waving his fingers like he's casting a spell.

"You fool," I say, snatching his sunglasses from his face. "Watch and learn, man."

Placing Deontay's shades on my head, I let the tips of the temples rest behind my ears as the pads sit comfortably just above my hairline. I roll my sleeves up a tad, and quickly throw a piece of gum in my mouth.

I take a light jog over to the two girls, who are probably about fifty yards down the road by now. I'm aware I might have my work cut out after Deontay's juvenile attempt at courting, but I don't mind a challenge. Like I said, a man always tries his best, no matter the odds.

"Excuse me," I say as I reach the two girls.

They turn around in unison, and I'm quite impressed. Deontay's got good taste. Orange Dress is pretty. She's got a little Coolie twang going on. She's a lot younger than me, but for his age group, she's a spice.

"How you doing?" I ask as the older girl takes a protective step in front of Orange Dress.

"We're fine," the older girl says, looking me up and down. "You?" Her eyebrows rise, and behind the tint of her shades, I can see a set of fierce eyes.

"I think you dropped this," I say, extending my hand that holds the lip gloss.

Orange Dress looks down at her open bag before her eyes return to me. "Oh, thank you," she says, all cute and innocent.

"Your eyes are beautiful, by the way. What colour are they?" I ask her.

She smiles. "Erm, brown."

"What's your name?" I ask as her bodyguard jumps in.

"Her name is Natasha," she says, directing my attention back to her. "She's my sister, and she's *eighteen*."

I look at this other girl, who seems fired up. But it's all part of my plan. Get the friend on side first. "My bad, I didn't mean anything by it. I was just saying she's got beautiful eyes," I say softly.

The bodyguard nods her head as Natasha nervously moves from side to side.

"I'm Rakim," I say, offering a hand to Natasha's sister.

She unfolds her arms, and after a second or two, she shakes my hand. "Priscilla," she says.

"That's a nice name. I like it," I say, still keeping a gentle hold of her hand.

"Thank you."

"So, do these sparkling brown eyes run in the family, then?" I ask as I look straight through Priscilla's lenses.

It takes a moment for a subtle smile to emerge on Priscilla's face as I let the gum in my mouth circulate.

She lifts her sunglasses.

"Nice to meet you, Rakim, and thank you for the erm... lip gloss."

"No problem."

We've attracted some attention as a man drives by, calling out to me in typical Jamaican fashion.

"I take it you're from around here then," Priscilla says.

I raise a hand to the driver as he goes by.

"Yeah, born and bred."

"You said that with pride, didn't you?" Priscilla says.

The praise from the driver, Priscilla's words, and everything in this moment make me smile. For a split second, I feel like I never left this place.

"Are you two hungry?" I ask.

The sisters both look at each other. "We've already eaten. We just came from that shop," Natasha says, pointing towards Burritos.

"For real? That's my spot, ya know."

"Is it?" Natasha says.

"Yeah, from long time."

"I haven't seen you there before," Priscilla says as she twiddles with her sunglasses.

"Yeah, I'm more of a night owl," I say, keeping my eyes firmly on Priscilla.

"Night owl, yeah... Is it?" she says.

"I would have offered you both to come and get something to eat with me and my cousin over there, but it looks like I'm a bit too late," I say.

"Your cousin?" Natasha asks, searching beyond my shoulder.

"Yo D," I call.

Pretending like he hasn't been watching the entire conversation, he lifts his head and looks around.

"Yo," he calls.

"Come."

He walks over, appearing much calmer and more collected now, which I thank God for.

"Deontay—Natasha, Natasha—Deontay."

"Hi, you all right," Natasha says with a warm smile.

"Yeah, I'm good, thanks. You cool?" Deontay replies as he shakes her hand.

"And this... This is Mademoiselle Priscilla," I say, introducing the older sister.

"You good?" Deontay asks.

He's lucky my comment has got the smile back on Priscilla's face.

I give the boy a stern look that says, *Don't fuck this up.*

"Nice to meet you," Priscilla says, raising a hand.

I turn to Natasha. "D'you mind if I borrow your sister for a moment?"

Natasha looks at Priscilla, who must give her some sort of encoded confirmation. "Sure," Natasha shrugs, and I walk Priscilla a few metres down the road.

"Rakim, is it?" Priscilla says.

"Yeah."

"Suits you."

We share some details, and I pretend to be interested in what she does, where she's from, and all the rest of it, but I'm not a fool. I know what kind of girl Priscilla is. Fiery, abrasive, and by the way, she's checking me out, kinda forward. Not that I got a problem with that. If I hadn't met Nia since coming out of prison, believe me, I'd have Priscilla's legs wrapped around me by tonight. But the reality is I have met Nia, and although Priscilla's sexy, she's just not in Nia's league. Nowhere near.

From the corner of my eye, I see Deontay pull out his phone, and I can only hope that he's sealed the deal. Any longer with Priscilla, and I might get myself into trouble.

"Look, I be real with you, Priscilla. I've just come out of prison—"

"—I can tell..." she says, eyes scanning my body.

Her forwardness makes me laugh.

"I'm just saying," she says. "Your arms, chest, shoulders, you've obviously been working... Hard."

"You're trouble, ya know," I say, wagging my finger.

Priscilla laughs, and she all but confirms my suspicions.

"Lemme take your number," I say.

She agrees, and I'm glad to end this conversation. This girl's got the big fella springing into life. I dial her number but hang up before the call connects.

We walk back over to Deontay and Natasha, who seem to be hitting it off. Natasha's laughing and Deontay's looking like his usual animated self, so I assume everything went well.

"We gotta keep it movin', ya know, but it was nice to meet you two," I say.

"Yeah, likewise," Natasha says.

"Byyeee," Priscilla waves as flirtatiously as she can.

Deontay licks his lips and backs away from Natasha. "I call you, yeah," Deontay says, and we make our way into the taco shop.

As soon as we get through the doors, Deontay starts jumping around like a kangaroo. "Oh, my days. She's peng, bro. Peeeehhh-ng!"

"You're welcome," I say.

"Did you get her sister's number?"

"Nah."

"What, why not? She was leng as well."

The plastic stool lets out an annoying screech as I sit down and look out the window.

"I got a girl, bro," I say.

"So..."

I shake my head at his immature response. It's funny. I was exactly the same once upon a time.

"Listen. Just 'cause a girl looks good, that don't mean nuttin', you feel me?"

Deontay puts one foot on the stool opposite me as he crouches.

"I got a good girl. Why do I need another one?"

He looks at me, puzzled, like I'm speaking a foreign language.

"You only get two good women in your life, ya know. Three if you're lucky. All the rest of the women come and go. They don't mean nuttin'

260

in the long run. That girl was peng, yeah, but she's hype. She's loud, and she's forward. Now, if she's like that with me, how many other men d'you think she's like that with?"

"True," Deontay says, nodding his head.

"A hype girl who likes to argue is the last thing a man needs when he's on the roads like we are... I ain't got no problem with Priscilla, but when I got a good one waitin' for me, what do I need her for? Girls like her you'll bump into everywhere, but my one's humble, goes about her business, don't cause man no drama, and I know I can rely on her. That's one in a million."

"Yeah, but—"

"—But nuttin' brudda. When you gotta girl like mine, you hold on to her tight, treat her good and always look after her, 'cause I'm tellin' you gyal like mine are a dying breed."

Hearing how I talk about Nia must resonate with Deontay, or maybe the tacos here are just so damn delicious because he spends the next ten minutes eating in silence.

We finish our food and get up to leave. "I'ma pay. Go wait in the car," I say.

After handing over the money for our food, I exit the shop to see Deontay in conversation with a bald-headed man. It takes a split second for me to realise it's Clinton, the barber.

"Yo mi breddah," Clinton says, looking flustered.

"Wa gwarn," I ask.

"Mi try fi ring you, but mi see mi nah have no credit. Rasclart Giff Gaff, always cut out when mi have sutt'n where important fi say," Clinton says.

"What's up?" I say, shoving my wallet into my back pocket.

"One ah them bwoy you was asking for."

"Who," I ask.

"Yuh remember, di Turkish bwoy."

"Yeah, what about him?"

"Him just left mi shop, big, hefty breddah."

261

I look at Deontay, who looks at me. "What? Which way'd he go?" I ask.

"That way," Clinton says pointing in the direction of the church.

"Ite, say no more. Love Clintz," I say, taking off with Deontay.

"Wait, what was he wearing?" Deontay shouts as he stops and turns in the middle of the road.

"Him have some kinda black hoody and denim jeans," Clinton calls.

Deontay throws a thumb up, and we set off.

It doesn't take long until we identify our target. He's on the opposite side of the road, roughly a hundred yards ahead.

"Stay on this side and catch up to get a look at his face," I instruct Deontay, who starts to speed up his walk as I cross the road and gain on the unsuspecting Turk.

We carry on for another minute or so as Deontay gets ahead of him from the other side of the road. I watch Deontay take out his phone and put it to his ear.

"Yo," I say, answering at once.

"Oi, fam, it's him."

"Who?"

"The guy. Remember from the flat when I got the stuff."

"When?"

"You know, the first time I came out with you. We were waiting outside that block, and those two men followed me."

"What, that guy?"

"Yeah?"

"You sure?"

"Yeah, a hundred. I 'member that ugly screw face."

"Ite, say no more. If he don't take the next turning, I'ma grab him. Come back me."

"Yeah, yeah."

I end the call and get closer to this guy.

He's on the phone talking in another language.

I'm near enough to hear his deep voice and even catch a whiff of that tangy-citrus barbershop fragrance that lingers in his wake.

Treading lightly and quickly as cars pass, the guy remains oblivious to my presence. There are fewer pedestrians in this quiet part of the high road, just flats on my left and a vast open green space on my right.

We approach a junction, and to my relief, the guy takes the turning.

I waste no time.

I sprint up to him and push him as hard as I can.

By the time he realises I've rushed him like it's a game of rugby, he hits the ground, and his phone goes flying. I swiftly assert myself on top of him, pushing my knee into his chest and controlling his arms.

"Get off me!" he shouts.

"Shut up," I order him as I let go of his arm to deliver a powerful blow to the jaw. He screams out as he tries to turn onto his side.

Now, I'm up close to him, I can see.

Deontay was right. It's the same guy who came out of the flats that day.

"Get off me," he yells under the cover of his arms.

"Who sent you after me?"

I look over my shoulder and see Deontay arriving. Thankfully we're the only three on the road.

"Nobody send me," he says.

"So why you come after me and my little bro?" I shout.

We wrestle with each other as he squirms to get free.

"You ain't going nowhere, fam," I tell him.

After nearly a minute of struggling, he starts to breathe heavily, and his attempts to free himself become much more laborious. Deontay decides to join in and pulls his arms away from his face. I clench my fist and threaten to punch him again.

"Who sent you after me?" I shout.

"Okay. Relax," he cries, coming to terms with the fact that he isn't wriggling out of this one.

"Tell me, then."

"Tell him, you pussy," Deontay screams.

"I don't know. I just get message from inside. They tell me whoever wants to be boss has to get the coke back," the Turk yells, his accent fluctuating from foreigner to Londoner.

"What?"

"You steal the food from the house. I have to get back."

"Stole what?" Deontay says as he looks at me.

"We didn't steal shit," I say.

I hear a voice call out, and I turn and see a couple of civilians pointing directly at us.

I shake the guy on the floor, banging his head against the concrete as he reaches to cover his face again.

"You steal the coke from the house. You steal it and don't pay. Boss says whoever gets it back can take over the area."

"What the fuck you talkin' about, stealing coke?"

"You and your friend," he says as his eyes travel towards Deontay.

I'm baffled.

"Nobody stole no coke. That was my food, cuz."

"No, no, no. It's not yours."

"Shut up," Deontay says as he tries to punch the man in the face.

"Coward," the Turk cries, who does his best to avoid the blow.

"Who told you we stole it?" I say.

"I see you. I see both of you."

"So how you know we were gonna be there?" I shout.

Deontay lets go of the man's arms and shoots up. It's not until I hear him call my name that I realise what's got him standing as stiff as a post.

A police car has just pulled into the road. Still crouched low, I just about make out the blue and yellow patterns on the side of the vehicle as it passes the gap between two parked cars.

Instantly, I grab hold of the Turk and pull him to his feet. He's got a cut on his head, a couple of grazes, and his hoody is all dishevelled. I do my best to fix his collar, but he knocks my hands away.

"Now you wanna get brave," I say.

"Fuck you, you bastard," he replies.

The police car stops in the middle of the road just a few metres from where we're stood.

The door opens, and out step two officers.

"What's going on, fellas?" a young, brown-haired man asks, probably no older than me. He scratches his shaven face and walks around the bonnet of a parked car to assess the scene.

The Turk looks at me and flicks up his hood.

"Everything's good," I say.

The second policeman steps onto the pavement, his thumbs stuffed underneath his stab-proof vest as he looks at Deontay, then at me, then the Turk. "What you all doing round here, then?"

"None your business," the Turk says.

"No need for the attitude. We're just asking you what you're up to?" the bald officer says, leaning his head forward.

The Turk attempts to walk off when one of the officers calls out. "Oi, fella, where you going?"

"I go home," he shouts.

"No. I'm talking to you. You're not going anywhere. Come here," the bald officer says.

He puts an arm in front of the Turk, who rolls his head in annoyance.

"What's his problem?" the younger officer asks, pointing his head towards the Turk.

Deontay shrugs, and I give the kid a stark look.

The younger officer proceeds to ask us for our details.

Deontay answers first. He gives a fake name and address. He knows the procedure. After a short pause, the officer asks me, and I copy Deontay's tactic.

"Why you stopping us, anyway?" Deontay asks.

"A woman just down the road reported an argument in the street. You chaps happen to know anything about that?"

We both shake our heads, which makes the officer smile for some reason.

"What's funny?" Deontay says.

"Nothing," replies the officer before turning away and pressing his ear into his walkie-talkie.

I look to my left and see the bald officer begin to search the Turk who protests in vain. As soon as his hood comes off, baldy changes his tone.

"What's those marks on ya face? Who did that?" the officer asks.

The Turk remains silent as I look at him, and my heart begins to bang like a drum.

Baldy picks up on the glare and makes a gesture to his colleague.

I see the brown-haired officer wink and then nod as he opens the door of his vehicle.

Deontay's eyes widen.

"What?" I whisper discreetly.

"I got half a g-pack plugged," he mutters.

"Well, this ain't no strip search, chill," I murmur before the young constable returns.

"Right, lads, you're gonna be searched under section one of PACE. I'll start with you," the officer says, addressing Deontay.

He identifies himself as PC Barlow before stepping towards Deontay and instructing him to spread his arms.

Deontay turns his head towards me, and I use all the telepathy I can muster to tell him to chill the fuck out. I know it's not the easiest thing to do when he's got fifty wraps of crack and heroin stuffed up his arsehole, but he doesn't really have a choice.

The bald-headed officer must have found something on the Turk because I'm distracted by an all too familiar phrase.

"... You do not have to say anything, but it may harm your defence if you do not mention something when questioned that you later rely on in court...."

266

I watch as the Turk pleads his innocence before a set of steel cuffs are secured around his wrists.

I shake my head.

I have no love for this guy, but still, I never enjoy seeing another man being arrested. I've felt that feeling way too many times, and it never feels good, helplessly wishing you were anywhere else in the world.

"Is not mine," the Turk yells as the officer speaks into his walkie-talkie, seemingly requesting assistance.

'Please don't let Deontay be next.'

I try to appear uninterested, but from the corner of my eye, I watch the officer's blue latex gloves pat against Deontay's leg, upwards towards his groin, before they begin to turn the waistband in Deontay's tracksuit bottoms inside-out.

'Please make sure he's got that plugged deep.' Otherwise, this stop-and-search is about to take on a whole new dynamic.

Less than a minute later, the officer appears to have finished with Deontay. "Right, you're free to go. Go on, get out of here."

My belly shrinks as I exhale heavily.

'Thank you.'

The officer hands Deontay his phone and a few other items before turning towards me and ordering Deontay to walk away. He takes one look at me, and the strangest thing happens.

"I'm gonna allow you to take off," he says.

I try not to seem too excited or too disappointed. I just want to get out of here now. I nod and turn to leave when the officer raises a palm, and I stop like clockwork. "If I see you around here again, though, mark my words, you will be getting stopped, and you will be getting searched, is that understood?" PC Barlow says.

"Yeah, man. Say no more," I say.

"All right, go on, on ya bike then, fella," PC Barlow says.

I take one more look at the Turkish man to mark his face and see the vengeance in his eyes beaming back at me. This isn't over, not by a long shot.

25

Rubbing my eyes, I sit up as my phone rattles away somewhere on the floor. I reach out blindly into the darkness of my bedroom and nearly tumble out of bed.

I turn the phone over to see the screen.

It's a number I don't recognise.

'Three-sixteen in the morning. Whose callin' man at this time?'

"Who's this?" I ask, clearing my throat as I speak.

"Yo, Rakz, it's me, Scribbler."

Like a defibrillator, Scribbler's voice zaps life into me.

"What—where are you? Why you callin' off some next number?"

"Man got shipped out, bro."

"What? When?" I say straightening my back against the headboard.

"Two days ago. Some joke ting."

"Why, though? You were calm over there. You ain't get re-categorised yet, alie?"

"Nah, not even."

"So, why they transfer you?"

"I don't know. Screws just came for man first thing in the morning, didn't even see the slip under my door until they were up in my cell."

I suck my teeth.

I know the feeling of being transferred with no warning. It's not nice at all.

Imagine you've been settled in your house for years. You've spent loads of time and energy decorating it, made friends with the neighbours, and even got yourself a job.

Then one day, without prior warning, ten men with handcuffs turn up at your front door, telling you, you've got fifteen minutes to pack whatever you can carry and that your home is no longer yours. You're being moved.

You have no idea where you'll be taken, what it will be like, or how long it will take to get there, but you have no say in the matter. You can protest, but do so, and you'll be beaten and removed by force.

That's what it feels like.

"Where you now, then?" I ask.

"Wakemead."

"Rah."

I never spent time at HMP Wakemead, but apparently, the screws there think they're ex-military commanders who run the place like it's a boot camp.

"I can't even talk too tight. I borrowed this tech for the night, but I forgot the charger. Battery soon done," Scribz says.

"Wait, Scribz. What's this about the food we got being stolen from some Turks?"

There's no response, just a faint buzz.

"Scribz..."

Again, he doesn't respond, which heightens my anxiety.

"Yo."

"Look, Rakz..." The flatness of his voice tells me all I need to know.

"Are you serious, cuz?"

"Bro, I was gonna—"

"—You robbed your connect!"

Scribbler sighs.

"You robbed your connect and didn't even fuckin' tell me?"

"Rakz, I was gonna tell you, fam."

"When...? You had man going up in that yard to take food that weren't even yours. *You* didn't even rob him—*I* robbed him. And now I gotta bagga Turks looking for me and Deontay, 'cause of some snaky shit you pulled."

There's no response.

I suck my teeth as I stand up. Wide awake now, I'm pacing around in the darkness.

"How you gonna do man like that, Scribz? After every'ting man's done for you, you're gonna put man in this position, mandem coming after me, and you don't even tell me. I got man coming after Deontay. I'm breaking this one's nose, rugby tackling that one, nearly gettin' nicked and sent back to jail all because your fuckin' greed, bruv," I shout.

Scribbler doesn't say a word.

"You violated man, Scribz, you know that."

"Bro, I was gonna work tings out with the connect, ask Jonesy. He knows. I just got shipped out, I can't get hold of no one."

"Nah, you violated man."

"Oi, Rakz, chill man. We both know it's never that."

"That's exactly what it is."

I stand in the middle of the room, eyes closed, head back, hoping Scribz is chatting shit.

"Bro, look. I'm sorry, init. I had to."

"Had to what? Rob the plug? Or not tell me?"

"Both, bro."

"Wickedest ting is... I don't even care about you finessin' the plug. You should've just fuckin' told me, so I know what to expect."

"You were already moving shaky. If I told you, you wouldn't have done it."

"So, why'd you *have to* rob him, then Scribz, go on?"

There's a pause as I await Scribz's response.

'Let's hear this shit.'

"It's my mum, bro..."

I stop pacing around.

"What about her...?"

"They gave her a year to live."

His words hit me like a blow to the gut, forcing me back onto the edge of the bed. "You serious?"

270

"Yeah, man. Around three months ago. Just before you come outta jail."

"Shit. Why didn't you tell me?"

"You can't *do* anything."

"So, what happened?" I ask.

"I was giving her the money to hold on to. Had about forty grand with her. Then one day, I asked her for a quick ten just to buy my sis a car and pay for the kids to go on holiday with their mum. She turns around and tells me, point black. It's gone."

"What?"

"Bro, she spent all the money."

"On what?"

"I dunno. Parties, holidays, shoes, handbags, restaurants. What do women spend money on?"

"Fuck's sake."

"She's going through it, my guy. She's got less than a year to live. Her mind ain't right."

"I know, but—"

"—How can I tell her anything? I'm in here. I'm probably the reason she's ill and that, in the first place, sitting in here. I should be out there helping her."

'Ain't that the truth.'

I don't say anything, but if anybody understands Scribz at this moment, it's me. Trust me on that.

We spend the next minute or so not saying anything until Scribz warns me about his phone battery again.

"Look Scribz, I'ma ask you once. How much you rob...? And don't lie to man, 'cause I know it weren't just no nine bar."

Scribz sighs again, and I prepare for the worst.

"A box," he says.

"Are you joking?"

"Bro, you said you wanted the truth. That's the truth."

This is bad. Real bad.

271

I assumed me and Deontay had taken everything Scribz had stolen, but it turns out that was just a quarter of it.

"You've lost your head. A box of food?"

"Obviously, I ran through half, then found out that my mum rinsed the money. I couldn't pay, so I consigned a next half. I was gonna sort it, then my worker got bagged. Feds took half the Ps he had with him. I only had a nine-bar left."

"All right, forget all that. How much you owe now?"

"Fifty, fifty-five..."

"Oi Scribz, you gotta sort this. I can't help you on this one."

"I ain't askin' you to, Rakz. I know."

I feel the anger shooting through my blood.

"I chat to you tomorrow, man."

"My bad, bro. I'm sorry. Man will sort it."

Right now, I have as much faith in Scribz as I do in the Tooth Fairy.

For the rest of the night, I barely sleep. Scribz didn't just use me like a pawn, he used everyone. After building a relationship with his suppliers and taking a batch of food on some buy now, pay later shit, he's fucked up his part of deal. Well, his mum did to be more specific but he's still culpable. The thing is guys like these Turks aren't stupid; they don't give you stuff on credit without having some correspondence for you or your place of business. It's like a bank. Which bank would give you a loan without having information on where they need to send the bailiffs in the event you fail to repay.

The thing that hurts the most though, is how Scribz manipulated me. He told me he needed a favour, and he knew my loyalty wouldn't allow me to refuse helping him out. That food me and Deontay took shouldn't have been ours to sell, Scribz hadn't even paid for it. That's why those two goons were waiting outside the block that day. They wanted their shit back. I don't blame them. In fact, I blame myself. I should've picked up on that one.

272

Now they've seen Deontay and me literally drive off with their product, these Turks obviously think we're to blame and now there's probably money on my head.

I think about Nia and how she may now be a target.

I think about Scribz's mum and try to understand how she must feel, knowing she's going to die.

My sentence changed my perception of life. I gave up all my plans and became engrossed in the present. That's all that mattered. As far as I was concerned, I had no future. I know it sounds mad but try being eighteen and being told that nearly all the years you've been alive you're going to need to live again, but this time in prison. Pretending there was nothing outside waiting for me was the only way I could cope.

But even with my sentence, there was light at the end of the tunnel. Even if I chose not to see it until years passed and the light got closer. Scribz's mum has no light. Her sentence is much worse. Hers is a death sentence.

Scribz has deceived me. But I understand why he did what he did. He feels guilty about his mum. I wish I could've been there for my mum. I missed her last days, and Scribz will have to endure the same pain. He saw me go through it. He knows first-hand how that shit can nearly break a man.

Maybe he knew what his mum was up to and thought he'd allow her the best few months of her life before she moves on. Reparations for all the stress he's ever caused her. It's about the best gift you can give from a prison cell.

The only problem in life is that every gift has a cost. And in Scribz's mum's case, it may have cost a life.

I wish I could do something, and once Deontay and I sell all the product we have left, maybe I can, but fifty thousand will clear me out. If I help Scribz I might as well say goodbye to The Gambia.

That's not to mention the fact it's going to take time to get rid of all the product. And with these Turks now pursuing us, convinced Deontay and me have stolen their food, I've just realised it's time I may not have.

26

Saturday evening, Nia and I are sitting across from one another at one of Mayfair's finest restaurants. An enchanting candle flickers and flashes like an exotic dancer on the table between us as I examine my surroundings.

This setting is like something out of another world. The closest resemblance to anything like this for me is those visiting halls back in prison. Everybody seated at their tables talking and eating reminds me of the visits before Mum died.

Instead of cheap plastic chairs bolted to the ground, though, this place is set out with dark walnut tables underneath bright spotlights that twinkle magnificently. A couple to my right pose for a photo as a waiter holds up a smartphone, capturing their matching smiles, the wagyu beef, and the sticks of asparagus on their plates.

I look over at Nia, trying to focus on how beautiful she looks in her bedazzling dress, but that fifty-thousand-pound debt weighs heavily on my conscience.

I can't seem to get it out of my head.

She lifts her glass in the air like she's signalling a taxi, and within seconds, a young man skims across the polished marble floors to provide a refill. Nia smiles at me, and I fake one back as the clinking of glasses amongst the murmuring and laughter on the tables around us disguises my unwillingness to converse.

To my left, a neon blue strip runs along the curvature of the bar like a futuristic meeting place for intergalactic dating. All the stools are occupied. Young and old are here this evening.

Hundreds of bottles from all regions of the globe decorate the wall behind the bartenders who dart this way and that way like busy worker ants, striving to accommodate every order.

I see why Leanne chose this place for me. It's clearly upmarket, designed for the wealthy to enjoy, but it doesn't carry the superciliousness she knows I detest.

The journey here in the Porsche, showing Nia the heated seats and the panoramic roof, was supposed to be an exciting feature. Maybe for her, it was, but my conversation with Scribz this morning hasn't left me for a second.

Our juxtaposition exacerbates as we plough through our three courses. Nia talks passionately about travelling to different countries with me, and I sort of just go through the motions.

Every time she notices my low mood, I compliment or offer her some of my food—nothing like a forkful of chocolate fondant and a bit of flattery to deter a woman's suspicions.

We finish dessert, and Nia takes hold of my hands.

"Are you okay, Rakim?" she asks with that maternal concern written across her face.

I give her hands a gentle squeeze.

"I'm good, babes. Just been a long day."

"Uh-uh. Don't be getting all tired on me now," Nia says, snaking her neck towards me as she tries to make me laugh.

"Why's that?"

"Because..." she says, leaning forward to kiss me. "It's my birthday, and the night's still young."

Our lips touch, and it takes my mind off my problems for a second. The taste of mango, salt, and alcohol swivel and swirl around my tongue, and an abundance of testosterone fires through my body.

Lost in our world of sensual seduction, the warmth of Nia's delicate palm on my cheek soothes my soul. She calms me, controlling my grittiness and luring me deeper into her world of pleasure and plentitude. Her hair smells divine. Cocoa, avocado, and almond oil, all combine to produce the aroma of a goddess.

It's only when the pianist, I've hardly noticed the whole night, takes it up a notch and the restaurant erupts into a chorus that I'm dragged from our sensual abyss.

Dozens of diners sing Happy Birthday as I look to my right to see a cake with a single golden candle sprouting from the centre. Men and women hold their phones in the air while others smile and clap, and Nia raises her glass like it's a Nobel Prize.

I put my hand over my face.

'Leanne got me with this one, still. Must be my comeuppance for embarrassing her little Taylor.'

The song finishes as Nia blows out her chunky candle, and a round of applause has her blushing.

"Awww. You two are the perfect couple," a waitress says.

"Yeah, she's lucky, init,' I say.

The waitress laughs and offers to take a photo of us. I hand her my phone and oblige. I put an arm around Nia as we come together across the table and smile at the camera.

"Watch when I get you home," Nia says, her devious eyes squinting at me.

I don't need another invitation. I finish the rest of my drink while Nia demolishes a slice of chocolate cake, and within five minutes, I've paid the bill, tipped the waiter, and we're back in the Porsche.

The alcohol must be flowing through Nia because I've never seen her like this. She rubs her hand up and down my thigh, teasing the big guy who is all but ready to be uncaged. The smell of fresh leather fades a little as I open the panoramic roof and let the cosmos cast its wonder upon us.

The night sky twinkles with a wealth of stars as I hurry to get home. At fifty miles per hour, this car still glides along smoother than a knife through warm butter. Even London's infamous potholes fail to hinder the drive.

"Thank you for my meal, Rakim," Nia says.

"It's cool."

She kisses my neck. She knows it's my spot, and she knows how to work it.

"Ni, you're gonna set me off, ya know."

"Good," she whispers as her tongue makes my torso tingle.

I place my hand on her thigh.

'If she don't stop, I might just crash.'

By now, the big fella's fully alert. I thank God for a traffic light as I slow down to a stop and kiss her back. She moans gratefully like I'm the most delicious dessert she's ever tasted.

'Forget the road. The lights can wait.'

Our feral instincts take over, and we snog like two drunken lovers, high off each other's pheromones in the seats of this a hundred and twenty grand car.

Maybe it's right, or maybe it's wrong, but I'm not even paying attention to the cars behind me. The light changes and a driver blasts his horn.

I raise a middle finger out of the sunroof, and Nia giggles as we continue to ignore him.

"Oh my God, Rakim, I feel bad," she says.

Her eyes are hazy from the multitude of cocktails and champagne she's downed. She looks at me, biting her lip.

Right now, she *is* bad. Being a good girl has gone out the window tonight.

The frustrated driver from behind zooms by, and we laugh as he throws us an insult in some foreign accent. I don't know why it seems so funny, but our laughing soon stops. In fact, everything does when I notice flashing blue lights in the rear-view mirror.

I pull away from Nia and look to my left.

"Shit."

A black BMW X5 is stationed metres behind us like a tank, its blue light spinning all around the high road.

Two police officers sit in the front.

I make out the driver, a white male with a heavy brow, gesturing for me to pull the car over.

"What's going on?" Nia asks.

I raise my hand through the open roof top and inch along to the side of the road until the tyres slowly scuff along the curb.

"Why are they stopping us?" Nia asks as she fixes her hair.

A few pedestrians on the street are drawn to what's happening. Some look at me, some at Nia, and some check out the car. I close the panoramic roof with a touch of a button and hear the thud of car doors being closed.

'What do these man want?'

The officer who was in driver seat approaches my window. As he crouches to peer inside, I catch a whiff of his aftershave.

"How you doing, sir?" he asks.

"I'm all right. What's going on?" I say.

The second officer approaches Nia's window and taps his knuckle against it.

The officer beside me puts a hand on the roof of my car and comes close enough for me to get a good look at his crooked nose and the mole that sits just below it. He twitches his pale, narrow lips and opens his mouth.

"I'll cut right to the chase. You were going pretty fast back there, and now you've obstructed the road at this traffic light. Any reason why?"

I see Nia attempting to lower her window, but I've locked it. She looks at me for help, but I ignore her.

"Speeding? I don't know about that, but I apologise for blocking the road. My Mrs dropped a bottle of deodorant. It was rolling around near the pedals. I didn't wanna try and drive with it there in case it got stuck underneath the brakes or suttin'. That's all dangerous, you feel me?" I say.

The officer gives me a look I've seen a thousand times. The one that implies he knows I'm lying but doesn't want to accuse me because he can't prove it... Yet.

"Is this your car, then?" he asks.

"Nah, it's a rental."

"Flashy. Must be pretty expensive...?"

"Bruv, you lot are CID. You don't care about traffic stops. What's this about?"

"Speeding cars kill more people than knife crime," he says sharply, and I think how a person who is entrusted with protecting the community says that with a smile on his face as if there's anything funny about it.

I look at Nia, and I'm reminded of her brother.

"So, are you the only person who drives this vehicle?" the officer asks.

"I just told you, it's a rental. That means different people rent it all the time."

"Okay. And when did you start renting it?"

I can see where this is going, and I feel my heart rate increasing. Even when I'm innocent, police have always had a way of making me feel like I'm guilty of a crime.

I clear my throat.

"Today. It's a special occasion," I say.

"Oh right," the officer replies as he looks over at his colleague on the other side of the vehicle.

"So, where are you heading off to tonight?"

"Just droppin' my Mrs home," I say, rolling my eyes at his unsolicited foreplay.

He continues asking me questions about the vehicle and the insurance before finally requesting my details.

I'm about to answer when Nia steps in.

"Excuse me," she says, drawing the attention of the officer on my side. "What's all this about? We were blocking the road, and he said sorry, can you leave us alone now, please?"

"Relax, lemme deal with it, Ni."

The officer who was at Nia's window comes to join the one with the mole. There's some chatter over the walkie-talkie, and the pair take a step back.

"What do they want, Rakim?" Nia whispers.

"Chill, babe. These lot are just bored. They'll be done soon, and we can go home," I tell her, trying my best to appear calm.

A couple of minutes pass as the rhythmic tapping of my hand against the steering wheel speeds up.

'Come on, hurry up.'

Finally, the officer with the mole returns to my window.

"What did you say your name was?" he asks.

"Rakim."

"R-a-k-i-m?" he asks, spelling it out.

"Yeah."

"Morrison?"

"Yeah."

The officer looks at his colleague, and Nia huffs as she folds her arms.

"Step out of the vehicle, please," the officer says.

Suddenly, his whole attitude changes. He's way edgier.

"What for, man?"

"Just turn the engine off and step out, please."

"What's going on?" Nia asks.

Reluctantly, I step out of the car. I look to my right to see a marked police car pull up behind the X5.

"What's this about?" I say, pointing towards the four officers that have just turned up looking like a gang of hitmen.

It takes a second for me to spot the holsters on the hip of two of the officers who've just arrived.

"Armed response. Are you lot taking the piss?"

"Put your hands down, please," the plain-clothed officer says, raising the grey sleeve of his cardigan.

"Nah, what's happening? You're pulling me, now you're askin' me to get out the car. And now you got these man coming over like you lot are some gangsters. Wa gwarn?"

"Rakim, mate, just calm down. Give us a moment, and my colleague will explain," a chubby-faced officer says.

"Just explain now, you man have already messed up my evening. I told you why I stopped in the road. If you think I was speeding, cool, give me a ticket and go about your business, init."

I'm halfway between anger and fear. I don't know what these lot are planning, but the Jamaican running through my blood will never let another man intimidate me, police officer or not.

Six of them form a semi-circle in front of me as a tall white man wearing a police hat steps forward, looking like the Devil himself.

"Are you ready to listen and stop talking?" he asks.

"Go on, wa gwarn then?"

"I'm Sergeant Dawkins from the Violent Taskforce at Croydon Police Station. We have intel that this car is being used in the supply of class A drugs," this piece of work says.

The words leave his mouth with an unnerving pleasure, as if he is pleased about harassing me like this.

"What you talkin' about?"

"The vehicle's gonna be searched under section..."

I ain't listening anymore. I watch as an officer asks Nia to step out of the vehicle.

"Leave her alone," I call as I go to stop him.

"Stay there, Mr. Morrison, please," a burly officer says, putting an arm in front of me.

"What's going on?" Nia asks as a female officer ushers her onto the pavement far enough away from me to ensure we can't hear each other.

Nia looks petrified as she glances over at me. Her hands rub against her bare arms as the chill of the night bites our skin.

"You lot are taking the piss. Ain't no drugs in this car," I say.

"It's a pretty nice car. What do you do for a living?" the sergeant asks as he noses around with his flashlight, moving the driver's seat forward.

"None of your business, man."

"Is that right?" he says.

I wish I could punch that conniving grin right off his face.

'10... 9... 8... 7.'

I get down to one and take a deep breath.

'Nia's gonna know man's up to suttin' now.'

Cars pass by, and I see the humiliation on Nia's face as she stands on the pavement.

'How can I let her be gettin' searched like this on road... On her birthday?'

She looks mortified as one officer holds her arm and pats her down while the other goes through her handbag like she's a criminal.

Two officers search my pockets while Sergeant Dawkins and one of his minions rummage through the vehicle.

Nia puts her face in her hands, and I call out to her, but she doesn't respond.

The officers offer some kind words and reassurances, but it all goes in one ear and out the other. They've ruined our night.

Nia's arms are crossed, and she's got a face like thunder.

Not being able to help her infuriates me more with every passing second.

"Let her go," I tell the officers. "She ain't done nothing."

"She was in a vehicle that we believe is concerned in the supply of illegal drugs. Therefore, she'll be dealt with accordingly and searched under section 23 of the Misuse of Drugs Act," Sergeant Dawkins responds like a fucking cyborg.

I shake my head. "You love this, init."

"Love what, Rakim?"

"Just harassing black men."

He smiles. "It's got nothing to do with being black. You're in a vehicle that we have good reason to believe may contain class A drugs," he says, trying to sound as believable as possible.

"Where you get this bullshit intel? 'Cause, there's no drugs in the whip."

He ignores my question, and after going through the boot and leaving papers, rubbish, and a load of crumbs over the upturned seats in the back, Sergeant Dawkins and his sidekick close the doors of the Porsche and join me on the pavement.

The smile has left Sergeant Dawkins' face. He looks at me with an unforgiving glare, and I look back, trying to see if there's even the slightest glint of any love or humanity behind those cold blue lenses.

But there's none. Not a shred.

"Has he been searched?" the sergeant asks one of his colleagues.

"Yeah, he's clean, sarge," an officer with *PC Cullen* tagged on his stab-proof vest says.

I sense the hint of regret in his voice, which just riles me up further.

"Let go of my arm. Now," I order PC Cullen.

I'm done with playing nice.

I shake his arm off me, nearly sending him tumbling over.

Nia turns and looks at me with disapproval, but my concerns have left the building.

"You're just gonna leave my car like that?"

"It's not your car, is it? It's a rental," Sergeant Dawkins says.

"Yeah, I'm renting it for the day, so what?"

"So, if you're not dealing drugs, then how can you afford it?"

"Are you dumb? You just searched the car, searched me, and searched my girl and found what? Nothing! And you're still accusing man of selling drugs."

The plainclothes officer who initially stopped me, steps in, attempting to be the voice of reason.

"Look, Rakim. Sorry, we've stopped you, but if I were you, I'd tell whoever rented me this car to stop selling drugs before he gets it seized, along with his freedom."

"Cool, so why didn't you just say that from the beginning instead of one, two, three, four, five, six of you, ganging up on man... Wasting taxpayers' money. Why don't you go out there and catch some peadophiles or some rapists or suttin'?"

I watch Nia walk over to the passenger door. Her face is smeared with blotches of mascara, just making my anger towards Sergeant Dawkins multiply.

My lungs pump hard, and I can't think straight. I need to get out of here before I completely lose it. Thankfully, Sergeant Dawkins hands me the keys.

"You're free to go, Mr. Morrison. Drive safe and have a pleasant evening," he says, cracking the fakest smile I've ever seen before turning away as if nothing's happened.

No apology.

Nothing.

I hear one of the officer's snigger, and something in me snaps.

"Fuckin' dickhead," I yell.

"What was that?" Sergeant Dawkins says, turning to face me.

"You heard, you fuckin' prick. You knew there weren't nuttin' in man's car. You see a black breh driving a hundred grand car and just wanna ruin his night. You're a stone-cold hater, and on my life, if you weren't a fed, I'd smash your head in," I say, pointing two fingers at him.

He places one hand on his taser as he steps closer.

"Go on, son, say that again, swear once more," one of the officers says with a Glock 17 tucked away at his side.

The demonic look in his eye tells me everything I need to know about him.

"Get in your car and drive off now before you get yourself nicked, you silly little boy," Sergeant Dawkins says.

I'm about to retaliate when I hear Nia's voice.

"Rakim, please," she cries, and I turn to look at her.

A set of wide, teary eyes looks back at me, filling me with shame.

Nia's never seen this side of me.

Passers-by have gathered to watch the stand-off like it's an old Western as Sergeant Dawkins hovers in front of me, waiting for me to retreat.

I shake my head and ease past him towards my car.

From my peripheral, I see him smirk. He's achieved the rise out of me he wanted. I'm the angry black man, and he's the white saviour of the neighbourhood.

I've failed.

"You wanna watch yourself with this one, love. You don't wanna be his next victim," he snares as his colleague chuckles to himself.

I press the unlock button and get into the vehicle. It's not until Nia's sat next to me and the door closes that it actually registers what the sergeant just said.

'Next victim...'

I avoid Nia's eyes, put my seatbelt on, and we drive the short distance home in complete silence.

We pull up outside her house, and she turns towards me, clutching her handbag like a precious artefact.

"What was that all about?" she says.

My hand stays on the steering wheel, and I keep quiet.

"Rakim, what's going on?" Nia cries.

I don't budge.

"Rakim, why are they searching up your car like that?"

I stay silent.

"Rakim, I said, why are they searching your car looking for drugs?"

"What did they ask you?" I say calmly, my eyes still looking straight ahead.

"Loads of stuff."

"Like what?"

"How long have I known you? Where do you live? What do you do for work? Do I sell drugs? Where did you get the car? Loads of stuff. What's going on?"

"What did you say?"

"Rakim, answer my question."

I press the button to demystify the now foggy windscreen.

"What question?" I ask.

"Do you sell drugs?"

I look at the innocence in Nia's eyes.

I don't want to lie to her, so I turn away.

"Rakim, why can't you just tell me?" she says, throwing her hands in the air. "You do, don't you?"

I sigh.

"Yeah," I mumble.

She lets her hands drop, and they clap against her thighs. "I knew it."

"I'm stopping now, though. I swear. I'm done."

"I knew it."

"Knew what?"

"The car, the shady phone calls. I knew there was something off with you."

I feel ridiculous for hiding it now.

"I was gonna tell you, I just—"

"—When? When were you gonna tell me? Because I'm guessing this isn't a new thing, you've had at least the past two months to say something. What? Did it just slip your mind?"

I can't argue with her. Right now, she's me this morning when I spoke to Scribz.

She shakes her head. "And what did that policeman mean when he said about your next victim?"

I take a deep breath.

"Rakim?" she calls.

I feel my blood rising.

"Leave it," I mutter.

"What did he mean? Who are you?" Nia says, trying to pull my chin to face her.

I'm getting hot, and I can feel my armpits sticking to my t-shirt.

"Let's just go inside," I say.

"No. Tell me."

I ignore her and move my face away from her hand.

"Rakim, tell me," Nia cries, pushing my shoulder.

"Just leave it, Ni."

"No, tell me now."

My throat has suddenly dried up.

'You can't tell her, man.'

"Rakim?"

The car feels like a sauna.

"Rakim?"

Nia's arms flail around as her voice penetrates my ears relentlessly. "Rakim, what did he mean? Rakim?"

I can't take it no more.

"Rakim?"

"Look, I fuckin' killed someone. That's what he meant!" I shout, turning towards her in a fit of rage.

Her face loses all colour, like she's just seen a ghost.

Her mouth hangs open, and her eyes remain frozen in time, unable to blink.

"You what?"

Seeing her reaction, for some reason, makes me continue.

"You heard me. I killed a man. I punched his head in until I fractured his skull and killed him. I've been in jail for the past twelve years... That's why you've never seen me. That's why I wasn't around when my mum died. And that's why them fuckin' feds won't leave me alone. Are you happy now?"

I punch the steering wheel, and Nia screams.

'You fuckin' idiot. It's all over now. You ruined it. All you had to do was keep your mouth shut in front of them feds.'

I can hear myself breathing as I stare out of the windscreen.

Shocked, Nia doesn't say a word for the next few seconds as the silence draws out like a fishing reel, seeming to last forever.

Then finally, she speaks.

"Why didn't you tell me?" she quivers.

I sit there, unable to answer.

"Rakim... Rakim... Rakim?" she persists, but I'm locked away in my own world.

"You killed someone, Rakim. You killed someone, and you went to prison for twelve years, and you didn't think to tell me? Why, Rakim...? Why? Why would you do that to me?"

I ignore her.

"Rakim...?"

I remain unmoved.

She sniffs and wipes a hand across her nose.

"You lied to me... From the day you met me, Rakim, all you've done is lie to me. You told me you didn't know who lived in that house when it was *your* house. You told me you didn't know your own mum. Now, you're telling me you're a drug-dealing murderer... What the hell is going on, Rakim? Who the hell are you?" Nia screams.

Guilt places two hands around my throat and chokes me, squeezing every inch of pride from my being. I feel so embarrassed. I can't believe Nia's found out like this. She must be regretting the day she met me, but I have no defence.

"Are you just gonna ignore me then? Because I swear if you don't answer me, we're done. I deserve answers, Rakim. Who the hell are you?"

"Get out."

Nia's mouth stops moving.

"What?"

"Get out."

"Are you for real?"

'I should have told her from the start. I fucked up. This is done.'

"Is that really how you gonna do me, Rakim? After everything. After I told you about my brother and what drugs have done to us, you've been selling that shit all the time. I knew something was up... Why did it have to be this?"

288

I ain't looking at her, but I can tell Nia's crying.

"All the lies you've told me. Now you can't even look me in the eye, and you wanna tell *me* to leave."

I stare ahead, not saying a word.

"Rakim, you better tell me something right—"

"—I just fuckin' told you. Get out!" I yell, turning towards her like a man possessed.

She cowers and quickly reaches for the door handle. A tear comes to my eye, but I wipe it before it can fall.

"I don't know who the hell you are, but stay away from me," Nia says as she exits the car. She forgets to close the door before turning back and looking at me.

"You're a fucking liar. I thought you were different, but you're not. You lied to me about so much. All those whispered words when we were in bed, were they lies too?

I can't even look at her.

"I hate you. Don't ever call me again," she screams.

Nia's words cut through me like daggers. All the false testimonies I've declared about myself. All the virtues and morals I built myself upon, honesty, loyalty, courage. I watch a fiction of the man I believed myself to be, crumble in the blink of an eye. An illusion shattered within seconds.

She hurries off, and I don't even move a muscle as the sound of a door slamming shut echoes through the dead of night. Disgusted with myself for not reciprocating Nia's virtuosity, I sit in the Porsche, me, myself and I, wondering how on earth I let a night of celebration turn into my worst nightmare.

'Smile through the rain and laugh through the pain.'

Yeah-fucking-right.

27

Demons don't live in dark places; they live in the minds of men. And guilt can be a powerful demon. Once embraced, it can wear away the bones, corroding the soul like a ravenous poison, seeking only to destroy and cause further misery. It may subside for days, months, even years, but unless true forgiveness for one's actions is attained, it never truly dissolves.

I thought I had forgiven myself for killing a man, but my inability to be open with Nia has proved otherwise tonight.

Sat on my bed for the past two hours, I've replayed tonight's events in my head countless times. I reach for my phone with every noise I hear, expecting Nia to call or text, but it doesn't come.

As I stand up, I feel different. Heavy. Lethargic. Angry. My guilt has returned.

I walk over to my wardrobe and reach inside one of my jacket pockets to find a half-empty bag of weed when I realise there are no cigarettes around me, which means no *spliff*.

"Fuck's sake."

'This is stupid. Nia only lives across the road. I could literally be there right now instead of drowning my sorrows.'

But her words ring in my head. 'Don't ever talk to me again.'

I suck my teeth, trying to put her to the back of my mind.

A couple more shots of Hennessy, my head hits the pillow, and I sink further into a drunken stupor.

My eyes close and time passes before a sharp pain slices through my head as I sit up too fast.

The brightness around the room tells me it's early morning and the humming in my dream turns out to be my ringtone.

I pick the phone up from the floor, hoping it's Nia.

"Yo," I say.

"Wa gwarn, brudda."

I suck my teeth. It's just Scribz.

"What d'you want?"

"Come on, allow all that, Rakz. I thought we squashed this ting."

I ain't in the mood for Scribz right now. My head's thumping and his words are like a bassline in my brain.

"What d'you want, Scribz? If you're thinkin' I'm gonna help you with your debt, you got shit twisted. You got yourself into this, *and* you dragged me into it."

"I'm not asking for your help," Scribz says, although his voice doesn't sound very convincing.

"So what's got you ringin' man at seven in the morning, fam?"

"You need to chill, my guy. It's good news."

I roll my eyes.

"What?"

"Obviously, man's got a new connect. I've been chattin' to him. He said he can drop me food. You just gotta go pick it up. I give you the shots, you get rid of it, and man should be able to pay this debt."

'This guy's not serious.'

"You think I'm taking any more food off you, bro? Are you sick in your head?"

"What's the problem?"

"The last food you had me pick up had people coming after me and thinking I'm some thief. Bun that, man. Keep your connect."

"Ah, bro. C'mon. If we move this together, we can pay off the Turks and get straight back to business. All I need is a month."

"You ain't got a month. They're already coming after man."

"I can pay them off every week."

"I don't need your food, Scribz."

He switches tactics.

"How you gonna survive then, Rakz? You gonna go get a job? Take orders in Starbucks or stack shelves in Sainsbury's like some wasteman. C'mon, bro, you're telling me this don't makes sense? Look, my bad 'bout before, but we can sort this ting together."

"You're not listening. I don't need your connect. I got my own. The food's better, and so is the price." Scribz pauses, and for the first time today, he's lost for words. "I'm doing my ting by myself, bro," I say.

"Who's your connect?"

"Don't worry 'bout that?"

"What it's like that, Rakz? Man bring you in an' now you wanna try cut man out."

"Ain't like that at all, Scribz."

"So, what's it like, brudda? 'Cause it come like you're forgetting who brought you in and put you on," he cries, clearly irate now.

"Relax, man will put some money aside for you and your mum, but *I'm* runnin' tings now. *I'm* callin' the shots."

"Are you dumb? You think you're sidelining me in my own operation—"

"—You sidelined your fuckin' self. You stole from the connect, and that's why you can't get any more food. And on top of that, you got man comin' after me and Deontay, making business way harder."

"So, what? You come outta jail, and you think you're gonna run tings, Rakz? You wanna be the boss?"

This is all just anger coming out of his mouth now. Irrational anger.

"What kind of boss pulls the moves you pulled, Scribz, seriously?" I say as calmly as can be.

"Ite, cool. Say no more," he says and hangs up the phone, ending his toddler tantrum.

I throw my phone to the bottom of the bed.

"Let him sulk, man."

Somehow, I manage to smash through two hundred press-ups before the throbbing in my head deters me from going on.

Once I've showered and eaten some leftover fried fish, my hangover abates.

I make my way outside, and as I reach the Porsche, I take a long look at Nia's front garden.

'What am I gonna say if I go over there, though? Apologise after she told me not to talk to her again... If I chase her, I look desperate... That's a wasteman ting and it's only downhill from there. She knows she'll always have man where she wants.'

I convince myself she'll come round eventually, get in the car and call Deontay. The dashboard lights up, and his voice echoes around the vehicle.

"Yes, yes, Rakz."

"Wa gwarn, D?"

"I'm good, broski. What you saying?"

"Listen, I need you to chat to Ribz and tell him to go and pick suttin' up for me."

"What? Now?"

"Yes, now, bruv."

"Ite, cool."

"I'ma text you the location and time from the other number."

"Cool. Aye, wait, Rakz."

"What?"

"Erm... You see later, yeah?"

"Yeah."

"You mind if I take the evening off, please, bro?"

"Evening off, for what?"

"You remember that girl man drew the other day."

"You mean the girl that *I* drew."

"Ite, the girl that *we* drew."

"We? Please. I put that on a plate for you."

"Yeah, but I finished it off, though," Deontay says with that adolescent tenor.

"What about her?"

"Basically... Man wanted to take her cinema and that tonight."

"Cinema?"

"Yeah."

"What happened to 'Netflix and chill.' Ain't that what you likkle youts do nowadays?"

"G, I don't have nowhere to Netflix and chill."

'Nowhere to Netflix and chill, and all man's thinkin' about is gyal.'

I shake my head. "Say no more. Take the evening off. Just make sure you get Ribz to cover your shift."

"Yeah, nah, of course. Love Rakz."

"Say nuttin', shout Ribz now. And take ten g's from the spot, give it to him."

"Ite, bro. Love."

I disconnect the call and fire up the engine, waking half the neighbourhood.

I glide through the roads until I hit the motorway. Then, I kick the car into sport mode and get my last little joy out of this beast.

As my head flies back against the headrest and I switch lanes like I'm Lewis Hamilton, I realise why people love these supercars so much. It's that sense of dominion over everyone else. A feeling that you're more than just a man. You're a superman in one of these, faster and more powerful than anyone of anything around you.

A near-lethal dose of adrenaline shoots through me as I speed dangerously fast, knowing one wrong move and I could spin into oblivion. The wind tears against my eardrums, and it's exhilarating. Cars transform into red, silver, and black specs in my side mirror as I race on, challenging myself to see how far I can push it before fear takes over.

I hit 145mph, and for the first time since last night, I'm smiling.

Twenty minutes later, I reach my destination.

I walk into Prestige Car Hire, and I'm greeted by Darkos' uncle. We stroll past sparkling luxury cars with laminated signs hanging in their windscreens before we end up in his office. We talk for a bit, and I hand him the keys to the Porsche.

"How'd you like it?" he asks with an excited grin like *he's* just been driving it for the past week.

"It was calm, man, but I need suttin' low key," I tell him.

We mull over a few options, and he eventually hands me the keys to a Silver Mercedes A-Class.

It's perfect.

Not too shabby, but certainly not too flashy.

"No need for the paperwork," he says, and within ten minutes, I'm out of there and in my new car.

I text Darkos, thanking him for the hook-up. He texts back with the thumbs-up emoji. I don't mention anything to him about the police stop. After all, he didn't mention anything about the car having a 'drugs marker' on it.

In hindsight, that's probably why he gave it to me so cheaply. Nobody ever does favours from the goodness of their heart in my line of work.

A couple of hours later, I'm at home, going through some of Mum's old stuff, when my phone rings.

'Nia?'

But it's just Deontay.

"Yo, D."

"Oi, Rakz, where are you, man?"

"At yard, wa gwarn?"

"Oi, bruv, I need to come to you now."

'What?'

"Where are you?" I shout, rising to my feet.

"I'm on the block, man."

"What happened?"

"Rakz, them man bored up Ribz."

"What? Who? Did he lose the money?" I ask.

The static across the phone, coupled with the wailing and roaring in the background, overpowers Deontay's response.

"Where you, Rakz?" is all I make out.

"I'm coming now."

I'm in shorts, a vest, and sliders, but I don't care right now. I grab the keys from the kitchen counter and jet out of my house.

I spin the Mercedes around and turn onto the high road.

It's at its busiest, and I have to creep along, stealing a few yards every so often in the baking sun.

"Move out of the way," I yell to the driver in front of me.

The rays splinter through my window, blinding me as I take a right turn and hear the blast of a horn. A car skids to a halt, and the woman behind the wheel bangs her hands against the dashboard, but I ain't got time to argue.

I turn down the road, park the car, and jog the rest of the way. I shimmy past hundreds of men and women, moving to jog on the road at some stages just to get through the sea of bodies.

'Ribz better not have lost my ten grand, man. I swear down.'

I arrive at Tunwell Estate to see two police cars parked at the first junction. Both vehicles are empty, so I pay them no mind and phone Deontay.

I tell him to meet me in one of the low-rise blocks tucked discreetly away behind the derelict remains of an old youth centre.

Minutes later, Deontay enters the block, his shoulder bag swinging back and forth as he repeatedly turns to look over his shoulder.

"Wa gwarn?" I ask.

He lifts those Men in Black shades that fail to hide the sweat running down his temple, and I see the fear in his eyes.

"Yo, them man caught Ribz, bruv," he says.

"You got the money?"

"Yeah, yeah, it's here," Deontay says, looking slightly stunned.

My heart settles.

"What should I do?"

"Nuttin', just chill."

"What?"

"What you gonna do?"

"Them man stabbed Ribz, bro. Man can't just sit here and let that slide."

"So, what you tryin' to do?"

"Let's go get them. They'll still be local. Come."

"There's feds on the block, and you're talkin' about ridin' out. Use your head."

"So, what? Man ain't gonna do nothing?" Deontay says, his arms spread like he doesn't understand.

"Who was it, some likkle dickheads he had beef with?"

"It was dem Turks. They saw us in the cab when we came out the estate and tried to rush the car."

"Serious?"

"Yeah."

"Hundred percent? You see their faces, yeah?"

"I see one of them, he looked Turkish, like, hairy, and he had that... like Spanish-y, Greek skin and that."

'Rah, is that how these man are movin' now.'

I sigh.

"Look, I'll deal with this. You just go grab a pack from the trap, init," I tell Deontay.

"But, wait, what about Ribz?"

I suck my teeth. "Bruv, Ribz was gonna get stabbed sooner or later. He's too hype. I told you about that yout'," I say.

I take the bag from Deontay and go to leave the block.

"Rakz, man can't just leave him. That's my guy."

"Well, where is he?"

"The ambulance came and took him to the hospital."

"Where'd he get stabbed?"

"In his shoulder and his arm."

"He'll be alright then."

"But Rakz..."

297

One hand holding the block door open, I turn to face Deontay. I let go of the door and pull up my vest to show him the massive scar that runs from the side of my chest along my back.

"You see this? I was sixteen years old, and man chopped me with a machete."

Deontay's head jerks back.

"I went hospital, then I discharged myself two days later and camped out for three nights straight until I caught this prick and shot him in the back. If the gun didn't jam on my daughter's life, he'd be six foot deep."

Deontay stands there in silence as I let my vest fall and turn to face him.

"Listen, I ain't out 'ere to put my life on the line for the whole fuckin' ends. *You're* my brudda. If a man touches *you*, it's curtains. Let Ribz deal with his problems. If he needs a machine, tell him to come holla me."

Deontay's arms hang by his side as he stares at the ground.

"You're setting up in the other spot tonight. Man's gonna send all the shots there," I say, handing Deontay the key.

"But Rakz, you said I could have the night off to go cinema."

"I know what I said, but is Ribz around to run tings?"

"Nah, but I already—"

"—No, he's not. So, it's your job, you feel me?" I say, leaning over Deontay to ensure he knows I'm not joking.

He moves his head from side to side, unhappy but unable to complain.

I put a hand on his shoulder. "Look, I'm done with all this soon, ya know."

Deontay raises his head, expressing a look of disgust.

I can't lie. It wasn't the reaction I was expecting.

"What? What do you mean?" he asks.

"I'm done after this pack. Out the game."

"Seriously?"

"Yeah."

"But we're making Ps."

"That don't matter when you get caught."

"We ain't gonna get caught," Deontay says.

"That's exactly what my bredrin Jonesy thought. And now guess where he is... Sittin' in jail doing sixteen years. You see us—you and me... We ain't no different. Nobody's untouchable out 'ere. Don't ever forget that."

Deontay kisses his teeth and looks away as his nostrils flare.

"Look, after this man's going Africa. I don't know how long for, but I need to get outta this place. Man stays here, it's only a matter of time before suttin' happens. I'm too old for this shit."

Deontay forgets himself for a minute and knocks my hand off his shoulder.

"Africa?"

"Yeah, Africa. Far away from all this."

"But what about me, cuz?"

"You got some money put away, alie?"

He looks from side to side.

"You must have at least a little ten stack by now."

He looks at the ground before raising his chin again. "I got a couple bags, but why can't we just keep doing this? Or at least give me the line when you go," he cries.

"Give you the line... You think I'm leaving you to stay out on these roads. Nah, there's no longevity in this ting, D, don't you get that? It's get in and get out. Man got in, and now I'm getting out."

"But what am I gonna do then?"

"Do suttin' better. Save your wage off this pack, then put it into suttin', I dunno. Suttin' you like to do."

"Why didn't you tell me this from the beginning?"

"Do I look like your son?"

"You should've told me."

"I don't need to tell you nuttin'. You're *my* young G, ya know! Not the other way round, don't ever forget that."

Immediately Deontay surrenders, and I realise why. My fist is clenched, and I'm standing over him like I'm about to punch his head off.

"Sorry," he says, his eyes replete with fear.

"Go to the trap, grab what you need, and then get to Sally's. I'ma shout you."

I hold out my fist, and he gives me the weakest fist bump he's ever given me before walking off.

As I march off, I feel everything slowly falling apart.

The Turks have started a war, Scribz has betrayed me, Deontay's head has been turned, and it's over with Nia.

This isn't how I planned any of this.

28

It's been a week since my argument with Nia. I assumed she would have texted or called me by now, but no. Nothing. I haven't even seen her in passing.

I didn't attend, but Jamal's funeral yesterday has put a harrowing thought in the back of my mind that won't subside. I need to see that Nia's okay. Pushing my pride to one side, I walk up to her front gate.

The curtains are drawn in the living room and the spare bedroom in the same manner they've been for the past three days. This isn't like Nia.

I knock at the door and wait a while.

"C'mon, Ni. Where are you?" I say, taking a step back to see if I can peek through a gap in the curtains upstairs.

I tap against a window and even call her name several times.

A few minutes later and nothing.

I shake my head as I walk back along the garden path. This girl must really hate me, or I'm just catching her at the worst possible times.

With one hand on the gate, another thought hits me like a blow to the face. *'Woah. What if these Turks have seen me with her and come after her? Shit.'*

I turn around and walk straight back up the pathway, pressing the bell as I pound the door with my fist. "Nia, Nia," I yell.

Soon enough, I hear the sound of a neighbour's door opening.

"Can I help you, sir?" calls an elderly man with a strong Caribbean accent. Hunched over, he hobbles out onto his porch dragging a plastic chair with one hand and carrying a walking stick in the other.

"Nah, it's cool, man," I say.

"My eyes may not work, but my ears definitely do, and you ah knock pon that nice likkle girl's house like you the Gestapo."

I look closer at the little man who feels all around the window seal on his porch before placing his chair down. He's frail with a subtle pot-belly visible behind his pale blue polo shirt. A pair of spectacles dangle below his chest, supported by the thin leather strap tied around the back of his neck.

"I was just tryin' to see if Nia was home, that's it. Sorry if I disturbed you."

He doesn't look at me, but he replies. "You nah affi be sorry. More men should be like you."

"How you mean?"

"Well, you ah chase after your woman. Good for you, bwoy," he says, pointing a trembling finger in my direction.

The man's gentle words calm me a tad.

I decide to exit Nia's front garden and continue this conversation privately. If anybody round here knows where to find her, her next-door neighbour is a good place to start.

"You mind if I open the gate?" I ask the elderly gentleman, who sits in his chair, his walking stick resting against his leg.

He gestures for me to enter, and it's not until I get about two metres from him that I freeze. "Oi... Uncle Dennis, is that you?"

He raises his head, and I look him in his milky-blue eyes.

"Who am I talking to?" he asks.

I run my hand over my head. "It's Rakim, Anthea's son."

Even though he's not my biological uncle, the joyous scream he lets out would convince most people otherwise.

"Rakim, where you been, bwoy? Come 'ere so mi can see you."

"Rah, Uncle Dennis. I never knew you lived here," I say as I hug him.

"Lord have mercy, you get big," he says, squeezing my forearm up to my bicep. "I bet you look like Terminator now."

I laugh.

"When did you move here? I thought you lived at the other end of the road."

He continues to hold onto my arm as he explains.

"Mi did use to live down at one hundred and seventy-three, but that was with mi wife."

"Okay, I hear you. How you been though, long time?"

"Mi nuh really come out mi 'ouse too much these days, but mi getting there. Mi carrying on, man."

"How's your wife?"

"Ahh, she get sick of my backside and divorce me, so mi ah shack up with mi new wife, right here."

I crack up as my mum's words play in my head. 'Uncle Dennis, one nasty old man', she used to say when he'd joke about how good some of the women, thirty years his junior, looked when they passed by.

It turns out he wasn't joking after all.

We talk about some of my fondest childhood memories, and he tells me how he completely lost his sight a few years ago. We talk about my mum, her funeral, and how his latest wife left him all alone in the world after falling victim to cancer last year.

I lean against the rail that leads down his porch steps and embrace the nostalgia.

"Remember when you used to give us them likkle sweets? Member them Weathers Original tings, me and Leanne always used to bug you for them."

Uncle Dennis smiles, and I feel a warmth from within. "How is your sister, she keeping well?" he asks.

"Yeah, she's fine."

"Good to'ear."

Uncle Dennis lifts his walking stick and points it towards Nia's front garden. "So weh happen with you an' your likkle girlfriend?"

"What d'you mean?" I say, playing dumb.

"She ah go back fi visit her mother," Uncle Dennis says.

"What, Nia left?"

"About a week ago. She come over and say not fi tell anybody, but mi can't have you just ah beat down the door like that."

'Is that how Nia's moving? She just left the country without even saying anything?'

Trying to convince myself of a silver lining, I take a moment to acknowledge the most crucial fact, at least she's safe.

"You know when she coming back?" I ask.

"Maybe a month, mi nuh really know."

I wipe the beads of sweat from my forehead.

"She's a sweet girl, that one. Nuh let her get'way."

"She must wanna get away. She's gone to the other side of the world," I shrug.

"Gwarn an' get her back then," Uncle Dennis says, raising a wrinkly finger. Bringing his hands together, he continues. "Take some piece of advice from an old man..."

"Go on," I say.

"Son, di biggest problem with your generation is that you never stick at anything. You always shift from one thing to another, one woman to di next, without seeing any of it through... Take it from a man who knows. Relationships aren't one bed of rose petals. They're hard work. But if she's worth it, then never give up because if you *do* give up, then *you're* not worth it."

I let the words marinate.

"... But wait, Uncle. How you really giving me advice about relationships? You been divorced twice," I say.

"Then, if mi ah divorce twice. Maybe you should listen to me before you end up just like me, old and alone."

Uncle Dennis always loved a sense of humour, and his smile indicates nothing's changed in that department, at least. I nod my head, happy to have had this conversation and feeling the most grounded I have in a while.

'I need to get away from this life, man,' I think as I'm reminded of who I am and where I've come from. Rakim before prison, before Nia, the Turks, and before all of this shit, I've found myself in the midst of.

I talk with Uncle Dennis for a bit longer before I say goodbye and tell him I'll stop by from now on.

A couple of weeks pass, and it's pretty much the same old, but still nothing from Nia. She's played on my mind daily, but I've kept myself occupied as a distraction.

There haven't been any more problems with the Turks. My guess is that the increased police presence in the area after Ribz being stabbed has deterred them. I'm not naive, though. I know they'll be back.

With Ribz just being released from the hospital a few days ago after treatment for a punctured lung and a hematoma in his arm, I've had Deontay working much harder than usual. I reckon another week or so, and I'll have my fifty grand. Once I do, I'll have two options: win Nia back and lure her to The Gambia with me or pay off the Turks on Scribbler's behalf and start again from scratch.

No alcohol or weed for a fortnight; I'm thinking clearer.

I've been out of prison for three and a half months doing this stuff, and it's brought money, yeah, but it's also brought a load of drama, and I can't help but think my circumstances are a karmic result of the life I live.

I mean, I sell crack cocaine and heroin at the end of the day. Two of the worst substances a human being could possibly put in their body. And although I may not physically hand over the drugs myself, I control their distribution. I facilitate an addiction that leads to thousands of deaths, destroys families, ruins communities, and fuels the robberies, prostitution, thefts, and homelessness that engulf impoverished neighbourhoods like mine and give them a bad name.

The addicts I may not see on a daily basis, but I know their stories all too well.

Jimmy, who calls at least four times a day, stole his mum's gold earrings last week. They'd been passed down his family for three generations, and he went and pawned them for forty quid.

Lisa's just had her three kids taken off her for the second time because she can't kick her addiction. And now they're lost to a care system until they're eighteen.

Kayla's buying more than ever which means she's selling her body more than ever. She was ten when she was sexually abused by her father. The only way she's ever known how to deal with it is by putting the shit I sell in a needle and injecting herself.

This is just a fraction of what I've discovered within the past twelve weeks, and as I leave another probation session, I feel The Gambia calling me. It's my only escape from this.

When I get back home and enter my house, Ping's in the hallway. "This come for you," he says as he hands me a brown envelope.

It's only the second letter I've received since I was released from prison. This one looks familiar, though.

"Bye," Ping says as he heads out the door.

I see the tape along the top of the envelope and turn it over. It's addressed to me, just like Ping said. It's been sent from prison, but I don't recognise the handwriting.

I take it into the front room and sit down on the sofa. As I open the envelope, a piece of paper falls to the carpet while another remains in my hand. I reach down and pick up the piece of paper from the floor. The writing on it is about half a page long, and at the top are the words 'READ THE OTHER LETTER 1ST.'

I follow the instruction and shift my attention to the sheet of A5 in my left hand.

Yo Rakz,

What's good, my brother? I hope you're doing alright out there, keeping your head down like you said you would. I bet you're loving the freedom, hitting the roads all swole, flexing on these girls. Lol. How's your people? Your sis and your nephews and that, they cool? What about your daughter? Have you spoken to her mum yet to try and pattern a visit?

I know we just spoke the other day, but I haven't been able to get through to you and keep u updated.

I thought I'd let you know the visit with my girl went well. It was just what I needed. I don't wanna jinx it or say too much, but hopefully everything goes to plan. Man might be looking at a retrial.

I pause for a moment.

I gulp as I feel my throat begin to dry up.

The letter is from Jamal.

A strange shiver ripples through my body, and I flip the page.

The other side is blank. No name, no nothing. He hasn't left any sort of farewell message.

It's odd, but I continue, nonetheless.

I can't lie, after you left Rakz, I was feeling pissed. Of course, man was happy you were gone, and that, dat goes without sayin. You deserve to be free. Twelve years my brother! I've only done three, and it come like I've been here half my life. I can't even picture twelve.

Imagine, I didn't come out of my cell for two days. Mandem were thinking I had beef on the wing. You were my main guy in here, fam. It's dead without you. I fuck with some others, but whenever I speak with them, they never really have me thinking the way you did. You got man through a couple bad nights, my bro. I didn't really get a chance to tell you before you left—serious love for that from my heart.

And I know this might not matter to you now you're out, and I know you're not gonna like it, but you kept it real with me, so I owe it to you to tell you something.

I get that feeling in my stomach. The one when your gut becomes hollow like you've descended too swiftly on a rollercoaster.

When I was in your bro's yard the other day...

'My bro?'

I rack my brains. Jamal always joked about Scribbler and me being brothers because we were so alike. '*He must be referring to Scribz.*'

307

Cryptic message deciphered; I continue reading.

... I see that yout' going through some papers. He was by himself, so I crept up on him. I was gonna get him back for the other day when he took my Game of Thrones DVD and ran off before bang-up like that shit was funny. So, these times I've sneaked up behind him and snatched his newspapers off him. Man starts wiling out try'na swing for man n ting. Then when I get a good look at a bit of the page, I understand why.

Right at the top, big, bold letters it...

The letter ends abruptly.

I turn it over again to ensure nothing is on the other side.

'What?'

I briefly put it to one side and pick the other letter up from beside me. I unfold the crease and instantly notice the different handwriting.

I scan the bottom of the page.

It's signed by Devonte.

"What does this guy want, man?"

Rakz my darg I hope you been gd keeping out of trouble, but you probably know I'm not about this writing life. That other letter was from J init. I found it when I dropped suttun behind the drawer in my cell. Then when I read it, I started doing my research. You know what he's talking about, init. That lanky brudda. I bet he probly told u he boxed me up over me violating him or something. Dumb yute. Not even. It was a sucker punch ting. Not gonna say much, but long story short, me and that lanky yout' got into it, and I got moved off the wing. I'm calm tho, Jonesy's on my wing and truss me. He's got a lot to tell u.

They put me on monthly visits becoz that lil madness, so hit Jonesy up yh, he said he put u on his list, so book a V, and he'll fill u in.

Roll safe, my darg and when ur settled an every'ting, come check me.

Devonte

Jonesy's deets:

Danny Jones

A1466BR

I scan over both letters again, picking out key points.

The prison officers read every letter before they get sent out, so ninety-nine percent of the time, people will write certain parts in code, the pieces of information they don't want the authorities to see.

Jamal's letter has me staring into oblivion.

'Scribz told me Jamal's visit with his girl went bad and that she left him.'

But Jamal's letter says the total opposite.

'What's going on? If Jamal could've got a retrial.... Why would he hang himself? And why would Scribz lie about it? This don't make sense.'

I read further on until I get to the part about newspapers. For the next few minutes, I strain my brain trying to figure out why Jamal and Scribbler would fight over newspapers.

'Newspapers... Newspapers... What's he on about?'

Then it clicks. "Ohh, papers."

Jamal must've saw Scribz going through his 'papers'—his paperwork, all the stuff to do with his case (information about his arrest, transcripts of his police interview, witness statements, his criminal background, etc.)

The letter makes sense now, but it still doesn't explain why Scribz would fight Jamal just because of that. The only reason a prisoner refuses to show his paperwork to a friend or cellmate is that he's either a snitch or he's in for some sick kind of crime like rape or sexual offences against children or something disgusting like that. But I know Scribbler. I've read his paperwork, and he's read mine. He ain't no snitch. And his crimes are far from preying on little girls.

He was convicted of kidnap, false imprisonment, and two counts of possession of a loaded firearm with intent to endanger life. He's serving an indeterminate sentence which means he has no release date, just a minimum term of fifteen years. After that, it's up to the Parole Board to decide when, if at all, he'll end up getting out.

Struggling to figure out what could have been so bad that it would cause Scribz to fall out with Jamal *and* Devonte, I read Devonte's short paragraph for the third time. It indicates Scribz has been lying. Again.

309

He told me Devonte was stealing his things, but apparently, that wasn't the case.

'Devonte might just be twisting Jamal's words. He might've found that letter and thought, rah, let me put a little spin on this, so Rakz don't think I'm a scumbag thief.'

He could be doing all of this just to get back at Scribz.

My thoughts run like a hamster on a wheel, working hard but getting me nowhere. I'm not sure who to trust right now.

"Wa gwarn for Scribz? I need to chat to this guy ASAP."

I search through my recent calls and find the number he called me off the other day.

Holding the phone tightly, my bicep threatens to pop as I wait for a connection.

The mobile phone you've called is switched off. Please call again later.

I suck my teeth. 'Scribz a snitch? I ain't buying that man.'

Scribz lied to me, and it was a sneaky move, but for him to be snitching in his paperwork? No way. That ain't Scribz.

Plus, who could he have snitched on? He's been in jail for over twelve years.

'But then Jamal said his visit went well. Why did Scribz lie?'

Something's off.

I don't know what Jamal and Devonte found out about Scribz, but I guess there's only one way to find out.

"I gotta go see Jonesy."

29

I arrive in the car park of HMP Huntingley around 2.15. After registering my arrival in the visitor's office, I place my phone, keys, and wallet in a locker and wait for my name to be called.

'This is weird.' It feels strange to be on this side of the prison walls.

Perched on the hand railing by the entrance of this cabin, I can't believe I'm going back into prison. I thought I was done with this place forever. I thought Scribz would be out five or six years after me, and there'd be no reason to ever return. But ironically, he's the reason I'm back.

By the looks of the company, I'm in, I've made it in good time.

A crew of gym junkies laugh and joke like schoolchildren while a group of glammed-up girlfriends and dejected baby mothers form a clique. They complement each other's outfits and moan about their journeys as a series of names are called over the speaker in quick succession. I hear my name and stand up as a couple of OAPs hurry to the front of the group that's amassed outside the visitor's building.

As soon as my feet cross the threshold of the reception, my mouth goes dry. My fingerprint and passport are checked, and I move along the conveyer belt of bodies. As I look around this old building, the smell of damp concrete and stale sweat clogs my airways.

I don't recognise any of the five officers in the reception, but they still look familiar. The sinister uniforms and the black steel toe-cap boots make the men look like wannabe drill sergeants and deprive the women of any sex appeal.

About fifteen of us are directed through an automated door that leads to a narrow hallway. After a straddler finally makes it in, I hear a sound I know well. Keys clink together in a rhythmic tempo as an officer

311

joins us in the hallway. Beads of sweat form on my forehead as the officer taps a window, and the metal door behind him slides shut.

We stay locked in an area as fine as a bus aisle as everybody shares one another's fragrance before we eventually shuffle through to a lobby.

The artificial lighting above shines down harshly on everyone, revealing flaws that some tried their utmost to conceal this morning.

A poster about charities and helplines for prisoners and their families to contact catches my eye. It seems this place is designed to give the families of those incarcerated a false sense of reality as they wait here. Attempting to create the illusion that inmates here receive all the support they need and that the prison establishment is one big happy family that cares about the men that live here.

I shake my head, and a fellow visitor smiles at me. "They might as well stick a picture of Santa up there with the Easter Bunny and the Tooth Fairy," he says, and I give him a half-smile.

Everybody in the lobby forms a queue for the final check before the visiting hall. A German Shepherd passes by, and I feel the soggy tip of its nose as it checks for traces of drugs. Satisfied, none of us have half a kilo of coke stuffed down our trousers, the door in front of us is opened. I follow a few t-shirts and jumpers through the entrance, and my entire body changes.

The indistinct chatter, the loud chants, the laughter flying around. I know I shouldn't, but I feel like I'm back home amongst my band of brothers.

Four separate rows of chairs and tables embellish the hall. One chair occupied by an inmate in an orange netball bib on one side of each table, and three empty chairs on the other. At the far end of each aisle are prison officers, spaced out evenly and strategically to keep order.

Scattered around a large, carpeted hall, heads rise like meerkats on a horizon, trying to find their partners for the next couple of hours.

I approach the desk and give my name.

"Table thirteen," a stubby woman says as her bleak brown eyes peer over the rim of her spectacles. "Next," she calls, directing me with her hand.

I hear my name being called and greet a couple of familiar faces while looking along the rows to find Jonesy.

Shaven heads. Plaits. Gelled comb overs. Scruffy corn rows.

'Where's this guy?' I think until I see Jonesy's steamy red cheeks deep in conversation with a man on the table next to him. He looks like a sunburned tourist.

"Jonesy?" I call out.

My voice barely gains any attention amid the hollering and excitement within this place.

It's not until Jonesy's friend brings my presence to his attention that I'm greeted with a set of open arms.

"Oi, oi, lad," Jonesy says, shooting up from his seat.

His gristly brown beard rubs against my cheek as he pulls me close.

"What's good, my brother?" I say.

Then from nowhere, a whiny voice interrupts. "Morrison, is that you?"

Jonesy and I release each other to see Mr F beaming like a little kid when daddy comes home.

I give a discreet nod, hoping he'll get the message.

Unfortunately, he doesn't.

'Why's this guy walking over like we're friends?'

"Fancy seeing you back here. How you doing, mate?" asks Mr F, extending a hand.

"I'm good," I say, my face straight as an arrow.

Mr F looks at Jonesy, who gives him a subtle greeting before another screw intervenes from afar to save Mr F's blushes. "Folkes, leave 'em. I need ya," one of his superiors calls.

Throwing up a thumb, Mr F still seems unaware that his unsolicited remarks are interrupting a meeting between two pals. "I'll catch up with ya before ya go then, yeah, Morrison?" he says before scampering off.

I'm like a celebrity in this place. The good, the bad, and the ugly all seem to love me.

"What, best pals?" Jonesy says pointing his head at Mr F.

"Never that."

"Talk to me then, son," Jonesy says as we both take a seat. "What's been going on? How's freedom? How many birds you shagged?"

"Trust you to jump in with the shagging straight away."

"Of course, mate. I don't do foreplay. I'm raw. No lube. Straight in," Jonesy says, directing his hand forward like an arrow.

"To be honest, fam, it's all right. Been taking it easy, ya know."

"You're such a boring cunt, Rakz."

I laugh.

"Well, if you hurry up and get out, you can show man the good life."

"That's what I'm talk'n 'bout. Thailand, Dubai, Cancun. I'm not coming back to this old dump for about six months straight."

"I don't blame you, fam. I been thinking about getting away myself."

"Surprised you haven't... Probation got you by the balls?"

"Nah, I done my whole term. The full twelve. Just got the one-year probation top-up. Go there, tell 'em what they wanna hear, and they leave me alone. As long as I ain't killing no one or becoming the next El Chapo, they don't really give a shit."

We go back and forth for a while, and gradually the intensity of our conversation ceases. It seems neither of us *wants* to address the elephant in the room.

"Yo, you want any chocolates or anything?" I ask, standing up.

"I'm on a diet, mate."

"Diet?"

"Yeah, get rid of this," Jonesy says, grabbing hold of a roll of flab above his waist. "Can't all be Hercules, like you."

I walk off to the corner of the room, where the prison employs a couple of inmates to stand behind a counter and serve tea and biscuits to visitors like it's their own private cafe.

314

You should see how serious some of these guys take it as well. God forbid they give you a black coffee instead of a hot chocolate. They'll be apologising for the next twenty minutes. I swear some of the lads doing this job are more repentant about messing up an order than the crime that actually put them here.

While I wait for my cup of tea and snacks, I begin mentally preparing myself for whatever Jonesy tells me. Whatever he says about Scribz, I've gotta be open-minded. I can't approach this with tunnel vision.

Minutes later, I'm back sitting across from Jonesy.

"That diet lasted long," I say as Jonesy tucks into a Mars bar.

"Cheat day," he muffles as he chomps away.

I put my plastic cup of tea on the table and straighten my back. Jonesy must sense the change in my demeanour as I notice the rotation of that mouthful of chocolate slow down drastically.

"So, what's going on with Scribz? Why's Devonte told man to book this V?"

Jonesy swallows his food and gestures for me to come closer.

I lean towards him like we're being spied upon.

"It's Scribbler," he says.

"Wa gwarn?"

"Well, you know, I moved wing a few weeks after you left us all. Get more gym time on this one. Then a month or so later, Devonte turns up telling me about he had a dust-up with Scribz over calling him out."

I look at Jonesy, baffled. "Callin' him out over what?"

"Rakz... He's a grass."

I hear the words, but it doesn't seem like it's me who's listening. It feels like I'm watching myself in a movie.

I squint my eyes as I try to process what Jonesy is telling me.

"A grass?"

"A grass, a snitch—"

"—I know what a grass is, bro. And what, you think that's Scribz?"

"Yeah, that's how it looks."

"How what looks? What's going on?"

315

Jonesy looks over his shoulder.

Lowering his voice to a whisper, he continues. "I didn't know how much you knew, but I'm guessing you ain't got a Scooby by that look on ya face."

I shake my head.

"Nah, wa gwarn?"

"All right, well, it's like this. About a month ago, two Turkish fellas turn up on the wing. One of them barely speaks a word of English, but the other one knows the lingo a bit. So, after a few days of seeing their faces around, I approach one of 'em. Turns out these two brothers, Burak and Hasan, run a Turkish firm that does business all over England and Scotland, moving mad bits of sniff, pills, dark, hash, weed, the lot."

"Yeah, so what's this gotta do with Scribz?"

"According to Burak, Scribz used to be a customer of his. I mean, he doesn't know him by face. These lot rarely even get seen. But roughly a year ago, under the direction of Scribz, a little black kid ran off with some grub that belonged to Burak.

"Scribz thought he'd got away with it until the Turks threatened his sister. He paid the debt, but since then, Burak and his people stopped working with Scribbler."

My face drops, and Jonesy picks up on my reaction. "Sounds like the sort of thing your mate does, right?"

Reluctantly, I nod.

"Don't you think it's funny how Scribz's old suppliers end up in here the week he gets transferred...? Burak's told me he knew Scribz was here, in this prison, and he's put fifty K on his head."

"What for if he got the money back?"

"You don't really know your mate, do ya?" Jonesy says as he unwraps another chocolate bar.

"Chat to me."

"So, you remember, Golem?"

"Who?"

"Golem... Ugly mug. Was Scribz's Offender Supervisor, hair thinning, eyes like a big fuck off owl. Looked like that little goblin from Harry Potter, Lord of the Rings, or whatever you call it."

"Oh yeah. I remember."

"Long story short, these Turks didn't only have a good thing going out in the real world, but they were operating on the inside for some time as well. And old Golem was bringing in all kinds of stuff for these lot about ten months before they even arrived."

"Swear down?"

"Yeah, they got a young guy, Emrah, who sells it on G-Wing. You know how it works, treble the price in 'ere."

"Yeah, for real."

"So, a little while after you left, Golem must have had a change of heart, the no-good-shit-cunt-slag, 'cause he turns around and says he can't do it anymore," Jonesy says before pausing to take a bite of his Mars. "Well, it doesn't work like that with these Turks. You're done when they say you're done. They've told Golem he's gotta get rid of this kilo or else, but he's refused. So, they've turned up at his daughters' school, given her a ride home, and threatened to kidnap her next time if he doesn't go ahead with it."

"How'd you know?"

"Mate, Golem fuckin' asked *me* if I'd get rid of it for him."

"For real?"

"Yeah, I thought he was try'na set me up, the cunt. Calling me into his office, fidgeting around the gaff, looking dodgy as fuck. Turned it down straight away."

"So, he went to Scribz and asked..."

Jonesy holds his arms out as if to say, 'Voila!'

"And Scribz took the box of flake?"

"Golem told Scribz if he can get rid of it, he'll bring it in, and for the trouble, he'll write a letter of recommendation that should be able to get Scribz an immediate release instead of D Cat when the time comes."

"Like that?"

"Yeah, Golem held weight in here."

"*Held?*"

Jonesy sniggers.

"What?"

"Scribz has only gone and robbed the cunt."

"What, instead of taking the coke and selling it, Scribz took it for himself?"

"Yeah. A few days later, I see Golem on the wing looking even worse than usual, and that's saying summink. He's all stressed and sweating, snapping at every little thing. Scribz even points him out to me, starts laughing, telling me about it."

I sit there processing everything. Voices, laughter, and infant cries bounce off the walls as I think of all the stories being told in this room.

But the thought in my head remains. '*I bet no one here is having a conversation like this.*'

Jonesy goes on.

"Scribz told Golem he'll take care of it on the outside and get someone to sell it. Lessens the risk. And because Golem ain't got a streetwise bone in his body, he's given Scribz the address of where the stuff is. Scribz didn't tell me anything else, but I'm guessing he took it sold it for himself because it's only when he realised who he'd robbed he changed his tune."

"Shit," I say, looking down at the table like I've just discovered the cure for cancer.

"What?" Jonesy asks.

I slowly lift my head and look across the table.

Jonesy's stout face cuts a frown as those rugged bristles circulate round and round while he chews.

"How well d'you know these Turks? You man friends?" I ask.

"Nah, I mean, they've done some business with a couple of my pals in the past, but that's it, just business."

He stops chewing and looks me directly in the eye like he knows I'm hiding something.

"Why?" he asks.

"Bro, I'm the one who took the food."

Jonesy freezes.

His eyebrows shoot up, and his mouth falls, revealing a glutinous trail of chocolate and caramel across his teeth.

"You're having me on?" he says.

All his charm has gone; for some reason, I sense he's more worried than me.

"Nah, seriously, why, wa gwarn?" I ask, impatient for a response.

"Rakz, I spoke with Burak earlier today... He's put fifty K on Golem's head."

"So, where's Golem?" I ask.

"He quit. Apparently. Or maybe... Maybe they've found him?"

"You think...? Nah, he would've given Scribbler up in a heartbeat. They would've gone after Scribbler."

"Yeah, but who would Scribbler have given up?" Jonesy says as he looks at me discerningly.

"Nah, he wouldn't. He told me he needed the money 'cause his mum was ill. She took all his money."

"Bullocks."

"So, you're saying when Scribz realised who he'd robbed, he snitched to the Governor, got himself a transfer, and put the message out to Burak and them man that I'm the one to blame."

"Exactly."

"Nah, man, he couldn't—"

"—Mate, when Scribbler found out who he'd robbed, he threw all his morals out the window."

The lights turn on behind Jonesy's eyes like he's just had a revelation.

"... What?"

"Fucking 'ell, maybe Devonte is right."

"Wa gwarn?" I ask.

"Well, Devonte said he found a letter from Jamal before J topped himself."

319

"Yeah."

"Jamal must have read through Scribbler's papers and found out he was a grass."

"You think?"

"Mate, Devonte told me Scribz was the one that found Jamal hanged."

"He never told me that."

"Shit! Devonte said he saw Scribz up on the landing outside Jamal's cell. What if Scribbler knew Jamal had found out he'd snitched on the Turks, and Scribz fucking killed him."

"But he hanged himself."

Jonesy looks fired up as he hits me on the arm.

"Rakz, you know like I do. It only takes ten minutes alone in a cell to choke someone out and wrap the bedsheets around his neck, tie them to the frame of the bunk, and you got yourself a suicide."

"Scribz? You really think he...?"

Suddenly I feel sick to my stomach. My insides are churning, and I feel like I'm about to throw up. It's the only thing that makes logical sense at this moment in time, but I don't want to ask. I don't want to know the answer.

"You should have seen his face when he found out who he'd robbed. After he grassed up Burak to the governor, I reckon Jamal found out. Then he's killed Jamal, left the cell, gone back, then ran outta there screaming, pretending he's found him like that."

The chatter in the room fades away.

It's just Jonesy and me. We sit there together, shocked beyond reprieve.

The vice around my lungs tightens by the second, forcing my heart to pump faster.

A prison officer calls out something about visits ending soon, bringing Jonesy and me back to the morbid reality.

"Look, Rakz, you gotta give the Turks their food back," Jonesy says. "They're a serious bunch, and they ain't just about the money. Their

320

pride's hurting. Burak's a sound geezer. Hasan's a bloody animal. If he finds out where you live, mate... Put it this way, I wouldn't wanna go to war with these lot."

"I ain't got the food. I sold it."

"What? Why?"

"It's food. What does a shotter do with food, bruv? I didn't know it was stolen. Scribz only told me after I'd stolen it. I had man coming after me, and my runner. Scribz, had no choice but to confess, the fuckin' snake." I slam my fist on the table. "Watch when I catch him."

"Forget about him for now. He's transferred out, probably doing voluntary with the nonces. Have you got the money?" Jonesy asks.

"Yeah."

"How much?"

"All of it."

"Well, maybe if I have a word and explain to Burak, you might get out of this."

"Just tell him it was Scribz."

"They thought it was Scribz, but if Scribz already told 'em it's you, and you got lads coming after you, they believe him."

"Can't you chat to them, tell them wa gwarn."

"I can try, but I hardly know the geezers. If you fork over the hundred grand, then maybe that'll settle it."

"A hundred grand? Bruv, it was fifty?"

"Not according to The Sultan. He's adamant he's a hundred grand out of pocket."

"How?"

"Fifty for what he would have made of the merchandise and another fifty for the hit he's put out. I reckon they took out Golem and got the wrong guy, they ain't gonna tell me, but that's all I can come up with."

"I ain't got a hundred bags, though. I've barely got fifty."

Jonesy looks to the side.

"Rakz, I'd help you if I could, but—"

321

"—It's cool. I know you got your own tings to pay for. You're in here. I'm out there. You should be the one asking me for money if anything."

Jonesy doesn't say anything but gives me that look that says, 'I'm glad you understand.'

"I didn't even plan any of this shit, and I'm here giving this guy all the money I've made," I say.

Jonesy appears sympathetic to my complaints, but his commiseration means nothing. It's not him who put money out on my head.

"What if I give him the fifty and get him the other fifty down the line?"

"It's not just about the money with these lot, Rakz. It's principle and pride. These lot are all fighting for whose gonna take control of the firm now that Burak and his brother are banged up. If Burak shows any weakness and lets you walk for this, he ain't just giving up fifty large, he's giving up his seat on the throne."

The next fifteen minutes is a blur. We go over Scribz's actions, how we can track him down, and a few possible ways Jonesy can approach Burak. He agrees to do so, and soon enough, we're shaking hands as Mr F calls for us to finish our visits.

"Look who's grown a pair," Jonesy says, trying to lighten the mood.

It doesn't work, though.

All I can think of is Scribbler's betrayal. I visualise myself smashing his skull with my fist.

'I loved this guy like a brother. I told him about Keziah and Shanice. He rode for me no matter what. How could he switch up on me just to get an early release?'

The pain slices through me like a guillotine.

I don't need to say anything. Jonesy sees the look on my face.

"I'll do my best to chat to Burak. I let you know, Rakz. Don't sweat it mate. Scribz done us all," he shrugs.

I know he means well, but right now; I'm not even as bothered about these Turks as I am Scribbler. My one true friend, my brother from another mother, murdered Jamal in cold blood, snitched to the

Governor, and sold me out. The thought hits me like a steam train. The force alone sweeps my legs, and they almost give way. I blink heavily as Jonesy holds me firmly.

"You all right, mate?"

The heat in this room is sweltering, I'm sweating, and my pulse is racing. I shake my head. "Yeah, I just gotta get outta 'ere."

I share one last embrace with Jonesy.

"I'll get at you. I let you know if I can do anything," Jonesy calls as I walk towards the exit.

I don't even look back. I can't, my head is spinning like a propeller. Stars flash around me, blinding me before everything turns a stinging white that burns the back of my eyes. I stumble out of the visiting hall and manage to use the wall to support my faltering legs.

I put a hand on my forehead, and suddenly everything goes black.

'What the...'

My eyes roll back, my legs buckle, and I hit the ground.

When I wake up, I'm seated on a plastic chair as a tight pressure cuffs my wrist. Some medic has my other wrist between her fingers, and I can feel eyes passing me by like I'm a circus attraction. I don't know what just happened but as I gaze at my shoes, my thoughts start making some sense. A lady's voice asks me if I'm okay, and after a few seconds it all comes flooding back.

'Scribz!'

30

Parked in my car on Deontay's estate, I check my phone.

One final pull of my spliff, and I toss it out the window before reaching for the half-depleted Hennessy bottle that rests on the passenger seat. A swig of that familiar-tasting cognac goes down swiftly, leaving an afterburn milder than I'm used to.

I gaze between the gaps of the high-rise flats around me that reveal a corporate utopia made up of gigantic carbon buildings and glass towers. Multi-story offices stand proudly as the bright city lights sparkle for miles into the distance, shining upon exquisite craftsmanship along the midnight skyline.

As the liquor settles in my chest, I try to phone Scribz again, but I withhold my number this time.

The phone doesn't even ring, just like it hasn't since yesterday. Still, I won't let this one lie.

Once I confirm Scribbler is not only a snitch but that he killed Jamal and tried to set me up, I'll count down the days until he's released, and however much money or time I have to put into it, I swear I'll make sure he pays for his betrayal.

I take another shot of Hennessy.

"Fuck Scribz."

Browsing through my phone, I see a photo of Nia and me. It's the one that the waiter took on Nia's birthday. She looks immaculate, from her smile to her hair to her bronze skin that looks like it's been dripped in syrup.

"How'd you manage to fuck this up, Rakz?" I ask myself.

With no answer to comfort me, I search for one in my bottle of Henny.

Just then, I notice movement from the corner of my eye and turn my head to see Deontay. He's strolling over lethargically like he'd rather be anywhere else in the world.

"Wa gwarn for you, walking like we've got all night?" I call.

"Nothing."

"Man's been tryin' to call you. You've had man sat here for ten minutes, bruv."

"My bad. You want the money, yeah?" Deontay says with a blank expression.

I look him up and down as he reaches my window. "Get in the car."

He ambles around to the passenger side and gets in.

"Wa gwarn," he says, lacking any sort of enthusiasm.

I don't give him any response for a few seconds. Instead, I just stare at him. His eyes move from left to right as he tries to appear like he's not intimidated, although he blatantly is.

"What's this?" he says as he reaches underneath his bum and pulls out my bottle of Hennessy. He hands it to me, and I take it without breaking eye contact.

"What's wrong with you, bruv?" I ask.

"Nothing," he mumbles.

"Stop chattin' shit. What's the problem?"

"I ain't got no problem."

His words are so insincere, which just pisses me off even more. "Is it 'cause man's had you doing bare extra shifts or suttin'?"

Deontay shakes his head.

"Or, what, 'cause I told you I'm leaving this trappin' ting behind and now we're nearly finished, you're gettin' all emotional and shit?"

"Nah, not even," Deontay says all defensively.

"We gotta make this dough quick, and then I'm out. I told you, there ain't no happily ever after in this game. You make your money and get out. Put it into suttin' proper, you feel me?"

Deontay doesn't say anything. He just stares ahead and shrugs.

I suck my teeth. "Just give me the money, man," I say, fed up with his bitch-ass sulking like I haven't helped this boy make more money in the past couple of months than he would have ever made standing on the corner of the street selling little twenty-bags of weed.

'People are so ungrateful, no matter how much love you show them...'

We sit silently for the next couple of minutes as I count through the money. Once satisfied it's all there, I break Deontay off his little paycheck.

He takes it and goes to get out of the car before turning back. "Rakz?" he says.

"What?"

"... Ribz was asking when you're gonna pay him because obviously he's done bare shifts with man, helping me out and ting and he ain't even been—"

"—What are you his mum now?"

"Nah, but—"

"—He'll get paid when I pay him."

One hand on the door handle, Deontay squints his eyes like he wants to say something.

"What you saying?" I ask, hoping he'll finally be a man and get whatever has been simmering within him since God knows when off his chest.

"Nothing."

I roll my eyes.

"So, where you going now? Seen as you're done for the night, cuz," I say, changing the topic.

"I dunno."

"Bruv, where you going all Armani'd out from head to toe?"

He shrugs his shoulders as he steps out of the car, still holding onto the door.

Shaking my head, I look at the photo of Nia once again.

"I'm gonna see Natasha, init," Deontay finally confesses.

"Oh-kay. What, you like her, yeah?"

He doesn't say anything. He must think that I was born yesterday if he thinks his silence will fool me. I can see the lovestruck emojis all in his eyes.

Then it dawns on me that it isn't too safe for him out here. The Turks may still be looking for him.

"How you gettin' to her yard?" I ask.

"Gonna walk."

"What are you, some homeless yout', wandering the roads of south London at this time? Jump in, man."

"It's not even far, bro."

"Just get in the car, man."

I notice his hesitation as his eyes turn to the Hennessy bottle stuffed in my pocket.

"Don't watch that. I'm a much better driver when I'm wavey."

Reluctantly, he agrees and gets back in the car.

"Where's this place?" I ask.

"Wait, lemme get the postcode," Deontay says, reaching into his pocket for his phone. "Ah, shit, it's dead. I beg you let me use your phone to call her quickly."

I suck my teeth. "Cool, but hurry up, man. I gotta take a piss."

I unlock my phone, hand it to Deontay and watch as he sits there trying to recite his girlfriend's phone number.

"Zero-seven-five-one-nine... Erm... eight-two... Or was it four?"

I roll my eyes.

"Listen, hurry up with my phone. I'm gonna go take a piss. Just have the postcode by the time I come back," I say before leaving the vehicle and finding a secluded spot behind a set of communal bins.

Minutes later, Deontay's back in my sight. The engine still hums as I open the door and get behind the wheel.

Deontay's sitting with his arms folded and a frown on his face.

"Wa gwarn, your gyal don't wanna see you?" I ask.

He shakes his head, refusing to look at me.

"What's wrong then?"

"Nothing, I got the postcode. Let's go," Deontay says bluntly.

I input the postcode into the sat nav, click my seatbelt, and glide off.

We spend the short trip listening to some old-school Max B and French Montana, which fails to mask the frosty atmosphere. Honestly, though, I can't be bothered to entertain Deontay's immature mood swings tonight. I've got more important things to worry about, including his safety.

We turn into the street where Natasha apparently lives. A six-storey block of flats just ahead on my right-hand side appears to be the destination. It's one of many low-rise brown brick blocks that sit a fair way back from the pavement. A small region of grass is in front of the block, overlooked by a tinted glass baluster on each floor.

I slow the car to a stop outside just before the block.

As Deontay takes off his seatbelt and sorts his cash out, I see the door of Natasha's block swing open. "Is that your girl's sister?" I ask, tapping Deontay's arm to get his attention.

He raises his head and looks out of my window. "Yeah, that's her still."

I lower my window discreetly, hoping Natasha's sister won't notice me checking her out. "She looks good, ya know," I tell myself.

I can feel the liquor working through me now. It's got me in that flowy state; my feelings are more intense, and my thoughts seem to have much less power over me.

I keep my eyes on her as I focus on her bashment dancer thighs, robust and rotund.

"What's her name again?" I ask Deontay.

"Priscilla, why?"

"She's lookin' dangerous."

Deontay stops counting his money to hold both hands out in front of him. "I thought you had a girl," he says.

"Don't worry about all that," I tell him. "Plus, lookin' ain't cheatin'."

"After you gave man one big old speech."

"Sekkle yourself, you're killin' my high," I say as my eyes follow Priscilla's legs up past the bottom half of her jungle-green playsuit. I wonder how on earth her delicate calves carry the weight of her bum. And that's not all I'm wondering.

"So what was all that talk about when you got a good girl, you don't need another one then? What was that about?" Deontay says, and I think he's forgotten who he's speaking to for a moment.

"Mind your rasclart business," I say, turning towards him with a look that immediately puts him in his place. "About you wanna call me out. You were the one who was tellin' me to do my ting, you don't remember? Tellin' me, she's peng reh teh teh."

His nostrils flare, and he shakes his head.

"You need to go and check your girl. Let off some steam," I tell Deontay as my attention sways back to Priscilla.

Deontay opens the door without responding, slams it, and storms off.

"This yout's so lucky that I'm waved right now."

I watch him walk towards Priscilla as grey smoke swirls around just above her head while she taps away at her phone.

As Deontay approaches her, she raises her head, and they begin talking. Now that I can get a better view of her face, I angle my head out the window a tad. Two large, hooped earrings wobble as she speaks with Deontay. I can't tell how many cornrows she's got in, but they look good against her honey-glazed skin as they run from her forehead to the afro that sprouts out the back.

Her pocket-sized frame in that vivid playsuit, she reminds me of the girls I used to see at Notting Hill Carnival way back in the day. A flyer in her hand to fan herself, some body paint, and a plastic horn, and she'd be ready for a celebration right now.

I observe as Priscilla and Deontay talk for another minute or so.

Then Priscilla turns to look in my direction. She leans her head forward and squints her eyes as Deontay walks off.

The light from the screen of her phone brightens the vicinity as she aims it in my direction.

I put my hand out of the window and watch her wave back.

"I gotta go say hi now," I tell myself as if I need any more encouragement.

I take a sip of my drink as I look at the photo of Nia and me once more and sigh.

'She's gone. She left you to go on holiday without even tellin' you. She's probably out there right now... What do they call it? Hot girl summer and that.'

I suck my teeth and shove the phone back into my pocket.

Priscilla pivots on one foot as I approach. I watch her slide her phone out of sight before taking a pull of what I now know isn't a cigarette.

The smell of the weed makes me feel at ease right away.

I press the button on my keys, and my car chirps as I stroll over. My light grey cargo pants have me feeling cool in the heat of the night, and my plain t-shirt matches the cocaine-white Air Force's, which I make sure not to scuff on the uneven pavement.

"What's going on?" I ask Priscilla, who's just a couple of metres away.

She examines me with her fierce eyes that set my insides ablaze. "Not much," she says.

"Thought I'd come over and say hello since I see you checkin' me from the car."

"You could've called?" she says, which I hope she means in a sporting manner.

My head is beginning to feel a little light, and I can feel my body rocking back and forth, but I'm still in control.

"Nah, you prefer me to see me in person, alie?"

Priscilla shakes her head, but I hold eye contact until I see the traces of a smile. 'Who's she kidding?'

"You know I'm right," I say.

"Whatever," Priscilla says, taking another pull of her splif. "What you been up to then anyway, mister... What was it...? Rashad, Rashaun..."

"Funny."

"I'm messing with you," Priscilla says. "I remember your name."

"I know you do."

"Wow, you got a big head, innit? Proper fancy yourself."

I smile.

After not seeing Nia in nearly four weeks, I can't lie; it feels good to flirt with a woman.

"Not even," I say calmly.

Priscilla's eyes examine me once again. But this time, for longer. And more detailed. She doesn't say it, but I can feel it.

"What you smoking?" I ask.

"This...? It's Cali. Biscotti. You wanna try?"

"Gwarn then," I say, holding the spliff between my two fingers and taking a deep pull. I hear the paper sizzle as smoke rises in front of my face. "It's nice still," I say.

"Of course. Only the best for me, darling."

"So, where you off to with all your flesh on show, the butcher shop?"

Priscilla rolls her eyes. "What are you, my dad?"

"Nah, just saying. A lot of thirsty niggas out 'ere ya know. If you wanted a ride, I don't mind droppin' you?"

Priscilla's head swivels to face me. She squints her eyes and pouts her lips like she's considering my offer. "Thanks, but I'm cool," she says.

"Ite."

"Plus," she says, looking towards my pocket. "You shouldn't be drink-driving, anyway. Tut-tut-tut."

"What are you, my mum?" I say, flipping her words on her.

She laughs as smoke rises in all directions, evaporating into the mild air. "No, but seriously you shouldn't. You don't wanna crash, do you?"

"I'll bear it in mind."

"Good."

The conversation dies down, and I feel my head gently rocking. I focus my eyes on Priscilla's sexy little face to provide some equilibrium when I spot her throwing me several swift glances in quick succession.

"What?" she cries, half embarrassed and half intrigued.

"You look good," I tell her.

I notice the blushing cheeks. The red is way more evident on her light skin. "Thank you, you look good too," she says.

'This is gettin' dangerous. She looks fuckin' good, and she's on it, too. You should cut. Go home. You know her type. She's only after one ting. You really wanna risk everything you've got with Nia over this little lightey?'

I stretch my eyes wide like it will sober me up and figure I should head off before things escalate.

But just then, Priscilla throws a curveball.

"I was gonna go to my girl's for a drink up, but she's pissing me off, taking bare long to reply, so... If you want, you can come up and chill for a bit, keep me company."

I lick my lips as I think to myself.

"Hmmm..."

Next thing I know, Priscilla has her arm linked with mine. "Rakim, you're tipsy."

"What d'you mean?"

"Come on, it's bait. You can barely stand still. I'm not letting you drive off like that. At least come upstairs and sober up before you get back in that car."

'This girl must think I don't know her game.'

She tries to lead me into the block, and to my surprise, her tiny frame does a decent job.

"Your strong, init?" I laugh.

"Don't get it twisted, mi likkle but mi talawa."

I stop resisting and allow Priscilla to pull me through the hallway. We both press the button to call for the lift, which soon turns into a silly childish game of who can push it last.

Laughing, I fend her off as she reaches for the button.

"You ain't gettin' it, chill," I say as white French tips, and dainty caramel fingers reach across me.

Seconds later, the lift arrives, and we enter.

Priscilla's got a grin on her face like a mastermind who's just pulled off an audacious plan.

Under the brightness of the lift, every intricate detail of Priscilla's scalp is visible. The pimples at the root of each watertight plait are moisturised and symmetrical. Not a strand is out of place. "Who done your hair?" I ask.

"My sis, you like?" she says, flaunting her head from side to side.

"Yeah, it's bad."

As I continue to pay attention, she catches me off guard and plucks my bottle of Hennessy from my pocket.

"Gimme that," I say, but she skillfully evades me, ducking under my arm.

She hoists the bottle up to the light.

"Half a bottle? Never thought such a big man like you would be such a lightweight?"

'This girl's trouble,' I tell myself as I go for the bottle.

"Don't watch that," I say, reaching over her head.

I manage to get hold of her hand, and an electrifying spark zaps through my body.

'Rah.'

Her skin feels even smoother than it looks as she turns towards me rotating her body like a graceful dancer until she's facing me.

Our hands remain touching, sharing a grip around the neck of the bottle.

I sense an apprehension behind her deep-set brown eyes. The place she hides her fear from the world. Within seconds, she transforms from wild and brazen to innocent and meek as she stands before me, willingly at my mercy.

I know this is a moment right now.

A fork in the road, leading to two completely different pathways and two entirely different lives.

'You don't wanna do this, fam. Think about Nia. You can't cheat on her, man. She doesn't deserve that,' says my conscience.

But then I think about how sexy Priscilla looks as she gently massages my hand with her thumb.

Her touch is soft.

Feminine.

Submissive.

Just how I like it.

She takes my other hand, and now I know I'm in trouble. There's no getting out of this. It's either kiss or be kissed.

My conscience goes to pipe up again, but my brain has its own sentiments.

'Nia's gone, bro. She won't know, anyway. You know you wanna take Priscilla to her bedroom and deal with that. Look at those thighs.'

Just as the battle within me reaches a climax, the lift stops.

Bing.

The doors open and standing right outside are Deontay and Natasha. Four eyes glare at Priscilla and me, holding hands like a couple of lovers about to tie the knot.

Deontay's expression quickly turns to one of revulsion as he tries to ignore what he's seeing and holds an arm out for his girlfriend.

I release my hand from Priscilla's grasp, and the bottle of Hennessy clatters against the floor of the lift, prolonging the awkwardness of the moment.

Priscilla clears her throat loudly.

"Where you going?" she asks Natasha, who politely eases her way into the lift as I pick up my bottle from the ground.

"Just to the shop," smirks Natasha, trying to hold back her laugh. It must be the first time she's caught her older sister in the act.

I stand up, greet Natasha, and spud Deontay, who doesn't even look at me. "You good?" I ask as I squeeze by Deontay. He nods his head, avoiding my eyes.

Maybe he's disappointed in me for going against my word, perhaps he's lost faith in me, but I'm just a man at the end of the day. I try my best no matter the odds, but I'm far from a role model. Ignoring his sour face, I follow Priscilla out of the lift and into the corridor.

"See you in a minute, Deontay, and make sure you look after my sister," Priscilla calls.

Deontay nods as I watch his black hoody disappear behind the steel doors.

Priscilla and I reach her front door, and a million things run through my mind. My head's spinning like a revolving door, and I can't hold a particular thought for no longer than a couple of seconds. I know I need to sit down, and as soon as Priscilla opens the door, I head straight for the sofa.

Music begins to play, and I feel my body becoming buried in the ambiance.

I have no idea what the rest of this night holds, but I'm confident that Priscilla wants me.

And to be honest, watching that bum jiggle as she walks by carrying two shot glasses, I think I want her too.

31

"Rakim... Rakim..."

I lift my head off a silk pillow and stretch my arms high and wide, feeling a dull ache as I twist my neck.

"Fuck."

A sharp pain shoots through my brain, and I squeeze my eyes until they won't shut anymore.

"Are you okay?" a female voice asks.

My eyes open to streams of light trailing along the carpet like narrow pathways.

Seated at the end of this double bed, I don't recognise, is a honey-glazed face. It takes a couple of seconds to click while the girl gives me that suspicious raised-eyebrow look.

"Priscilla?"

"You remembered my name. Well done," she says.

A one-eighty swivel tells me I'm in Priscilla's bedroom.

'What the...? Don't tell me I...'

I look down at the coarse hairs on my chest before feeling under the covers.

'At least I still got my boxers on.'

Priscilla mentions something about shots, vodka, and whisky, but her words are far too harsh against the pain that batters my forehead.

It's not until she mentions Nia that she gets my attention.

"What did you say?" I ask.

"I said, are you gonna call Nia today then?"

"What?"

"Don't play dumb, Rakim."

She must recognise the look of bewilderment on my face as her tone simmers.

"You really don't remember?"

"Remember what?"

"Wow. You really are a lightweight," Priscilla says before standing up to reach over and pick up a mug that sits on a chest of drawers.

I sit up against the headrest, letting the covers fall onto my lap.

"What happened?" I ask.

Priscilla goes on to tell me how I spent half of the night telling her about Nia, about our argument and asking for an opinion on whether I was right or not to hide the last twelve years of my life from my girlfriend.

"You idiot," I mumble to myself.

Priscilla shakes her head as she hands me a white porcelain mug.

I blow away the blanket of steam that accompanies the mug, take a sip, and place it on the bedside table.

With her hands clasped together, Priscilla turns to me.

"Sorry," I say.

"It's not that deep," Priscilla says with a soft smile.

"Yeah, I should've told you, though, still."

"You did. That's the problem."

"What was I saying?"

"Wow, where do I start...? You kept going on about how you had messed things up with Nia. And how you shouldn't have lied to her, how you only meet good girls like her every—"

"—Nah, leave it, leave it."

Priscilla laughs.

Probably at my embarrassment.

"It was actually quite cute. You were upset about your girl, said you'd messed things up, and wish you never shouted at her and told her to leave."

'This is gettin' worse by the second. She got man soundin' like some joke-man out 'ere.'

337

"Yeah, it was Nia this, Nia that," Priscilla says.

"For real?"

"Yup."

I watch Priscilla sigh and notice how her smile gradually leaves her face.

Removing the duvet from my legs, I scoot over to sit next to her.

"You good?" I ask.

She nods and signals me to hand her the mug of tea, which I do.

"... On the level, sorry I never told you. I dunno why I came up 'ere in the first place. Maybe you just reminded me of what I'm missin', I don't know, but it was a stupid move."

"It's fine. You don't have to apologise. I invited you up at the end of the day when I barely know you, so I can't blame you if you tell me you got a girl, init."

Looks like I misjudged another one; I never thought in a million years that Priscilla would be the understanding type.

"So, nothing happened between us?" I ask just to confirm.

Priscilla shakes her head, stands up, and hands me the mug of tea.

"Just for the record, Nia sounds like a nice girl. I take it that's why you never bothered to call me?"

I avoid the question, but I reckon my face says it all.

"It's minor, don't worry."

"We cool then, yeah?" I ask.

"I mean, you told me in the end, init. It's not like we had sex, and then you told me afterwards. That would've made you a fuckboy," Priscilla says sternly.

I don't know how to respond to that one, so I take a long sip of my tea.

"Stupid? Yeah. Lightweight? Yeah. But fuckboy, nah. You're a sweet guy, Rakim," Priscilla says as she kisses my forehead. "We're cool."

Looks like my heart really does belong with Nia after all.

"I've gotta go to work anyway, so hurry up and finish that. Your cousin's downstairs, waiting for you," Priscilla says before leaving the room.

'Shit, I forgot about Deontay.'

I put the mug on the side, grab my folded pile of clothes from the chest of drawers, and get dressed in record time. I take eight thousand pounds wrapped in tiny elastic bands from the pocket of my cargo pants and analyse it briefly. The bands are tied in the same style, which saves me the hassle of counting the money again.

Once I've made sure I've got my keys, phone, and other belongings, I leave the bedroom. I say goodbye to Priscilla, who responds from the bathroom, and I close the front door behind me.

Deontay's waiting in the hallway on the ground floor, looking fed up. If he thinks I owe him an explanation, or I'm even interested in his emotional state right now, he better think again. I'm a drug dealer that needed a worker, not a psychiatrist who wanted a patient, so today, he'll do well to keep that miserable, passive-aggressive behaviour far from me.

"Come, let's go," I say as I hurry past him, hoping there isn't a ticket on my Benz.

He follows me out of the block, and we walk to the car. The breeze hits me as I reach my vehicle, feeling sharper than usual.

'No ticket. Good.'

I unlock the door as Deontay stands on the opposite side of the car.

With one arm leaning casually on the roof, he asks me, "Did you fuck her?"

I look him up and down as his eyes stay fixated on me.

"Get in the car," I say.

We both get in the car, and I have to take a moment.

"Wa gwarn with you?" Deontay asks as I throw my head back against the headrest.

"My head's banging."

I lower the window, take a deep breath, and push the button that fires up the engine. Within seconds, the interface lights up with a green phone icon, and a number I don't recognise flashes on the interface.

The car stereo sounds like a thousand telephones rattling up against my ear until I answer the call.

"Rakz, it's Jonesy. Look, I can't talk, mate, but the long and short of it is those Turks ain't having a bar. They want the full hundred grand to reverse the hit—" Jonesy blurts.

"—Yo, yo, yo. One sec," I say.

"Put a tune on, man," I tell Deontay as I disconnect the call from the Bluetooth system.

He cuts a suspicious look as I step out of the car and close the door behind me.

"Chat to me," I say.

"Listen, I had a word with Burak, but with all his people getting wrapped up, he needs the money. Now."

"So, what, you can't speech him?"

"No chance, mate."

"I don't have a hundred racks, though, bro."

"Can you get ya hands on a brick of flake and what, sixty, seventy in cash? He might take that."

"Might?"

"Yeah, otherwise...?"

"Otherwise, what?"

"Well, it's either that or you roll up your sleeves and go to war with these cunts."

I fling my head back until I'm staring up into the perfect blue sky and let out a sigh of exhaustion.

I'm tired of this. Fighting and warring just to survive. I've been doing it all my life. Before prison, throughout my sentence, and now I'm out, I'm right back in the thick of things.

"Nah, they got too much on me. Scribz has probably told them my address already, the pussyhole," I say.

Just hearing that name brings about a world of rage.

"Now's the best time. Their men are gettin' nabbed left, right, and centre," Jonesy says.

I choose to fight against these lot, then I know there are only two ways it ends for me. Either a prison cell or six feet underground. And that's not to mention the danger I'll bring upon Nia, Deontay, Leanne and my nephews.

"Nah, I'm done with this warring ting, man. There's gotta be another way."

"You just gotta pay 'em then, Rakz," Jonesy sighs. "Now he knows we're affiliated, I'm a target too, and I'm skint, mate."

"What?"

"Yeah, confiscation order came through. Three-hundred and forty-seven thousand or another seven years."

"Shit."

"Listen, I gotta go, mate. I'll ring ya tonight."

"Make sure."

Jonesy ends the call, and I feel I'm in no better position than I was two days ago.

'These lot want a hundred grand to reverse the hit back to Scribz. How am I gonna get a hundred bags? And am I really gonna get Scribz killed?'

Questions run through my brain, and I know I've got a lot of contemplating to do as I get back in the car.

"Wa gwarn, what was that?" Deontay asks.

"Don't watch that."

I press down on the accelerator, and the car zips off.

We arrive at Deontay's estate within ten minutes, and I order him out of the car to go and collect the twenty-five grand I have stashed away at a traphouse in Ribz's block.

While I wait, I try Scribz's phone again. Surprise, surprise—no answer.

Deontay returns looking shifty, and I'm reminded of the day I sent him into that building to take the drugs Scribz had told me about.

341

The day this all started.

Deontay gets in the car, and we waste no time. The first stop is Prestige Car Hire.

We arrive, and I tell Deontay to wait in the car.

Darkos isn't about as usual. Instead, his uncle greets me with a courteous grin.

We talk for a couple of minutes before I hand him the bag containing thirty-three thousand pounds. He doesn't check it as a mark of respect and gives me a piece of paper with a time and location of where I can receive the next drop.

I haven't told him I'm getting out of the game yet. I've figured that can wait. It isn't him I need to be telling, anyway. Darkos is the man for that conversation.

But before I speak to Darkos, I have to weigh my options.

I may need to lead Darkos on, take this product and use it to pay off the Turks. It's either that or I go to war with them. Or I postpone my retirement from selling drugs, get Deontay to break down this kilo, and get back to business.

The last option may not even be viable, though. These Turks have already waited over two months for their money. I can't see Burak taking kindly to waiting another month for me to get rid of this while he sits down in a prison cell.

He may think I'm playing him.

I would if someone stole from me and then told me he needed a month to get the money.

He's already seen Scribz do a runner. What's to say I'm any different?

Trust in the streets is as rare as water in the desert. It's not a currency you can confidently conduct business with. When transactions are done in my world, there aren't any contracts, emails, or signed agreements that force a person to honour their word. If a man takes something on credit and says he's going to pay you on a specific date, and that date comes, and he doesn't pay, you can't sue him or take him to court.

It doesn't work like that in the streets when practising illegal activities. You get the police involved, not only are you now labelled a snitch, which is about the worst possible reputation a man can carry, but you've implicated your involvement in a crime.

The only way to deal with those who break their agreement is violence. Shootings, stabbings, kidnapping family members, it all sends a clear message. And nothing is off the table. It's all fair game.

I know, through Jonesy, that Burak and his brother won't hesitate to go to any length to get their money, so I gotta be tactical. I'll hold on to this kilo, and if I have to use it to pay the Turks, then so be it, even if it does put me in debt with Darkos. I'd rather deal with Darkos' wrath than a bunch of foreign drug lords who don't know me from Adam.

I tell Darkos' uncle to tell his nephew to throw in a machine with the product, and the man looks at me like I'm speaking another language.

"He'll know what I'm talkin' about. Tell him I'll throw in another three grand on the rebound."

When he hears 'three grand,' his uncle smiles and shakes my hand.

I leave the showroom and get back into my car.

Deontay fires a volley of questions at me as we make our way back to our neck of the woods.

'Am I still in the game? Am I planning on expanding? Do I know who tried to attack him, blah, blah, blah?'

Eventually, I get annoyed and tell him to stop asking questions.

We arrive at his estate, and I pull into a small car park.

"Go and get Ribz to bring out the rest of the dough," I tell Deontay.

He hurries off and returns with this fool, Ribz.

I've seen some get-ups in my time, but this one takes the biscuit. It's twenty-eight degrees out here, and this clown is wearing a level three bulletproof vest with shades and a woolly hat.

"Yo, akhi," he says, although neither of us are Muslim.

I nod and hold my hand out of the window. "There you go, killer," Ribz says.

I take the bag and open the zip to ensure the money is there.

"Oi, what, can man get a likkle advance my brudda?" Ribz asks.

"I told Deontay, you'll get paid when I pay you."

"Deontay, yeah?" he laughs.

"Yo, listen, likkle man, go wait over there. I'll hit you later," I tell Ribz.

"Say niz," Ribz says, taking his hyperactive self away to join the rest of his gang that's congregated around an entrance to one of the tower blocks.

I tell Deontay to go and do as many deals as possible to get rid of the remaining product, spud him and tell him I'll call him in an hour.

He gives me a strange look, the kind of look you give someone when you think they're up to something.

It lasts a couple of seconds before he bops off to get to work.

I don't even bother trying to decode his antics. Instead, I drive back to my yard, slowing down as I pass Nia's house. Her curtains look just the same as they did yesterday.

I wonder what she's doing right now when I'm drawn to the Audi Q7 parked outside my house.

This is all I need right now.

Leanne doesn't notice me pull up. She's in a world of her own, probably playing Candy Crush, doing online shopping, or whatever you do when you're the wife of a millionaire.

I exit my vehicle and walk up towards Leanne's window. "You all right?" I say, tapping loudly.

She brings a hand across her chest, and I shake my head as the window comes down.

"Don't do that, Rakim. You scared me."

"Says the one that turns up out of the blue whenever she wants."

Leanne opens the car door, forcing me to step back. After removing her sunglasses, she shakes her hair like she's just had a dip in the sea before putting them back on.

"Why you here, Lee?"

"Is that really how you're going to welcome your sister?"

Seeing my non-reaction, Leanne continues.

"Well, aren't you going to invite me in?"

I scratch my neck as I look around. "Now's not a good time, Lee."

Leanne dismisses my words with her hand. "No. You tried that last time. What's going on?"

"Nothin'. You just caught me at a bad time."

"Uh-uh. I'm not buying that. I know you, Rakz, something's up. What is it?"

Knowing Leanne isn't about to let this one lie, I'm aware we could be standing in the street for a while.

"I'm about to go out, that's why."

"Don't lie to me."

"I ain't lying."

Leanne gives me a straight face.

"Rakz, you're my little brother. Do you know how many times I've seen you do that face? I know when you're lying. Now, tell me what's going on. Why don't you want me up in the house? It's still partly my house, for goodness' sake," she says, throwing her arms in the air.

I think about who could be watching us having this conversation, and I notice a black Volvo parked about a hundred yards to my right.

It looks like there's somebody in the driver's seat.

Or are my eyes playing tricks on me?

"Rakz, are you gonna open the door, or what?" Leanne cries once more.

A blue 4x4 drives by, and the driver looks at us.

'Who's that?' I think until I spot the child in the backseat.

'This is way too bait out 'ere.'

Admitting defeat, I usher Leanne inside.

I close the door behind her as she natters on about the relief of being back in Mum's house and how she feels like a stranger because she hasn't been 'allowed' here in three months. I let her prattle on, hoping her jabbering will take her mind off of me, but as I return to the living room, I realise I'm mistaken.

Standing in the centre of the room, her hand pressed against her hip like a schoolteacher, Leanne looks at me.

"What's going on, Rakz?"

I look around at the ashtray, the newspapers, the cash, the Rizzla papers, and the empty bottle of Remy and begin to understand Leanne's concern.

The sofa moulds to the shape of my body as I relax and reach for a spliff from the ashtray.

Leanne's eyes closely follow me. "Rakim, are you okay?"

I light my spliff, take a pull and figure it might just be easier to be real with Leanne right now. As I blow the smoke around the room, I half expect Leanne to go and open a window, but instead, she takes a seat on the other end of the sofa.

I extend my exhalation, picturing my problems floating away before my eyes.

"It's nothing man can't handle, Lee," I say.

Concerned, she places her handbag on the floor.

"Rakz, what have you got yourself into?"

I look at her from the corner of my eye. "Nothing," I say.

"Rakim, tell me."

I sigh.

"... It's nothing. I was helping someone out, ya know, a favour, but unfortunately, it got me into a little predicament."

I regret telling Leanne straight away. She starts panicking, reaching for her phone, then sitting up to check outside the window like MI5 are about to sneak up on us. It's not until I raise my voice and order her to be calm that she settles.

"Rakz, I can help you out if you need money."

"I'm good, Lee. Plus, you don't have any money, anyway."

"Well, Taylor does. I'm sure he wouldn't mind lending—"

"—Please."

She must have hit her head if she thinks I'm borrowing his money.

Leanne slides across closer to me, and I can see the worry in her eyes.

'I knew I shouldn't have let her in.'

"Do you owe someone money?" she asks.

"No."

"Is someone trying to harm you?"

"Nah, nuttin' like that, man," I say, getting annoyed at these police interview-style questions.

"Well, why do you look like you've been living off of weed and whisky for the past few weeks?" she asks, her arm moving in front of her like she's introducing me to my own living room.

I take a pull of my spliff.

"You were right, init."

"Right about what?"

"You were just right."

"About what?"

"... About Nia."

I observe Leanne's entire body become lighter. Her shoulders fall, and the anxious look on her face vanishes as soon as she hears Nia's name.

"What happened?" she asks.

I take another pull.

"Rakz, come on, what's going on? If there's trouble in paradise, maybe I can help?"

"You were just right. She's too good for me."

Leanne gasps. "Don't tell me you blew it."

I shrug.

Leanne hits my arm.

"Oooh, Rakim, what's wrong with you? Nia's such a lovely girl. How on earth did you manage to mess things up with her?"

Happy I've thrown her off course, I tell Leanne how Nia left me after we had an argument. Giving me some sisterly advice and educating me about women, Leanne's like a dog with a bone.

I continue to smoke my weed as Leanne tidies the place up, all the while lecturing me about the importance of being truthful with women and being emotionally available, blah, blah, blah.

Within fifteen minutes, she has the room looking brand new.

"There you go," she says, proud of her work. "Oh gosh, I've come over all hot now," she adds as she fans herself with her hand and I fetch her a bottle of water from the fridge.

"I can't believe you're just gonna let her get away. I was looking forward to inviting you both over for dinner," Leanne says.

"That's how it goes sometimes," I say nonchalantly.

Leanne shakes her head.

"Give me that," she says.

"What?"

She reaches over to me and plucks my spliff from my mouth. With the elegance of a seasoned smoker, she takes two pulls and blows the smoke around the room.

I stare at this rare occurrence for a few seconds before she hands me back my spliff.

"Who would've thought I'd see the day when the wife of Taylor buns a spliff with her no-good brother?"

"Shhhh," Leanne says, putting a finger in front of her lips. "It's our secret." She lies her head back and slips her heels out of her shoes. It's the most relaxed I've seen her in ages.

I smile as the world goes silent for a short while. It's just me, Leanne, and a cloud of smoke.

"Hey Rakz," Leanne says, all calm and mellow.

"Yeah."

"Do you remember when we were kids, and Mum took us to that school fete?"

"Which one?"

"When we got our faces painted."

I think back. "Slyly," I say.

"You got yours painted like a lion, and I was a panda."

"Yeah, I remember," I say with a smile. "We came home, and Dad started switching. Talkin' about face painting being some demonic ritual an' that."

"Yeah! You do remember?" Leanne says overjoyed.

I nod as I finish the last of my spliff.

"We were sat right there. Right there," she says, pointing to where a glass table now rests.

"For real," I mumble.

"Wow. That's crazy. All those years ago," Leanne says.

I sit there, reminiscing for a moment, until Leanne rolls her neck on the headrest to look at me. "You know I'm thinking of selling this place." Her words should shock me, but maybe it's the high I'm feeling. I don't even fully process it. "What do you think?" she asks. Then before allowing me to respond, she continues. "Taylor reckons the way the market is so aggressive right now; we could get at least five hundred thousand for this place. Maybe even more."

"That's a lot of money."

"Yeah, well, Taylor said with his team on board, he could get it on the market within a few weeks, and we could possibly get it sold within a couple of months. Apparently, there's a lot of interest around here nowadays."

"You're saying it like you've made up your mind already."

"We have," Leanne shrugs. "But obviously, I wanted to consult you first. I mean, this is your home, after all."

I think about that word.

Home.

And what it really means.

I always thought home was a place where families create everlasting memories. The place where we laugh, cry, sing, and play. Where we dance together and try weird foods for the first time. The place where we argue, fight, slam doors, and then make up and love each other again. That sacred place where we learn so many amazing things that prepare us to take on the world. Things that seem so simple at the time. But the reason why they're amazing is that we learn them together.

I'm all alone here now—just me. And Ping, of course, but he isn't family.

This house is supposed to be my solitude. A place where the Buraks of the world can't harm me, where the Scribblers of the world can't betray me, where the police can't harass me, where the Nias can't abandon me, where the Deontays can't frustrate me, and the Supercoons can't judge me.

But lately, this castle, my very own space to reflect and meditate, has felt like a waiting room. A mere steppingstone before the impending desolation that awaits me. Mum always said, 'A man cannot serve two masters.' He must choose if he serves God and the way of the family or serves only his personal desires and appetites because a house without God is a foundation destined to crumble.

I try to think of a reason why this house still feels like a Godly home, but I struggle.

"You know, Lee, if you'd asked me a few months ago, I would've told you, no way, but right now, all this place holds for man is memories. Memories of the past. And I love Mum and all the times we spent running round this yard, but Mum's gone. You've left and made a life for yourself with your family. I'm never gonna be able to move on with my life unless I cut ties with my past. There ain't nothing left for me here."

We talk for a bit longer, and the more we do, the more we both agree that the house should be sold. It would leave me without a place to live, but with a quarter of a million in my pocket, my dream of moving to The Gambia need be a pipe dream no longer.

By the end of the conversation, it's a no-brainer.

Leanne gets up to leave, and I follow suit, remembering I've got business to take care of.

I chaperone Leanne to her car while she informs me that she'll get Taylor on the case as soon as she gets home.

She winds down the window as I stand nearby. "Make sure you come by in the week, please. Ricky and Nath are off to Taylor's mum's for a week soon, and they've been pining after you," she says, rolling her eyes.

"Yeah, tell 'em I'll be over soon."

"I will do," Leanne says, firing up the engine. "Oh, and Rakz," she continues as she stops adjusting her mirror for a second.

"What?"

"Don't ever let me hear you say Nia's too good for you. She's a good woman... But you're also a good man. Please don't ever forget that," Leanne says.

She holds a hand out of the window to touch my arm before the car pulls off. "Take care. I'll speak to you soon."

Leanne disappears, leaving me standing on the pavement, wondering what my future holds.

I take a look over at Nia's house. The curtains are still drawn.

I suck my teeth.

"Let me go check Deontay, man."

32

"So, I have to click this button down to shoot, yeah?"

"Yes, man," I say for the third time as I watch Deontay standing there with a Glock 19 in his hands.

Under the cover of darkness, he aims it towards a tree about ten metres ahead as he fiddles with the lever at the side of the slide. He finally works it out, and the lever drops, allowing the slide to move forward and click into position.

"Bruv, we ain't got all day," I tell Deontay as I glance over at the entrance to the park where Ribz maintains a lookout.

I've already shown Deontay how to load the bullets into the double-stack magazine and how to remove the slide to clean the spring, barrel, and firing pin. Now, after watching me fire the pistol twice, it's his turn.

He keeps both hands securely wrapped around the handle and presses the trigger. I watch his head jerk away from his body as he closes an eye, and a loud bang explodes through the air.

"Oi, fam, this will take a man's head off," Deontay cries.

I lift his arms, pointing the gun back towards the tree. "Not if you don't hit the fuckin' target, bruv," I say, looking at the unscathed silver birch in front of us.

"Listen, I told you how to aim. Line up the rear sight and that likkle bit of metal sticking up on the end of the barrel," I say. "Now aim at the tree and press the trigger. Easy though. It's sensitive... You gotta touch it gently. You know, the way you touch your girl."

Deontay nods his head. There's a bang, followed by what sounds like wood snapping. Taking my advice on board, he hits the tree dead in the centre.

"Oi, lengman style," he shouts, raising the gun in the air. "C'mon, man's a sharpshooter out 'ere, cuz."

I roll my eyes.

"Ite, cool. Gimme it now," I tell him and carefully take the gun from him. I press the magazine release and ensure the chamber is empty before taking a quick look around and putting the gun in my rucksack.

"Let's get out of here," I say, and we head towards the exit.

Back in my car, Deontay asks if Darkos can provide us with any more guns, and his question seems to set Ribz off. The two of them spend the next ten minutes asking me about different types of weapons and how many rounds they can fire per minute, like I'm a firearm specialist or something.

I ignore most of their questions and let them argue amongst themselves. "You man play too much Call of Duty," I say as Ribz swears on his life that an SMG rifle is more powerful than an MP5 as if he's ever seen either.

I reach a junction, and all three of us are forced to hold our breath.

"Yo, there's Jakes there," Deontay says.

Adjacent to the traffic lights to my right-hand side is a marked police car.

'Shit.'

"You man, don't move," I command.

The nerves in my leg fight to keep control of the accelerator as my foot trembles against the pedal. Depending on which light goes green next, at this three-way traffic light, either we'll be behind the police, or they'll be behind us.

Only cab drivers, night-shift workers, and foxes roam the streets at this time round here. A black man in a car with two dark-skinned boys all dressed in black, we're definitely getting pulled.

Deontay grips the bag tightly and puts a hand on the door handle.

"Oi, chill out. If they see you movin' about, you look even more bait," I tell him.

Ribz goes to speak, but the fierceness in my eyes silences him as we wait for what seems like an eternity. I swear I can hear hearts thumping.

The policewoman in the passenger seat looks over in my direction.

We catch each other's glance, and I raise an eyebrow as if to say hello.

She doesn't respond but just looks straight ahead.

'Please let them go first,' I pray.

Seconds feel like hours, until finally, my prayers are answered, and the police car glides off.

"Boyy," Deontay cries as he dramatically puts a hand on his chest.

I open a window, and the whole vehicle breathes a sigh of relief.

'I gotta get out of this place. I can't keep doing this, man.'

Minutes later, we're on Tunwell Estate, and I pull over into the car park by Ribz's block.

I let him out of the car, and after reiterating he'll get paid when I decide, I order him to take the bag with the gun, store it in one of my stash houses and bring down the duffle bag containing the kilo of cocaine and heroin.

"Yo, listen, D," I say, turning towards Deontay.

"That burner's just for you to protect yourself, ya know. Don't be giving it to nobody, don't tell anyone you got it there, and don't even think about using it unless you phone me first and I give you the green light, you understand?"

Deontay knows me by now to know when I'm deadly serious. He nods his head hard and fast. "Nah, I hear you," he says.

"Make sure you do, ya know. Guns ain't toys, but I ain't lettin' nobody run up in our spot or catch you slippin' either, you feel me?"

"Yeah, I feel you."

"Good... It's only for a couple of days until I sort some things out."

"Cool. What about the reload? When we gonna move this ting? Man needs to make some money."

"I told you, I'm out the game. You know my plans; I'm going to The Gambia."

Deontay's whole body deflates. "Are you being serious?"

"Course I am. I told you."

"So why did you just grab another box of food, bro? How does that make sense?"

I look out my window before turning back towards Deontay. "Don't worry about that," I tell him.

He huffs like he can't believe what he's hearing. "So, you're just done. I thought we were just getting started."

"We might move this one. We might not. But you saved up like I said, right?"

"Yeah, I put a little something away, but—"

"—Well, there you go, use that to do suttin' else 'cause I'm tellin' you, there's more to life than doing this shit."

Deontay shakes his head as he reaches for the door handle. He opens the door before turning back towards me and giving me one of the strangest looks he's ever given me.

"You're leaving every'ting behind for your girl, init?" he asks.

I study him for a second.

His heavy brow and flared nostrils, it's like he's angry I've chosen somebody over him.

"It ain't just because a girl, trust me. We just passed feds back there. Imagine they stop me, and I get nicked. They'll bury me."

"We ain't getting bagged though, G."

"Look, I get it, you're young, you still think you're gonna conquer the world like Scarface, but I'm older than you. I've *been* doing this. And when you been doing this ting as long as me, you don't change... You just get tired—tired of ducking police—tired of the beef. Tired of the same people ringing you with the same dramas... I'm tired, D. Tired of doing this shit, bro. And I'm tellin' you, you stay in this game too long, it traps you, you can't leave it alone, no matter how much money you make. I've seen it all before. Where d'you think I just came from? I was surrounded by guys who couldn't leave this shit alone. Remember I told you about my bredrin Jonesy, he just found out he's gotta pay nearly four hundred racks, or he's gotta do another seven years. That's twenty-three fuckin' years."

Deontay looks ahead, face still stubborn, but I can see he's listening.

"That ain't no life," I continue. "Trust me. Find suttin' else to do, bro. I don't know what but find suttin'."

"So, you're just gonna cut and go to fucking Africa?"

"Yeah, bro. And when I'm set up over there, come take a likkle holiday, visit man. You know, no matter what, man's always got love for you. Just say the word, and man will get you a ticket. You can come see with your own eyes. There's more to life than south London."

Still staring ahead, Deontay remains silent.

I hear footsteps getting louder and turn to see Ribz. He hands me the bag through my open window and gets on his phone.

Seeing Deontay's back in one of his moods, I decide it's time to leave. "Yo, listen, I'ma shout you and let you know wa gwarn with this food," I say, still unsure of what I plan to do myself.

"Cool," Deontay mumbles as he spuds me and gets out of the car.

I watch him walk back to his dreary block with Ribz and drive out of the estate.

Once back home, I check my messages.

48 hours, he said. Big J.

According to Jonesy, I've apparently got forty-eight hours to come up with one hundred grand.

I spend half an hour counting up fifty-eight thousand, four hundred and sixty pounds, which has me feeling a lot more comfortable than I did a couple of days ago.

With almost sixty grand and a kilo of high purity class A, I'm in a good position to settle my debt with the Turks.

I don't want a war and taking off with the money makes no sense. It will only lead to an army of Burak's men looking for Deontay, and I'd never leave him in that position.

I know I'll have to repay Darkos at some stage, but I'm not worried about that. It was me who introduced him to the hefty Albanians that propelled him to the cocaine-slash-arms-slash-luxury-car-dealer he is today. And if he forgets that when I tell him, he's gonna have to wait for his money, I'll be sure to remind him.

I lay down on my bed, and my conversation with Leanne about selling the house fills me with more confidence that everybody will come out of this unharmed.

'Once I get the money from the house, I can pay Darkos with interest and still have enough for a new life in The Gambia.'

I start thinking about what I'll do when I get over there.

'I could open a gym. Or if I can get Nia on board, maybe even a restaurant or she could teach yoga... She needs to come back, man.'

I take another pull of my spliff and look at the clock.

1.34 a.m.

By the time I've finished my spliff, I'm half asleep.

I hear the toilet flush, then Ping's footsteps in the hallway before his door closes.

Five minutes later, I'm out like a light.

33

Brrr-brrr.

I open my eyes, but it's still dark. The house is so tranquil the vibration on my bedside table sounds like a jackhammer.

I reach over and pick up my phone. It's nearly four o'clock as I try to identify who the eleven digits across the screen belong to.

"Yo, who's this," I croak.

"What you saying? You got your connect. Now you're done with man, yeah?"

"Is that...? Wait, Scribz."

"You did man dirty, Rakz."

I climb to my feet and feel my body overcome with a wave of anger. My heartbeat has shot up, and suddenly, I'm wide awake. I've envisaged this moment so many times; what I wanted to say to this guy, but he's caught me off guard.

"Hello," he cries.

I clear my throat. "So what, you're a snitch, yeah, Scribz?"

"What?"

"You heard me. Don't even try deny it. I know."

"Know who you're talking to, brudda," Scribz warns me.

"I know who I'm talkin' to. A little snitch."

"Who's been chatting shit to you?"

"You ain't gotta worry 'bout that. Just know that man knows what you are and what you done."

"I'ma give you one chance to apologise—"

"—Apologise? What, you're a tough snitch now, yeah?"

"So your taking next man's word over me... Me?"

358

"Shut up, man. I heard every'ting. I know how you finessed Golem, then how you robbed the Turks and put it on me. I know, bruv... I fuckin' know!"

"You don't know shit, you snake."

"Me? *You're* the snake. You set man up to steal that food, and then when them Turks got on to you, you snitched to get a transfer, you little pussy, don't think man don't know about you."

Scribz blows his top and starts screaming down the phone. "Alhamdulillah, you're pissed when I see you. On my life, you snake. You come outta jail, ask me to bring you in, then get a new connect and cut man out like I never saved your life. You member that, or you forget that shit?"

Scribz has me pacing around the room, shouting into my phone. How can this prick dare to set me up, snitch on his suppliers, and still talk like he's a badman?

"How d'you do, Jamal? After he clocked you snitched on Burak. You choke him out or what?

Any control I had over my temper has gone.

This ain't usually me, but Scribz has drawn me out. There's no turning back now. Saliva flies around the room as we hurl insults at each other back and forth, nobody really listening to anything the other says until he slips up.

"I should'a let them man slice you up in the shower and took them two packs a' burn they offered man."

"Yeah...? So, what, you been plotting on man since the day we met... And I'm the snake? You know what Scribz, you *were* my nigga. Now you're nuttin'. You sold man out to them Turks, and I know you done suttin' bookey with Jamal. I saw the letter—"

"—You wanna come on my phone like you're bad. You think you're bad because you killed some little dickhead. Trust me, you don't know badness, rude boy. On my life, when I touch road, you're a deadman, Rakz. Think you can take my line, take my customers, and disappear. Watch brudda, 'member I told you, you're a dead man!"

"You better hope *you* don't see me when you land road, 'cause on my Mum's grave, I'ma put six bullets through your fuckin' head."

The phone goes dead, and I slam it on the ground.

It takes me nearly an hour before I stop cursing and sporadically punching the air.

'Watch when I catch this guy.'

I try counting from ten to one, but it doesn't work.

"I need some air, man," I tell myself.

After grabbing a bottle of water from my fridge, I find myself sitting in my front garden, my hands still shaking.

"This guy snitches, sets me up, then wants to lie about it and go on like I'm the snake. Watch when I catch him, I swear down."

'How can man snake me after everything we been through?'

My fist refuses to unclench, and I feel my pulse banging relentlessly against my skin, begging me to untighten my grip.

I wish I could see Scribz right this minute and pummel his face. I thought my best friend, my ride-or-die, would always be there for me and vice versa. Everything I've done for him, and now I'm here tryin' to picture the rest of my life without him.

I think back to all those times we laughed about screws getting violated on the landing, all those times we whipped up tuna, mackerel, and potatoes together, all those times we played blackjack deep into the night and spoke about his mum and my daughter.

I feel my eyes begin to burn. My vision becomes blurrier, and my throat dries up as I look above.

'Why always me? Why?'

I wish Nia was here to soothe my pain as I focus on the ethereal glow the moon shares with me tonight. Sitting proudly in the sky, she watches over a city that sleeps as the distant caws of birds and the howls of foxes form my only company. With every exhale, I cast a mist in front of me as I peer over at Nia's house.

I want to go back to bed; I'm tired, but I'm fuelled by my rage.

"Fuck Scribz," I hear myself reiterate at least a dozen times over the next half an hour. Betrayed by my brother... Again.

'How did I not see this shit?'

I begin to second-guess myself and question if Scribz really is a snake.

I've had all the evidence. Scribz admitted he lied to me, and Jonesy has told me why. I've seen the letters from Jamal and Devonte, but some part of me still clings to the hope that Scribz isn't lying.

I hate myself for even thinking it.

Only Mum had me feeling like this when she left this earth, and I despise my weakness for sparing a single spec of consideration and compassion towards this traitor.

I take a deep breath and stand up.

"Fuck Scribz. I'ma give the Turks the money tomorrow, and I'll tell 'em exactly where to find him. On my life, this prick's gonna pay."

34

Tomorrow arrives, and I don't roll out of bed until past one o'clock. I grab my phone from the bedside table and see a text from Leanne.

Morning, even though I doubt you're up. Just to let you know, Taylor's team will be in Mum's place from next week. Just to get it sale-ready before he works his magic. Soo looking forward to this. Have a gd day. Mwah x

I read through her text with about as much excitement as I feel before a dentist appointment.

Tossing my phone on the bed, I soldier through staggered sets to complete a hundred press-ups. But by the time I reach one hundred and fifty, my mind's taken back to HMP Huntingley.

Then back to Scribz.

I suck my teeth and go jump in the shower.

Once dry and clothed, I spark my spliff and decide to get some fresh air. Mum always told me a good meal can fix anything, so I head towards the High Road.

The drab grey sky above spares a minute to allow an arrow of sunshine to pierce the unending queue of rain clouds as I stroll along without a care where I end up.

Swallowed by the grey abyss, the light disappears as I reach the entrance of American Shakes. I push open the door and take a seat. It's not so much a seat as a stool, and it's not so much a restaurant as a diner. In fact, the whole place is set out like an American diner. The chequered floor, the black leather stools, the neon lights, even down to the rustic jukebox over in the corner.

Apart from some young teens and a couple of families with small children, the place is basically empty.

Hunched over like a silverback on a pogo stick, I must look so out of place in this joint. A young blonde waiter approaches me and introduces herself before listening to my demands. She gives me a look that questions what a man like me is doing in a place like this by himself in the middle of the day, but I don't even sweat it.

The simple answer is pancakes plus milkshakes equal my mind off of Scribz.

Ten minutes later, I'm tucking into an extra-large helping of thick American-style pancakes, doused in icing sugar, topped with freshly sliced strawberries, and glazed in a generous helping of maple syrup. The whole thing tastes like a slice of heaven. There's a reason why they call this comfort food.

I devour the pancakes, order a giant portion of cookie dough to go, and finish slurping my milkshake while I wait. The few youngsters in here are loud. They talk about everything from TikTok to Kanye's latest outburst to where they want to go shopping today.

'Some of these lot must be like fourteen, fifteen... I wonder what they think they'll be doin' when they're my age.'

The thought has me reflecting on how things never seem to pan out the way you think they will. You can plan and plan, but at the end of the day, what is to be, will be. It's the inexorable karmic way of the universe that governs all our lives, putting us in specific places at specific times to make choices that will ultimately determine the course of our existence.

One of Mum's famous lines plays in my head.

'Man makes plans, and God laughs, so just be grateful for every day you have on his earth.'

I never dreamed I'd be sitting here eating pancakes at thirty. Shit, I didn't even think I'd reach thirty. I always knew I'd have a child early on in life, but I genuinely thought I'd be gunned down, and she'd only live her life with a fragmented memory of who I was and how it felt when I held her.

363

Funny how things went; I only got two years with Keziah, but it wasn't my death that ruined our relationship. It was another man's death.

I used to have such a disregard for my own life because I was certain it would end in my twenties. Looking back, it made me take so many things for granted.

I was stubborn, reckless, and ultimately, my temper landed me in prison. Still, miraculously, through everything, through all the people I've experienced die—friends and family, through all times I could've been killed myself, and all the times I probably deserved it, I'm still here.

It's crazy. I've seen people in prison slit their wrists and set themselves alight after getting a hefty sentence. Some go insane and get sectioned, some turn to crack, spice, and other drugs, and others, through no fault of their own, fail to make it out of those gates.

These are the tales from prison that never make the news, but take it from me, a man who has nothing to gain by lying to you; it's way more common than you'd imagine. Not everybody can outlive a life of crime, murder, and violence with their health and sanity intact.

But I did it.

And I did it all by myself.

I may not have many achievements, but I can say with pride and honour that reaching thirty years old as the man I am, with what I've been through, is a goddam achievement. I guess my only one to date, but I'll take it.

The girl behind the counter signals me, and I rise to my feet. I pay for my cookies and leave her a generous tip that has her gawking at me totally different from when she first laid eyes on me.

I leave the shop to see the day has brightened up a little, though spots of rain still decorate the grubby pavements. I figure I'll walk back home and finish these cookies before I call Jonesy and set up a meeting to pay Burak's men when a twist of fate stops me dead in my tracks.

Right in my path, a few metres ahead of me is Nia.

Infused with that tropical sunshine, her skin radiates like an exquisite diamond on a dull day.

After fiddling inside her bag, she looks up.

"Nia," I say, startling her.

She stands there in shock for a moment, looking as if a strong gust of wind could sweep her away.

"You okay?" I ask.

Nia straightens her spine, squaring her shoulders my way. She shakes out her hair and then clears her throat. "I'm fine," she says, her words as blunt as the back of a knife.

"When d'you get back?"

She pulls at the strap on her handbag, shifting it further up her shoulder.

"A few hours ago," Nia says, avoiding eye contact.

"Okay... W-well, how was your holiday? Did you—"

"—Look, Rakim, what do you want? I'm busy."

"My bad. Can we talk?"

Nia shakes her head as she goes to power past me. Her glittery sandals slap the pavement as her refusal slaps me in my face. "I'll see you around, Rakim. Bye."

My heart stutters, and my stomach drops to my feet.

'Did she just air man like that?'

A sudden fit of rage comes over me, and I reach out and grab hold of her arm. "Ni!"

"Let go of me," she cries.

I instantly recoil and show her a submissive palm while my other hand holds onto my box of cookie dough.

"Sorry, I just need to talk to you, Ni. Please?"

"Talk about what, Rakim. What do we have to talk about? Because the last time I wanted to talk, you told me to get out of your car. Do you remember that?"

By now, we've attracted some attention; a man asks if Nia's okay, seeing the look of distress on her face, and I give him the death stare.

'*You better take your hand off my woman before I fuck you up.*' The words nearly blurt out, but I play it smarter this time. Refraining from displaying any aggression, I allow Nia to deal with it.

"I'm okay," she says, and after giving a cheerless smile and asking if she's sure, the man crawls back under the rock he came from.

A lone tear trickles down Nia's face, and that familiar feeling of guilt returns to my gut.

"I'm sorry, Ni."

"Sorry for what, Rakim?" Nia says, widening her eyes to stop the inevitable tears. "What are you sorry for? Lying to me, pretending to be someone you're not. Shouting at me. Ruining my birthday. Which one? Which one are you sorry for?"

"I'm sorry for everything, Ni. C'mon, you know me, I never pretended anything when I was with you. It was all real. On my life. You've been away for a month, and I've missed you bad. Every day I checked your window, hoping you'd drawn your curtains, just to see if you were okay. I called, texted, knocked on your door, you name it. Ask your neighbour. He'll tell you. He's the reason I knew you were away."

"So? What does that mean? You missed me when I left, so I'm just supposed to fall back into your arms now after you lied to me about everything?"

"I ain't sayin' that."

"You could be lying right now for all I know."

"I'm not lying," I say, taking a step closer to Nia and putting a hand on her bare arm. Her wannabee hero looks at me again, but I ignore him. It's been so long since I just touched Nia's skin.

She moves her arm away, but I reach for her palm and gently take her hand.

"I'm sorry I didn't tell you the truth. I wanted to, believe me," I say, not allowing Nia to avoid my eyes.

"Why didn't you then?" she cries as if it should be the simplest thing in the world.

"Because, Ni."

"Because what?"

"I was scared."

"Scared?"

"Yeah, man. Big old man like me, scared."

We stare at each other for a moment, and I see all the heartache and betrayal she's feeling behind her pupils, somewhere deep inside. I've taken a part of her, twisted it, churned it, and all but snapped it in two.

That bond we had, her trust in me, it's withered, damaged, and dying... But it's not beyond repair. It remains intact, just. Threadbare and as fragile as a dream, it gives me a glimmer of hope. Nia hasn't wholly forsaken me after all.

"What could you possibly be scared of?" she asks in an exhausted whisper.

"I don't know. Losing you."

The tears stream down Nia's face as she battles to prevent her onslaught of emotions. She dabs her cheeks with the back of her wrist.

"Why would you lose me by being honest with me, Rakim? I don't get it."

"Can we just talk about this back at mine?" I ask, holding up the box of cookie dough as an enticing treat.

I hope for a smile, but it's not forthcoming.

"I trusted you, Rakim. I trusted you, and you lied to me."

"C'mon Ni, I fucked up, I get it. But I ain't stopped thinkin' about you since you left and how I messed things up. And I'm here now, tryin'... Tryin' to make things right. At least just hear me out."

She pulls her hand away from mine and grabs the strap of her handbag.

"I thought about you too while I was away. You had me questioning myself if I was in the wrong, if I did something for you to treat me like that, but now I know that I didn't because I would never hurt you like that, Rakim. Ever."

"At least let me walk you wherever you need to go," I plead.

"My brother needs me, and I need to be there for him. I can't deal with you right now. I've got other things in my life to take care of... I'll see you around, Rakim," Nia says, threatening to crush my world.

But the words of Uncle Dennis and Leanne play in my head; I'm not letting Nia go this easy.

"What d'you want me to do, Ni? You want me to get down on one knee and beg, 'cause I'll do it. I'll do it in front of all these people, ya know."

As the sky opens up and I feel the droplets of rain begin to fall upon my skin, I kneel down.

Nia uses her hand to shelter herself from the rain while she looks at me, and her eyes open wide.

"What are you doing, Rakim? Get up."

"Nah, man. I ain't gettin' up until you give me a chance to explain myself."

There're dozens of eyes on me, and I must look like I've lost my goddam mind kneeling down on this wet pavement but fuck it.

The rain pelts against the bus stop to my right like a drummer lost in his element as Nia moves towards me.

"Rakim..." she says, reaching for my hand to pull me up.

"Are you gonna hear me out?"

"Rakim, you're embarrassing me in front of all these people. Please, get up."

I look Nia dead in the eye. "These people?" I say, circling my finger. "I don't care about any of these people. I care about *you*."

Nia crosses her arms, and I look around and see the smirks, the phones, and the watchful eyes of men, women, and children. Heads turn as passers-by evade me on either side of the pavement.

"What d'you lot think, does man deserve a second chance?" I yell.

There's some murmuring, and a few eyes flit around, but nobody says anything with any conviction.

'Nah, there's no way I'm gettin' parred in public in front of all these people. They better answer.'

368

I raise my voice and repeat myself.

"I said, do I deserve a second chance, or what, you lot?"

The bass of my voice thunders so loudly that it commands a response. Hearing my untamed roar, the crowd begin to cheer in my favour as jubilant chants for Nia to listen to my words ring out.

'Yeah.'

'Give him a chance.'

'Listen to him.'

"Oh my god," Nia says between gritted teeth.

From behind the hand that covers her mouth, I see the subtle glimpse of a gorgeous smile, and I know I've nearly won the battle. "Okay, Rakim," she says.

"Wait, what?" I say, putting my hand to my ear as if I can't hear her.

"I said, okay, okay. We can talk. Jheeze, just get up. Please."

Rain steadily dripping down my forehead, I rise to my feet and hear the support and applause surrounding me.

"Thank you," I say, waving an arm to my loyal servants.

"Rakim, what the hell are you doing?"

"The people have spoken, Ni. You can't go against the people."

"I can't believe you."

"I told you, I'm here for the long run. I'm not going anywhere."

Nia bites her lip as she shakes her head in disbelief.

Neither of us seem to care about the rain as we look into each other's eyes.

"All right, Rakim. Fine. Come over to mine later, and we can talk."

I put my hands together like I'm about to pray.

"That's all I wanted."

"I don't know what's got into you, Rakim, but please don't ever embarrass me like that again."

I give her a confident wink and let go of her hand as she goes to turn away. "I'll see you tonight, yeah," I say, backing away slowly as I keep eye contact.

Probably quite unsure of what actually just happened, Nia rubs her brow before turning away and walking off.

I stand in front of my faithful fans and take a bow.

A boy, whose phone camera has been aimed at me for the past two minutes, approaches me and holds out his hand for a high-five. I oblige as he lauds me like I'm a superstar. I hand the boy my box of cookies and he looks like the happiest kid in the world.

Then, with a new-found buoyancy in my step, I spud him and bounce off to jog the whole way home.

35

7.58 p.m., and I put my phone on flight mode. Jonesy, Deontay, Burak, they can all wait. Tonight's about me and Nia, no one else.

I've spent the day attempting to make this evening as special as possible.

I visited Leanne's house earlier, where I discovered Ricky had seen a video on Snapchat of me winning Nia back. After Leanne caught wind of it, she got all emotional and congratulated me. Being so overjoyed, she didn't hesitate when I asked her to lend me some money.

I only asked for five grand, but she insisted on transferring me double, and for the first time in my life, I lapped up her offer. She'll get it back when we sell the house, but for now, I've got social media to thank for her generosity. Something I never thought I'd say.

The product is safely stuffed away at the back of my wardrobe along with the fifty-something grand I've put aside to settle my debt tomorrow.

Shrewdly, I replaced an eighth of the kilo with bicarbonate of soda, which means Deontay will have 125 grams of the real stuff to sell when I give it to him tomorrow.

I know once I work my magic in the kitchen with that, I'll see a minimum of twenty thousand, which will keep me ticking over nicely until Supercoon works *his* magic and sells Mum's house.

I look at myself in the hallway mirror as I prepare to leave my home. The man looking back at me looks on point. Face shining, like I've just returned from a tropical expedition, traps like hills on a horizon, sturdy and robust. Beard neatly trimmed and a hairline sharper than the edge of Samurai sword. Thanks to a little trip over to Slickz earlier, I look like an African Adonis.

And with a bouquet of flowers, a hamper of chocolates, and a special surprise in my possession, there's no way Nia's gonna be able to resist me tonight.

I leave my house carrying a bunch of flowers and make my way over to Nia's.

Confidence sky-high, I knock at the door, and seconds later, it's opened.

"Miss Barbados."

"Are you for real, Rakim?" Nia says, trying her best to contain her smile.

"Of course, I am. Here you go," I say, handing her a bunch of pink roses and a basket of chocolates.

Shaking her head and covering her mouth with her free hand, Nia gives me those inviting eyes. "Thank you, come in," she says and closes the door behind me.

I lean in for a kiss, and she gives me her cheek.

'Who's she kiddin' though? She knows I'm smooth with it. And I ain't even begun yet.'

She heads off to the kitchen, and I slip my shoes off.

"You're welcome," I say. "Just a little apology for ruining your birthday, ya know."

"Well, thank you, they're appreciated. I love roses," Nia says, trying to sound all formal.

"You need any help?" I ask from the kitchen doorway.

"No, it's cool. I got this," she says while hunting through the cupboards to locate a vase.

I've clearly made way more effort than Nia's casual mint green loungewear this evening, but whoever said that effort is proportionate to outcome lied.

With her hair tied in a bun, her tight-fit joggers on, and a cropped hoodie that displays her trim belly, Nia embodies the perfect yoga-teacher slash housewife.

I watch her for a moment.

Remember how I told you I conclude a lot about a woman from her feet. Well, Nia's are the benchmark of benchmarks. They look like they've just been manufactured in a lab - pristine and perfectly symmetrical. The glossy green paint on her toenails doesn't display a single chip, smudge, or crack and synchronises with her outfit. Her skin is smoother than Belgian chocolate, and there isn't a single blotchy patch of discolouration. It's all just beautifully brown. From heel to toe, she has not one imperfection.

"You still there?" Nia says as the cupboard closes and reveals that megawatt smile.

"Just admiring the view," I say.

"Uh-hmm. Well, go and sit down in the living room. I'll be through in a moment."

"Cool."

I obey her command and take a seat in the living room.

As I stare at the coals in the fireplace, I get lost for a moment. The flames crackle and ignite to perform a tribal dance celebrating my return. Swooping and swaying enchantingly, metres from my outstretched feet, they've got me feeling like a king back in my palace.

'Home sweet home.'

Minutes later, Nia comes in to join me, sitting down on the armchair adjacent to the sofa I'm on.

"You okay?" I ask.

"Yeah, I'm good," she says, crossing her legs as she fiddles with the drawstring on her hoodie.

"No wine tonight, nah?" I ask, noticing the water in Nia's glass.

"Nope."

There's an awkward silence for a moment.

"You look nice, by the way," I say.

"Thanks."

"I missed this."

Nia raises her eyebrow and rubs her belly before reaching for her glass. "What was that little performance about earlier, then?" she asks, swiftly changing the topic.

"What you sayin' you didn't like it?"

"It wasn't the best serenade, but you made your point, I guess."

I shrug, thinking when to reveal the surprise I've got stuffed away in this carrier bag. We engage in some small talk until a random question from Nia pulls me away from my thoughts.

"If I was to go away, Rakim, what would you do?"

"What?"

"If I went back to Barbados, what would you do?"

I sit up straight and give Nia a look of confusion. "Are you goin' back?" I ask.

"Answer my question first."

"Okay. Well, when you say what would I do, what d'you mean?"

"How would you feel about it?"

I exhale.

"Obviously, I wouldn't want you to leave. I didn't even know you were plannin' to go *this* time."

"There was a reason for that."

"Why?"

"I actually booked it for my brother and me. You remember I told you he came out of prison, and he's just determined to mess up his life?"

"Yeah, yeah."

"Well, I was gonna take him there, pretend it's a holiday and just leave him there with my mum and my gran."

"For real?"

"Yeah, me and mum had it all planned out. We'd spoil him when we got over there, take him to all the nice beaches and restaurants, do all the tourist stuff, get him thinking it's the best holiday ever. Then when the day came to fly back to England, I wouldn't tell him, and I'd just leave with his passport."

"Rah, so what happened?"

"The day before we were due to fly, he told me he's not coming."

"Why not?"

"Said he wants to stay here, doesn't wanna go back home."

"Why?"

Nia shrugs.

"It was hard enough to get hold of him; he was ignoring my calls for so long I was just happy he answered the phone... But I think he's done with us, and I don't know why. He's my little brother. I'm meant to be the one who looks after him. And now I'm supposed to just what...? Let him throw his life away?"

Seeing Nia get a little emotional, I move closer towards her.

"Aye, chill. It ain't your fault."

"You'd always say that, though, Rakim. You'd say that no matter what I did, wouldn't you?"

"Nah, I just mean, you can't force him to do what you want him to do. D'you want me to talk to him, Ni? 'Cause I will. I'll go round there now, maybe comin' from me he might listen."

"No, definitely not."

"Why d'you say it like that?"

"It's not you. It's just if he ever found out I had a boyfriend..."

"What?"

"He definitely won't talk to me then."

"Why?"

"It's just how he is. Ever since Trevan died, he's felt like he's gotta be my protector or something." Nia breathes deeply, and I reach out, but she moves away.

"What's the matter?" I ask.

She leans further into the comfort of her armchair. "... You still haven't told me."

"Told you what?"

"About your past. About who you really are?"

I sigh as my eyes hit the floor.

"Earlier, you said you were scared. What did you do that was so bad?" asks Nia.

"You know what I did."

"Yeah, but what happened? Why?"

My eyes hit the floor as I think about Dr Hartley, the psychiatrist that came to interview me in prison before my trial. He asked me all these strange questions about regular sporadic outbursts, suicidal thoughts, and the history of violence in my family, all to determine if I was fit for trial.

Apparently, he was on my team, but I swear to God, it never felt like that.

I look up and see Nia studying me as she holds her glass close to her lips.

"You really wanna know?" I ask.

"I don't want to... But I feel like I need to. To understand why. To understand who you are."

"That's not who I am no more."

Nia keeps her eyes on me, holding a hopefulness behind her lenses.

"Fair enough." My lips retract as my hands come together. "It happened a long time ago. And when I say long, I don't mean just in terms of years. I mean, in terms of the person I was back then, you feel me?"

Nia nods her head, and I sense the anticipation within her.

"So I was with this girl, my baby mum—"

"—You mean the mother of your child, not baby-mum. I hate that word."

"You know what I mean."

"Go on."

"I'ma give you the short version, cool?"

"I just wanna know, Rakim. As long as you're honest."

Other than Scribz, I've never sat down with anybody and explained the fullness of that terrible night.

I take a deep breath.

"So yeah," I begin. "Me and Shanice, the mother of my child, were supposed to go out this one night. I think Keziah must've been like two at the time 'cause we dropped her with my mum. Anyway, instead of going out with Shanice, I went to a rave with my bredrins. It ended up being kinda dead, so we cut after about an hour.

So, after I left, I saw these missed calls from Shanice. I called her back, but she wasn't answering, so I called Mum, and she told me Shanice had left the house already. These times I'm thinkin' where the hell is she."

"How old were you?" asks Nia.

"Seventeen, eighteen."

"Okay."

"So, me and my two bredrins phone around to try get hold of Shanice. Then my bredrin, Preddie, receives a call from his cousin tellin' us he just saw Shanice at the same rave I just came from. Apparently, she knew I went there and was askin' about me, was I whining with any girls, who was I talkin' to, all'a that.

Preddie's cousin told me she left the rave with some yout' called Jermaine. I knew Jermaine. He was a cool guy, he wasn't my close bredrin, but he definitely wasn't my enemy. And he wasn't competition to me in any kind of way. He just wasn't built like that, he was a music guy, but anyway, everybody loved Jermaine. He was just one a 'dem guys, friends with everyone.

Preddie and FatMack, my two bredrins I'm with, start teasing me sayin' Jermaine's tryin' to move to Shanice, he's gonna take her from me reh teh teh.

I manage to get through to Shanice and tell her to come and link me. Preddie and FatMack leave to go off and do whatever, and after about ten minutes, I see Jermaine come along with Shanice. I look at the two of them and suttin' just feels off.

Anyway, the three of us end up chillin' together. Shanice goes inside, and I start sizing up Jermaine just to make sure there's nuttin' bookey going on under my nose. Once I'm convinced it's me being parrow, I relax and join Shanice inside.

We make up, and I go back outside to use her phone to call a cab. Then when I'm scrolling through her phone, I see a message from this Jermaine guy... Shit, I still remember the exact words 'til this day."

"What did it say?"

I shake my head; I don't know why but I'm embarrassed to repeat the words. "... It said, 'You're beautiful in every way, and if I was there, I'd take care of you,' with a little kiss at the end."

Nia covers her mouth.

"See me, though...? I was a hothead when I was young, so you can imagine when I read that message, I went mad. I turned around, and everything they were doing instantly became sexual, the looks, the laughs, the hand movements. It was like they were just takin' the piss out of me right in front of my eyes. I marched over to them, and Shanice saw the look on my face. You know the one?"

"Yeah."

"She used to call it the death stare, where I'd just be locked onto someone. Everything else would just disappear like I was going in for the kill."

Anyway, Shanice saw it coming, but unfortunately for Jermaine and me, in hindsight, he didn't.

I boxed him in the side of his head, and he dropped to the ground. Before he could get back up, I was on top of him, smashing his face in. I must've punched him about twenty or thirty times; I don't remember. I just remember seeing blood coming out of his ears, his nose, and eyes, everywhere.

Then, when someone pulled me off him, his face was fucked. Just swollen. Purple. Brown. Red. His hair was covered in blood. His lip all buss up. It's like it was him, but it wasn't him. There wasn't any life left in him. His soul was gone. I beat him to death.

378

Bare people were screaming all around man, but it all felt like one long ringing in my ear. Everything just happened so quick. I don't even remember runnin' off."

My throat threatens to clog up, and my eyes narrow as I pause to take another deep breath, and Nia puts a hand on my arm.

"It's weird 'cause I say I never meant to kill him, and even the court agreed. That's why they gave me a twelve for manslaughter. But the fucked-up thing is when I saw that text, the only thought going through my mind was that 'I'm gonna kill him.' It's all I wanted to do.

The prosecution argued that I could've stopped after two or three punches, but my barrister, good old Mr Marshall-Hicks, managed to swing it around and say how Jermaine and I were both intoxicated. He got some doctor or whatever to state that once in the moment, a person isn't necessarily in control of their emotions, which doesn't prove pre-meditation. He even got nuff of the witnesses to crumble by accusing them of being drunk on the night in question and saying they couldn't be trusted to recall the events accurately."

I sip my drink before continuing.

"My bredrins were gassin' me saying it was a good thing, but I remember thinkin', Jermaine's dead, over what, a text. How can that be a good thing?

My barrister didn't care about that, though, and he didn't care about me. He got that little pyrrhic victory for himself and then went off to brag to his mates about how he got his 'client' a twelve instead of life. And yeah, I was grateful. I mean, I could be rottin' in jail right now, but d'you think he ever came to visit his 'client' or wrote to him, nah. He was probably living it up while I was contemplating if I should hang myself.

See, it was never about helping me, right or wrong, justice or injustice. It was just another case for him, for all of them, the jury, the judge, and the CPS. They all went home and carried on their lives, as usual, the next day.

All of them, apart from me.

379

I spent over ten years of my life tryin' to come to terms with every'ting, and it still haunts me. You wouldn't know it, but it does.

So, when you asked me in the car to talk about it, it just came flooding back. That's why I bugged out. I wasn't ready to tell you. I thought you'd look at me the way Jermaine's mum looked at me all through the trial, the way the prosecution portrayed me. A criminal with no regard for human life, a worthless piece of shit who deserved to be the one in a coffin and not the other way around."

Nia holds my hand.

"Rakim, I would never think that of you."

"It's cool, Ni, I know what I am, and I know what I'm not. Through you I've learned what really matters. I'm able to sit here and be honest with you. I can kneel down in the middle of the street and not care what anybody thinks of me. You made me want to change how I think about life. I never forgave myself for killing Jermaine and never thought I deserved anything else than what I got."

I feel the warmth of Nia's palms around my hand. Her longing gaze offers her pity, but I stay rigid, evading her eyes as I go on.

"See, some people who take a life don't care. They weren't raised to know any better. Me, though, I had a mum who loved me, taught me right from wrong, and instilled certain morals within me from a young boy. Mum constantly repeated those commandments, telling me about the wages of sin and how only God has the right to take a life. When I killed Jermaine that day, I killed a part of myself. That part that can look in the mirror or lie down at night and say with absolute conviction that I'm a good man who's worthy of a good life. My soul is tainted. All I say nowadays is that I try my best, no matter the odds. And even my best will never be enough 'cause I can't go back in time and change things."

"You are a good man, Rakim. Trust me, you are," Nia says, leaning closer to me.

"I killed a good yout' over a text message. Didn't even give him a chance to explain, nuttin'. I just punched him and punched him until I

380

fractured his skull, punctured his brain, and left his eye hanging out of the socket. What's good about that?"

Nia looks at me, but she doesn't know what to say after hearing the graphic detail.

"I'd been to Jermaine's house bare times; his mum had brought us drinks when some of the mandem were recording there. I saw her at parents' evenings. I knew his little sister, his brother. All of them were there in the court thinking what kind of sick monster kills his own friend and leaves him so fucked up he has to have a closed casket. Then to get away with murder, must've broken his sister because she slit her wrists two days later. She was only sixteen years old. And that's another body on my conscience."

I see the look on Nia's face and regret mentioning any of this, but we're here now. There's no turning back.

I take a sip of her water before she hurries out to the kitchen to bring me something a bit stronger.

She returns with a bottle of whisky and pours me a glass, which I down in one gulp. She sits next to me on the sofa and lays my head down across her lap, my face staring up at the ceiling as she caresses my head, gently moving her hand across my ears, around my cheeks, and up to my shaven scalp.

Silence befalls the room, and minutes pass while I try to expel the image of Jermaine from my mind.

"You gotta forgive yourself, you know, Rakim. If you don't, then you'll never accept reality."

"I know, I know."

"I mean, what happened was terrible. I wouldn't wish that on anyone, but does it define you as a person? No. You've made me feel so special since the day I met you, and if you hadn't mentioned any of the things you've told me tonight, I would've never known you'd been through all this."

"For real?"

"No, never. Why do you think I was so shocked when you told me?"

"I'm sorry about that," I say.

Nia cracks an innocent smile and plants those velvet-soft lips on my forehead. "You served your time, that was your punishment, and you took it like a man, so people can say what they want, right or wrong; you've paid for what you did."

"Yeah."

"You went to prison for twelve years, Rakim."

"Yeah."

"That's a long time."

"I know."

"How did you even manage?"

"I had to, init."

"I mean, wasn't it hard?"

"Of course, but it's like anything in life; after a while, your brain becomes accustomed to it, I guess."

"But being in prison for all those years, you've done so well to come out and be so... normal. And I'm not trying to sound patronising. I'm just telling you the truth."

"You think I'm normal?"

"Yes, one of the most normal men I've met. You're calm and humble."

"Yeah?"

"Put it this way, if you hadn't told me, I'd have no idea you just spent twelve years in prison.

"Thanks."

"What was it like?"

"The first years were the hardest, not because I was new to it or I was young and vulnerable or anything like that, nah. I was wild, reckless, and wasn't scared of anyone. And true what charge I came in on, man knew I was good with my fists. I went Y.O—"

"—What's that?"

"Young Offenders."

"Oh."

"I went there first. I was eighteen, so I was one of the oldest, so nuttin' like that was really an issue for me. It was more the not knowing. That killed me. Before my trial, I swear I couldn't sleep. I used to lay awake thinking all kinds of stuff. Thinking, 'What if I get life? Will I ever see my daughter again? What about if she grows up without a dad, has no guidance, and becomes a hoe—'"

"—Ah Rakim, don't."

"You asked, Ni. I'm givin' you the real. These kinda things happen. I've seen it. And this is the stuff that was going through my head. I used to pray I'd get found not guilty just to be back with Shanice."

"You still wanted her after all that?"

"We had a baby together. We basically lived together. She was the only girl I had any chance of clinging to. I used to wonder how many years she would be able to hang on for if things went left. Would she leave me after four years, five years, what? Would she even last that long? What if she was out one night and met a guy she liked who made her laugh? What would happen then? Would my daughter be callin' a next man daddy? I used to think of how I'd let my Mum down and worry about how Leanne would cope with my nephews by herself. What age would they be when I saw them again? All these things would just drive me insane every night. That was the worst thing for me, the uncertainty. So, when I got sentenced, it was a sort of relief in one sense. Then, on the other hand, I knew that no matter what, I would be living as a prisoner, in a cell for the next ten years or whatever. That was the next thing I had to deal with."

"That's crazy."

"Over time, it gets easier, you get into a routine, and it becomes your life. The letters stop, the visits stop, then you stop really caring about what people are up to on the outside because you have a new family— your friends on your wing. And then the female screws become the girls, the ones to impress, the ones that give you the purpose to put on some muscle, so you can walk back to your cell and feel just a little bit of what you used to feel when you were a free man and women would give you the eye."

"So that's why you got all this, yeah?" Nia says as she squeezes my biceps and my chest.

"Maybe to begin with. But after a few years, exercise became my way of blocking out everything on the outside. That's when your world becomes a prison. You talk about prison. You complain about prison. You laugh with prisoners about other prisoners. Nothing outside really matters. Only when somebody's going home, you remember, rah, this ain't actually our home. We still got a home out there."

"Did you forget about your life outside?"

"The memories were always there, but after years and years, that's all they became, just memories. Irrelevant distant memories."

"Wow," Nia says, like I've given her some profound insight.

"Yeah, it's not nice."

"I'm happy you're out now anyway, and my home is your home for as long as you want."

"Yeah, man."

"You wanna know something?" Nia says tentatively.

"What?" I say turning my head to look in her eyes.

She holds back a smirk. "... You know you could've come to Barbados with me."

"What d'you mean?"

"I mean, once I found out my brother wasn't coming, I changed the ticket to your name," Nia says.

I sit up, nearly headbutting Nia as she jerks backward to avoid a collision with my head.

"Are you serious?"

She smiles, slapping me gently on the shoulder. "Well, that's what happens when you're so rude, and you tell me to get out of your car."

I shake my head and resume my position.

"Now you tell me, ya know."

"Well, I had a banging time all by myself anyway, so there," Nia says, poking her tongue out.

"You basically wasted your money to spite me?"

She avoids the questions, knowing she'll sound silly.

"Anyway... You weren't ready to meet my mum and my gran just yet," she says.

"Do they look like you?" I ask.

"Behave yourself. My mum's nearly sixty."

"Yeah, but you know them Bajan women be looking twenty-two when there all sixty-five an' that."

Nia frowns. "My mum would never date a man like you," she says.

I laugh. Hard. "What's wrong with a man like me?"

"You're just too English," Nia says.

"Ah, Nia, you make me laugh."

"You'd never stand a chance."

I rub my hand across Nia's back, feeling like I could lay on her thighs all night. "What about if I bought her a really nice present?"

"Please, she doesn't need your presents."

I use my head to point towards the carrier bag that's gone unnoticed since I arrived.

Nia leans forward, trying to peer inside.

"What's that?" she asks.

I stretch my arm around to pick it up and pull out a box, gift-wrapped in pink glittery wrapping paper.

"For me?" asks Nia.

"Or your mum, whoever wants it."

Putting her ear to the box, she shakes it lightly, and her smile lights up the room. She unwraps the present slowly and cautiously as an air of suspicion hangs over her knitted brows.

I maneuver myself to sit upright and watch the excitement on her face turn into astonishment.

Her jaw drops.

"Oh my God, are you joking?" she says when she sees the dark green leather box with the word Rolex scrawled across the middle in gold print. "Rakim, I can't take this."

"Don't even try that," I say, and by the tone of my voice, Nia knows this isn't up for debate.

She pops the cap and plucks a rose gold 26mm Rolex Datejust from the box.

"You sure your mum wouldn't want my gifts?" I ask.

Nia turns towards me. "Rakim, I can't. This must have—"

I'm not having it, though. I secure it around her wrist, and Nia bites her lip as the Swiss craftsmanship hypnotises her like it does nearly every woman on this planet.

"Thank you, Rakim."

I take my phone out and tell her to strike a pose. Her beautiful eyes dazzle me, and the unsulliedness of her smile tells me I'm worthy of forgiveness. Not just from Nia but from myself.

"Happy birthday. D'you like it?"

"It's beautiful. I love it," Nia says.

"Good."

"And I love you too," she says, running her hands over my cheeks and bringing my face towards her to kiss me softly.

I pull away, leaving a look of shock on her face.

"That ain't it," I say, causing Nia to blush.

"Rakim... Are you serious?" "Of course."

"Rakim, I'm sorry I said you ruined my birthday."

I ignore the ramblings that stem from Nia's excitement and show her my phone screen.

She squints her eyes to form a steady focus. "Banjul International Airport..." Nia hums before she looks at my straight face. "No, you didn't, Rakim. Are you for real?"

"You ready for some yoga on the beach?"

"We're going Gambia. Are you serious?" Her scream sends shockwaves rippling through the entire house, and I reach to cover my

386

ears. "When... When are we going?" Nia says, snatching the phone from me.

A quick mental calculation, and she's destroying my eardrums once again.

"Two days. We're going in two days. Oh my God, Rakim, I swear, I fucking love you."

Nia squeezes me tightly, and we fall onto the floor, rolling over. I laugh as she plants hundreds of kisses all over my face, refusing to let me go.

"Thank you so much. I mean it from the bottom of my heart. I love you, Rakim."

"I love you too, Ni."

36

My chest goes up and down like a trampoline as Nia and I lay side by side on her bedroom floor, completely naked. Each heavy breath she takes eases my mind, letting me know she's content with recuperating for the meantime.

Her head on my shoulder; she circulates her finger around my solar plexus.

"Is it warm?" I ask.

"Yeah. Very."

"That's all you, ya know... Fulfilling my desires."

"Is it?"

"I swear down, you know how sexy you look right now?"

"Uh-uh, I haven't even done my hair or anything."

"You don't need to. Real talk. If that's what the downward dog's like, we're doin' yoga on the beach every single mornin', afternoon, and night when we reach The Gambia."

Nia laughs and then kisses the side of my chest.

"You make me laugh, Rakim."

"Nah, I'm being serious, Ni. You don't know how good you look," I say, lifting my head to examine the pinnacle of the female anatomy.

This one was undoubtedly constructed by a caring, patient, and loving God who must have summoned all the beauty of the universe when he carefully created Nia; she looks flawless.

"Well, thank you, you're not too bad yourself," she says as she frees an arm from under my back.

She takes her brand-new watch from the dresser next to us and begins to admire the sapphire crystal glass.

"Can I wear this when we go swimming in Gambia?" she asks so innocently, running a delicate finger around the smooth pink dial.

"Of course. You can dive like a hundred metres with them."

"Thank you again, Rakim. I know you didn't have to."

"It's cool."

She holds the watch to her ear, which sparks a laugh from me.

"It's real, Ni. You ain't gotta listen for no ticking."

"Oh, is that why it doesn't tick?"

I shake my head. "It glides. The fake ones tick."

"Ohh, right."

I climb to my feet, and Nia displays her elasticity by bending her leg past her shoulder to rub her foot against my calf muscles.

"You look good naked, you know, Rakim."

"Not as good as you," I say, turning to get another look at Nia's exposed body. "I'm gonna grab some water. You want anything?"

"Yeah, bring me some, too, please."

"Cool."

I pass by the monotone humming of the dryer and head downstairs to the kitchen.

Coupled with the whirring from the boiler, whatever Nia is saying is drowned out as I pour two glasses of water.

Before I go back upstairs, I check my reflection in the kitchen window.

'She wasn't lying, Rakz. You look good naked.'

Ego inflated, I head upstairs, hoping for more sweet loving. As I reach the third or fourth stair, I hear Nia's voice.

I stop moving to concentrate.

A high-pitched squeal puts me on high alert.

"Nia!"

I rush up the remaining stairs as water sloshes over the sides of the two glasses in my hands.

"Yo Ni," I yell.

She doesn't answer, but I can make out her words when I reach the hallway.

"Where are you...? Hello... Hello," she shouts as I burst through the door.

She's holding her phone to her ear, and something's struck the fear of God through her.

"Yo wa gwarn?" I say, placing the two glasses on the dresser. "You, okay?"

"Rakim! They've got Daniel."

"What?"

"They just rang me... They've got Daniel," she screams.

Her hands are shaking as she aimlessly presses buttons on her phone.

"Wait, calm down. Who's got Daniel?"

"I don't know, Rakim," she shouts. "They just rang me. They said they've got him."

"Who's *they*, Nia? I don't know what you're talkin' about."

"I don't know. Wait!"

"Who's—"

"—Shhh... Wait." She puts the phone on loudspeaker.

It rings several times before being disconnected.

Immediately she calls back.

"Who you callin'?" I ask, still oblivious to what's going on.

She bites at her fingernail as she hovers over the phone.

"Come on, Daniel, answer."

"Nia," I say, grabbing hold of her arms. "What's going on? Who's got your brother? Where is he?"

Nia shakes me off and reaches for her underwear. Moving from left to right, panicking, she tries to redial her brother for the fourth time.

"Nia?"

"What am I gonna do?"

"What the fuck's going on? Talk to me."

Her heart must be on the verge of exploding as she slips her knickers back on a takes a couple of steady, controlled breaths.

"I don't know, they just called me and t-t-told me they've got Daniel," she says as she breaks down and falls into my arms, a snivelling mess.

"Calm down, Ni, calm down. It's cool, it's cool."

She buries her face between my chest and my arm, sobbing uncontrollably as panic turns to pity.

"They took him, Rakim. They took him."

My heart thrashes at my chest, but I know I must remain calm.

"Who's *they*, Ni?"

"I don't know," she mutters.

I lift her head gently, keeping both hands on her cheeks. "What did they say?" I ask.

Tears flood down her face as she blows her nose on her hand. "They said... They've got... Daniel... And if I don't give them money, they're g-g-gonna kill him," she says before breaking down again.

"Shhh. Look, Ni, nobody's gonna kill your brother, all right? Look at me," I say, following her head as I try to regain eye contact.

"I'll sort it. I got you. But you gotta tell me exactly what they said."

"I just told you, Rakim!"

"Okay. Okay."

I reach across the dresser and pick the phone up. "Is this the number, yeah?"

Nia nods her head, and I press call. It rings a few times, but nobody answers.

"I'ma try again."

Two more attempts but no answer.

"All right, Ni. Did you speak to him when they called?"

She wipes the never-ending stream of tears that fall and sniffs again.

"Did you speak to him?" I ask.

"No... I mean yes, yes. He said, 'help,' that's it."

"All right, okay," I say, trying to appear calm. Inside I'm a shambles, though. I don't know how I'm staying so composed. I have no idea who her brother is or what's going on, and here's my woman—distraught and undoubtedly expecting me to alleviate her devastation.

391

"Was that all they said, yeah?"

"Yeah, then they hung up."

I reach into my pocket and switch my phone off of flight mode.

"What are you doing?" Nia asks.

"I'm calling off my phone. Maybe they'll answer if they think it's someone else."

"What if they don't answer, though? What if they—"

But as I dial the number, Nia becomes mute.

I stare at the phone and a wicked coldness shoots through my body.

Neurons fire through my brain, tryin' to clarify what I'm seeing.

The hairs on my arms spring up, and the room strikes me with brightness.

Frozen to the spot, I blink hard before my eyes read the name on my screen again.

'No way. He can't be...'

"What it is, Rakim?" Nia says.

Daniel isn't just Daniel, Nia's brother.

He's Deontay.

37

On the fourth ring, a voice answers, and I jump to my feet.

"Who speaking?" a slurred foreign accent says.

Nia springs to my side, and I instantly signal her to be quiet, running my finger across my throat.

"You called my phone. You got my little brother there. Who is this?" I say.

"Your brother?" the voice says unexpectedly.

"Yeah, Daniel..."

"You have the money?"

"Who is this?" I thunder.

I see Nia miming orders from my peripheral, and I have to turn my back on her to concentrate.

"You have money or no? If you no have money in one hour, your brother is dead man."

"Listen, listen. How much?"

"Hundred."

"Hundred what?"

"One hundred thousand."

It takes a second for the words to register and I have to double-check I'm not surrounded by a plethora of cameras and a man sat on a director's chair.

"How much?" I ask.

"One hundred thousand," the slobbery voice repeats.

Nia's eyes tell me she's counting on me—they're locked onto me like I'm the Son of God. Quickly I gather my thoughts and regain composure.

"Done. Where am I coming?"

"You have the money?"

"I got all the money right here," I say assertively.

The voice on the other end of the phone goes silent.

"Yo," I say.

"I text where you come. One hour."

"Wait... wait. Let me speak to Daniel first, make sure he's—"

"—Just bring money and come alone."

The phone goes dead, and straight away, Nia fires her questions. "What did they say? Is Daniel okay? Where is he?" she asks more intently each time.

"Listen," I say, taking control of the room. "They want a hundred grand."

"A hundred grand?" Nia's eyes nearly burst out their sockets. "What's going on, Rakim? Who are these people?" she asks.

"I don't know. But I'm gonna find out, Ni. Don't worry."

"How?"

"I'll sort it."

I push my legs into my joggers and pull my socks over my feet.

"What, you just have a hundred grand stuffed under your mattress?" Nia asks like it's the most ridiculous thing she's ever heard.

"Not under my mattress, in my wardrobe," I say as I kiss her forehead.

"Where you going?"

"I'm gonna grab the money. Wait here. I'll be back in two secs. I'm taking this too," I say as I snatch Nia's phone from the bed.

"Be quick, Rakim, please."

"I'll be back in two minutes, tops. Just get your clothes on."

I dash downstairs and out of the house. Once I reach my door, I turn the key and dart up the stairs like a bullet train. I grab the duffle bag from the wardrobe in my room and rip the zipper open.

A quick scan tells me it's untouched. Fifty-eight thousand and a kilo of heroin and cocaine. I zip the bag back up, throw it on the bed, and phone Deontay.

"C'mon, c'mon... Pick up D."

Voicemail.

"Fuck."

I try again. Same outcome.

I suck my teeth and phone Priscilla as I pace around.

"Yo," I say as she answers.

"What's with the booty hour phone calls? Things didn't work with Nia?"

"Priscilla, have you seen Deontay?"

"That's what you calling me for?"

"Look, I ain't got time for this. I think he's in trouble."

Her tone changes. "No, I ain't seen that boy since he was here with you."

"What about your sister? They speak all the time, alie?"

"What's going on?"

"Has she seen him or not, man?"

"Hold on, lemme ask her... Tash... Tash?" Priscilla calls. "Have you seen your boyfriend recently?"

I pray this isn't what I think it is. But there's only so much prayers God can answer for one man.

"No, she hasn't."

"Shit."

"What's wrong with him? What's going on?" Priscilla asks.

"I ain't got time to explain. If any of you lot speak to him or see him tell him call me ASAP."

"Okay, but—"

I hang up the phone.

38

This wasn't how things were supposed to go. I was supposed to have forty-eight hours to come up with the money to pay off Burak's men.

"Who are these people? What's going on?" Nia cries.

Her voice is non-stop in my ear as she bombards me with question after question. But I'm in my own zone, behind the wheel, ploughing straight through red lights like they don't exist.

A horn blasts as I narrowly avoid a turning car, and I feel Nia's body crash against my left shoulder.

"Careful, Rakim!" she shouts.

I chuck a hard right and hear my car tyres screech in agony as the rubber burns black tread marks into the tarmac of Tunwell Estate.

"Rakim, where are you going?" Nia asks, clutching my wrist as I park up abruptly.

"Just wait here. Lock the doors. I'll be back in two seconds," I say.

Her fear-filled eyes cling to me.

"Two secs, Ni. I promise."

This is far from how I planned tonight's events. Nia didn't want to believe this side of me existed just a month ago, but ironically, it's going to take all my street knowledge and ruthlessness to get her beloved brother out of this alive.

I close the car door and run towards Ribz's block. I try calling him, but he doesn't pick up.

'Don't tell me these Turks have nabbed Ribz as well.'

Grit-grey clouds lurk over the streets, warning me of an impending rainfall. The only audio, stray cats and vermin scratching through empty bins and darting off when they hear my footsteps.

396

A fox lets out a series of harrowing howls that sound like they're right next to me as wild winds whoosh by, and I pull my hood back over my head to persevere.

I reach the entrance to Ribz's block and force open the block door with a tug so powerful that it rips the two magnetic strips apart and nearly dislocates my shoulder.

"Shit."

The pain sears through my body, impelling me to scream, but I don't. The luxury of complaining is one I cannot afford at this moment. Time is of the essence.

I race up the stairs to the third-floor flat and use my key to open the door. I march through to the master bedroom, which is nothing more than a neglected space with a torn carpet, mouldy furniture, and a grimy mattress spread across the floor.

I bend down and search for the slit in the mattress where my gun is stashed. If these Turks think they're gonna kidnap Deontay and hold him hostage, they're in for a surprise.

In the streets, a man is only as good as his word. Burak's word was that I had forty-eight hours. It hasn't even been twenty-four, and these lot have made their move. The worse thing is that I'd arranged to pay them, so why they've gone and kidnapped Deontay, I mean Daniel, baffles me.

Fuck that for now. The gloves are off.

I reach inside the mattress and feel around, but a couple of sharp springs force me to slow down. Gently, I run my hand across some tattered foam until I feel the strap of a bag.

"These man think they're gonna nab D, and I'm just gonna let it slide? Never."

I pull the bag out. "I swear, soon as I get..."

The bag feels way lighter than it should.

I unzip it, and there's nothing but blackness.

The gun's gone.

"What the fuck?"

I spend the next few minutes ransacking the place, hoping the gun will miraculously fall from the top of a wardrobe or jump out from behind a pillow, but luck isn't on my side tonight.

"How's Deontay gettin' kidnapped when he's carrying a burner?"

I don't understand. The whole point of me giving Deontay the gun was to protect himself in situations like this.

"... I bet he's given it to Ribz or one of his dickhead friends."

I suck my teeth as I try Ribz again, but there's no answer.

As soon as I end the call, my phone lights up. It's Nia.

"Where are you, Rakim? They just text me where they're keeping Daniel."

"Swear down."

"Yeah, hurry up. We've gotta go."

"I'm comin' now," I say as I grab a small lock knife from the chaotic mess around me. I'm like a cheetah down the stairs hopping two or three at a time, and before I know it, I'm back behind the wheel of my Merc.

"What were you doing up there?" Nia asks.

"Don't worry. Give me your phone."

I read over the address several times.

43 Darwin Avenue. It's not a road I'm familiar with, so I put it in the satnav.

A female voice announces our destination is fourteen minutes away. Although intended to placate, her conciliating voice has the complete opposite effect on me.

'Fourteen minutes?'

I need to be there *now*.

I turn to Nia.

"Look, I'ma drop you back at mine. You can—"

"—No, I'm coming with you."

"Nia, are you mad? You're not coming."

"Rakim, that's my brother, who's probably tied up in some warehouse. I'm coming."

"Listen, this shit ain't no game, Nia. This is dangerous. It's real life," I exclaim.

"I know. And I'm not leaving my brother."

"Nia, I beg you just—"

"—Rakim!" Nia screams, making me jerk my head to the side. "I've lost one brother. I'm not gonna sit back and lose another one. I'm coming with you."

Seeing that I'm fighting a losing battle and wasting time, I give Nia a dour look.

"Why you gotta be so stubborn?"

"Stubborn? Daniel's my brother. You don't even know what he looks like. What's gonna happen if you go in there and it's not him? You gonna risk your life for someone you don't know?"

She doesn't even know how wrong she is. I know exactly who Daniel is, meaning I'm just as invested in this as her. I want to say something, but it will only make matters worse, and this is neither the time nor the place.

I suck my teeth.

"There you go. Just drive," Nia orders, pointing ahead like she's the colonel of this two-man army.

Minutes go by, and Nia's sadness has become a silent focus. I hear her steady breathing as I whizz towards Darwin Avenue. The night of the city passes by, and I look out the window, knowing I'd give anything not to be in this car right now.

A quick glance at the satnav tells me I have eight minutes to concoct a plan.

With no gun, no backup, and now subjected to an unfamiliar environment, I'm most definitely the disadvantaged party here.

The seconds tick by, and we get closer to our destination. I feel the uneasiness in the car grow as I tap away at the steering wheel, hoping Deontay's still alive and kicking.

I call the number the Turks called from, but the phone doesn't ring.

'They must've got rid of the phone, so it can't be tracked.'

For a moment, I question whether I brought the money and the drugs, and my heart skips a beat.

The nerves are kicking in big time now. My hands are sweating, and Nia's eyes keep flitting between me and the ETA on the interface.

4 mins.

"Is Daniel gonna be okay?" she asks.

"Yeah, he'll be fine, don't worry. They don't want him."

"How do you know?"

"Ni, I know loads of guys like this. They don't care about your brother; they just want the money. I'll pay them, and we'll be gone.

"You sure?"

"Yeah, your stayin' in the car, though."

"But—"

"—Your stayin' in the car, Ni," I say, raising my hand like a guillotine ready to strike down on any festering response. "You wanted to come, you're here, but I'm not puttin' you in danger. I'll get your brother out. Just trust me. Okay?"

I turn and look into Nia's hopeful eyes.

"You promise?" she asks.

"On my life."

My words seem to have the desired effect.

Still clueless as to how this will unfold, all I have to go off is past experience. The problem is, though, I've never been on the victim's side. I've always been the hostage taker.

I think back to what Squeeze used to tell Preddie and me.

'Rule one, get the money first... Rule two, make sure you check it.'

I wonder if these Turks will take the same approach.

'The guy on the phone sounded eager for the money. Maybe he won't check it all. Maybe they don't have time. Maybe I should bring the food in and leave the money in the car.'

"We're one minute away," Nia says as I lower my window to cool down.

This area is far from how I expected it to be. Instead of an enormous run-down council estate, with alleyways and pathways meandering off in numerous directions, it's an everyday residential area. Even Nia seems to pick up on the oddness of the location.

"Here?" she says, clearly expecting something far worse.

Jonesy talked Burak and his men up, but I'm starting to think maybe they're amateurs.

On each of the several occasions I was entrusted with watching over a person who'd failed to pay a drug debt, the location was either a warehouse, a garage on an industrial estate, or a block of flats. As I turn onto Darwin Avenue, the terraced houses on either side don't fit the bill at all.

'Why these man wanna kidnap Deontay now?' The question still bothers me.

I rack my brain for an answer, and only one name springs to mind.

Scribz.

'Fuckin' snake.'

The thought of him hits me like a ten-tonne truck. It could only be him. He's the only one who knew about Deontay working with me other than the Turks. We both made it clear we wanted each other dead when we argued on the phone; only he may have acted first, which gives him the upper hand.

The more I think about it, the more it makes sense.

I know he's a snitch, so now he needs me out of the way. He can't risk anybody else getting wind of what he really is; snitches don't last in prison.

It's all coming together now.

Scribz gets the Turks to kidnap Deontay, I come running. The Turks get the two people they think stole their product, the two they saw that day, me and Deontay.

Then instead of Scribz, the disloyal thief, he becomes Scribz, the hero, when the Turks get their product and their money back, and every bit of coke and cash turns out to be right where Scribz said it would be.

He appears an honest criminal, the guy who even gave up his own friend as a show of loyalty to his suppliers, making him a trustworthy asset to Burak and his gang. Then he's back in business.

Yeah, Scribz played this one to a tee.

We arrive at the destination, and I slow the car to a halt about thirty metres from the address. Parked on the road adjacent to Darwin Avenue, I've got a good view of number 43. It's a three-storey building like all the others I can see on the street, and my guess is it's a house conversion, split into three separate flats on three levels.

I decide to wait a few minutes just to conduct a quick re-con. With some luck, I'll catch the twitch of a curtain or somebody leaving the house, and maybe I'll get a better idea of what I'm up against.

I switch the engine off, and the car goes quiet.

"What could Daniel possibly have done to get himself involved in this?" Nia asks, shaking her head as if wondering how she's ended up here tonight.

"I don't know, Ni, but don't worry, he'll be fine."

"But how's he getting mixed up in this, Rakim. I thought he was just selling little bags of weed. What's he done to owe somebody a hundred grand?"

Her words remind me of the first time I met Deontay. The day I bought one of those little bags of weed.

"It's not he's fault, Ni. People get involved in stuff not really thinkin', and before they know it, they're in way over their heads. But don't worry, I'll sort it."

"A hundred grand, though, Rakim."

Every word that comes out of Nia's mouth injects a little more guilt into me.

"I've got this, Ni. Don't worry."

"I'm never gonna be able to pay you back," she says.

I swivel my body to face her.

"Pay me back? Are you mad?"

"But it's a lot of money..."

402

"Listen," I say, taking hold of Nia's hands. "Money's just paper. It comes and goes. As long as I got you, I don't care about nuttin' else. I'ma go in there, get your brother back, then tomorrow he's on the first flight to Barbados. If I have to take him there and throw him on the plane, myself, I swear, I'll do it."

I wrap my arms around Nia and squeeze her tightly. "Everything'll be all right, Ni. I promise."

As I pull away, I'm drawn to the curtains on the second floor of number 43.

"Yo, did you see that?" I ask.

"What?" Nia says, releasing herself from my embrace.

"The curtains just moved."

"Where?"

Confident I know which flat Deontay is located in, I grab the duffle bag containing the drugs and the money from the back seat.

"Rakim, where you going?"

"I just saw the curtain move. Daniel must be in on that second floor there."

As I go to get out of the car, I freeze.

'Maybe I should take the money and leave the food.'

"What's wrong?" Nia asks, seeing me pause.

'But if they check the bag and want me to go get the rest, then I'm riskin' getting Nia involved... Nah, lemme just take every'ting.'

"Rakim?" Nia cries.

"Ni, look at me and listen, yeah."

I stare deep into Nia's eyes until I'm sure I've got her full attention. There can't be another thought floating around in her head right now.

"Stay here. No matter what, don't come in after me."

"Yeah, okay."

"I'm not joking, Ni. Whatever happens, don't get out of this car," I say as if I'm relaying orders to an infant.

She gives an obedient nod before leaning in and kissing me.

"Be careful, Rakim, please."

"The time's two-thirteen. If I ain't back in fifteen minutes, start blasting the horn as loud as you can, flash your lights, whatever you need to do, that'll wake up the whole street. These lot ain't gonna do nuttin' if they know there's loads of eyes on them, you understand?"

"Okay, I got it."

"Good. Lock the doors."

"I love you, Rakim. Be safe."

"I love you too, Ni. I'll be back soon. Just stay here," I say.

Then I close the door, pull the strap of the duffle bag over my shoulder, and make my way towards the house.

39

The sound of my trainers plopping in and out of puddles that daylight has long abandoned follows me. I reach number 43 and scamper across the pathway over weeds and withered plants that time forgot.

Leaning back, I try to get a better view of the second-floor window.

There's no sign of life, and for a brief moment, my mind turns on me, and I start second-guessing whether I saw any movement by that window up there in the first place. Confused, I press all three buzzers one after the other.

'What if these Turks are tryin' to set me up? What if they just wanna kill Deontay and me and take the money?'

I guess it's a risk my lock knife and I will have to take.

I pull the strap of my duffle bag over my head. Holding it in my hand, I go to press the buzzers again when a voice responds. It's the same voice I heard over the phone, a bit more muffled through the static of the intercom, but it's the same voice. The one that sounds like it belongs to a greasy, debauched foreigner.

"You have the money?" he asks.

"Yeah, it's in the bag," I say.

"I open door."

There's a buzz, a click, and then the door opens.

I've got one foot over the threshold of the unlit hallway as I hear the order. "Put bag on floor and close the door."

"Leave the bag?"

"Yes. Leave bag and go," the Turk says.

"I ain't leaving the bag without my brother. Send him out, and I'll leave it right here."

"Leave bag," the voice bellows.

This man seriously wants me to abandon my life savings in the hope of him honouring his word. No way.

"I'm not leaving the bag until I see my brother."

"Leave bag, or you *never* see your brother," he shouts.

"Look, I only come for my brother, that's it. I'm unarmed. No gun, no weapon, nuttin'. Just me."

I wait, but there's no reply.

"Hello, hello," I call.

Nothing.

I press all three buttons again and wait.

Carefully placing the duffle bag in the doorway to stop it from closing, I take a couple of steps back and look up towards where I saw movement from the curtains.

Tap, tap, tap.

My head immediately swings around towards the ground-floor window.

Right in front of me. On the other side of this glass panel. With a knife being held to his temple, stands Deontay.

There's a terror I've never seen before present in his eyes. Relief and joy battle against despair and fear. Deontay's less than a metre away, but he might as well be a mile.

Suddenly, I feel useless, and it takes all of my willpower to refuse to embrace the pity and guilt that threaten to consume me.

'This ain't the time for feeling sorry.'

My eyes move towards the fat Turk next to Deontay, and I feel my blood boil and my muscles tense. He's exactly how I imagined him. His hood fails to cover a heavy set of eyebrows and he has a black bandana tied around his mouth that doesn't do much to conceal his scruffy beard.

He shoves Deontay towards the window, and I watch as my friend reluctantly draws the curtains.

"D?"

It's no use, though. As quickly as Deontay appears, he disappears. Back to the wretchedness of the dingy flat.

My jaw clenches tight like a vice grip, and I feel the anger rise in me like a great volcano.

'All right, cool. These man want war.'

I press all three buzzers again.

My shoulder aches, but I ignore the pain, and within seconds, the same voice answers. "You see your brother, now leave money and go," the Turk says.

I kick the bag further into the darkness of the hallway, ensuring it's still within my reach should I have to snatch it for any reason. Then keeping myself between the door and the outside, I reply.

"The money's there outside your door. Let my brother go."

"You go first."

"Send him out," I order.

"Where the money? You don't fuck with me?" the Turk says raising his voice.

He's getting irate now. Jittery. He's worried I'll try something, and he won't get his money.

"Listen, I just want my brother. Send him out and take the money. It's there."

The intercom goes silent for a few seconds, which seems like forever. Every moment passes in slow motion.

I hear the monotonous drips of water that splash against the concrete ground. I hear birds hooting in the distance. The unspoken whisper of the wind. Every sound is magnified beyond measure as I wait in the deafening silence. Then there's contact from the other side.

"I coming. You stay away. You fuck me, you brother dead."

"No problem. Let's do this," I say calmly.

The door at the end of the hallway sneaks open, and a figure emerges.

"You stay back," warns the heavyset shadow.

407

With my body taking up the doorway of this converted house, the moonlight behind me provides the only illumination inside the hallway. It's enough to make out the outlines of a face but not enough to read the writing on the letters scattered on the floor at the foot of the staircase.

"The money's right there," I say, pointing to the bag a few feet in front of me.

Tentatively, the Turk edges forward.

That's when the sparkling silver gleam of a massive blade twinkles as it meets the moonlight.

The Turk has his hood up, and his bandana still covers most of his face.

I need to think fast.

My brain starts working like a ghetto Einstein, fitting together all the parts of the equation.

The first thing I note is the zombie knife he's carrying—a wannabee gangster's weapon of choice, super popular amongst the younger generation. I remember it from all the drill lyrics amongst the millennials back in prison.

The second piece of the puzzle is *how* he's holding the knife. Like it's a bottle of water, the blade pointing upwards towards the ceiling. I doubt this kid's ever used a knife before.

Finally, the edginess in his movement and his tremorous voice, he's scared. He isn't the one running this scheme.

He gets within reaching distance of the bag and, pointing the knife in my direction, lowers himself while keeping his eyes on me.

"You stay, don't come no close," he yells.

I don't break eye contact. I don't even blink as he wraps his gloved hand around the handle of the bag. His hand that holds the knife lifts his hood back slightly in order to keep his eyes on me, and as he does so I realise there's something off about this whole thing.

'Why are Burak and these big-time dealers allowing this fat little kid to handle a six-figure handover?'

This isn't right.

The Turk picks the bag off the ground, and I watch his arm shake like a blade of grass as he ascends to his feet. I lift my hoody from my belly, exposing my waistline. "Look, no gun, nothin'."

"You go back!" shouts the Turk.

He has the bag now, but I still don't have Deontay. I could go for the bag and rush at him, but one wrong move against that twelve-inch serrated blade, and I'm in big trouble. With a knife like that, it doesn't take a seasoned pro to do some severe damage, just a wild swipe.

'C'mon Rakz, think.'

I take a step into the hallway.

"Back, go back!" the Turk screams.

"Look, you got the bag. Where's my brother?"

"You go, or I kill you," he says, stabbing the knife into thin air.

I show the guy my empty palms. "Calm down," I say, trying to gain a few inches with another step.

He backs towards the door of the flat, and by now, I'm confident this guy has never used a knife before. If he knew what to do, he would've attacked me by now.

My instincts kick in—*when you spot a weakness in your enemy, exploit it.*

This guy has the money, but he's not away scot-free yet. I can guess what's going through his mind. He didn't expect someone with my courage. Someone willing to take things as far as I am.

He's obviously out of his depth, yet he still hasn't called out for anybody to come back him up.

Then that's when it occurs to me. '*Shit... This prick is doing this all alone.*'

He was the voice on the phone, the voice on the intercom, and the now he's the guy collecting the bag. Until now, I haven't seen or heard another soul apart from Deontay.

It makes perfect sense.

'*How'd I only just clock?*'

This isn't the workings of Burak.

This Turk's on a rogue mission by himself. That's why he has no backup with him, that's why we're in this strange location, that's why he's shaking like a leaf, and that's why he kidnapped Deontay before the forty-eight hours were up.

'Fuck... He probably knew I had forty-eight hours, which meant he only had a small window of time. All he had to do was get me here without Burak knowing, pretend this is all on behalf of his bosses; then, once I hand over the money, that hundred grand goes straight into his pocket, he goes off the radar, and Burak thinks I didn't honour my word.'

Not only did I get played by Scribbler, but I've also been played by a man who barely speaks English and is probably ten years my junior.

Scribz's betrayal hurt my heart, but this one hurts my pride.

I step closer as he continues to back away. "Go back!" he says, taking a crazy swing with his machete, forcing me to jump out of the way.

This yout' has shown some courage and cunningness to outwit both his boss and me; I'll give him that. But the downside of youth is the lack of experience and wisdom. You see, there's a thin line between bravery and stupidity, intelligence and arrogance. And now I know this guy is all by himself in this; my confidence has skyrocketed.

"Chill," I say.

"You come close, you die."

He's all but reached the door now, and I'm still too far away to pounce on him.

'Man can't let him take my food. If I lose that, I'm into Burak for a hundred grand and Darkos for thirty-five. That's as good as dead.'

If he gets through that door, it could well be game over. For all I know, there's a back door in the flat that leads to a garden. If he goes through that, climbs a fence, and takes off, I'll never see him or my money again.

"Yo, brother, look, I know what you're doing. D'you think Burak's not gonna find out?"

The Turk doesn't say anything but just gives me an odd look.

410

"I know… You want the money for yourself, but if you take that, Burak'll find you. And if he doesn't, you know it's your mum and your family he's coming for."

Up against the door now, the Turk pauses. I'm unsure if he understands what I'm saying, but I have no other play right now. He scrunches his face up and lowers his bandana. "Burak," he says.

"Yeah, Burak."

He shakes his head, pulls his bandana back up, and reaches for the door handle.

My last chance.

I have to gamble.

"Yo, brother, I'm sorry… But there's no money in there, fam," I say, pointing at the bag that dangles between him and the door of the flat.

He looks at me blankly.

"The bag… No money," I say, putting on the best pitiful face I can muster.

"No money?"

It must work this time because the face in front of me changes. All the life appears to have drained from it.

I inch a bit closer as I continue the façade. "I'm sorry. I lied. I just wanted my brother back. I don't have a hundred thousand pounds. There's no money."

The Turk looks down at the bag, and in that split second, I seize my opportunity. Throwing caution to the wind, I launch towards him, my arms protecting my face.

To my surprise, this coward uses the knife to guard himself instead of stabbing me. But even as a fat lump, it's nearly impossible to repel two-hundred and forty pounds of muscle flying at you, and I bulldoze through him like he's not even there.

We both hit the ground with a tumultuous clamour. I lift my head as the young man groans in anguish. I don't know where the knife is. All I can hope is that I haven't been stabbed.

411

As his arm swings towards me, I assert myself on top of this chubby yout'.

'Shit, he's still got the knife.'

From below me, he waves it around frantically. I feel something skim the side of my head, and I duck lower, my face pressing against his flabby chest as I use my hand to control his flailing arm.

"You think you're gonna rob me?" I shout as I easily overpower him, pushing his hand that holds the knife to the ground. He yells something in Turkish, but I'm not listening. I manage to get upright, knees either side of his torso. I cock my right arm back and let my fist go to work.

Repeatedly, it smashes into his fragile doughy cheek, again and again. By the fifth or sixth punch, he stops screaming.

My eyes seem to have adjusted to the darkness by now, or maybe because we're super close, I can see the blood oozing from the face below me. His bandana hangs loosely around his neck and a blackish-red wound by the side of his head stands out about the width of a golf ball.

But it's only when I notice he's out cold that I stop attacking him. I look at him, and for a moment, I swear it's Jermaine.

Quickly I snap out of my anger-fuelled daze. I climb to my feet as I fight for my breath. I grab the bag from the floor and pick up the knife. It's decorated with streams and spots of blood. It's caught one of us. I touch the throbbing pain in my head, and low and behold, I feel the gash.

It's not deep, but blood's trickling from it. I suck my teeth as I run my hand over it, which sends a stinging pain around my skull, making me flinch.

'It's just a slice.'

I'll deal with that later.

Right now, I need to get Deontay and get the hell out of here. I step back, and not for the first time in my life; I send a firm boot through a flimsy front door that flies wide open.

"Deontay," I shout as I enter a hallway without light.

'What is it with these vampires?'

I feel across the wall for a switch and press it, but nothing happens.

"Deontay," I call again.

"Rakz!" a voice shouts from somewhere to my right.

I follow the voice down the corridor, where I make out a few door handles on either side of me.

"I'm coming," I cry.

I rush along, looking from side to side in desperation.

"D?" I shout again when I spot a door that emits light from the gap between the carpet.

I turn the handle and enter.

The door swings back, and I freeze.

My body goes as stiff as a board.

The knife drops out of my hand, clattering against the floor.

"Deontay?"

40

"What's good, brudda?" Deontay says, the fear completely gone from his face.

Looking like the Grim Reaper in black trainers, a black jacket, black joggers, black gloves, and a black ski mask pulled just above his eyebrows, he stands metres away.

I stare at him in shock.

I wondered where my gun had gotten to. And now the answer is literally staring me in the face.

"What—what you doing?" I ask.

"You think I don't know," Deontay says.

"Are you mad, bro? Put the gun down, man," I say as I walk towards him.

"Don't fucking move," he screams, cocking back the slide of the Glock just the way I taught him.

The menacing sound stops me in my tracks.

"Oi, D, what you doing? What you on?"

Deontay emerges from the kitchenette area, thumping his left hand across the countertop while his right-hand aims the barrel directly at me. As he moves into the living room area, I watch his sinister figure pass the crimson-painted walls.

He plucks a walkie-talkie from his jacket pocket, and for a moment, a ridiculous thought that he's an undercover fed runs through my mind.

"Is this a joke, fam? Are you serious?"

He says something on the walkie-talkie before putting it on the countertop beside him.

The blood has begun to leave a sticky, dry trail by the side of my face that feels tight against my skin.

414

"D?" I shout, not understanding what the hell's going on.

"Shut the fuck up, man," Deontay yells.

Looking at how he's gripping that gun, I feel a real rush of fear. I know how sensitive that trigger is, and his index finger is right on it. "

"Look, D, I don't know what this is about, but we have to go. Put the gun down."

"How long have you been fucking my sister?"

I tilt my head back. "What?"

"How long?" he shouts.

"Is this about your sister, bro? I never knew. On my life, I swear, I just found out today."

"You see you; you talk a lot of shit."

"I'm keepin' it one hundred. I never knew she was your sister."

"Stop chatting wass. I see the picture and the calls on your phone. I see the text about, 'You just gotta leave your bro to sort his own life out.' You knew, don't lie. You wanted man out the way so you could fuck my sister and take her away with you to Africa."

'This yout' must've gone through my phone and got shit twisted?'

"Fam, you told me your name's Deontay; how would I know you two are related? Listen to what you're sayin'? There's no logic in it."

"Shut the fuck up," Deontay roars, and I hold my hands up.

"Oi, easy with that gun, D."

"Move over there," Deontay says.

Being ordered around by this boy is almost unbearable. My ego wants to slap him, but that's not an option. He has the power right now.

I nod my head and suck it up. "So, what you're gonna shoot me, 'cause I'm in love with Nia?"

"Don't say my sister's name. I'll smoke you right now. About love, you snake."

"Snake? Are you sick in your head? You're the one holdin' the gun to me, bro. I come all this way to fuckin' save you," I shout, momentarily letting my anger get the better.

I see Deontay shake a little. He knows I still carry authority no matter how badly the odds are stacked against me. That gun might give him some false confidence, but there's only one master and one apprentice in this room.

He pushes the back of his sleeve into his teary eye. "You love my sister, but you're banging Priscilla up in her yard these times. Man should clap your head off."

"So that's why you were movin' all weird that night?"

"How you saying you love my sister, but you're fucking Priscilla?"

"I never touched Priscilla."

"You chat shit. You slept in her bed."

I suck my teeth. Loudly. "Ask her or ask your girl. Nuttin' happened. I love Nia; I don't give a shit about Priscilla."

There's a creaking noise to my left, and we both instantly swing our heads to investigate.

The door opens, and in steps Ribz, walkie-talkie in hand and a callous grin across his face.

"Yes, yes, my nigga," he says, walking over to stand next to Deontay.

My heart drops to the floor, and a gaping canyon opens within the pit of my stomach. "You?"

"Yeah, me, cuz," Ribz says proudly.

I nod my head sarcastically.

"What you saying, you fuckin' pussy?" Ribz says.

"What's this about Ribz?"

He looks at the bag I'm holding. "What d'you think it's about, fam? The money."

I ignore him and look at Deontay.

"This is what you're doing, D? You're gonna rob man over what?"

Deontay's gripping tightly on the gun. His nostrils are flared, and his bottom lip wavers as his conscience and ego stay locked in a brutal war.

"You were gonna take my sister and fly away, yeah? Just both of you. That's why you wanted to leave the game, alie? So, you can take my sister away from me. Not even tell man. Just cut and leave me here after

416

man made you all this money. You wanna leave me here broke and take the only person who really loves man?"

"You got it twisted, bro. It ain't like that, D. Come outside. Ask Ni; she's in the car. She'll tell you herself."

"Oi, shut up and run the bag," Ribz says as he walks towards the door and picks up the large knife.

'Fuck.'

"Ribz, brudda. You don't wanna do this, trust me."

"Brudda, yeah? What, were we 'bruddas' when them man shanked me up, and you told Daniel, 'it was gonna happen, anyway?' Didn't even check me in hospital to see if I was cool."

I look at him, fully aware of what he's doing.

The pride emitting from him; this was his plan. Deontay's weak mind has just been coerced.

"You don't wanna do this, Ribz."

"Was I your brudda when you didn't wanna pay man, huh? All those sales man was hitting for you. All the work that man put in, and now you wanna take all the money and cut. Fuck that, gimme the bag," Ribz says holding the knife in the air, threatening to come closer.

I shift my weight to my right to ease away from him and pull out my lock knife.

"If you wanna do this, then make sure you're ready to die; I'm tellin' you, Ribz. 'Cause, we're stabbing it out 'till the end. 'Till one of us is dead. You feel me?"

My words reverberate around the room, and Ribz knows I mean business. I watch his cocksure attitude leave him as he looks over at Deontay for confirmation.

"Oi, burst him, man," Ribz says.

I look Deontay dead in the eye.

"Burst him," Ribz cries.

Deontay's breathing heavily; his mind must be going mad. But he knows me; he can't shoot me.

"Just give him the bag, Rakz," Deontay says.

417

"I can't do that," I say, tightening my grip on the handle.

"Run the bag!" Deontay shouts with a wicked look. I know more than most; vengeance creates killers, but I can't let Deontay follow in my footsteps.

Calmly, I shake my head.

The throbbing pain by my eyebrow is getting worse, and I notice a tingling feeling in my left shoulder, which I reckon is another wound.

"I'll clap you in your head, Rakz. Last time. Give me the money."

"D... There ain't no hundred racks in 'ere, bro."

"Don't try that one."

"I'm being real."

"What's in there, then?" Deontay asks.

"Fifty grand a brick of food," I tell him.

Ribz's eyes light up. "That's calm; we're up," he says, looking at Deontay with a villainous grin.

I let out a nervous laugh.

"What you man gonna do with a brick of food and fifty bags?"

"Don't watch that," Deontay mumbles, and I can tell he hasn't thought this through.

"Man'll fucking sell it," Ribz cries.

"Ribz, you can barely sell rocks and pebs for tens and scores, let alone a brick. You're a worker, not a boss."

That one riles him up.

His ego damaged; he raises the knife and begins to stalk me. I squeeze the handle of my lock-knife as we both move around the room until I find myself with my back facing the door with Ribz in front of me. "Do your ting then, badman. Gwarn!" I say, but he's reluctant to make the first move.

"Oi, Ribz, fall back," Deontay orders.

"Nah, fuck all this. Clap this guy, 'for I take the gun and clap him myself," Ribz says.

"Rakz, give me the food," Deontay demands.

418

I'm tired of this back and forth now. I'm beginning to feel light-headed, and I'm struggling to keep my focus.

"What d'you think your gonna do when you sell this weight then, you man? What, you're gonna go back to Darkos and get more? Or... Or you gonna go to the Turks? Because they're the only ones with grub round 'ere. Soon as they know you got a brick of food, they'll know it's you man, who robbed them. You do know that don't you? And what you gonna do then? 'Cause I ain't protecting you no more. Nobody knows you two, and your names don't carry any weight. You're two little kids tryin' to step into man's world. It won't run."

Ribz cackles like I've turned into a comedian all of a sudden.

"What's funny? Other than you man thinkin' you're some cartel bosses."

"You're funny," Ribz says. "You seriously thought I didn't have this patterned? You're old and soft. You're washed out 'ere Rakz, your time's up. Man don't need your links," he says.

I can tell by how he's pronouncing every syllable that he's taking pleasure in knowing something that I don't. He wants to drag this out. Let it last as long as possible. Savour the reaction on my face when he finally drops the punchline.

"So, who you gonna get your food off when you man start runnin' the ends, huh?"

"Man's got Jonesy, cuz," Ribz says.

My head jerks back, and the revelation brings a smugness more arrogant than I imagined to Ribz's face.

'Jonesy?'

I turn my attention to Deontay. "My bredrin, Jonesy?"

Deontay shrugs, and I can see the guilt written across his face. "We give him the cash now, we move the food, and boom, he's our connect," Deontay explains.

"But what... How did you...?"

My anger strangely ceases, and I'm taken over by pure curiosity.

"He took the number from your phone, brudda," Ribz cackles.

Seeing the shock and disbelief on my face, Ribz can't wait to continue. "Jonesy needs the Ps for some confiscation order ting. He sold you out quickly, fam," Ribz says, loving that he manipulated this whole scheme.

I shake my head as the news hits home.

'Fuck me. Scribz was tellin' the truth; he didn't snake me. Jonesy was making that shit up all along. It's been him pulling the strings, organising this payoff. How didn't I see that?'

I shake my head. Hard. Trying to stay alert.

"Just give man the food," Deontay says. "You're done out 'ere Rakz."

"You know Burak, and the Turks just gonna come after both of you, ya know," I say.

"There is no Burak," Ribz smirks.

The double blow takes the wind from me, and all I can think about is being back in Nia's bedroom.

'Shit, Nia.'

I look towards the window, but the curtain is drawn.

'Fifteen minutes must have passed by now. Where is she? Why ain't she blastin' the horn?'

The thought of Nia sparks some life back into me as I feel the adrenaline resurface.

"If there's no Burak, who's that outside?" I say.

"He's working for us, cuz. We had a little beef but soon as man told him he could get ten bags for helping us, we squashed it," Ribz exclaims.

Deontay keeps the gun aimed at me, and I'm wary of that trigger.

"D, you don't wanna do this, I'm tellin' you. You're gonna ruin your life. Thirty years in the big house when feds catch you. You gonna ride that?"

Deontay shrugs, tryin' to act tough, but he isn't fooling anybody.

"Thirty years, yeah, you're solid like that? What's gonna happen to your sister when you're rotting in prison? Who's gonna look out for her? You think Nia will ever forgive you for this?" I ask.

"This is long, D. Let's just take the money and move one time," Ribz says.

"Forget this guy," I say, pointing my knife at Ribz. "He's a fuckin' wasteman. You're a hustler. You're smart. What's this dumb yout' got going for him? Fuck all. That's why he's planned this. And look, he couldn't even do that properly."

I watch that smirk instantly vanish from Ribz's face as his hostile glare locks onto me.

"Look at you," I say, turning towards Ribz. "You can't even rob a bit of coke, you wasteman."

Ribz has no comeback, so he resorts to anger.

"Oi, D, shoot this prick. We'll take the food and bounce," he thunders.

Deontay's trembling, though, he's tryin' to look unbothered, but he's as transparent as a windscreen.

"Shoot him," Ribz bellows as saliva flies from his mouth.

Deontay's wrist trembles.

All I can think about is that sensitive trigger.

'Please don't make that gun go off,' I pray.

"This yout' doesn't care about you; he's banging your sister. Man's ready to leave us man here so he can live good while we stay in the hood, struggling. Fuck this guy, clap him," Ribz cries, placing his knife on the countertop while he forces his propaganda down Deontay's ear.

"I ain't staying here by myself. I got nowhere to go," Deontay says.

"D, you're my brother; I done told you this. You can come with us. Or stay here at my yard or yours, whatever you want, fam. You know how long Nia's wanted you back?"

"She was the one who kicked me out."

"She made a mistake, bro. We all do. Put that ting down before you make a big one you can never come back from."

The realness of my words seems to resonate with something inside Deontay, which sends Ribz crazy.

"Oi, this guy's moist, talking all this shit about retiring. No more chat, give me the gun, D," Ribz says reaching over towards the pistol.

"Nah, chill," Deontay says evading Ribz's hand.

"Bro, if you ain't gonna clap this washed up yout', I'll do it. Right here, right now."

"It's true, Ribz. What we gonna do after we flip the food?" Deontay says.

"We got Jonesy!" Ribz shouts.

This time it's my turn to cackle.

"I've known Jonesy for three years. We've been through the good and bad times and look how quickly he sold me out. What the fuck you think he's gonna do to you?"

Ribz knows he can't argue with logic as he scowls me like a raging demon.

"Ribz," I say. "I'll give you five grand. That's five times your wage. And we forget this ever happened."

He stares at me, tryin' to work out if I'm genuine.

"That's the only way you're coming out of this paid, you feel me?" I tell him.

There's a moment of silence as Deontay and Ribz look at one another.

"What you saying?" I ask, hoping Ribz is ready to bury his pride and listen to reason.

Deontay shrugs, ready to concede.

"I'm saying..." Ribz says, super theatrically. "Fuck you; I'm taking the whole ting. Gimme the gun, D."

"Nah, dead it, Ribz," Deontay says.

"Give me the gun."

"Let go, man."

"You let go."

"Bruv, you're gonna let it off."

"Give me the fuckin' gun, man."

As they wrestle each other, I feel a presence behind me.

Footsteps and panting.

I go to turn my body but the sound of thousand fireworks blasts through the room, echoing like a thunderclap from the Hammer of Thor.

My instincts take over, and I hit the floor with a face dive. Faint voices bicker around me, but my ears are ringing; everything's half-muted below a powerful droning noise. I cover my head with my hands when I hear a second explosion.

A bright spark illuminates the room as a shell case springs up in the air spinning around like a coin toss. The melee between Deontay and Ribz unfolds in super-slow motion. Deontay swivels, and his face becomes a scene of unequivocal terror. His eyes widen, and he looks as if Death himself has come to snatch his soul and drag him to the underworld for all eternity.

I turn my head to look at the doorway, and all the horrors of hell are unleashed before me.

"Nia!" I shout as I clamber to my feet. "Ni, Ni!"

41

Slumped against the door, Nia clutches at her belly.

I rush over to her while she groans in agony as her body inches down the door. "I got you; I got you," I say, putting my arm under her back and lowering her to the ground.

She's in shock; her eyes flicker as she struggles to breathe. "Ni, Ni, look at me, look at me."

"Ra—Rakim, help me."

"I got you, Ni. Stay with me, babe."

Violent shouts surround me.

"Rakim, help me, please," Nia begs.

She lifts her blood-soaked hand that looks like a scene from a slaughterhouse.

"Daniel," she cries as her attention is drawn away from me.

I push her hand back over her wound and apply pressure.

"Arghh, Rakim, it hurts," Nia squeals as she tries to move.

"I know, I know, but I gotta stop the blood," I say, pushing down harder.

"I'm sorry, Rakim. I just wanted—"

"—Don't worry, Ni, it's cool. I got you."

"Call a fuckin' ambulance," I yell at the two idiots across the room.

"You shot my sister," Deontay screams as the arguing between him and Ribz continues.

I yell at them to call an ambulance, but they're consumed in their beef.

Nia squeals again, and I turn to attend to her.

"Rakim, please. Don't leave me. I'm sorry I got out of the car. I just wanted to help." I rub my hand across her cheek, the blood smearing over her face as tears stream like waterfalls of sorrow and pain. "I'm sorry," she reiterates. "I just—"

"—Shhh... It's okay, Ni, I'm here. I ain't going nowhere."

Her hand takes hold of mine.

"Squeeze my hand. Don't let go, all right," I tell her. "You're gonna be all right, I promise you."

Thankful for her yoga skills, I watch as she begins to take long, deep breaths.

"Keep breathin'. You're doing good. The ambulance is gonna be—"

Bap!

We both shudder at the sound of another gunshot. I throw myself in front of Nia's defenceless body as she lets out a harrowing cry that pierces my eardrums.

When I turn my head, Deontay's trembling with the gun in his hand.

"D?" I cry.

He's anchored to the ground, frozen in time as he stares at the floor.

My eyes follow Deontay's gaze to a set of trainers pointing towards the ceiling. I follow the legs upwards to reveal Ribz's lifeless body laid out across the shaggy brown carpet.

"D, what did you do?"

"Daniel," Nia cries, stretching out her hand.

"Fuck, is he dead?" I ask the question, but I already know the answer. I've seen a dead body before.

I stare into the soulless pupils of a face that once knew happiness and laughter. That boy that jumped around with excitement is gone. Nothing but a cold corpse remains—another soul for the Devil, stolen in a flash.

"D, put the gun down," I say.

He's paralysed, though, glued to the spot.

"Deontay?" I call.

"He shot my sister," Deontay mutters in a torpid trance.

"D, put the burner down and come here."

"He shot my sister," Deontay repeats.

"Daniel," Nia screams.

Seeing Nia begin to regain her composure, I get myself in a squat position. "Keep pressure on the wound; we're gettin' up. You ready?"

Taking a deep breath, Nia nods her head to my count.

"One, two, three," I put my arm under her back and lift her off the ground as she lets out an excruciating cry.

Carrying her in my arms like a sleeping infant, I walk over to the sofa and carefully lay Nia down. "One sec, Ni," I tell her as she strains with her all her might to get comfortable.

Deontay's still in his own world, lost in the image of his once-upon-a-time friend as I approach him.

"D, give me the gun," I say, reaching out my hand.

Keeping eye contact, I slowly take the gun from him. By now, I can hear the sound of impending doom as sirens wail in the distance. "We gotta move."

I look around the room.

"Is there anyone else in this building?" I ask Deontay.

He ignores me.

I put the gun on the countertop and stand right in front of Deontay, blocking his view of Ribz's body. "Look, D, you gotta go; feds are coming."

I shake him by the shoulders, and it works like a jump-start. "Rakz," he says, now back in the room. He looks over at Nia and tries to run over to her. "Nia," he yells, but the force of my hands yank him back.

"You gotta go, D. Feds are on their way," I say.

"I ain't leaving my sister."

Deontay rushes past me and starts to break down as he sets his sights on his wounded sister.

"Nia, I'm sorry. I'm so sorry, Nia. I never meant for all this to happen," he says.

"It's okay, Daniel. It's fine," Nia says.

The two squeeze each other like they never want to let go until Nia lets out another painful cry.

"Daniel!" I shout. "I've got Ni, trust me. I'm not leaving her; I've got her, bro. If you stay here, you're going jail... For life. You just shot Ribz in the head."

Deontay looks at the body on the ground and holds his head with regret.

"He's dead, D. You gotta go."

Tears run down Deontay's cheeks. "But I didn't mean to... It was an accident, bro. The gun just went off," he says.

"I know, I know, but none of that matters. You gotta move."

Deontay looks over at Nia and reaches out a hand. "I'm sorry, Nia. Please don't die," Deontay begs.

"Go, Daniel, I'll be fine; I'm with Rakim. Just go. Please. I love you," Nia calls.

I push Deontay towards the door, but his legs remain stubborn.

"I got this," I shout.

"What about you, though?" Deontay asks as he frantically tries to wipe away the tears that fall down his chin.

"Don't worry about me. Just go."

"Rakz?"

I scamper across the room, pick up the duffle bag and take Nia's phone from her pocket. I unzip the bag and throw in my phone, Nia's phone, and my lock knife.

I hand the bag to Deontay. "Take this and go. I ain't tellin' you again."

The sirens are much louder now. I hear dogs barking and feel like the street's about to explode into chaos.

Deontay looks down inside the bag. "You brought the money... And the coke."

"Of course," I say, one hand on his shoulder. "Bruv, I'd never leave you, fam. I done told you, you're my bro. For life."

Deontay's lip trembles as fluids leak from his nose and eyes. A grizzly mess, he snivels hard as he hugs me tight.

"I love you, Daniel," Nia shouts.

"I love you too," Deontay calls.

"Now go, my brudda. Call the ambulance as soon as you're free. I got Nia. We're good."

Deontay nods, and after one more look at Nia, he pelts it out the door.

I hurry over to Nia, who seems to be hanging in well. I hold her tight, keeping my bloodied hands over her wound.

"Where you gonna go?" she asks as tears fall down her crimson-stained hoodie.

"I'm staying right here. I ain't going nowhere."

"But Rakim," Nia protests before the pain in her abdomen gets the better of her.

"Listen, Ni. Your brother's got his whole life to live. There's nearly a hundred grand in that bag. He can start a whole new life. And so can you."

"I don't want a new life, though, Rakim. I want you."

"You have me, Ni. You always will. But look at where my life led you. Right here. You deserve better than this, and I tried my best, but I couldn't give it to you."

"No, Rakim. Don't do this to me."

The sirens are overwhelming now. The whole street must hear them screaming. Flashes of blue, white, and red-light spin around the room, shooting through gaps in the curtains.

"Rakim. Go before they come, quickly."

"I told you, Ni. I'm here for the long run. And I meant it," I smile.

I feel my eyes welling up. They're burning, and I have to blink hard to stop the tears from falling. I should be scared. And a part of me is, but another part of me has never felt more at peace in all my life.

"Please, Rakim. You have to go. You've got time."

Nia's a total mess now. Mascara, blood, tears, everything's spread across her face like a child's oil painting. But as I look her in her eyes, she looks more beautiful than ever.

"Please?" she begs, but I hush her.

Squeezing her tightly, I whisper in her ear. "I love you, Ni."

Her emotions flood all over me. My t-shirt is drenched, but I couldn't care less.

A stampede of steel-toe cap boots thuds against the floorboards as voices on walkie-talkies get closer.

"Rakim," Nia manages to say, nearly all cried out. "You have to go."

Streams of black ink stain the flushed skin under the horror in Nia's eyes.

I move my head back, and my eyes narrow as she presses on her wound. There's something she's not telling me.

"What's going on, Ni?"

A door booms off its hinges as Nia clasps my hand with all her might. Keys clank. Bodies rustle as they frantically race through the corridor until the door crashes against the wall.

I look up. Guns. Helmets. An army of black swarms the room. Roars of armed police drown out everything.

I look back at Nia.

"Rakim, I'm..."

42

WEDNESDAY 5th MAY 2010

7.03 p.m.

"Shanice, hurry up, man," I call from the bottom of the stairwell before strolling back to the kitchen and hoisting myself up onto the countertop.

Swinging my keys around my finger, I contemplate my plans for tonight.

'Lemme call Preddie.'

I pull my phone out of my pocket and make the call.

"Yo, Preddie."

"Rakz, my g. What you telling me?"

"Man's just at my yard. What you on?"

"I'm cooling, gonna get ready in a bit."

"So, what's this rave gonna be sayin' then, live?" I ask.

"Yeah, it'll be lit, trust me. It's my cousin's girl's thing, and she's a dancer.

"Yeah?"

"Yeah, she dances in carnival and them ting there."

"For real?"

"Yeah, so you know what that means, innit?"

"What?"

"B-yaarree gyal," Preddie says.

I laugh as I slide down off the countertop and discreetly close the kitchen door. The Patois always seems to come out in Preddie's voice as soon as he mentions anything about girls.

"D'you know any of these gyal, like you seen 'em?" I ask.

"Nah, but my cousin's twenty-two, so they'll all be older than us."

"Hmm..."

"What?"

I put my phone between my ear and shoulder, grab my Rizzla and weed from the cupboard and start rolling my spliff.

"I dunno, Predz... I see some of the hippos you like to fuck with–legs looking kebab meat an' ting."

"You joke-man, I like thick girls. I don't do skinny girls."

"I keep tellin' you, *thick* and *fat* are two different things, bro."

"You ain't seen the ting I'm dealing with now. If you knew, you wouldn't say shit," Preddie says, trying to claw back some respect.

"Whatever, man, what time you tryin' to reach, fam?"

"My cousin said come for like nine. You coming, yeah?"

"Maybe, maybe."

"Shanice finally letting you out?"

"Funny guy. It's called being a family man. I keep her happy. She keeps me happy. You feel me?"

"Keep her happy... Okay, shout me later, init."

"Safe."

I end the call, and I'm just about to spark my spliff when the door opens.

"Keep me happy, yeah?" Shanice says with her head cocked to the side.

"Oi, you look sexy in that dress, come 'ere," I say, moving towards her.

"Naah, Rakim, don't be trying to come over here all touchin' me up, messin' up my makeup," Shanice says using her arm to keep me at bay.

"Don't watch that," I say as I wrap an arm around her waist.

"You know how long it took me to get ready?"

"I don't even care. You look bad in that dress," I say, easing my body up against hers.

The compliment does the trick.

"You think?" Shanice asks.

"Mmmm... No lie."

The lacey feel of her dress between my fingers. That thin veil between skin and skin has already set me off.

Shanice giggles as I start to kiss her neck.

"Rakim," she squawks as I squeeze a handful of her bum, licking her neck from collar to ear.

"Rakim, you're gonna ruin my makeup."

"Listen, I'm tryin' to lift up this dress and ruin this floor."

"Rakim!"

Laughing, she performs a Houdini-like escape from my arms.

"Come, we just stay in," I say as Shanice starts to fix her hair in the reflection of the glass panel on the back door.

"And do what?"

"Go upstairs, put Keziah down. Man will order some food and—"

"—No, Rakim. I just got all dressed up."

"Keep the dress on. Take the thong off, but the dress can stay," I tell her.

"No way. Not happening. I haven't been out in over a month. There's no way I'm cancelling this night with you. Ring your mum. Tell her we're on our way."

I suck my teeth as Shanice moves past me and leaves me alone in the kitchen. Just me and my feral cravings.

Seconds after her mum's departure, in waddles my two-year-old daughter, Keziah, moving like a baby penguin.

Grunting and groaning, she shoves her Sippy cup at me. "You can't just come in 'ere demanding tings. You must think you're a big woman." Keziah grins as I crouch to a squat and take her cup.

Then, like a true woman, she's off like a greyhound as soon as I hand her what she wants.

"You just like your mum, ya know," I mutter as I follow her into the living room.

After we finish watching one of her cartoons, I wipe her face and pick her up. She gives me her rendition of Twinkle Twinkle Little Star as I put her shoes on, and we leave the house.

"I'm waitin' in the car," I call out, unbothered if Shanice hears or not.

Keziah in the back and me in the driver's seat, I fire up the engine and wait.

'I can't even be asked to go for this meal. This is long, man.'

A few minutes later, Shanice exits the block looking like a celebrity sporting a tight lacey dress, sleek black heels, and a YSL handbag, all courtesy of me, yet she still wants to call the shots tonight.

She looks from side to side, searching for me, and for a moment, I feel to just drive off, drop Keziah at Mum's, and hit this rave with the mandem.

Shanice pulls out her phone as I press my foot down hard on the accelerator, and the car roars like a lion.

I pull up to Shanice and see the look of disdain on her face.

"Range Rover, Rakim, really?"

"It's hard, init?"

With her arms crossed, she shakes her head and takes her place in the passenger seat.

She mutters to herself for the next few minutes, and I do my best to ignore her, but the monotonous moaning becomes unbearable after a while.

"Why you gotta be such a hater?" I snap.

"Get over yourself, about hater..."

"You are."

"Please. What have I got to hate on?" Shanice asks. Her neck pivots as her eyebrows shoot up expectantly.

"You see man pushin' a bad-boy whip, and now you're hating, init? You want man to be driving round in some beatdown Fiesta so no other girl will check man out, alie?"

Shanice rolls her eyes and resumes her position, seated with her arms folded, staring ahead with a face like someone just passed wind under her nose.

I look over at Keziah in the backseat, who's fighting her sleep, before turning back to look at Shanice. "Wa gwarn with you, what's your problem?" I ask.

"This car. It's just bait, Rakim."

I suck my teeth.

"Why you gotta be the one who's all flashy, showing off what you got all the time? We get it. You got money. Why you gotta show the world?" Shanice says.

"Oh, my days. Are you my mum or suttin'?"

Shanice frowns. "If I was, I'd teach you some manners."

We're only a few minutes from Mum's, but this girl has already killed my vibe.

"Squeeze let man drive it for the day, and that's what I'm doing. If you don't wanna roll, feel free to walk, init."

My statement's met with silence.

"That's what I thought. 'Cause when I copped you that dress, bag, shoes, and that necklace you got on, that weren't 'too flashy,' was it? Now I'm taking you out to some stupid restaurant I don't even wanna go to tonight, and you're still moaning."

"Woah... Number one, ain't nobody forcing you to take me out Rakz, don't ever get it twisted like say I'm begging for your dry company."

"Dry?"

"Yeah, all you gonna do is be on your phone all night, anyway."

"Who's on their phone right now, though," I say, watching as she quickly puts it in her bag.

"Only 'cause you're always talking and texting on yours... Who are you giving all your attention to, Rakim? 'Cause it ain't me."

"Ah, shut up, man."

"You shut up. You know it's true. Your phone's just gonna be ringing and all—"

Shanice goes to continue her rant, but I've had enough. I crank the volume up to the max, letting Styles P and D-Block drown out this mosquito that's persistent on sucking my blood with her non-stop nagging.

We arrive at Mum's, and no sooner than I stop the car, Shanice slams the door as hard as she can before storming up the pathway, leaving me to deal with Keziah's grizzling.

'Fuck this girl, man.'

I battle with the buckle on Keziah's car seat, eventually picking up my baby and soothing her before walking the short distance to Mum's.

The front door's already open.

Shanice has obviously started unloading on Mum. It's her favourite tactic; get in first, slag me off and get Mum on her side.

I step into the hallway, Keziah feeling like a deadweight on my shoulder.

"Mum?"

As I presumed, she's in the kitchen, playing psychologist to Shanice, who spills out all of our business.

It's one thing about Shanice I can't stand. She's always the victim. No matter what. I don't hear the whole conversation that's taking place in the kitchen, but from the snippets I do catch, I get the gist—'I don't care about her', 'I'm only worried about my making money with my friends, 'I'm not ready to settle and have a family.' The usual bullshit.

I suck my teeth, and Mum signals for me to come over.

I place Keziah on the sofa, kiss her forehead, and walk into the hallway.

Standing at the kitchen doorway, I refuse to enter.

Never step into a den of hungry wolves.

And these two together are like a pack, pride, and ambush all wrapped into one.

I don't know what it is about Mum. She just seems to have this unquestionable soft spot for Shanice. Maybe it's just her nature, always trying to see the best in people. I mean, Shanice had a tough upbringing; I'll give her that. Being sexually abused while bouncing around from foster home to foster home, dumped with people who saw her as a monthly income instead of an actual human being who needed raising, nurturing, and caring for, couldn't have been easy.

But when she arrived at my school—a thirteen-year-old empty shell, it was me who defended this girl from the teasing and the bullying. When girls and boys used to make fun of her dry hair and all the other things on the list of what was wrong with her (and believe me, there were many things), it was me who stuck up for her and put a stop to that.

It was me who brought her out of that dark place that was her entire world and showed her how to have fun, put a smile on her face, made her laugh, walked her home, and made sure nobody ever picked on her again. I saw potential in her, brought her around Leanne's friends, and got her looking like a supermodel and not that skinny, nappy-haired girl she used to embody.

And did I stop there?

No, I made her my girlfriend and gave her my time and affection. Then when she got pregnant at fifteen and was ready to go and terminate the baby, I talked her out of it, told her I'd be there for her, that I'd look after her and the child, no matter what. And 'til this day, I've been doing just that.

But what do I get for my troubles—an earful of moaning and complaining, that's what.

"What's up?" I ask as Mum and Shanice both acknowledge my presence.

"What's going on with you two?" Mum asks.

"Nothing," I say.

Shanice shakes her head.

"Well, Shanice doesn't seem to think that's di case, so what is it you nah tell me?" Mum asks.

"Mum, there's nothing," I say, holding an arm out towards Shanice.

"Rakz, you know that's not true."

"You're the one with the problem, so you tell me then, wa gwarn?" I say.

"You know how I feel. I've told you," Shanice replies.

"What?"

"You're always choosing other people over us."

"Are you dumb?"

"Rakim! Watch how you talk in my house," Mum says, pointing that stern index finger at me.

"How do I choose other people over you?" I ask.

"You always do, Rakz," moans Shanice.

"How?" I say, my lemur eyes pleading for an explanation for this nonsense.

"Well. You're never home. You're always out, doing God knows what with God knows who. You never come through on any of your promises. You just don't care," Shanice says, and I feel my resentment growing.

It's a cheap shot.

She knows the things Mum despises, my waywardness being at the top of the list, and she's made sure to throw that one out there just to trigger Mum.

'How can this ungrateful bitch, say I don't care. I... Me...? Not care. She's taking the piss.'

"I'm the *only* person in your life who cares about you, yet I'm the worst, yeah? All you do is moan and nag. What else do you do?"

"... Apart from raising your child, cooking for you, washing your clothes, and looking after our house?" Shanice replies, ticking off each answer on her fingers.

"Rakim, why don't you listen to the girl instead of try fi be right all di time, huh?" Mum says.

"Ah, Mum, I can't listen to nonsense," I reply.

437

"Mi tink some things that you say is nonsense, Rakim. But mi still listen, you know why?" Mum barks.

I sigh, knowing there's a Bible verse coming.

"Because... The way of a fool is right in his own eyes, but a wise man listens to advice."

'I knew it.'

"Now mi nah know, what di problem is between you two, but you nah go get nowhere if you can't talk about tings without all of this fussing and fighting," Mum says before turning towards me.

"And God knows mi tried with you, Rakim," Mum says, looking me up and down. "And mi still pray every day that he'll take you outta di life you live. Mi nuh know why you want fi run go wild when you have a woman and a child deyah home who love and need you. God bless you with my beautiful likkle granddaughter, and still, you want fi live fast life like you ah go be eighteen forever," Mum continues before stopping for emphasis. "Well, mek me tell you this bwoy... 'Ear mi good because mi nah go tell you again. Fast life ah go be the death of you!"

I've just about had enough.

"Look, sorry, Mum, but I didn't come here for no lecture. Not from you and especially not from *you*," I say, pointing at Shanice, the instigator of Mum's sermon. "So, if all you're gonna do, is blame me, then cool, I'll remove myself from this little party... I got a better one to go to, anyway. Later," I say and turn away to leave the house.

I hear Shanice mumble something, but I don't even care. I tried to do something nice for the girl, and all she wants to do is criticise me. As for Mum, well, Mum is Mum. I know she loves me, but her opinion of me will never change. I've heard that speech a hundred times, and I'm still alive and doing well for myself. I don't need no church or no God looking out for me. My team is strong. We ain't like the others who fall apart and crumble. We're a different breed. I'ma show, Mum. One day I'll be rich, have everything I ever wanted, and finally prove to Mum that I was right.

10.54 p.m.

Standing under the darkness that only offers illumination from phone screens and the dim light it steals from the hallway, I'm leant against a wall of this living-room-turned-dancefloor, checking out the skin on show.

However, nothing appeases me.

The DJ shouts something through his mic before the music starts again, and everyone returns to dancing.

Body lotion, sweat, alcohol, fried chicken, and weed mix together in the air to form a deadly concoction that's even more potent in the humidity of this room.

"I knew Predz was gassing, man. This rave's dead, cuz," I say, looking at FatMack.

He takes a pull of his spliff before passing it to me. "You wanna cut?" he asks.

"Yeah, stand in front of man quickly, though. Man's gonna swipe this bottle of Hennessy."

They don't call him FatMack for nothing. He stands between those who are enjoying this afro-beats nonsense and the extended table that's spread with all types of alcoholic beverages and plastic cups.

Like a solar eclipse, he blocks anybody's view of me as I stuff an unopened bottle of Cîroc under my jacket before reaching over and snatching a bottle of Hennessy.

Smoothly I hand it to FatMack, who stuffs it inside his hoodie. So large is he I hardly even notice the bulge in his clothing from the bottle. It just sort of blends into his physique. We exit the room, leaving this bunch of losers to continue their evening.

I bully my way through the overcrowded hallway until I see an old friend.

"Yes, yes, Rakz, what you saying?" Jermaine says, greeting me with a hug.

"Long time, you good?"

439

"Jheeze, you shining, fam," he says, noticing the thick gold bracelet sitting comfy around my wrist, no doubt.

"You know me, cuz. The grind don't stop."

"I feel you, I feel you."

"What you doing with yourself, still got your studio and ting?" I ask.

"Yeah, just working with some new artists and that, they got good bars, good flow, and the work rate's high, so hopefully, all our hard work can pay off soon."

"I hear that."

"How's Shanice and the baby?"

"They're good, bro."

Jermaine nods at FatMack, who winks back at him.

"What, you just came on a mandem-only flex tonight, no wifey?" Jermaine says with that conspicuous grin.

"Listen, I don't know what I was thinking. Them girls up in there are dead."

"No way," Jermaine says.

"Bro, see for yourself," I say, patting his shoulder as I pass by him and head for the exit.

"Good to see you, my brudda. Come by soon, man. Don't be a stranger," Jermaine shouts.

"Yeah, yeah, safe, J. We'll link up soon."

"Say hello to Shanice as well," he calls.

Once outside, the cold cuts at my skin like a sharp blade. "Oi, phone Preddie and tell him to link man by the chicken shop, man," I tell FatMack.

I pass a few girls who decorate the front garden of this house with their bright red dresses, blue and green weaves, fake gold earrings, and glittery heels. FatMack stops to talk to one of them, using his famous 'Sexiest Fat Man Alive' line, but it seems it doesn't work this time as I hear him break out into cussing.

"Come we cut," FatMack says.

"Where's Preddie?"

"He texted me just now and said he's coming."

We cross the road and jump in my car. As soon as I push the start button and press the brake, I hear cries from the other side of the road.

It's a couple of the hood rat chicks that just turned down FatMack. Apparently, he's hot property now he's sitting next to me in a 2010 plate Range Rover Sport.

He calls one of them over, and like a dog being summoned by its owner, she hurries across the road. Her arm in front of her chest to contain her breasts, she approaches the passenger window.

FatMack takes the bottle of Ciroc from me and takes a long sip.

"You all right? Where you lot going?" the girl asks.

I give her a once over.

'Not my type, but she's all right.'

Paying little mind to their conversation, I check my phone and see two missed calls from Shanice.

"Can she jump in?" FatMack asks.

The look on my face says it all.

"Go bring your two girls over," FatMack says, and the girl's eyes seem to light up. She whistles for her friends to join her as I hit FatMack on his arm.

"They can't get in. I'm linking Shanice, fam. What you doing?" I whisper.

"Don't watch that," FatMack says. He winks at me and screws the cap back on the bottle of Cîroc. Then turning towards the girl and her two friends, FatMack turns ruthless. He takes hold of the main girl's hand and kisses it softly as her friend giggles, thinking there in for the night of their lives. Then looking her straight in the eyes, he breaks the news, "Listen, babes, you're gonna have to walk home still. Ain't no space in the car for gold diggers."

I smile as the look on the girl's face drastically changes. Her eyebrows shoot up, and her mouth hangs open. She looks at her friends in shock as FatMack hits me, and I take the hint. Zooming off, we leave the girls

441

looking like a trio of fools in the middle of the road fighting away exhaust fumes with no ride home.

Laughing, we make our way to a little chicken and chip spot a few minutes down the road. I take a seat inside as FatMack orders some food.

'Nothing like chicken and chips on a late night.'

Ten minutes later, a bell ringing in the doorway announces Preddie's arrival.

I get straight into it.

"Predz, don't ever invite me to one of your people's dead shoobs again," I say, making my voice loud and clear.

"I can explain, fam," Preddie says.

FatMack cracks up before a chicken wing disappears in his mouth and comes out with just the white of the bone remaining.

"G, all them girls were clapped. What kinda dancers your cousin's girl move with, 'cause they ain't no fuckin' dancers?"

Preddie cracks an awkward smile as FatMack laughs even harder before continuing his assault on his portion of wings.

"Nah, there were some decent tings there still."

"Predz, don't..."

"There were."

"You were going on like they were frontline carnival dancers. Brudda, they're the ones way, way at the back tryin' to squeeze into costumes ten sizes too small for them. The ones nobody wants to see."

"You chat shit, Rakz."

"Alie Fatz, you know them rubbed out Auntie's tryin' to relive their youthful days," I say, sending FatMack into a coughing fit as he nearly chokes on his food.

"You're just gassed 'cause you got Shanice. Think your girl's the best ting on ends 'cause she's a lightey," Preddie says.

I roll my eyes. "Whatever."

Preddie takes the bottle of Hennessy from the table and sips it as I try phoning Shanice.

The phone rings, but there's no answer.

I try again.

Still, she doesn't pick up.

'How's this girl callin' me then not picking up my calls?'

"Did you man teeth this from my cousin's yard?" Preddie asks as he places the bottle of Hennessy back on the table.

"Yeah."

He puts his palm across his face.

"Rakz, how you teething bottles like you ain't got thirty pound to your name?"

"It ain't about what I got to my name, bruv. It's about your cousin inviting man to some dead rave. He should've been paying *me* to come there. So, since he wasted my time, man'll take this bottle as compensation."

The next half an hour or so passes with me, FatMack, and Preddie trading insults, laughing, and finishing the bottle of Hennessy before passing the bottle of Cîroc around.

A little tipsy, I step outside onto the pavement leaving Preddie and FatMack to their conversation.

The evening breeze hits my face, and it feels oddly fresh tonight.

The roads are still amok with people, and I look around under the streetlights to see joy, laughter, and happiness on the faces of spools of revellers lapping up the city's nightlife.

I try Shanice again.

Still no answer.

'Let me ring Mum.'

The phone rings several times before Mum answers.

"What time you call dis?" Mum croaks.

"My bad, Mum. Is Keziah okay?"

"She's fine. She sleeping, and so was I. What do you want?"

"... Sorry 'bout earlier, Mum. I didn't mean to just leave like that. I was just angry."

Mum sighs, and I hear movement as if she's just sat up in her bed. "Rakim, you need to sort your life out," she says. I'm your mother, and mi will always love you, but if you don't fix up, you gon' ruin your life."

"I love you too, Mum. I beg you tell Shanice to answer the phone, please?"

"Shanice isn't 'ere, Rakim."

"Where is she?"

"Mi thought she was with you."

"Nah..." I suck my teeth. "Sorry for waking you, Mum. I'ma call her now."

"Okay. Well, goodnight. And don't be out too late, son."

"I won't. Bye."

I go back inside the shop and get Preddie and FatMack to help me call around to find Shanice's whereabouts.

It doesn't take long until Preddie gets hold of his cousin. With a smile on his face, he hands me the phone.

"Yo," I say.

"It's Michael, Ricardo's cousin."

"Yeah, I know. Man just came from your likkle rave."

"He said you were looking for your girl, right?"

"Yeah, you seen her?"

"Light skin, slim, long curly hair?"

"Yeah, yeah."

"She wearing some black lacey dress?"

"Yeah, where's she?"

"She was asking about you, apparently?"

"Asking what?"

"Just asking people if they had seen you. Were you dancing with any girls? You know what chicks be like."

"Where's she now?"

"I just see her leaving my yard with Ricardo's friend."

"Who?"

"Slim guy. Had a white t-shirt on. Got one cheesy smile on his face."

"... Jermaine?"

"Yeah, I think that's his name, still."

"Where'd they go?"

"I dunno. I just saw her leaving about five minutes ago. I'm outside the front of my yard, but I can't see her. She probably going home."

"Ite, cool. If you see her again, tell her to call me."

"No problem."

I end the call and go back inside the shop.

This time it's Preddie's turn to taunt *me*.

"What, Jermaine whining up with your girl, yeah?"

"Funny guy."

"Oi, man like Jermaine's got himself a new spice."

I don't bite, though; I know Preddie's game.

"What you reckon, FatMack? Jermaine's better looking than Rakim alie?" Preddie says.

FatMack laughs, shrugging his shoulders. "They're about as ugly as each other, fam."

"Number one, Jermaine could never step to Shanice. Number two, he ain't got nuttin' on man, he's a college boy, he ain't about this life. And number three, the nigga likes his life. He knows I'd kill him if he ever tried a ting."

Preddie continues to tease me, and although I know it's all banter, a part of me begins to question why Shanice is ignoring my calls and what she's doing, leaving the rave with this boy.

We were all friends in school, and both Shanice and I, know Jermaine's family, but if they're leaving together, where the hell are they planning to go.

I pull out my phone and realise the battery is nearly dead, so I use FatMack's phone and call Shanice.

This time she answers.

"Hello," she says.

"Where are you? It's Rakim."

"What do you want?"

445

"Shanice, drop the bad girl attitude. Where are you? Mum told me you left the house."

"Yeah, is that a problem? You went out and left me, so I went out."

"You went out to do what? Follow me or prove a point. Which one?"

"You really think it's all about you, init Rakim?"

"So why were you at the dance then?"

Shanice pauses. She didn't know I knew she was there. I can sense it from her reaction. Or lack of one.

"Why were you at Michael's girl's rave? You were following man, alie? Came there to check on me."

"I went there to see if you still wanted to go out," Shanice shouts. "I tried calling you to tell you I was coming, but you wouldn't answer. I didn't wanna be locked up in that house with your mum and Kez. I told you tonight was supposed to be my night off, and look, you chose your friends over me yet again."

I let my tone simmer. "Well, where are you now?" I ask.

"I'm walking down the road, gonna get something to eat and then go back home."

"Who you with?"

"I'm with Jermaine. My phone's mash-up, it keeps switching off by itself. I told him, and he knew you wouldn't want me walking by myself with a dead phone, so he said he would walk me back to your mum's."

"Why didn't you just call me to pick you up?"

"I told you, you weren't answering your phone. What's with all the questions?"

FatMack's phone receives a call, and I immediately recognise the name.

It's Squeeze.

I show FatMack the screen, and he urges me to hurry up and get off the phone.

"Look, Shanice. FatMack needs his phone back. Mine's dead. Come by Select Chicken. You know the spot?"

"Yeah," Shanice says.

"How long 'til you're here?"

"About five, ten minutes. Is it just you and Fatz?"

"Nah, Preddie's here too."

"Please tell him to go, Rakim. I really don't wanna talk with him around."

I roll my eyes, but with the alcohol settling inside me, I can barely be bothered to respond, let alone argue.

"Cool, I'll see you in a bit."

I hand FatMack his phone, and he moves with more urgency than I've ever seen, throwing the empty bottle of Hennessy into the bin and brushing himself down.

His conversation quickly gets loud and abrasive, and he goes outside.

"Yo, Predz," I say when I'm interrupted.

"Oi, Rakz. Squeeze is outside. He wants to chat to you," FatMack calls from the doorway.

I leave the shop to see a blacked-out Mercedes with tinted windows parked a few metres down the road. The passenger window rests slightly ajar, booming out hot-blooded ragga lyrics. I stretch my neck from side to side as I approach the window and crouch down.

The window lowers slowly, revealing a cloud of thick grey smoke as I move my head back.

"You good, fam?" I ask.

As the smoke evaporates around me, I see the trademark jet-black sunglasses across a gaunt, hard-skinned face. Only Squeeze can wear sunglasses at night inside a car and make it look normal. It's like they're glued to his skin.

"You have mi keys?" Squeeze asks.

I shove my hands in my pockets and pull them out. Reluctantly, I go to hand them over when Squeeze raises a palm. His long claws scratch at the sinister scar that runs across his eye and down his cheek.

"D'you want 'em, bro?" I mutter.

He doesn't say anything. Instead, he locks those pitch-black lenses onto me for a moment. I study his tightly braided corn-rows and the thick gold chains that hang from his scrawny neck and veiny wrists, wondering what's in store for me or what I'm about to be tasked with.

"Hold them, my yout'," Squeeze says, blowing smoke in my direction.

I thank him and go to leave when I feel a grip on my arm. I turn back, and the sunglasses are lifted. Not by much. But enough to see the soulless, wicked glare behind one of Squeeze's pupils. The one that works.

Pointing a gnarly finger at me, he gives me my warning. "Make sure you bring it back inna one piece."

"Yeah, yeah. Course, man."

His firm grasp keeps my arm captive for a few moments longer as he stares into my eyes.

I know the drill, so I keep eye contact. No smile. No words. Just remain still and let the moment pass. Once satisfied, I've understood, Squeeze lets my arm go and summons FatMack.

I spud FatMack and straighten out the sleeve of my coat before returning to the chicken shop.

"Wa gwarn, brudda? Preddie asks.

"Nuttin'," I say before quickly changing the topic. "I'm linking Shanice. What you on?"

"What, she coming here?"

"Yeah, yeah. Need to chat to her alone, you feel me," I say.

Sluggishly, he rises from his stool and stands up. "This girl's got you on smash, man. You need to leave her," he says.

I'm not sure if it's him or the alcohol talking, but either way, a little resentment lingers in his words.

"You're drunk, fam," I tell him.

"Maybe," he says as he stretches his arms to the sky. "All I know is she says jump, you say how high."

"Whatever, go run along. Squeeze wants you."

We spud each other, and he leaves the shop but not before looking back at me and shaking his head. Then he disappears out of sight.

As I wait for Shanice to arrive, I look at the time on my phone.

'Why's this girl taking so long?'

A few souls saunter into the chicken shop before ordering their meals and either hanging around or waiting outside.

I spark a quick conversation with bossman behind the counter to take my mind off Jermaine and Shanice, but something still niggles at the back of my mind.

'Why did Shanice not answer my calls? And why did Jermaine keep mentioning Shanice's name? Asking if she's okay...? Tellin' me to say hello to her.'

I don't know if it's the skunk, the alcohol, or Preddie's words, but something's got me feeling way more paranoid than usual.

11.47 p.m.

Five minutes later than they should have arrived, I look out the window to see Jermaine and Shanice. They're walking together about a metre apart. Passers-by stroll past them without a second look. If they were any other pair tonight, they could be a perfect couple, blending into the scenery.

Jermaine's moving his hands around as he explains something to Shanice and for some reason, she looks captivated by his speech. With every moment that passes, it's as if she falls deeper and deeper into his hypnotic spell.

He continues talking as they get closer, unaware of my watchful eyes. I want to know how his linguistic allure captures her, holding her prisoner to his every word. I can't even hear what they're talking about, but I just know it isn't anything *we* talk about. Thinking about it, we've barely had a meaningful conversation in... I can't even remember.

They're taking their time as if they never want this little stroll to end. Shanice's arms are crossed, and she looks unbothered by everything, including me.

'*Rakz, chill out, man. It's just Jermaine. You know she ain't into him. Preddie's just got in your head.*'

Standing at the doorway of the chicken shop, it's Jermaine who notices me first.

"Wassup, Rakz, you good?" he says, spudding me.

"Yeah, man," I say, scanning him up and down, searching for anything that seems off. Any slight look. Any sign of guilt or nervousness, I'll be on him like a vulture on a dead carcass.

That cheesy smile forms across Jermaine's face, which cools my anger a tad. I've seen that smile so many times to know it's Jermaine in his ordinary state.

My shoulders drop as Shanice raises a hand.

"You okay?" I ask her.

450

She nods as she moves past me into the warmth of the shop.

Still outside with Jermaine, I take my chance to interrogate him. "Where you lot go?" I ask.

"I just saw her outside the dance. She said she was going home. She came there looking for you, init, but you'd already left."

"Did you see her with anyone there?"

"Nah, she got you, fam. She ain't dancing with nobody, come on."

"Just askin' ya know."

"Nah, I feel you. I was just showing her this new beat I made and telling her about how my sister just won her kickboxing competition."

"Yeah?"

"Yeah, the girl's only fifteen. She's knocking people out," he laughs.

Me and Jermaine carry on our small talk as Shanice sits inside, her head in her phone. After a few minutes of listening to Jermaine talk, I'm confident I'm being overly paranoid.

If Preddie was tryin' to draw me out earlier, it worked. I take a look at Jermaine and realise what I knew all along. He's just not on my level. We're two different breeds. He's a Labrador, and I'm a Pitbull. And as much as Shanice goes on like she likes to be in control, she doesn't want a pet she can manage. She needs a rugged man, not a computer geek.

My chest feels much less tense, and I feel stupid for misjudging the situation.

I go inside, and Jermaine follows me. Shanice's eyes flit between me and her phone as Jermaine talks about a song he needs to master by tomorrow.

I walk over to Shanice and stand in front of her.

She looks at my straight face, staring into my eyes until a little smile forms on her face.

"What?" she says, all innocent and softly emitting those feminine pheromones. Her candid tenor instantly turns me on. "You have a good time at the rave then?" she asks, flicking her hair around as she does a terrible job of tryin' to appear unmoved.

"Nah," I say.

451

"Why's that? I thought you would've loved it?"

"I was just thinkin' about you."

"Oh, whatever, Rakim, you use that line every time you piss me off."

"That's 'cause it's true."

"Sure."

I lean closer to her, and her smile returns. She tries to hide it, but it's too late.

"You miss me? That why you come over to Michael's yard, come collect your man?"

"Maybe," Shanice says as her eyes refuse to look at me.

They don't need to though; her diffident smile says it all.

I eventually get her eyes back on mine, and by now, Jermaine doesn't even exist.

All those stupid worries of the past fifteen minutes evaporate like steam by an open window. I touch Shanice's cheek, and she puts her hand on my leg, stroking it up and down as I stand over her. "I don't wanna fight with you, Rakim," she says.

"Neither do I."

"It's just sometimes you can just be such an arsehole, I dunno what to do."

"Listen, don't worry. It's done now. We good, yeah?" I say, bringing my forehead to touch hers.

She nods.

"Nah, give me a proper answer."

After a quick smile, she pecks my lips to seal the deal.

"*Love is in the air...*" a drunk guy sings, dancing across the chequered floor like a gentleman from a long-forgotten era.

Jermaine laughs and joins in as Shanice and I ignore them, remaining in our little world.

"Should we go back home? We can go get into bed, bun a zoot and watch a film?" Shanice asks.

"Ite. Cool. I'm kinda waved, though, but I can still drive."

"Where's your car parked?"

452

"Just on the next road."

"Just get a cab. You can get it in the morning."

"You reckon?"

"Um-hmm. I don't want you to crash," Shanice says as she wraps her arms around me and lays her head against my chest.

I reach for my phone to see the black screen.

"Gimme your phone, my battery's dead." Shanice hands me her phone and gets up to say goodbye to Jermaine, who's just collected his food.

As I see them talking through the reflection in the shop, I decide to take my call outside. I walk down the road a little, and after ordering a cab, I contemplate something.

'Should I look through her phone?'

It's something that's never occurred to me to think of doing in the three years we've been together, and instantly my heart starts beating. I don't want to be that untrusting boyfriend, but Shanice's actions tonight have warranted my suspicion.

'Nah, this ain't me. I don't do this. Shanice is real, man. I know she is.'

But then the demons of doubt begin to work their sorcery.

'But what if I'm wrong? What if I look and I find something about her and a next man?'

Conflicted, I take another look at Jermaine and Shanice. She hasn't even noticed me standing here with her phone.

Surely, she wouldn't be this casual about me holding her phone if she had something to hide.

'Maybe she's just acting casual? When deep inside, she's scared, but she knows if she shows it, she'll give herself away.'

My heart's pumping harder as Preddie's comments return to torment me.

'Shanice could just be lying.'

A weird feeling compels me as I eventually succumb to unlocking the phone.

Scrolling through the messages, there's some from me, a couple from her girls, Mum, the bank, T-Mobile, and one from FatMack. I open the one from FatMack, and I remember telling him to send it last week.

As I delve deeper into her phone, flicking through photos and analysing the details of her call log, a heavy feeling spreads through my body. I'm unsure if it's guilt or embarrassment, but this feels wrong. Even my fingers shake as if they know they shouldn't be participating in this act of distrust and cowardice.

I look into the shop to see Jermaine and Shanice still in conversation. She's totally oblivious to what I'm up to, which just adds to my guilt.

This is not a part of my character.

'I should just go back inside.'

But as I mess about with the phone, I come across a tab named *Hidden Messages*.

My gut goes hollow, and I look over at Shanice.

She's moving her head, swaying from side to side as Jermaine shows her something on his phone.

I take a deep breath and open the folder.

My eyes zoom in to see a text from Jermaine.

My heart doubles its beat, and my hand begins to shake. I can taste my tongue. It feels like I'm watching this happen to somebody else.

I pray my world doesn't come crashing down tonight, but logic screams otherwise. It's stored in a hidden folder, for God's sake.

I open the message.

And as I read it, I see my future snatched away from me.

You're beautiful in every way, and if I was there, I'd take care of you x–it says.

I read it again.

Then again.

Then again.

A bloodthirsty rage rises within me like a spirit of a rebellious nation.

That old saying plays in my head, 'There's no smoke without fire.'

454

I turn to look at Shanice and Jermaine. Their skins brush and I picture them fucking. They share a glance; I imagine them kissing. She dips her hand inside his box of fries, and it's like she's sliding a hand inside his boxers.

The death stare has taken control of me. I can't contain it anymore.

I shove Shanice's phone into my pocket, and like a man possessed, I march over to the pair of them.

They're standing in the doorway of the shop, and when Shanice's eyes turn towards me, I see the look on her face.

'That's right... I've found your dirty little secret.'

But my beef ain't with her.

It's with this sly little rat who tried to move to my girl, then dared to hug me and look in my eye like we were friends.

'This guy's gone and broke my whole family.' It's all the fire I need.

Petrified, Shanice goes to alert Jermaine, but before she can get his attention, I throw a mighty blow straight into his temple, sending him crashing to the floor.

Next thing I know, I'm on top of this prick, letting my fists go berserk, one after the other.

Bam-bam-bam-bam-bam-bam-bam-bam-bam-bam-bam-bam-bam.

Before I know it, he's not even trying to defend his face. But I don't stop, I keep going and going and going until my lungs burn and my arms are exhausted.

Huffing and puffing, I can't swing them anymore.

I stop shouting and that's when the harrowing screams unmute themselves.

'Oh my God!' *'Someone help'* and *'Call the police'* form a medley of chants, hitting me from all different angles, confusing me.

A forceful tug from behind me brings me to my feet, and it's only once I'm dragged off Jermaine, I look at the battered boy below me.

He's not moving.

He's not flinching.

He's not breathing.

455

He's just lying there like he's passed out in a drunken sleep.

Blood trickles out of his swollen eye. It's almost closed shut.

His face is ballooned and completely covered in blood. I've never seen his skin this dark.

The side of his mouth is all mushy as it spills blood, and his right ear leaks a pinkish-white fluid.

Ghastly wounds reveal flesh and tissue, and as his head stays statue-still, facing the road, Shanice screams a scream that will live long in my memory until the day I die.

I turn to look at her.

She's trembling. Crying.

Her fingers in her mouth, she's screaming at what I've done.

All around, horrified eyes stare me down.

Men hide their girlfriend's faces from the hideous scene. People shout and scream, and the world around me hones in on me.

I'm sweating, and my heart's palpitating.

White lights from phone screens beam at me like I'm centre stage on Broadway.

I look at my quivering knuckles. They're stained with Jermaine's blood—purplish-red, glutinous, and thin, marked with cuts and bruises from the impact with his skull.

I look back at Jermaine lying lifeless on the floor, and that's when it clicks.

'Shit... He's dead.'

THURSDAY 6th MAY 2010
04.06 a.m.

There are some moments in life that define a person's existence. They usually happen in the blink of an eye but when they do happen, they leave an everlasting imprint. A person is no longer the same. They are split in two—everything they were before this moment and the person after the defining moment.

So far, nothing has made the TV. Just another black boy killed. Nothing new to the British public.

I think about Jermaine's mum and picture her reading the headlines in the newspaper in the morning.

Teenager beaten to death on busy South London street.

I'm still asking myself how. How and why.

Shanice lays across the sofa in Mum's living room, thanks to a heavy dose of Mum's sleeping tablets. It's a blur how we got back here.

I remember being in the car with Shanice shouting and screaming while she hit me as I sped back to Mum's, but other than that, I can't tell you which route I took or anything. I just keep reliving the incident, thinking of what I could've done differently.

'*I could've stopped after the first punch. I could have walked away and never spoken to Shanice again.*'

Instead, I chose vengeance—the main ingredient of my upbringing on these roads. An eye for an eye, a tooth for a tooth, and a life for tryin' to take my woman.

I go through all the possible outcomes in my head, had I never gone down that stupid phone.

The worst part is that I'd lost the thing by the time we got home. I couldn't even confront Shanice with the evidence. We argued, and she admitted she enjoyed the attention but only saved the message because it reminded her of how I used to talk to her. I know I should be angrier towards Shanice, and on any ordinary day, I would've cut ties with her, but today is no ordinary day.

457

Jermaine's dead, and the hunt for me is on.

Right now, Shanice is all I have.

Keziah and Mum are asleep upstairs, but they're both early risers. Another couple of hours, and they'll be awake. Keziah will be none the wiser, but Mum... She's gonna lose her shit when she finds out what's happened. All those times she prophesised something along these lines, now it's come to fruition. She'll disown me.

I take a look at the smashed screen on my phone.

'*C'mon, man.*'

Preddie's late.

Shanice doesn't know it, nor does Mum, but I'll be on a flight to Jamaica in a few hours. Preddie and Squeeze have set it all up for me.

I'll fly from Gatwick and arrive at Kingston, where Preddie's uncle will collect me from the airport. From there, I'll take orders from Squeeze's people out there. Not much different from what I do over here, I guess. It's a different way of life, but at least it *is* a life.

I'm not spending the rest of my days locked in a cell for this. I didn't even mean it.

I pace around the living room, trying to remain as quiet as possible. I want to go upstairs and kiss my baby goodbye, but I can't risk waking Mum.

'*When I'm sorted in Jamaica, I'll send for Keziah and Shanice.*'

I flick through the channels to take my mind off the madness of tonight, eventually settling on a documentary about endangered species.

I try to focus, but I can't.

All I can think of is Jermaine.

I run my hand over my forehead when my phone rings. Swiftly, I grab it from the arm of the sofa before it wakes the whole house up. Luckily, those pills continue to work their magic. Shanice doesn't move a muscle.

"Yo," I answer.

"Man's outside, brudda. Come," Preddie says.

"Two minutes."

"Hurry up. And only bring what you need. Phone, passport, one change of clothes."

"What about the rest of my tings?"

"You change your clothes yet?"

"Yeah, yeah, done that. They're in a black bag."

"Bring that. We'll get rid of it on the way."

"Cool."

I end the call and slip my trainers on before checking my jeans and jacket pockets.

"Phone, yeah. Keys, yeah. Wallet, yeah."

The bundle of cash inside my pocket settles my nerves a little.

I dart back into the living room and take one look at Shanice, who remains in her own world. Her eyes are puffy and swollen from crying and her lips are all dry, but I don't wake her. I don't touch her, I don't even say anything. I just stare at her, watching the rise and fall of her body.

'She's gonna be pissed when she wakes up.'

There's nothing I can do about that, though.

'Please make her understand. Please keep her strong, God. If not for me, then for Keziah.'

I look at the photo of Mum and me on the mantlepiece, and that's when it hits me, the gravity of what I'm about to do.

I'm off to a country where I barely know anybody, and my survival and welfare rest in the hands of Preddie's uncle, who I've never even met. I look to the ceiling and wish I could just go back to earlier this evening.

'I should've just gone out to eat with Shanice, man.'

Now I may never see her, Mum, or Kez ever again.

The ringtone from my phone snaps me out of my daydream. I silence the call and take one more look around the living room. Every piece of furniture, photo, and even the little marks on the wall and scuffs on the carpet all speak to me, telling me not to go.

My pocket vibrates again, and I know Preddie's eager to get going. Then with a heavy heart and a deep breath, I leave, shutting the door behind me.

"What took you so long, man?" Preddie asks.

"Nuttin'. Who dropped you here?" I say, looking up and down the street.

"Man got a cab. Don't worry. He parked couple roads away."

"This is fucked up, Predz," I say.

"I know, brudda." He puts a hand on my shoulder. "Shit happens, though. Just gotta get outta here, fam."

I shake my head.

"You got the keys?" Preddie asks, and I hand him the keys to the Range.

He opens the boot, and I give him the black bag containing my bloodied clothes and trainers.

Glad to escape the bitter early morning wind, I settle into the comfort of the leather seats, turn the heater on and hug myself.

We set off, and I watch Mum's house become smaller and smaller until, eventually, Preddie turns a corner, and my whole childhood disappears.

About ten minutes pass without either of us saying a word until Preddie breaks the silence.

"Oi, don't worry, Rakz. Jermaine deserved that, fam," he says turning to look at me.

"What?"

He must notice my reaction 'cause he quickly backtracks.

"Nah, I mean, like... Not deserve to die, but to get fucked up, at least. Come on. You said it yourself back in the shop, remember?"

I think back to my words.

Preddie's right.

460

I actually said the words *'I'd kill him if he tried'* when we heard about him walking Shanice home.

I go quiet for the next few minutes as I try to drown out my thoughts.

"You got every'ting, yeah?" Preddie asks.

"I think."

"Phone, money, passport?"

I recheck my pockets. "Shit, ain't got my passport."

Preddie shakes his head. "How you gonna forget your passport," he laughs.

"Had bare tings on my mind, man."

"Where is it?"

"It's at Shanice's. We got time?"

Preddie checks the time. "Yeah, we're good. Direct me."

I navigate the way to Shanice's, and with little traffic on the roads, we reach the flat in less than ten minutes.

"What time's the flight?" I ask Preddie before I leave the car.

"Erm..." he says as he checks his phone. "10:25."

"We got hours," I say, confused.

"Yeah, you can't chill 'ere, though. Feds clock it was you who duppied Jermaine they're coming straight to this yard."

"So, where we going then?"

"Squeeze got a little spot not too far from 'ere. Told man to drop you there until it's time to catch the flight."

Feeling mentally and physically drained from my thoughts and the levels of alcohol in my blood, I don't bother asking any more questions.

I come out of Shanice's block in a change of clothes, with my passport tucked in my pocket along with five grand in cash.

Within minutes of setting back off, I'm resting my head against the window, my eyelids closed. When I open my eyes, we're at the destination.

I check the time to see it's ten past five.

461

As I look out the window, I notice that little sleep has given way to the first signs of daylight. Birds deliver their morning medleys, chirping like it's just another day, and I turn towards Preddie.

"That's the yard there, my brudda," he says, pointing his head towards a little terraced house across the road and dropping a silver key into my hand.

"What, you're not coming in?" I ask.

"I gotta drop this whip to Squeeze, fam. He's vexed. He just got this, and now he's gonna have to sell it."

"Why?"

"You drove it before the Jermaine ting, and then you cut from the scene in this car. If boidem catch it speeding anywhere on camera and link the number plate to the murder, then Squeeze is getting dragged into it."

'I never thought about that.'

Knowing Squeeze, the best way to try and appease him has always been cold, hard cash. I take a grand out of my pocket and hand it to Preddie. "Give this to him. Tell him I said sorry and if he needs anything from man, just let me know when I touch down on the other side."

"Ite, brudda," Preddie says.

I leave the car and stretch my arms, letting out a lengthy, overdue yawn.

"Wait," Preddie says as I go to shut the door. "Give me your phone."

"Why?"

"If you get caught with that, you're pissed. Police will check it, and it will show you were outside the chicken shop when Jermaine got killed."

I look at Preddie's eager arm that leans across the passenger seat.

"That's thirty years, G. Life!" he says.

I sigh and hand it over.

"A cab will come to get you at seven-thirty. Don't worry, G. By tomorrow, you'll be on the beach sipping a rum and coke with your feet up," Preddie says as if this is supposed to be a relaxing vacation.

He undoes his seatbelt and shakes my hand.

"Make sure you check for my mum, Shanice, and Keziah."

"Of course, G."

"Tell them I'll call them as soon as I land, yeah."

"Give it a week or suttin' just in case jakes are sniffing around, ya get me."

As I go to shut the door, I notice something underneath the passenger seat and lower my head.

'That's Shanice's phone.'

"Yo, count through that money quickly, brudda. Make sure there's a grand there," I tell Preddie, who nods and follows my instruction.

While his attention is diverted, I drop the silver key underneath the seat.

So deep in concentration is Preddie that he doesn't realise I emerge with not only the key but Shanice's phone too.

I stuff it in my jacket pocket, and once Preddie's finished counting, he writes down his uncle's phone number and address on a piece of paper and hands it to me. "If you don't spot him at the airport, just phone that number or take a taxi to that address. Someone will be there waiting for you."

"Ite. Cool."

We share one last embrace, and he tells me to go get some sleep before speeding off.

Once I get inside the house and close the door behind me, I feel the cold sense of loneliness that consumes this place. The walls are a coffee-stained white, and the hallway smells of damp clothes. I zip my jacket up. It's freezing here, and there are no lightbulbs either. Out of everything, the sofa doesn't look too bad, so I attempt to find solace upon it.

Staring up at the ceiling, I count all the spots of mould I can find before I examine the dated floral patterns of the carpet. On a bookcase to my right, one of the shelves is littered with old books, a heap of copper coins, some old batteries, and an alarm clock that still blinks.

'At least I can keep an eye on the time.'

The silence has me drifting further into my thoughts.

'What's Keziah gonna think when she wakes up, and I'm gone? Then, what about when she doesn't see me for week? What if I never see her again? How's Shanice gonna manage? Is man really just leaving her? What's Mum gonna think when she finds out?'

The questions reap havoc upon my brain, and I decide to close my eyes. It doesn't take long for the tiredness to seep back in, and the aftereffects of the alcohol to send me off.

Even while asleep, I can feel my mind ticking, thinking about this, and worrying about that.

What feels like ten hours turns out to be just under two, I discover as I open my eyes and check the time on the alarm clock.

07:16.

I shake myself out of my somnolence, knowing the cab should be arriving soon. As I rise to my feet, I feel the uncomfortable feeling of something digging into my hip. I reach inside my pocket and retrieve Shanice's phone.

As I do, my finger presses the button at the top, and miraculously, the apple logo pops up on the screen.

"What the fuck?"

When I picked it up from under the seat earlier, the screen was just black, and I assumed the battery was dead.

'Maybe it was just off... I swear Shanice said suttin' about it turnin' off by itself.'

The screen comes to life, displaying a photo of her and Keziah that I took at Brighton Beach last summer.

The time reads 07:20 and indicates that the device only has 7% battery.

I punch in the passcode and think about dialling Mum. But after second thought, I stop myself in my tracks.

'Nah... Preddie said leave it a week.'

I'm just about to exit the call log and send a text when something weird catches my attention.

There're two missed calls from Jermaine.

One recorded at 03:17.

And a second at 03:35.

'What?'

"How the hell can Jermaine be calling just four hours ago? I saw him dead on the floor last night. Preddie, FatMack, the whole ends know he's dead. How can...? Unless..."

'... Somebody's got his phone.'

"Shit."

If that's the case and this person's calling Shanice, they must know I was involved.

My heart starts to thump.

But as I take a closer look at the digits underneath Jermaine's name, I realise something.

"Wait a minute... I swear I know this number."

The eleven digits in front of me look super familiar. I go over them again, reading them out. "Zero-seven-five-one-nine-six-six-two-one-eight-three."

It's the 'one-eight-three' part that gets me.

"I know this number."

A notification flashes at the top of the screen, telling me only five percent battery life remains.

Now the time reads 07:24.

The cab should arrive any minute.

I know I won't have another chance.

"Fuck it."

I press call.

The number rings four times, and on the fifth ring, I nearly collapse.

"Yo, Shanice, where you?" the voice answers as my soul's ripped from my chest.

"... Shanice, babe, where you?" the voice says, snatching the air from my lungs.

The words rob me of my heartbeat for a moment as my body goes as light as a feather. "Preddie?"

"Who's this?"

"Preddie, is that you?"

"Wait... Rakz?"

I hear muffling in the background then the phone goes dead.

"Preddie... Preddie!"

My hands are shaking, and I can barely hold the phone as the realization strikes me like a dagger to my chest, tearing my heart in two.

It was Preddie all along. He was the one texting Shanice.

I try to call back, but Preddie's number doesn't even ring.

"Preddie... Preddie the fuckin' snake. All this time, it was him."

I reach into my pocket and feel my passport when I hear a noise from outside.

I look at the clock, which reads 07:28.

The cab's here, but I can't go now. This trip's cancelled.

'I can't leave Shanice with Preddie. How do I know he won't... Wait, what's that noise by the door?'

I go to the hallway to inspect.

"Shit is that—"

Boom!

The door flies off the hinges, smashing against the wall.

"Armed police! Get on the fucking ground!"

An army of assault rifles, black balaclavas, bulletproof vests, and lasers charge at me as I drop to my knees and surrender.

Game over.

43

Bang.

My cell door slams against the wall, waking me from a vivid dream. It's one I've had a lot recently—the day I got arrested for killing Jermaine McPherson.

Seventeen years since Preddie set me up, and it still haunts me.

Don't worry, though. Preddie never drove off into the sunset with Shanice. He picked a fight with the wrong guy outside a club and got stabbed to death back in 2012.

After all that, I guess I should've seen it coming with Deontay, right? Maybe if I had, I wouldn't be back in prison. Maybe, you're right. Or maybe my heart's just too big for my own good, and I always see the best in people. Perhaps it's in my blood, just like Mum. Who knows?

Anyway, that's the past. Can't change that shit now.

"Morrison, you got a visit, mate," Mr Constantine says. We call him Mr C for short.

I tuck my feet into my sliders and rise from my bed. Rubbing my eyes, I look over at the pristine condition of the top bunk. Denny must be at work.

"Get ready while I go and grab the rest of 'em, and I be back 'ere in five, yeah?" Mr C says before tapping the door frame and walking off.

'Visit? He must've got the wrong cell.'

I haven't had one of those in years. Coming up to four years, to be precise.

I walk over to the doorway and the untranslatable roar that governs the landing on any given day forces me to yell as loud as I can.

"Yo, Mr C, who's visiting man?"

467

He shrugs as he spins to face me. Walking backward, he calls, "No idea, mate. I'm just the errand boy."

I return to my cell and study a blurred reflection in the cracked mirror that takes centre stage above the sink. Smudges of dried toothpaste decorate all four corners of the tiny square thing as the distorted image that looks back at me is vastly different from the Rakim who last went on a visit.

I still carry the weight, and my shoulders are still solid, but it's more my skin and my hair. A shade paler and a lot nappier.

After I was convicted for the murder of Kamari Wilson-Bell (known to me as Ribz), I was recommended to serve a minimum of thirty-four years. When the judge handed me that sentence, I figured my appearance was no longer at the top of my list of priorities.

I take my flannel from the shelf, wash my face, and brush my teeth.

Still wondering who's visiting me after all these years, I change out of my shorts into a black Nike tracksuit.

As I sit down on my bunk, I spot an envelope poking out from amongst the paperwork on the bottom shelf of a unit that acts as a wardrobe, dresser, and filing cabinet. Everything else on the shelf is neatly aligned, but this letter sticks out at a strange angle. It's subtle, but it's the kind of thing you tend to notice when living in such a confined space for so long.

I lace up my trainers and investigate further.

The letter is addressed to me.

'It must've come while I was sleeping. Denny must've put it with my stuff, thinking it fell.'

It's the only logical explanation because it wasn't here this morning.

I don't recognise the handwriting, but I open it anyway.

6th July 2027

Rakz

Longtime, my brother.

First of all, I gotta apologise for what happened between us. I know it wasn't all my fault and probably wasn't all yours either, but I know on my part, I let

468

pride get in the way of us as brothers. And for that, I can say with my chest I'm sorry.

You have to understand the whole thing with that snitch business, you thinking I snaked you and Jamal killing himself, and I assume you do if you've discovered the truth by now, to hear you accuse me of that licked me hard, fam. I couldn't believe you'd think I was that kinda yout'. After everything we'd been through together, I thought you knew me. But I've come to realise the separation between these walls casts a very different perspective of reality. Men like us tend to see things through our own lenses, whether inside or outside. We're always right even when we're wrong, and I reckon that's perhaps how you saw it due to you being free and me being locked up, not to mention Jonesy, who was feeding you all that bullshit. Don't watch, though. It's cool. I get it now.

Anyway, with that off my chest, I wanted to remind you that you got a brother for life in me. I heard about your sentence a couple of months after it happened, and I won't lie, I fucking cried, bro. Yeah, first time man like me cried in over 15 yrs. I cried because I know you, and I know you don't deserve it.

I couldn't believe they done u like that. But we stay strong and prevail. Insh'Allah, you receive some kind of intervention from the Most High, and justice prevails because I know you never killed nobody. Whatever happened, I can put my life on that.

We've been around killers all our lives, bro. From when we were both just youts on road to becoming big men in jail, we know what killers look like. We've seen them and felt their presence. It might sound stupid to the nosey minimum wage screw that's reading this before it gets to you, but I know even after catching a manslaughter charge and a murder charge—you, my brother, are not a killer.

And that's why Allah shall deliver you from the peril you currently find yourself in. (Don't laugh at my language btw I've been working on this letter for fucking weeks. Bought a dictionary, a thesaurus, and every'ting).

If you didn't realise by the envelope and when I said I BOUGHT a dictionary and a thesaurus, I'll be clearer.

I'm out.

469

My D-Cat came through eighteen months ago, and I ended up getting fully released last month. I'm working as a personal trainer and keeping my head down. (Not that lazy yout' in the gym no more, bro lol).

I'll leave you with the real purpose of my letter, though, because my language isn't the only thing I worked on, and you're not the only person I tracked down, either. You'll probably get a visit in the next couple days. Couldn't let you think we don't love you, my brother. Keep your head up.

And remember—Laugh through the pain, smile through the rain.
Your brother till the grave
Scribz

"Rah, Scribz is out."

It's been five years since I had any contact with Scribz whatsoever; the last time we spoke, we threatened to kill each other, yet hearing myself say those words brings an instant smile to my face. One I haven't felt in such a long time, it feels awkward, almost forbidden, as if I'm breaking some sort of taboo by expressing my happiness.

Some commotion on the landing briefly draws my attention away from the letter, so I push the door until it's nearly closed and drown out the riotous sounds.

'After all this time, Scribz still knows me.'

Prison is a small place where people have nothing to do, so they talk. They talk and talk, and news gets around.

It turns out Jonesy told the Turks where to find me so they could get back the food that Scribz stole. Scribz was working it out with them until Jonesy grassed him up for having a phone and got him shipped out. All that stuff Jonesy told me on the visit was all bullshit. He needed money to pay his confiscation order, so he told me to gather a hundred grand however I could, then tried to get Ribz to rob it from me and give it to him under the pretence that he'd become Ribz's supplier.

Only thing is, it didn't go down that way. Ribz got shot in the head, and I got convicted of it. As for Jonesy, fuck knows where he is. He just better hope its nowhere near me. I'm a lifer now, which means it ain't nothing to me to catch another thirty-four years, if you catch my drift.

I grab a load of papers and place the letter amongst the rest of my mail.

As I reach up to stuff everything back on my shelf, one of the letters falls into the sink.

"Shit."

I pluck the letter out of the soaked envelope, and luckily it only has droplets of water over it. Words and emotions on a piece of paper are sacred in prison, and I double-check to be sure this one isn't damaged.

The second I see the handwriting, it brings back a plethora of memories.

It's from Nia.

I walk over towards my cell door and look out on the landing. Jason, who lives opposite me, throws a hand up. I nod back, then look across my floor, up to the floor above, before scanning the floor below.

There's no sign of Mr C, so I sit back down on my bunk and shuffle backward until my back rests against the wall. Using my foot, I push the door to shut out the noise, then unfold the letter.

I start by reading the date.

14th July 2024

"Three fuckin' years ago... Where did that go, man?"

I bite my lip as I recall the words in this letter. I know them well; I've read them over a hundred times. But every time I do, nothing changes. Nothing fills that chasm of guilt and contrition entrenched within me. A scar forever imprinted on my soul that's resurrected any time I think of Nia and my six-week-old seed she carried. The one killed by the gun that *I* handed Deontay.

I take a deep breath and begin.

Dear Rakim,
I hope you're okay and you're looking after yourself.

471

I want you to know from the bottom of my heart that I don't think any less of you for shutting me out. I'm doing okay. It's been hard coming to terms with your sentence, but I know now that there are some things a man, especially one like you, must do by himself. You've made your decision, and I will respect that. This will be the last letter I will send you. You won't hear anything more from me after this unless you decide to respond.

It's so difficult to write to these words, it's taken me four attempts. I really don't know what to say, and I just end up breaking out into tears and ruining the letter.

I want you to know that you will forever be ingrained and embedded within my soul and my heart. And that my love for you will never die.

Rakim, I was so closed off to the idea of finding love before I met you.

I used to wonder if there was something wrong with me. Something wrong with the way I am as to why I'd always experience heartache and suffering in relationships.

I used to try my hardest to be the perfect woman, but my efforts were exerted in the wrong avenues. I had conditioned myself to use two traits in a man to overlook his other shortfalls. To provide and to protect. There isn't a man I've met who exemplified a fraction of who you are. You showed me a man I could love... can love.

You've shown me what it means for a man to truly love a woman—a woman for whom you'd lay down your life and die without a second thought. You're a lover in every sense. A man with so much generosity in your heart it bleeds out of your skin.

I could see your heartache at being cast off to prison so young, losing your mum, not seeing your daughter, and the unbearable load of taking a life taught you so many rules and codes that you bound around your soul like steel breastplates.

I know this because we are two lovers of the same heart. Two performers on the stage of life harmoniously existing in one another's symphony. I do not doubt that it is divine intervention that brought us together.

The day I first met you, I had been thinking about your Mum, so I went to her grave that morning to lay some flowers there. Then on my way home, I met

472

you, and stuck to your hand were lilies. The same flowers I had just laid at your mum's headstone. And when you stood up and looked at me, I felt a connection so primal and magnetic it took hold of my body. I looked into your eyes, and for the first time in my life, I understood what love at first sight meant.

Within a few weeks, I felt myself falling like a skydiver. The bass in your voice, the feel of your chest against my head as I rested on you, the solidarity in your whole body anytime you picked me up and carried me, the sincerity in your words and the love and warmth in your eyes all encapsulated me.

Your charm and your cheekiness got me every time my emotions got the better of me. Your chocolate skin and soft lips eased me whenever I felt unworthy or uneasy. Your wisdom and your intelligence lifted me up whenever I felt down. Your courage and fearlessness made me feel safe, warm, and protected whenever I was scared or anxious. And your ambition and determination inspired me to do more whenever I felt useless or idle.

Rakim, without knowing, you have made me the woman I am. You've shown me the standard a man should operate at. Your life was more challenging than most (twelve years a slave in that place), but you never let it crush your spirit. So many guys talk the talk, but when it comes down to it, they aren't who they pretend to be. You showed me you were the most unselfish, loyal, and loving person that night you did what you did, and, in another reality, right now, you're laying with me on this hammock in Gambia watching the sunset as our son runs around on the beach.

I pray you reach a point to forgive yourself one day because it was not your fault; you had no idea I was pregnant. And as God gives life, so it is he that takes it away. (A wise woman we both know used to say that).

When I lay in my bed alone at night and catch a whiff of your freshly trimmed hair or skin or remember your smile or laugh, I wish many things could've gone differently. I sometimes even think Daniel should be where you are, and you should be here next to me, keeping me warm, but that's me being selfish. I know that.

You said you were always here for me, and I felt betrayed when you went away, but I feel guilty and alone now. I'm working daily to rid this guilt from my psyche, but I can't lie it's hard.

473

I love you, Rakim. And I will always be here for you no matter what, no matter how long. If you ever change your mind and wish to reach out to me, please do.

You are the sweetest, kindest, wisest, strongest, most honest, and most courageous man I've ever known. I'm the luckiest woman to have even shared a few months with your special soul. And no matter how many years you stay in prison, they can never take that away from you, Rakim. Remember that.

Signing off now. Love you,

Always and Forever

Nia xxxxxxxx

P.S. Hope you liked the photo of 'Deontay.' He says hello and thank you for everything.

I squeeze my eyelids together.

Hard.

"Damn, man. Why'd I read that?"

I look at the photo of Deontay that's stuck on my wall. His effervescent grin almost jumps out of the page as he poses on a jet ski in the waters of Barbados. He's wearing the cap I bought him, and all I can do is laugh as the bottom of my eye begins to shudder.

'Man like Deontay ya know.'

I hold Nia's letter tightly, and the whole prison ceases to exist as I close my eyes and picture being with her.

"Morrison, you ready?" Mr C says, disturbing my rare moment of bliss from the doorway.

"Yeah, man. One sec."

I swiftly fix the collar of my jumper while silently cursing Mr C for interrupting my peace. On the other hand, I suppose I should thank him for not allowing my tears to flow before this visit.

We take the long walk through my wing, then through C Wing, and I'm placed into a holding cell along with three other inmates.

Over the next twenty minutes, more and more prisoners are inducted into our little box of a room. One guy keeps rapping in the corner as another tries to converse with me about how the prison cafeteria only serves left-leg thighs, so it can't be real chicken. I roll my eyes, thinking of how many times I've heard that one.

A few names are called for their visits, and for several of the men locked in this stuffy room, who don't hear their surname, it's a complete injustice. Riled up, one of them kicks the door with all the force he can muster. I'd like to shut everyone up, but the more pertinent matter of who's in that visiting hall governs my focus.

A part of me prays that it's Nia.

And it could be.

She visited me right up until my trial. Literally, the day before it commenced. It was only after my sentence that I stopped coming out of my cell for visits and replying to her letters. She tried bombarding me with bookings and letters for another year, but I didn't fold through her persistence. I couldn't let her waste the rest of her life waiting around for me to come out. But after reading that letter today, I sincerely hope it's her.

But then it could be Deontay. He's on my visitor list.

'Or could it be Shanice...? Nah.'

She's long gone.

I go through all the possibilities in my head. Leanne, Taylor, Deontay, Nia, FatMack.

'Rah... Imagine it was FatMack that Scribz tracked down, and he came back from Jamaica to visit me. If it is, then Scribz is a G.'

I think about what I'll say to each person, and I get a weird buzz inside my stomach. I look at my foot, and it's tapping to its own beat. I haven't felt like this in ages.

'Calm down... It's probably just a mix-up or some charity worker.' I have to extinguish this feeling. Hope can't exist in a place like this.

My name's called, and I stand up and leave the holding cell. After a quick pat down, I put on a lime green netball bid and hand my ID card over to the prison officer whose job it is to collect them before visits. The officer checks it out as if I've just handed him a dodgy tenner, then nods me through to the visiting hall.

I sit at my designated table and note the optimism on the faces of the other men in here.

'I remember those days,' I think as I reminisce. 'These lot are getting out one day.'

They talk loudly across the room, sharing details of who's visiting them and what they're gonna talk about and I feel completely ostracised. Not that I care, I don't know any of the faces in this hall that well, anyway. I nod at a few before crossing my arms and looking up at the ceiling.

Minutes go by, and the room begins to flood with people from the outside world. Glammed-up girlfriends, chaotic children, couples arguing about where they've put their tokens.

As more visitors pile through, I try to identify a familiar face, but it's a strain to do so at the angle I'm at.

My eyes focus on the swirling patterns on the grey table in front of me when I see a pair of glittery trainers pass by. I look up, hoping to see Nia, but it's just some girl with dreadlocks.

I turn back to look at the group by the reception desk.

It's much smaller now, but I still can't see anybody I know. "Miss," I call out to a female officer.

"Yes," she replies.

"Can you see who's come to visit me, 'cause I think I've been ghosted, and I ain't tryin' to wait here. I'll go back to my cell."

She sighs, then reluctantly asks me my name.

"It's Morrison. Rakim Morrison."

"All right, just hold fire. I'll speak to the officers at the desk and find out for ya."

"Nice one."

My arms crossed, I stare into oblivion, thinking there's either been some sort of miscommunication, or this is a practical joke. Either way, this is long.

'This woman needs to hurry up. I wanna go back to my cell. I don't need to be out 'ere like this. I could be...'

476

"Hey," a timid voice says pulling me from my silent tirade.

I look up.

"You all right?" I say, clocking the girl with the dreadlocks. I look at her from head to toe quickly. She fits the bill perfectly; fresh-out-of-uni Official Prison Visitor that gets some sort of kick out of shedding her pity upon us poor, lonely lifers.

Her eyes flit around, and she appears as if this testosterone-fuelled place is about to swallow her alive.

"Did you say your name is erm... Rakim Morrison?" she asks.

I study her closer. She's got a cute little smile and an athletic frame, even underneath her red and black lumberjack-style shirt. "Yeah, why? Who are you?" I ask.

She looks intimidated by my questions, but I'm not in the mood for no do-gooders tryin' to make me feel better about myself today.

"Well... Erm... My name is Morrison, too," she says.

I watch her scratch her face and realise the birthmark on her hand.

"Wait."

I freeze.

'This can't be real.'

She sees my reaction, and I hear her nervous gulp.

I want to speak, but my throat won't squeeze out the words. My mouth hangs open gormlessly like I'm waiting in a dentist's chair.

Then from my right, I see another two figures emerge.

"What, Ricky... Nathan?" I've nearly lost the power of speech; my words come out as a whisper.

I look back at the face of a girl I haven't seen in over a decade as she rubs her arm.

"It's me... Keziah Morrison... You're my dad."

She looks just like me. All those photos of me as a kid.

She's me.

A part of me.

But I don't know her.

I don't recognise the girl in front of me.

"What... What's going on?" I say, trying to stop myself from trembling. "What is this? Where's your Mum?" I ask the boys.

"We came alone," Ricky says.

I turn towards my daughter. "Kez, how did you...?"

A pint-size man pops up from behind Nathan carrying a tray of treats, and everything finally clicks. "Mi couldn't abandon you fi ah second time, King," Clinton the barber says.

Keziah and Ricky's eyes turn towards Nathan, who takes a step forward. That weary teen he was five years ago is dead and gone. Infront of me stands a tall, broad twenty-year-old man with a goatee and a three-piece suit.

"What's going on?" I ask, rising to my feet.

Then Nathan opens his mouth. "We've been on your visitor list from when we were children. Your friend told us where you are."

"I told your mum to never bring you man here again."

"Uncle Rakim, I've seen your case papers. I showed them to my girl's dad. He's a judge, and he said you should never have been put away."

"What?"

Keziah steps in, and every worry I ever had about how she would turn out disappears like a whisper in the wind. "He's right," she says.

I turn towards my daughter. "Kez, I'm sorry I left you," I tell her.

"It's okay. Don't worry, Dad... We're getting you out of here."

Author's Notes

'A thirty-year-old gangster, who had served over a decade in prison for manslaughter, had only been released from prison for less than five months, when he murdered a seventeen-year-old boy in cold blood; shooting him in the head at point blank range in a drug deal gone wrong. Today, callous monster, Rakim Morrison was jailed for life with the judge recommending he serve a minimum of thirty-four years' – Any tabloid or news report on any given day.

It was not my intention to glamourise or condemn any of the events or characters in this book, but to simply give a glimpse into a reality that is commonplace across a city I have lived in my whole life. A Life Not Lived is a story so familiar and relatable for hundreds and thousands of fathers, mothers, brothers, and sisters throughout London and beyond, yet so appallingly and accurately underrepresented in literature. Told through the eyes of a man who lost his freedom to the prison system at eighteen years old, it was my goal to portray a different perspective to the narrative pushed through the media by reporters, politicians, and others who have opinions of men like Rakim Morrison but have never walked a mile in his shoes, spent a day in his life or even had a meaningful conversation with somebody like him. Above all, it was my aim to show that effect is not without cause, that behind every murder and every man convicted of such a crime, lies an alternative story. And that all stories, however they appear, have a beginning, and will one day have an end.

"Life has many different chapters,
don't let one bad chapter ruin the book"
- Buddha

Acknowledgements

When I first told people I was writing a book I had almost finished two manuscripts (this one and another that I aim to release in 2023). The overwhelming response I was met with was one of shock, surprise, and disbelief. Understandable, I guess, when you've never written a novel before or barely even read one.

However, the question that I seemed to hear the most was, 'Do you find it hard?' Now I would've loved to respond to the expectant faces by telling them it was the hardest thing I've ever done, and it was all blood, sweat and tears. And it was (at times). But if truth be told, it was one of the most free-flowing, natural things I have ever done. From the moment I wrote the first sentence–ideas, characters, and everything else just followed.

This isn't to say that I never experienced challenges along the way. That would be a lie. I encountered many bumps in the road but the overriding desire of seeing this book through to its completion never subsided. And I believe that driving force alone–determination–is one of the most powerful forces in this universe with the strength to supersede any doubt or obstacle that life presents. The ability to never give up. To continue. To strive, no matter what the odds stacked against you may be, is a lesson, which I know, we can all learn from.

With that said, there are a number of people I'd like to give a shout out to for without them, this book would have never materialized. They are as much as a part of this as I am. Firstly, my brilliant editor Victoria Straw; I'd like to thank you for all the hours you put into making this book an actual thing. Thank you for all the ideas you gave me (especially in relation to character development and plot). Thank you for all your constant encouragement and wisdom. Thank you for your patience with me as a first-time writer and for your detailed explanations to any query I had. Thank you for your feedback that kept me grounded and focused on my goal, you feel me...? You are one of the main reasons, people are reading this right now, so thank you once again.

Thank you to my cousin, Bradley McWhinney (studiob92.co), for your work on the design of the cover. Talent runs in the family, cuz. All those fonts, and photos I had you going through, back, and forth... We made it click in the end, so kick back, and read this while having a beer on me. Thank you to all my brothers and bredrins I spoke to who encouraged me to keep pushing as we shared our experiences in the system and on the roads.

Thank you to all those around me who motivate me to do better every single day. Thank you to my children for inspiring me to do something they can be proud of, especially my eldest daughter, a creative genius in her own right, Aliyah Peter. Shoutout to my eldest brother for your non-stop bombardment over the years about the importance of harnessing a creative talent and the positive physical and spiritual results. Many nights we've sat and reasoned about these things and your words have stuck with me. Thank you for all the people I've ever met in my life, good and bad, who allowed me to experience life the way I have. 'If I could start from scratch, I wouldn't change shit.' Without my experiences, I would never have written this book.

Thank you to the one woman, who's always there, regardless of time, day, or year. You gave me the idea to start writing a few years ago when you told me your idea for a book. That conversation sparked something within me, and I can categorically say without you I would've never started this journey. Above everything, you've always got my back, and more than most you've sat and endured a million different ideas a million different times when all you really wanted to do was sleep, so love for your patience and your commitment. Without you, this would not have been possible. You know who you are.

And last but not least, thank you reader. If you got to this point, hopefully you read the whole book and didn't just skip to this page (if you did that then, I guess the only thing I can thank you for is your financial contribution). I know my novel is not for everyone, but the reason I write is to not only share a story with whoever decides to read it, but to hear people's opinions. Perceptions differ greatly, and two people rarely have exactly the same response. Characters, stories, plots, and settings in books tend to bring parts of us to life; one part in particular that lies dormant in way too many adults–imagination. We create our own world when we read and everybody's world is different, which produces infinite different viewpoints.

So, whether you liked this novel or you hated it is not my main concern. I'm just humbly appreciative that you gave it the time of day and for that your opinion is just as valid as the next. Hopefully more of my books will see your shelves or your audible list in the not-too-distant future. Until then, look after yourself.

Glossary

For those who fail to understand any of the language within this book, please refer to the glossary below. The terms listed in this glossary are not necessarily official interpreted translations. Depending on numerous factors (location, heritage, age, gender, language, dialect etc) people use and define words differently, however within the context of this book, their meanings are as follows:

Alie – "Don't you agree?"

Allow me – "Leave me alone" (either in a playful, jovial manner or a plea to be left alone)

Bag(s) – grand(s) Depending on context used i.e., "you got eighteen bags to put down for a **half**"

Bare – A lot *(depending on context used)*

Battymen – Homosexuals (derogatory slur)

Bloodclart – Jamaican Patios word that can be used as an expletive to show distaste or anger similarly to rasclart **OR** to express shock/awe.

Boidem – Police

Catching bodies – Killing people

Don't watch that – Don't worry

Wa Gwarn – "What's going on?"

Gyal - Girl

Half – Half a kilo *(if not used in normal context)*

Ite – All right

I'ma – I'm going to/I will

Lightey – A fair skinned person of colour

Mandem – Group of male friends

Mi cyah – I can't

Nigga/nigger (friend, brother if said in context of "my nigga")/Nigger (racist slur or referring to a black person who behaves as if he's white; coon, bounty etc.)

Nuh – Don't

Pickney – Child

Rah – "Wow"

Rah boy – Expression of shock or being in awe

Rasclart – Jamaican Patois swear word used to express distaste or disgust towards someone or something.

Reh teh teh – and so on and so forth

Stoosh – A person particularly female who is stuck up (thinks they are better than others usually based on appearance)

Ting – Thing

Tizz – Prison slang for illicit mobile phone

Wa'am – "What's wrong/what's up?"

Woi – Wow

Printed in Great Britain
by Amazon

23330733R00280